Country Bookshops
£2-99 -10% then

THE MARY POPPINS OMNIBUS

Mary Poppins has delighted children and grown-ups for generations. Of Mary Poppins herself, the *Times Literary Supplement* wrote: "She is the embodiment of authority, protection, and cynical common sense; her powers are magical. Basically she is the Good Fairy, whom we are all seeking."

The Mary Poppins Books

Mary Poppins
Mary Poppins Comes Back
Mary Poppins Opens the Door
Mary Poppins in the Park
Mary Poppins in Cherry Tree Lane
Mary Poppins and the House Next Door

P. L. Travers

MARY POPPINS

·

MARY POPPINS COMES BACK

·

MARY POPPINS IN CHERRY TREE LANE

Illustrated by Mary Shepard

An Imprint of HarperCollins*Publishers*

Mary Poppins and *Mary Poppins Comes Back*
were first published in the UK by Peter Davies in
1934 and 1935, and published by
William Collins Sons & Co. Ltd in 1958.
Mary Poppins in Cherry Tree Lane
was first published in the UK by
William Collins Sons & Co. Ltd in 1982.
This edition published in Great Britain by Carnival,
a division of HarperCollins Publishers Ltd in
1999 for Bookmart Ltd, Enderby, Leicester.

1 3 5 7 9 10 8 6 4 2

Lions is an imprint of
Harper Collins Children's Books,
part of HarperCollins Publishers Ltd,
77-85 Fulham Palace Road,
Hammersmith, London W6 8JB.

Copyright © reserved P.L. Travers 1934, 1935 and 1982
Illustrations copyright © Mary Shepard 1934, 1935 and 1982
Cover illustration copyright © Piers Sanford 1994

The author asserts the moral right to be identified
as the author of this work.

ISBN 0-261-67206-1

Printed and bound in Great Britain by
Caledonian International Book Manufacturing Ltd, Glasgow

Conditions of Sale
This book is sold subject to the condition
that it shall not, by way of trade or otherwise,
be lent, re-sold, hired out or otherwise circulated
without the publisher's prior consent in any form of
binding or cover other than that in which it is
published and without a similar condition
including this condition being imposed
on the subsequent purchaser.

MARY POPPINS

Revised Edition

Inside a little curly frame was a painting of
Mary Poppins

CONTENTS

To my mother
1875-1928

Chapter One

EAST WIND

IF you want to find Cherry Tree Lane all you have to
do is ask the Policeman at the cross-roads. He will
push his helmet slightly to one side, scratch his head
thoughtfully, and then he will point his huge white-
gloved finger and say: " First to your right, second to
your left, sharp right again, and you're there. Good-
morning."

And sure enough, if you follow his directions exactly,
you *will* be there—right in the middle of Cherry Tree
Lane, where the houses run down one side and the Park
runs down the other and the cherry-trees go dancing
right down the middle.

If you are looking for Number Seventeen—and it is
more than likely that you will be, for this book is all
about that particular house—you will very soon find
it. To begin with, it is the smallest house in the Lane.
And besides that, it is the only one that is rather dilapidated and needs a coat of paint. But Mr. Banks, who
owns it, said to Mrs. Banks that she could have either

a nice, clean, comfortable house or four children. But not both, for he couldn't afford it.

And after Mrs. Banks had given the matter some consideration she came to the conclusion that she would rather have Jane, who was the eldest, and Michael, who came next, and John and Barbara, who were Twins and came last of all. So it was settled, and that was how the Banks family came to live at Number Seventeen, with Mrs. Brill to cook for them, and Ellen to lay the tables, and Robertson Ay to cut the lawn and clean the knives and polish the shoes and, as Mr. Banks always said, " to waste his time and my money."

And, of course, besides these there was Katie Nanna, who doesn't really deserve to come into the book at all because, at the time I am speaking of, she had just left Number Seventeen.

" Without by your leave or a word of warning. And what am I to do?" said Mrs. Banks.

" Advertise, my dear," said Mr. Banks, putting on his shoes. " And I wish Robertson Ay would go without a word of warning, for he has again polished one boot and left the other untouched. I shall look very lopsided."

" That," said Mrs. Banks, " is not of the least importance. You haven't told me what I'm to do about Katie Nanna."

" I don't see how you can do anything about her

since she has disappeared," replied Mr. Banks. "But if it were me—I mean I—well, I should get somebody to put in the *Morning Paper* the news that Jane and Michael and John and Barbara Banks (to say nothing of their Mother) require the best possible Nannie at the lowest possible wage and at once. Then I should wait and watch for the Nannies to queue up outside the front gate, and I should get very cross with them for holding up the traffic and making it necessary for me to give the policeman a shilling for putting him to so much trouble. Now I must be off. Whew, it's as cold as the North Pole. Which way is the wind blowing?"

And as he said that, Mr. Banks popped his head out of the window and looked down the Lane to Admiral Boom's house at the corner. This was the grandest house in the Lane, and the Lane was very proud of it because it was built exactly like a ship. There was a flagstaff in the garden, and on the roof was a gilt weathercock shaped like a telescope.

"Ha!" said Mr. Banks, drawing in his head very quickly. "Admiral's telescope says East Wind. I thought as much. There is frost in my bones. I shall wear two overcoats." And he kissed his wife absent-mindedly on one side of her nose and waved to the children and went away to the City.

Now, the City was a place where Mr. Banks went every day—except Sundays, of course, and Bank

Holidays—and while he was there he sat on a large
chair in front of a large desk and made money. All
day long he worked, cutting out pennies and shillings

and half-crowns and threepenny-bits. And he brought
them home with him in his little black bag. Sometimes
he would give some to Jane and Michael for their
money-boxes, and when he couldn't spare any he

would say, "The Bank is broken," and they would know he hadn't made much money that day.

Well, Mr. Banks went off with his black bag, and Mrs. Banks went into the drawing-room and sat there all day long writing letters to the papers and begging them to send some Nannies to her at once as she was waiting; and upstairs in the Nursery, Jane and Michael watched at the window and wondered who would come. They were glad Katie Nanna had gone, for they had never liked her. She was old and fat and smelt of barley-water. Anything, they thought, would be better than Katie Nanna—if not *much* better.

When the afternoon began to die away behind the Park, Mrs. Brill and Ellen came to give them their supper and to bath the Twins. And after supper Jane and Michael sat at the window watching for Mr. Banks to come home, and listening to the sound of the East Wind blowing through the naked branches of the cherry-trees in the Lane. The trees themselves, turning and bending in the half light, looked as though they had gone mad and were dancing their roots out of the ground.

"There he is!" said Michael, pointing suddenly to a shape that banged heavily against the gate. Jane peered through the gathering darkness.

"That's not Daddy," she said. "It's somebody else."

Then the shape, tossed and bent under the wind, lifted the latch of the gate, and they could see that it belonged to a woman, who was holding her hat on with one hand and carrying a bag in the other. As they watched, Jane and Michael saw a curious thing happen. As soon as the shape was inside the gate the wind seemed to catch her up into the air and fling her at the house. It was as though it had flung her first at the gate, waited for her to open it, and then lifted and thrown her, bag and all, at the front door. The watching children heard a terrific bang, and as she landed the whole house shook.

" How funny! I've never seen that happen before," said Michael.

" Let's go and see who it is!" said Jane, and taking Michael's arm she drew him away from the window, through the Nursery and out on to the landing. From there they always had a good view of anything that happened in the front hall.

Presently they saw their Mother coming out of the drawing-room with a visitor following her. Jane and Michael could see that the newcomer had shiny black hair—" Rather like a wooden Dutch doll," whispered Jane. And that she was thin, with large feet and hands, and small, rather peering blue eyes.

" You'll find that they are very nice children," Mrs. Banks was saying.

*Holding her hat on with one hand and carrying
a bag in the other*

Michael's elbow gave a sharp dig at Jane's ribs.

" And that they give no trouble at all," continued Mrs. Banks uncertainly, as if she herself didn't really believe what she was saying. They heard the visitor sniff as though *she* didn't either.

" Now, about references——" Mrs. Banks went on.

" Oh, I make it a rule never to give references," said the other firmly. Mrs. Banks stared.

" But I thought it was usual," she said. " I mean— I understood people always did."

" A very old-fashioned idea, to *my* mind," Jane and Michael heard the stern voice say. " *Very* old-fashioned. *Quite* out of date, as you might say."

Now, if there was one thing Mrs. Banks did not like, it was to be thought old-fashioned. She just couldn't bear it. So she said quickly:

" Very well, then. We won't bother about them. I only asked, of course, in case *you*—er—required it. The nursery is upstairs——" And she led the way towards the staircase, talking all the time, without stopping once. And because she was doing that Mrs. Banks did not notice what was happening behind her, but Jane and Michael, watching from the top landing, had an excellent view of the extraordinary thing the visitor now did.

Certainly she followed Mrs. Banks upstairs, but not in the usual way. With her large bag in her hands she slid gracefully *up* the banisters, and arrived at the landing at the same time as Mrs. Banks. Such a thing, Jane and Michael knew, had never been done before. Down, of course, for they had often done it themselves. But up—never! They gazed curiously at the strange new visitor.

"Well, that's all settled, then." A sigh of relief came from the children's Mother.

"Quite. As long as *I'm* satisfied," said the other, wiping her nose with a large red and white bandanna handkerchief.

"Why, children," said Mrs. Banks, noticing them suddenly, "what are you doing there? This is your new nurse, Mary Poppins. Jane, Michael, say how do you do! And these"—she waved her hand at the babies in their cots—"are the Twins."

Mary Poppins regarded them steadily, looking from one to the other as though she were making up her mind whether she liked them or not.

"Will we do?" said Michael.

"Michael, don't be naughty," said his Mother.

Mary Poppins continued to regard the four children searchingly. Then, with a long, loud sniff that seemed to indicate that she had made up her mind, she said:

"I'll take the position."

"For all the world," as Mrs. Banks said to her husband later, "as though she were doing us a signal honour."

"Perhaps she is," said Mr. Banks, putting his nose round the corner of the newspaper for a moment and then withdrawing it very quickly.

When their Mother had gone, Jane and Michael edged towards Mary Poppins, who stood, still as a post, with her hands folded in front of her.

"How did you come?" Jane asked. "It looked just as if the wind blew you here."

"It did," said Mary Poppins briefly. And she proceeded to unwind her muffler from her neck and to take off her hat, which she hung on one of the bedposts.

As it did not seem as though Mary Poppins were going to say any more—though she sniffed a great deal —Jane, too, remained silent. But when she bent down to undo her bag, Michael could not restrain himself.

"What a funny bag!" he said, pinching it with his fingers.

"Carpet," said Mary Poppins, putting her key in the lock.

"To carry carpets in, you mean?"

"No. Made of."

"Oh," said Michael. "I see." But he didn't— quite.

By this time the bag was open, and Jane and

Michael were more than surprised to find it was completely empty.

" Why," said Jane, " there's nothing in it!"

" What do you mean—nothing?" demanded Mary Poppins, drawing herself up and looking as though she had been insulted. " Nothing in it, did you say?"

And with that she took out from the empty bag a starched white apron and tied it round her waist. Next she unpacked a large cake of Sunlight Soap, a toothbrush, a packet of hairpins, a bottle of scent, a small folding armchair and a box of throat lozenges.

Jane and Michael stared.

" But I *saw*," whispered Michael. " I'm sure it was empty."

" Hush!" said Jane, as Mary Poppins took out a large bottle labelled " One Tea-Spoon to be Taken at Bed-Time."

A spoon was attached to the neck of the bottle, and into this Mary Poppins poured a dark crimson fluid.

" Is that your medicine?" enquired Michael, looking very interested.

" No, yours," said Mary Poppins, holding out the spoon to him. Michael stared. He wrinkled up his nose. He began to protest.

" I don't want it. I don't need it. I won't!"

But Mary Poppins' eyes were fixed upon him, and Michael suddenly discovered that you could not look at

Mary Poppins and disobey her. There was something strange and extraordinary about her—something that was frightening and at the same time most exciting. The spoon came nearer. He held his breath, shut his eyes and gulped. A delicious taste ran round his mouth. He turned his tongue in it. He swallowed, and a happy smile ran round his face.

"Strawberry ice," he said ecstatically. "More, more, more!"

But Mary Poppins, her face as stern as before, was pouring out a dose for Jane. It ran into the spoon, silvery, greeny, yellowy. Jane tasted it.

"Lime-juice cordial," she said, sliding her tongue deliciously over her lips. But when she saw Mary Poppins moving towards the Twins with the bottle Jane rushed at her.

"Oh, no—please. They're too young. It wouldn't be good for them. Please!"

Mary Poppins, however, took no notice, but with a warning, terrible glance at Jane, tipped the spoon towards John's mouth. He lapped at it eagerly, and by the few drops that were spilt on his bib, Jane and Michael could tell that the substance in the spoon this time was milk. Then Barbara had her share, and she gurgled and licked the spoon twice.

Mary Poppins then poured out another dose and solemnly took it herself.

"Rum punch," she said, smacking her lips and corking the bottle.

Jane's eyes and Michael's popped with astonishment, but they were not given much time to wonder, for Mary Poppins, having put the miraculous bottle on the mantelpiece, turned to them.

"Now," she said, "spit-spot into bed." And she began to undress them. They noticed that whereas buttons and hooks had needed all sorts of coaxing from Katie Nanna, for Mary Poppins they flew apart almost at a look. In less than a minute they found themselves in bed and watching, by the dim light from the night-light, the rest of Mary Poppins' unpacking being performed.

From the carpet-bag she took out seven flannel nightgowns, four cotton ones, a pair of boots, a set of dominoes, two bathing-caps and a postcard album. Last of all came a folding camp-bedstead with blankets and eiderdown complete, and this she set down between John's cot and Barbara's.

Jane and Michael sat hugging themselves and watching. It was all so surprising that they could find nothing to say. But they knew, both of them, that something strange and wonderful had happened at Number Seventeen, Cherry Tree Lane.

Mary Poppins, slipping one of the flannel nightgowns over her head, began to undress underneath it as though it were a tent. Michael, charmed by this strange new arrival, unable to keep silent any longer, called to her.

"Mary Poppins," he cried, "you'll never leave us, will you?"

There was no reply from under the nightgown. Michael could not bear it.

"You won't leave us, will you?" he called anxiously.

Mary Poppins' head came out of the top of the nightgown. She looked very fierce.

"One word more from that direction," she said threateningly, "and I'll call the Policeman."

"I was only saying," began Michael, meekly, "that we hoped you wouldn't be going away soon——" He stopped, feeling very red and confused.

Mary Poppins stared from him to Jane in silence. Then she sniffed.

"I'll stay till the wind changes," she said shortly, and she blew out her candle and got into bed.

"That's all right," said Michael, half to himself and half to Jane. But Jane wasn't listening. She was thinking about all that had happened, and wondering. . . .

And that is how Mary Poppins came to live at Number Seventeen, Cherry Tree Lane. And although they sometimes found themselves wishing for the quieter, more ordinary days when Katie Nanna ruled the household, everybody, on the whole, was glad of Mary Poppins' arrival. Mr. Banks was glad because, as she arrived by herself and did not hold up the traffic, he had not had to tip the Policeman. Mrs. Banks was glad because she was able to tell everybody that *her* children's nurse was so fashionable that she didn't believe in giving references. Mrs. Brill and Ellen were glad because they could drink strong cups of tea all day in the kitchen and no longer needed to preside at nursery suppers. Robertson Ay was glad, too, because Mary Poppins had only one pair of shoes, and those she polished herself.

But nobody ever knew what Mary Poppins felt about it, for Mary Poppins never told anybody anything. . . .

Chapter Two

THE DAY OUT

"EVERY third Thursday," said Mrs. Banks. "Two till five."

Mary Poppins eyed her sternly. "The best people, ma'am," she said, "give every *second* Thursday, and one till six. And those I shall take or——" Mary Poppins paused, and Mrs. Banks knew what the pause meant. It meant that if she didn't get what she wanted Mary Poppins would not stay.

"Very well, very well," said Mrs. Banks hurriedly, though she wished Mary Poppins did not know so very much more about the best people than she did herself.

So Mary Poppins put on her white gloves and tucked her umbrella under her arm—not because it was raining but because it had such a beautiful handle that she couldn't possibly leave it at home. How could you leave your umbrella behind if it had a parrot's head for a handle? Besides, Mary Poppins was very vain and liked to look her best. Indeed, she was quite sure that she never looked anything else.

Jane waved to her from the Nursery window.

"Where are you going?" she called.

"Kindly close that window," replied Mary Poppins, and Jane's head hurriedly disappeared inside the Nursery.

Mary Poppins walked down the garden-path and opened the gate. Once outside in the Lane, she set off walking very quickly as if she were afraid the afternoon would run away from her if she didn't keep up with it. At the corner she turned to the right and then to the left, nodded haughtily to the Policeman, who said it was a nice day, and by that time she felt that her Day Out had begun.

She stopped beside an empty motor-car in order to put her hat straight with the help of the windscreen, in which it was reflected, then she smoothed down her frock and tucked her umbrella more securely under her arm so that the handle, or rather the parrot, could be seen by everybody. After these preparations she went forward to meet the Match Man.

Now, the Match Man had two professions. He not only sold matches like any ordinary match man, but he drew pavement pictures as well. He did these things turn-about according to the weather. If it was wet, he sold matches because the rain would have washed away his pictures if he had painted them. If it was fine, he was on his knees all day, making pictures in coloured chalks on the side-walks, and doing them so quickly that often you would find he had painted up one side of a street and down the other almost before you'd had time to come round the corner.

On this particular day, which was fine but cold, he was painting. He was in the act of adding a picture of

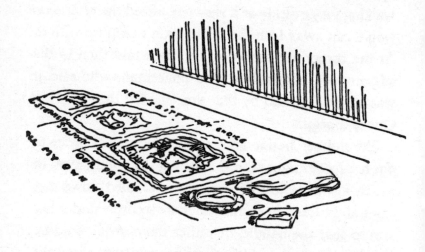

two Bananas, an Apple, and a head of Queen Elizabeth to a long string of others, when Mary Poppins walked up to him, tip-toeing so as to surprise him.

" Hey !" called Mary Poppins softly.

He went on putting brown stripes on a banana and brown curls on Queen Elizabeth's head.

" Ahem !" said Mary Poppins, with a ladylike cough.

He turned with a start and saw her.

" Mary!" he cried, and you could tell by the way he cried it that Mary Poppins was a very important person in his life.

Mary Poppins looked down at her feet and rubbed the toe of one shoe along the pavement two or three times. Then she smiled at the shoe in such a way that the shoe knew quite well that the smile wasn't meant for it.

" It's my Day, Bert," she said. " Didn't you remember?" Bert was the Match Man's name—Herbert Alfred for Sundays.

"Of course I remembered, Mary," he said, "but ——" and he stopped and looked sadly into his cap. It lay on the ground beside his last picture and there was tuppence in it. He picked it up and jingled the pennies.

" That all you got, Bert?" said Mary Poppins, and she said it so brightly you could hardly tell she was disappointed at all.

" That's the lot," he said. " Business is bad to-day. You'd think anybody'd be glad to pay to see that, wouldn't you?" And he nodded his head at Queen Elizabeth. " Well—that's how it is, Mary," he sighed. " Can't take you to tea to-day, I'm afraid."

Mary Poppins thought of the raspberry-jam-cakes they always had on her Day Out, and she was just going to sigh, when she saw the Match Man's face. So, very cleverly, she turned the sigh into a smile—a good one with both ends turned up—and said :

"That's all right, Bert. Don't you mind. I'd much rather not go to tea. A stodgy meal, I call it—really."

And that, when you think how very much she liked raspberry-jam-cakes, was rather nice of Mary Poppins.

The Match Man apparently thought so, too, for he took her white-gloved hand in his and squeezed it hard. Then together they walked down the row of pictures.

"Now, *there's* one you've never seen before!" said the Match Man proudly, pointing to a painting of a mountain covered with snow and its slopes simply littered with grasshoppers sitting on gigantic roses.

This time Mary Poppins could indulge in a sigh without hurting his feelings.

"Oh, Bert," she said, "that's a fair treat!" And by the way she said it she made him feel that by rights the picture should have been in the Royal Academy, which is a large room where people hang the pictures they have painted. Everybody comes to see them, and when they have looked at them for a very long time, every-body says to everybody else: "The idea—my dear!"

The next picture Mary Poppins and the Match Man came to was even better. It was the country—all trees and grass and a little bit of blue sea in the distance, and something that looked like Margate in the background.

"My word!" said Mary Poppins admiringly, stooping so that she could see it better. "Why, Bert, whatever is the matter?"

For the Match Man had caught hold of her other hand now and was looking very excited.

"Mary," he said, "I got an idea! A real *idea*. Why don't we go there—right now—this very day? Both together, into the picture. Eh, Mary?" And still holding her hands he drew her right out of the street, away from the iron railings and the lamp-posts, into the very middle of the picture. Pff! There they were, right inside it!

How green it was there and how quiet, and what soft crisp grass under their feet! They could hardly believe it was true, and yet here were green branches huskily rattling on their hats as they bent beneath them, and little coloured flowers curling round their shoes. They stared at each other, and each noticed that the other had changed. To Mary Poppins, the Match Man seemed to have bought himself an entirely new suit of clothes, for he was now wearing a bright green-and-red striped coat and white flannel trousers and, best of all, a new straw hat. He looked unusually clean, as though he had been polished.

"Why, Bert, you look fine!" she cried in an admiring voice.

Bert could not say anything for a moment, for his

31

mouth had fallen open and he was staring at her with round eyes. Then he gulped and said : " Golly!"

That was all. But he said it in such a way and stared so steadily and so delightedly at her that she took a little mirror out of her bag and looked at herself in it.

She, too, she discovered, had changed. Round her shoulders hung a cloak of lovely artificial silk with watery patterns all over it, and the tickling feeling at the back of her neck came, the mirror told her, from a long curly feather that swept down from the brim of her hat. Her best shoes had disappeared, and in their place were others much finer and with large diamond buckles shining upon them. She was still wearing the white gloves and carrying the umbrella.

" My goodness," said Mary Poppins, " I *am* having a Day Out!"

So, still admiring themselves and each other, they moved on together through the little wood, till presently they came upon a little open space filled with sunlight. And there on a green table was Afternoon-Tea!

A pile of raspberry-jam-cakes as high as Mary Poppins' waist stood in the centre, and beside it tea was boiling in a big brass urn. Best of all, there were two plates of whelks and two pins to pick them out with.

" Strike me pink!" said Mary Poppins. That was what she always said when she was pleased.

"Golly!" said the Match Man. And that was *his* particular phrase.

"Won't you sit down, Moddom?" enquired a voice, and they turned to find a tall man in a black coat coming out of the wood with a table-napkin over his arm.

Mary Poppins, thoroughly surprised, sat down with a plop upon one of the little green chairs that stood round the table. The Match Man, staring, collapsed on to another.

"I'm the Waiter, you know!" explained the man in the black coat.

"Oh! But I didn't see you in the picture," said Mary Poppins.

"Ah, I was behind the tree," explained the Waiter.

"Won't you sit down?" said Mary Poppins, politely.

"Waiters never sit down, Moddom," said the man but he seemed pleased at being asked.

"Your whelks, Mister!" he said, pushing a plate of them over to the Match Man. "*And* your Pin!" He dusted the pin on his napkin and handed it to the Match Man.

They began upon the afternoon-tea, and the Waiter stood beside them to see they had everything they needed.

"We're having them after all," said Mary Poppins

in a loud whisper, as she began on the heap of raspberry-jam-cakes.

"Golly!" agreed the Match Man, helping himself
to two of the largest.

"Tea?" said the Waiter, filling a large cup for each
of them from the urn.

They drank it and had two cups more each, and
then, for luck, they finished the pile of raspberry-jam-
cakes. After that they got up and brushed the crumbs
off.

"There is Nothing to Pay," said the Waiter, before
they had time to ask for the bill. "It is a Pleasure. You
will find the Merry-go-Round just over there!" And
he waved his hand to a little gap in the trees, where
Mary Poppins and the Match Man could see several
wooden horses whirling round on a stand.

"That's funny," said she. "I don't remember seeing
that in the picture, either."

"Ah," said the Match Man, who hadn't remembered it himself, "it was in the Background, you see!"

The Merry-go-Round was just slowing down as
they approached it. They leapt upon it, Mary Poppins
on a black horse and the Match Man on a grey. And
when the music started again and they began to move,
they rode all the way to Yarmouth and back, because
that was the place they both wanted most to see.

"I'm the Waiter, you know!"

When they returned it was nearly dark and the Waiter was watching for them.

" I'm very sorry, Moddom and Mister," he said politely, " but we close at Seven. Rules, you know. May I show you the Way Out?"

They nodded as he flourished his table-napkin and walked on in front of them through the wood.

" It's a wonderful picture you've drawn this time, Bert," said Mary Poppins, putting her hand through the Match Man's arm and drawing her cloak about her.

" Well, I did my best, Mary," said the Match Man modestly. But you could see he was really very pleased with himself indeed.

Just then the Waiter stopped in front of them, beside a large white doorway that looked as though it were made of thick chalk lines.

" Here you are!" he said. " This is the Way Out."

" Good-bye and thank you," said Mary Poppins, shaking his hand.

" Moddom, good-bye!" said the Waiter, bowing so low that his head knocked against his knees.

He nodded to the Match Man, who cocked his head on one side and closed one eye at the Waiter, which was his way of bidding him farewell. Then Mary Poppins stepped through the white doorway and the Match Man followed her.

And as they went, the feather dropped from her hat and the silk cloak from her shoulders and the diamonds from her shoes. The bright clothes of the Match Man faded, and his straw hat turned into his old ragged cap again. Mary Poppins turned and looked at him, and she knew at once what had happened. Standing on the pavement she gazed at him for a long minute, and then her glance explored the wood behind him for the Waiter. But the Waiter was nowhere to be seen. There was nobody in the picture. Nothing moved there. Even the Merry-go-Round had disappeared. Only the still trees and the grass and the unmoving little patch of sea remained.

But Mary Poppins and the Match Man smiled at one another. They knew, you see, what lay behind the trees. . . .

When she came back from her Day Out, Jane and Michael came running to meet her.

" Where have you been?" they asked her.

" In Fairyland," said Mary Poppins.

" Did you see Cinderella?" said Jane.

" Huh, Cinderella? Not me," said Mary Poppins, contemptuously. " Cinderella, indeed!"

" Or Robinson Crusoe?" asked Michael.

"Robinson Crusoe—pooh!" said Mary Poppins rudely.

"Then how could you have been there? It couldn't have been *our* Fairyland!"

Mary Poppins gave a superior sniff.

"Don't you know," she said pityingly, "that everybody's got a Fairyland of their own?"

And with another sniff she went upstairs to take off her white gloves and put the umbrella away.

Chapter Three

LAUGHING GAS

"ARE you quite sure he will be at home?" said Jane, as they got off the Bus, she and Michael and Mary Poppins.

"Would my Uncle ask me to bring you to tea if he intended to go out, I'd like to know?" said Mary Poppins, who was evidently very offended by the question. She was wearing her blue coat with the silver buttons and the blue hat to match, and on the days when she wore these it was the easiest thing in the world to offend her.

All three of them were on the way to pay a visit to Mary Poppins' uncle, Mr. Wigg, and Jane and Michael had looked forward to the trip for so long that they were more than half afraid that Mr. Wigg might not be in, after all.

"Why is he called Mr. Wigg—does he wear one?" asked Michael, hurrying along beside Mary Poppins.

"He is called Mr. Wigg because Mr. Wigg is his name. And he doesn't wear one. He is bald," said Mary Poppins. "And if I have any more questions we will just go Back Home." And she sniffed her usual sniff of displeasure.

Jane and Michael looked at each other and frowned. And the frown meant: "Don't let's ask her anything else or we'll never get there."

Mary Poppins put her hat straight at the Tobacconist's Shop at the corner. It had one of those curious windows where there seem to be three of you instead of one, so that if you look long enough at them you begin to feel you are not yourself but a whole crowd of somebody else. Mary Poppins sighed with pleasure, however, when she saw three of herself, each wearing a blue coat with silver buttons and a blue hat to match. She thought it was such a lovely sight that she wished there had been a dozen of her or even thirty. The more Mary Poppins the better.

"Come along," she said sternly, as though they had kept *her* waiting. Then they turned the corner and pulled the bell of Number Three, Robertson Road. Jane and Michael could hear it faintly echoing from a long way away and they knew that in one minute, or two at the most, they would be having tea with Mary Poppins' uncle, Mr. Wigg, for the first time ever.

"If he's in, of course," Jane said to Michael in a whisper.

At that moment the door flew open and a thin, watery-looking lady appeared.

" Is he in?" said Michael quickly.

" I'll thank you," said Mary Poppins, giving him a terrible glance, " to let *me* do the talking."

" How do you do, Mrs. Wigg," said Jane politely.

" Mrs. Wigg!" said the thin lady, in a voice even thinner than herself. " How dare you call me Mrs. Wigg? No, thank you! I'm plain Miss Persimmon *and* proud of it. Mrs. Wigg indeed!" She seemed to be quite upset, and they thought Mr. Wigg must be a very odd person if Miss Persimmon was so glad not to be Mrs. Wigg.

" Straight up and first door on the landing," said Miss Persimmon, and she went hurrying away down the passage saying : " Mrs. Wigg indeed!" to herself in a high, thin, outraged voice.

Jane and Michael followed Mary Poppins upstairs. Mary Poppins knocked at the door.

" Come in! Come in! And welcome!" called a loud, cheery voice from inside. Jane's heart was pitter-pattering with excitement.

" He *is* in!" she signalled to Michael with a look.

Mary Poppins opened the door and pushed them in front of her. A large cheerful room lay before them. At one end of it a fire was burning brightly and in the centre stood an enormous table laid for tea—four cups and saucers, piles of bread and butter, crumpets, coconut cakes and a large plum cake with pink icing.

"Well, this is indeed a Pleasure," a huge voice greeted them, and Jane and Michael looked round for its owner. He was nowhere to be seen. The room appeared to be quite empty. Then they heard Mary Poppins saying crossly:

"Oh, Uncle Albert—not *again*? It's not your birthday, is it?"

And as she spoke she looked up at the ceiling. Jane and Michael looked up too and to their surprise saw a round, fat, bald man who was hanging in the air without holding on to anything. Indeed, he appeared to be *sitting* on the air, for his legs were crossed and he had just put down the newspaper which he had been reading when they came in.

"My dear," said Mr. Wigg, smiling down at the children, and looking apologetically at Mary Poppins, "I'm very sorry, but I'm afraid it *is* my birthday."

"Tch, tch, tch!" said Mary Poppins.

"I only remembered last night and there was no time then to send you a postcard asking you to come another day. Very distressing, isn't it?" he said, looking down at Jane and Michael.

"I can see you're rather surprised," said Mr. Wigg. And, indeed, their mouths were so wide open with astonishment that Mr. Wigg, if he had been a little smaller, might almost have fallen into one of them.

"I'd better explain, I think," Mr. Wigg went on

calmly. "You see, it's this way. I'm a cheerful sort of man and very disposed to laughter. You wouldn't believe, either of you, the number of things that strike me as being funny. I can laugh at pretty nearly everything, I can."

And with that Mr. Wigg began to bob up and down, shaking with laughter at the thought of his own cheerfulness.

"Uncle Albert!" said Mary Poppins, and Mr. Wigg stopped laughing with a jerk.

"Oh, beg pardon, my dear. Where was I? Oh, yes. Well, the funny thing about me is—all right, Mary, I won't laugh if I can help it!—that whenever my birthday falls on a Friday, well, it's all up with me. Absolutely U.P.," said Mr. Wigg.

"But why——?" began Jane.

"But how——?" began Michael.

"Well, you see, if I laugh on that particular day I become so filled with Laughing Gas that I simply can't keep on the ground. Even if I smile it happens. The first funny thought, and I'm up like a balloon. And until I can think of something serious I can't get down again." Mr. Wigg began to chuckle at that, but he caught sight of Mary Poppins' face and stopped the chuckle, and continued:

"It's awkward, of course, but not unpleasant. Never happens to either of you, I suppose?"

Jane and Michael shook their heads.

" No, I thought not. It seems to be my own special habit. Once, after I'd been to the Circus the night before, I laughed so much that—would you believe it? —I was up here for a whole twelve hours, and couldn't get down till the last stroke of midnight. Then, of course, I came down with a flop because it was Saturday and not my birthday any more. It's rather odd, isn't it? Not to say funny?

" And now here it is Friday again and my birthday, and you two and Mary P. to visit me. Oh, Lordy, Lordy, don't make me laugh, I beg of you——" But although Jane and Michael had done nothing very amusing, except to stare at him in astonishment, Mr. Wigg began to laugh again loudly, and as he laughed he went bouncing and bobbing about in the air, with the newspaper rattling in his hand and his spectacles half on and half off his nose.

He looked so comic, floundering in the air like a great human bubble, clutching at the ceiling sometimes and sometimes at the gas-bracket as he passed it, that Jane and Michael, though they were trying hard to be polite, just couldn't help doing what they did. They laughed. *And* they laughed. They shut their mouths tight to prevent the laughter escaping, but that didn't do any good. And presently they were rolling over and over on the floor, squealing and shrieking with laughter.

"Really!" said Mary Poppins. "Really, *such* behaviour!"

"I can't help it, I can't help it!" shrieked Michael, as he rolled into the fender. "It's so terribly funny. Oh, Jane, *isn't* it funny?"

Jane did not reply, for a curious thing was happening to her. As she laughed she felt herself growing lighter and lighter, just as though she were being pumped full of air. It was a curious and delicious feeling and it made her want to laugh all the more. And then suddenly, with a bouncing bound, she felt herself jumping through the air. Michael, to his astonishment, saw her go soaring up through the room. With a little bump her head touched the ceiling and then she went bouncing along it till she reached Mr. Wigg.

"*Well!*" said Mr. Wigg, looking very surprised indeed. "Don't tell me it's *your* birthday, too?" Jane shook her head.

"It's not? Then this Laughing Gas must be catching! Hi—whoa there, look out for the mantelpiece!" This was to Michael, who had suddenly risen from the floor and was swooping through the air, roaring with laughter, and just grazing the china ornaments on the mantelpiece as he passed. He landed with a bounce right on Mr. Wigg's knee.

"How do you do," said Mr. Wigg, heartily shaking Michael by the hand. "I call this really friendly of you—bless my soul, I do! To come up to me since I couldn't come down to you—eh?" And then he and Michael looked at each other and flung back their heads and simply howled with laughter.

"I say," said Mr. Wigg to Jane, as he wiped his eyes. "You'll be thinking I have the worst manners in the world. You're standing and you ought to be sitting—a nice young lady like you. I'm afraid I can't offer you a chair up here, but I think you'll find the air quite comfortable to sit on. I do."

Jane tried it and found she could sit down quite comfortably on the air. She took off her hat and laid it down beside her and it hung there in space without any support at all.

"That's right," said Mr. Wigg. Then he turned and looked down at Mary Poppins.

"Well, Mary, we're fixed. And now I can enquire about *you*, my dear. I must say, I am very glad to welcome you and my two young friends here to-day— why, Mary, you're frowning. I'm afraid you don't approve of—er—all this."

He waved his hand at Jane and Michael, and said hurriedly:

46

"I apologise, Mary, my dear. But you know how it is with me. Still, I must say I never thought my two young friends here would catch it, really I didn't, Mary! I suppose I should have asked them for another day or tried to think of something sad or something——"

"Well, I must say," said Mary Poppins primly, "that I have never in my life seen such a sight. And at your age, Uncle——"

"Mary Poppins, Mary Poppins, do come up!" interrupted Michael. "Think of something funny and you'll find it's quite easy."

"Ah, now do, Mary!" said Mr. Wigg persuasively.

"We're lonely up here without you!" said Jane, and held out her arms towards Mary Poppins. "*Do* think of something funny!"

"Ah, *she* doesn't need to," said Mr. Wigg sighing. "She can come up if she wants to, even without laughing—and she knows it." And he looked mysteriously and secretly at Mary Poppins as she stood down there on the hearth-rug.

"Well," said Mary Poppins, "it's all very silly and undignified, but, since you're all up there and don't seem able to get down, I suppose I'd better come up, too."

With that, to the surprise of Jane and Michael, she put her hands down at her sides and without a laugh, without even the faintest glimmer of a smile, she shot up through the air and sat down beside Jane.

"How many times, I should like to know," she said snappily, "have I told you to take off your coat when you come into a hot room?" And she unbuttoned Jane's coat and laid it neatly on the air beside the hat.

"That's right, Mary, that's right," said Mr. Wigg contentedly, as he leant down and put his spectacles on the mantelpiece. "Now we're all comfortable——"

"There's comfort *and* comfort," sniffed Mary Poppins.

"And we can have tea," Mr. Wigg went on, apparently not noticing her remark. And then a startled look came over his face.

"My goodness!" he said. "How dreadful! I've just realised—the table's down there and we're up here. What *are* we going to do? We're here and it's there. It's an awful tragedy—awful! But oh, it's terribly comic!" And he hid his face in his handkerchief and laughed loudly into it. Jane and Michael, though they did not want to miss the crumpets and the cakes, couldn't help laughing too, because Mr. Wigg's mirth was so infectious.

Mr. Wigg dried his eyes.

"There's only one thing for it," he said. "We must think of something serious. Something sad, very sad.

There they were, all together, up in the air

And then we shall be able to get down. Now—one, two, three! Something *very* sad, mind you!"

They thought and thought, with their chins on their hands.

Michael thought of school, and that one day he would have to go there. But even that seemed funny to-day and he had to laugh.

Jane thought: "I shall be grown up in another fourteen years!" But that didn't sound sad at all but quite nice and rather funny. She could not help smiling at the thought of herself grown up, with long skirts and a hand-bag.

"There was my poor old Aunt Emily," thought Mr. Wigg out loud. "She was run over by an omnibus. Sad. Very sad. Unbearably sad. Poor Aunt Emily. But they saved her umbrella. That was funny, wasn't it?" And before he knew where he was, he was heaving and trembling and bursting with laughter at the thought of Aunt Emily's umbrella.

"It's no good," he said, blowing his nose. "I give it up. And my young friends here seem to be no better at sadness than I am. Mary, can't *you* do something? We want our tea."

To this day Jane and Michael cannot be sure of what happened then. All they know for certain is that, as soon as Mr. Wigg had appealed to Mary Poppins, the table below began to wriggle on its legs. Presently

50

it was swaying dangerously, and then with a rattle of china and with cakes lurching off their plates on to the cloth, the table came soaring through the room, gave one graceful turn, and landed beside them so that Mr. Wigg was at its head.

"Good girl!" said Mr. Wigg, smiling proudly upon her. "I knew you'd fix something. Now, will you take the foot of the table and pour out, Mary? And the guests on either side of me. That's the idea," he said, as Michael ran bobbing through the air and sat down on Mr. Wigg's right. Jane was at his left hand. There they were, all together, up in the air and the table between them. Not a single piece of bread-and-butter or a lump of sugar had been left behind.

Mr. Wigg smiled contentedly.

"It is usual, I think, to begin with bread-and-butter," he said to Jane and Michael, "but as it's my birthday we will begin the wrong way—which I always think is the *right* way—with the Cake!"

And he cut a large slice for everybody.

"More tea?" he said to Jane. But before she had time to reply there was a quick, sharp knock at the door.

"Come in!" called Mr. Wigg.

The door opened, and there stood Miss Persimmon with a jug of hot water on a tray.

"I thought, Mr. Wigg," she began, looking searchingly round the room, " you'd be wanting some more hot—— Well, I never! I simply *never*!" she said, as she caught sight of them all seated on the air round the table. " Such goings on I never did see! In all my born days I never saw such. I'm sure, Mr. Wigg, I always knew *you* were a bit odd. But I've closed my eyes to it—being as how you paid your rent regular. But such behaviour as this—having tea in the air with your guests—Mr. Wigg, sir, I'm astonished at you! It's that undignified, and for a gentleman of your age —I never did——"

" But perhaps you will, Miss Persimmon!" said Michael.

" Will what?" said Miss Persimmon haughtily.

" Catch the Laughing Gas, as we did," said Michael.

Miss Persimmon flung back her head scornfully.

" I hope, young man," she retorted, " I have more respect for myself than to go bouncing about in the air like a rubber ball on the end of a bat. I'll stay on my own feet, thank you, or my name's not Amy Persimmon, and—oh dear, oh *dear*, my goodness, oh *DEAR* —what *is* the matter? I can't walk, I'm going, I—oh, help, *HELP*!"

For Miss Persimmon, quite against her will, was off the ground and was stumbling through the air, rolling from side to side like a very thin barrel, balancing the

tray in her hand. She was almost weeping with distress
as she arrived at the table and put down her jug of hot
water.

"Thank you," said Mary Poppins in a calm, very
polite voice.

Then Miss Persimmon turned and went wafting
down again, murmuring as she went : " So undignified
—and me a well-behaved, steady-going woman. I
must see a doctor——"

53

When she touched the floor she ran hurriedly out of the room, wringing her hands, and not giving a single glance backwards.

"So undignified!" they heard her moaning as she shut the door behind her.

"Her name can't be Amy Persimmon, because she *didn't* stay on her own feet!" whispered Jane to Michael.

But Mr. Wigg was looking at Mary Poppins—a curious look, half-amused, half-accusing.

"Mary, Mary, you shouldn't—bless my soul, you shouldn't, Mary. The poor old body will never get over it. But, oh, my goodness, didn't she look funny waddling through the air—my Gracious Goodness, but didn't she?"

And he and Jane and Michael were off again, rolling about the air, clutching their sides and gasping with laughter at the thought of how funny Miss Persimmon had looked.

"Oh dear!" said Michael. "Don't make me laugh any more. I can't stand it. I shall break!" "Oh, oh, oh!" cried Jane, as she gasped for breath, with her hand over her heart. "Oh, my Gracious, Glorious, Galumphing Goodness!" roared Mr. Wigg, dabbing his eyes with his coat-tail because he couldn't find his handkerchief.

" IT IS TIME TO GO HOME." Mary Poppins' voice sounded above the roars of laughter like a trumpet.

And suddenly, with a rush, Jane and Michael and Mr. Wigg came down. They landed on the floor with a huge bump, all together. The thought that they would have to go home was the first sad thought of the afternoon, and the moment it was in their minds the Laughing Gas went out of them.

Jane and Michael sighed as they watched Mary Poppins come slowly down the air, carrying Jane's coat and hat.

Mr. Wigg sighed, too. A great, long, heavy sigh.

" Well, isn't that a pity?" he said soberly. " It's very sad that you've got to go home. I never enjoyed an afternoon so much—did you?"

" Never," said Michael sadly, feeling how dull it was to be down on the earth again with no Laughing Gas inside him.

" Never, never," said Jane, as she stood on tip-toe and kissed Mr. Wigg's withered-apple cheeks. " Never, never, never, never . . . !"

They sat on either side of Mary Poppins going home in the Bus. They were both very quiet, thinking over the lovely afternoon. Presently Michael said sleepily to Mary Poppins:

"How often does your Uncle get like that?"

"Like what?" said Mary Poppins sharply, as though Michael had deliberately said something to offend her.

"Well—all bouncy and boundy and laughing and going up in the air."

"Up in the air?" Mary Poppins' voice was high and angry. "What do you mean, pray, up in the air?"

Jane tried to explain.

"Michael means—is your Uncle often full of Laughing Gas, and does he often go rolling and bobbing about on the ceiling when——"

"Rolling and bobbing! What an idea! Rolling and bobbing on the ceiling! You'll be telling me next he's a balloon!" Mary Poppins gave an offended sniff.

"But he did!" said Michael. "We saw him."

"What, roll and bob? How dare you! I'll have you know that my Uncle is a sober, honest, hard-working man, and you'll be kind enough to speak of him respectfully. And don't bite your Bus ticket! Roll and bob, indeed—the idea!"

Michael and Jane looked across Mary Poppins at each other. They said nothing, for they had learnt that

Crept closer to her and fell asleep

it was better not to argue with Mary Poppins, no matter how odd anything seemed.

But the look that passed between them said : " Is it true or isn't it? About Mr. Wigg. Is Mary Poppins right or are we?"

But there was nobody to give them the right answer.

The Bus roared on, wildly lurching and bounding.

Mary Poppins sat between them, offended and silent, and presently, because they were very tired, they crept closer to her and leant up against her sides and fell asleep, still wondering. . . .

Chapter Four

MISS LARK'S ANDREW

Miss Lark lived Next Door.

But before we go any further I must tell you what Next Door looked like. It was a very grand house, by far the grandest in Cherry Tree Lane. Even Admiral Boom had been known to envy Miss Lark her wonderful house, though his own had ship's funnels instead of chimneys and a flagstaff in the front garden. Over and over again the inhabitants of the Lane heard him say, as he rolled past Miss Lark's mansion : " Blast my gizzard ! What does *she* want with a house like that?"

And the reason of Admiral Boom's jealousy was that Miss Lark had two gates. One was for Miss Lark's friends and relations, and the other for the Butcher and the Baker and the Milkman.

Once the Baker made a mistake and came in through the gate reserved for the friends and relations, and Miss Lark was so angry that she said she wouldn't have any more bread ever.

But in the end she had to forgive the Baker because he was the only one in the neighbourhood who made those little flat rolls with the curly twists of crust on the top. She never really liked him very much after that, however, and when he came he pulled his hat far down over his eyes so that Miss Lark might think he was somebody else. But she never did.

Jane and Michael always knew when Miss Lark was in the garden or coming along the Lane, because she wore so many brooches and necklaces and earrings that she jingled and jangled just like a brass band. And whenever she met them, she always said the same thing:

"Good-morning!" (or "Good-afternoon!" if it happened to be after luncheon), "and how are *we* to-day?"

And Jane and Michael were never quite sure whether Miss Lark was asking how *they* were, or how she and Andrew were.

So they just replied: "Good-afternoon!" (or, of course, "Good-morning!" if it was before luncheon).

All day long, no matter where the children were, they could hear Miss Lark calling, in a very loud voice, things like:

"Andrew, where are you?" or

"Andrew, you mustn't go out without your overcoat!" or

"Andrew, come to Mother!"

And, if you didn't know, you would think that

Andrew must be a little boy. Indeed, Jane thought that Miss Lark thought that Andrew *was* a little boy. But Andrew wasn't. He was a dog—one of those small, silky, fluffy dogs that look like a fur necklet, until they begin to bark. But, of course, when they do that you

know that they're dogs. No fur necklet ever made a noise like that.

Now, Andrew led such a luxurious life that you might have thought he was the Shah of Persia in disguise. He slept on a silk pillow in Miss Lark's room; he went by car to the Hairdresser's twice a week to be shampooed; he had cream for every meal and sometimes oysters, and he possessed four overcoats with checks and stripes in different colours. Andrew's ordinary days were filled with the kind of things most people have only on birthdays. And when Andrew himself had a birthday he had *two* candles on his cake for every year, instead of only one.

The effect of all this was to make Andrew very much

disliked in the neighbourhood. People used to laugh
heartily when they saw Andrew sitting up in the back
seat of Miss Lark's car on the way to the Hairdresser's,
with the fur rug over his knees and his best coat on.
And on the day when Miss Lark bought him two pairs
of small leather boots so that he could go out in the
Park wet or fine, everybody in the Lane came down to
their front gates to watch him go by and to smile
secretly behind their hands.

"Pooh!" said Michael, as they were watching
Andrew one day through the fence that separated
Number Seventeen from Next Door. "Pooh, he's a
ninkypoop!"

"How do you know?" asked Jane, very interested.

"I know because I heard Daddy call him one this
morning!" said Michael, and he laughed at Andrew
very rudely.

"He is *not* a nincompoop," said Mary Poppins.
"And that is that."

And Mary Poppins was right. Andrew wasn't .
nincompoop, as you will very soon see.

You must not think he did not respect Miss Lark.
He did. He was even fond of her in a mild sort of way.
He couldn't help having a kindly feeling for somebody
who had been so good to him ever since he was a
puppy, even if she *did* kiss him rather too often. But
there was no doubt about it that the life Andrew led

bored him to distraction. He would have given half
his fortune, if he had one, for a nice piece of raw, red
meat, instead of the usual breast of chicken or scrambled eggs with asparagus.

For in his secret, innermost heart, Andrew longed
to be a common dog. He never passed his pedigree
(which hung on the wall in Miss Lark's drawing-room)
without a shudder of shame. And many a time he
wished he'd never had a father, nor a grandfather, nor
a great-grandfather, if Miss Lark was going to make
such a fuss of it.

It was this desire of his to *be* a common dog that
made Andrew choose common dogs for his friends.
And whenever he got the chance, he would run down
to the front gate and sit there watching for them, so
that he could exchange a few common remarks. But
Miss Lark, when she discovered him, would be sure
to call out :

" Andrew, Andrew, come in, my darling ! Come
away from those dreadful street arabs ! "

And of course Andrew would *have* to come in, or
Miss Lark would shame him by coming out and *bringing* him in. And Andrew would blush and hurry up
the steps so that his friends should not hear her calling
him her Precious, her Joy, her Little Lump of Sugar.

Andrew's most special friend was more than
common, he was a Byword. He was half an Airedale

and half a Retriever and the worst half of both. Whenever there was a fight in the road he would be sure to be in the thick of it; he was always getting into trouble with the Postman or the Policeman, and there was nothing he loved better than sniffing about in drains or garbage tins. He was, in fact, the talk of the whole street, and more than one person had been heard to say thankfully that they were glad he was not *their* dog.

But Andrew loved him and was continually on the watch for him. Sometimes they had only time to exchange a sniff in the Park, but on luckier occasions—though these were very rare—they would have long talks at the gate. From his friend, Andrew heard all the town gossip, and you could see by the rude way in which the other dog laughed as he told it, that it wasn't very complimentary.

Then suddenly, Miss Lark's voice would be heard calling from a window, and the other dog would get up, loll out his tongue at Miss Lark, wink at Andrew and wander off, waving his hind-quarters as he went just to show that *he* didn't care.

Andrew, of course, was never allowed outside the gate unless he went with Miss Lark for a walk in the Park, or with one of the maids to have his toes manicured.

Imagine, then, the surprise of Jane and Michael when they saw Andrew, all alone, careering past them through the Park, with his ears back and his tail up as though he were on the track of a tiger.

Mary Poppins pulled the perambulator up with a jerk, in case Andrew, in his wild flight, should upset it and the Twins. And Jane and Michael screamed at him as he passed.

"Hi, Andrew! Where's your overcoat?" cried Michael, trying to make a high, windy voice like Miss Lark's.

"Andrew, you naughty little boy!" said Jane, and her voice, because she was a girl, was much more like Miss Lark's.

But Andrew just looked at them both very haughtily and barked sharply in the direction of Mary Poppins.

"Yay-yap!" said Andrew several times very quickly.

"Let me see. I think it's the first on your right and second house on the left-hand side," said Mary Poppins.

"Yap?" said Andrew.

"No—no garden. Only a back-yard. Gate's usually open."

Andrew barked again.

"I'm not sure," said Mary Poppins. "But I should think so. Generally goes home at tea-time."

Andrew flung back his head and set off again at a gallop.

Jane's eyes and Michael's were round as saucers with surprise.

"What was he saying?" they demanded breathlessly, both together.

"Just passing the time of day!" said Mary Poppins, and shut her mouth tightly as though she did not intend any more words to escape from it. John and Barbara gurgled from their perambulator.

"He wasn't!" said Michael.

"He *couldn't* have been!" said Jane.

"Well, you know best, of course. *As* usual," said Mary Poppins haughtily.

"He must have been asking you where somebody lived, I'm sure he must——" Michael began.

"Well, if you know, why bother to ask me?" said Mary Poppins sniffing. "*I'm* no dictionary."

"Oh, Michael," said Jane, "she'll never tell us if you talk like that. Mary Poppins, do say what Andrew was saying to you, *please*."

"Ask *him*. He knows—Mr. Know-All!" said Mary Poppins, nodding her head scornfully at Michael.

"Oh no, I don't. I promise I don't, Mary Poppins. Do tell."

"Half-past three. Tea-time," said Mary Poppins, and she wheeled the perambulator round and shut her mouth tight again as though it were a trap-door. She did not say another word all the way home.

Jane dropped behind with Michael.

"It's your fault!" she said. "Now we'll never know."

"I don't care!" said Michael, and he began to push his scooter very quickly. "I don't want to know."

But he did want to know very badly indeed. And as it turned out, he and Jane and everybody else knew all about it before tea-time.

Just as they were about to cross the road to their own house, they heard loud cries coming from Next Door, and there they saw a curious sight. Miss Lark's two maids were rushing wildly about the garden, looking under bushes and up into the trees as people do who have lost their most valuable possession. And there was Robertson Ay, from Number Seventeen, busily wasting his time by poking at the gravel on Miss Lark's path with a broom as though he expected to find the missing treasure under a pebble. Miss Lark herself was running about in her garden, waving her arms and calling: "Andrew, Andrew! Oh, he's lost. My darling boy is lost! We must send for the Police. I must see the Prime Minister. Andrew is lost! Oh dear! oh dear!"

"Oh, poor Miss Lark!" said Jane, hurrying across the road. She could not help feeling sorry because Miss Lark looked so upset.

But it was Michael who really comforted Miss Lark.

Miss Lark was running about in her garden, calling:
" Andrew, Andrew! Oh, he's lost!"

Just as he was going in at the gate of Number Seventeen, he looked down the Lane and there he saw——

"Why, there's Andrew, Miss Lark. See, down there —just turning Admiral Boom's corner!"

"Where, where? Show me!" said Miss Lark breathlessly, and she peered in the direction in which Michael was pointing.

And there, sure enough, *was* Andrew, walking as slowly and as casually as though nothing in the world was the matter; and beside him waltzed a huge dog that seemed to be half an Airedale and half a Retriever, and the worst half of both.

"Oh, what a relief!" said Miss Lark, sighing loudly. "What a load off my mind!"

Mary Poppins and the children waited in the Lane outside Miss Lark's gate. Miss Lark herself and her two maids leant over the fence, Robertson Ay, resting from his labours, propped himself up with his broom-handle, and all of them watched in silence the return of Andrew.

He and his friend marched sedately up to the group, whisking their tails jauntily and keeping their ears well cocked, and you could tell by the look in Andrew's eye that, whatever he meant, he meant business.

"That dreadful dog!" said Miss Lark, looking at Andrew's companion.

"Shoo! Shoo! Go home!" she cried.

But the dog just sat down on the pavement and scratched his right ear with his left leg and yawned.

"Go away! Go home! Shoo, I say!" said Miss Lark, waving her arms angrily at the dog.

"And you, Andrew," she went on, "come indoors this minute! Going out like that—all alone and without your overcoat. I am very displeased with you!"

Andrew barked lazily, but did not move.

"What do you mean, Andrew? Come in at once!" said Miss Lark.

Andrew barked again.

"He says," put in Mary Poppins, "that he's not coming in."

Miss Lark turned and regarded her haughtily. "How do *you* know what my dog says, may I ask? Of course he will come in."

Andrew, however, merely shook his head and gave one or two low growls.

"He won't," said Mary Poppins. "Not unless his friend comes, too."

"Stuff and nonsense," said Miss Lark crossly. "That *can't* be what he says. As if I could have a great hulking mongrel like that inside my gate."

Andrew yapped three or four times.

"He says he means it," said Mary Poppins. "And what's more, he'll go and live with his friend unless his friend is allowed to come and live with him."

70

"Oh, Andrew, you can't—you can't, really—after all I've done for you and everything!" Miss Lark was nearly weeping.

Andrew barked and turned away. The other dog got up.

"Oh, he *does* mean it!" cried Miss Lark. "I see he does. He is going away." She sobbed a moment into her handkerchief, then she blew her nose and said:

"Very well, then, Andrew. I give in. This—this common dog can stay. On condition, of course, that he sleeps in the coal-cellar."

"He insists, ma'am, that that won't do. His friend must have a silk cushion just like his and sleep in your room too. Otherwise he will go and sleep in the coal-cellar with his friend," said Mary Poppins.

"Andrew, how could you?" moaned Miss Lark. "I shall never consent to such a thing."

Andrew looked as though he were preparing to depart. So did the other dog.

"Oh, he's leaving me!" shrieked Miss Lark. "Very well, then, Andrew. It will be as you wish. He *shall* sleep in my room. But I shall never be the same again, never, never. Such a common dog!"

She wiped her streaming eyes and went on:

"I should never have thought it of you, Andrew. But I'll say no more, no matter what I think. And this

—er—creature—I shall have to call Waif or Stray or——"

At that the other dog looked at Miss Lark very indignantly, and Andrew barked loudly.

"They say you must call him Willoughby and nothing else," said Mary Poppins. "Willoughby being his name."

"Willoughby! What a name! Worse and worse!" said Miss Lark despairingly. "What is he saying now?" For Andrew was barking again.

"He says that if he comes back you are never to make him wear overcoats or go to the Hairdresser's again—that's his last word," said Mary Poppins.

There was a pause.

"Very well," said Miss Lark at last. "But I warn you, Andrew, if you catch your death of cold—don't blame me!"

And with that she turned and walked haughtily up the steps, sniffing away the last of her tears.

Andrew cocked his head towards Willoughby as if to say: "Come on!" and the other two of them waltzed side by side slowly up the garden path, waving their tails like banners, and followed Miss Lark into the house.

"He isn't a ninkypoop after all, you see," said Jane, as they went upstairs to the nursery and Tea.

"No," agreed Michael. "But how do you think Mary Poppins knew?"

"I don't know," said Jane. "And she'll never, never tell us. I am sure of that. . . ."

Chapter Five

THE DANCING COW

JANE, with her head tied up in Mary Poppins' bandanna handkerchief, was in bed with earache.

"What does it feel like?" Michael wanted to know.

"Like guns going off inside my head," said Jane.

"Cannons?"

"No, pop-guns."

"Oh," said Michael. And he almost wished he could have earache, too. It sounded so exciting.

"Shall I tell you a story out of one of the books?" said Michael, going to the bookshelf.

"No. I just couldn't bear it," said Jane, holding her ear with her hand.

74

" Well, shall I sit at the window and tell you what is happening outside?"

"Yes, do," said Jane.

So Michael sat all the afternoon on the window-seat telling her everything that occurred in the Lane. And sometimes his accounts were very dull and sometimes very exciting.

"There's Admiral Boom!" he said once. "He has come out of his gate and is hurrying down the Lane. Here he comes. His nose is redder than ever and he's wearing a top-hat. Now he is passing Next Door——"

" Is he saying ' Blast my gizzard!'?" enquired Jane.

"I can't hear. I expect so. There's Miss Lark's second housemaid in Miss Lark's garden. And Robertson Ay is in *our* garden, sweeping up the leaves and looking at her over the fence. He is sitting down now, having a rest."

" He has a weak heart," said Jane.

" How do you know?"

" He told me. He said his doctor said he was to do as little as possible. And I heard Daddy say if Robertson Ay does what his doctor told him to he'll sack him. Oh, how it bangs and *bangs*!" said Jane, clutching her ear again.

"Hull*oh*!" said Michael excitedly from the window.

"What is it?" cried Jane, sitting up. "Do tell me."

"A very extraordinary thing. There's a cow down in the Lane," said Michael, jumping up and down on the window-seat.

"A cow? A real cow—right in the middle of a town? How funny! Mary Poppins," said Jane, "there's a cow in the Lane, Michael says."

"Yes, and it's walking very slowly, putting its head over every gate and looking round as though it had lost something."

"I *wish* I could see it," said Jane mournfully.

"Look!" said Michael, pointing downwards as Mary Poppins came to the window. "A cow. Isn't that funny?"

Mary Poppins gave a quick, sharp glance down into the Lane. She started with surprise.

"Certainly not," she said, turning to Jane and Michael. "It's not funny at all. I know that cow. She was a great friend of my Mother's and I'll thank you to speak politely to her." She smoothed her apron and looked at them both very severely.

"Have you known her long?" enquired Michael gently, hoping that if he was particularly polite he would hear something more about the cow.

"Since before she saw the King," said Mary Poppins.

"And when was that?" asked Jane, in a soft encouraging voice.

Mary Poppins stared into space, her eyes fixed upon something that they could not see. Jane and Michael held their breath, waiting.

"It was long ago," said Mary Poppins, in a brooding story-telling voice. She paused, as though she were remembering events that happened hundreds of years before that time. Then she went on dreamily, still gazing into the middle of the room, but without seeing anything.

The Red Cow—that's the name she went by. And very important and prosperous she was, too (so my Mother said). She lived in the best field in the whole district—a large one full of buttercups the size of saucers and dandelions standing up in it like soldiers. Every time she ate the head off one soldier, another grew up in its place, with a green military coat and a yellow busby.

She had lived there always—she often told my Mother that she couldn't remember the time when she hadn't lived in that field. Her world was bounded by green hedges and the sky and she knew nothing of what lay beyond these.

The Red Cow was very respectable, she always behaved like a perfect lady and she knew What was What. To her a thing was either black or white—there was nothing in between. Dandelions were either sweet or sour—there were never any moderately nice ones.

She led a very busy life. Her mornings were taken up in giving lessons to the Red Calf, her daughter, and in the afternoon she taught the little one deportment and mooing and all the things a really well brought up calf should know. Then they had their supper, and the Red Cow showed the Red Calf how to select a good blade of grass from a bad one; and when her child had gone to sleep at night she would go into a corner of the field and chew the cud and think her own quiet thoughts.

All her days were exactly the same. One Red Calf grew up and went away and another came in its place. And it was natural that the Red Cow should imagine that her life would always be the same as it had always been—indeed, she felt that she could ask for nothing better than for all her days to be alike till she came to the end of them.

But at the very moment she was thinking these thoughts, adventure, as she afterwards told my Mother, was stalking her. It came upon her one night when the stars themselves looked like dandelions in the sky and the moon a great daisy among the stars.

On this night, long after the Red Calf was asleep, the Red Cow stood up suddenly and began to dance. She danced wildly and beautifully and in perfect time, though she had no music to go by. Sometimes it was a polka, sometimes a Highland Fling and sometimes a special dance that she made up out of her own head. And in between these dances she would curtsey and make sweeping bows and knock her head against the dandelions.

"Dear me!" said the Red Cow to herself, as she began on a Sailor's Hornpipe. "What an extraordinary thing! I always thought dancing improper, but it can't be since I myself am dancing. For I am a model cow."

And she went on dancing, and thoroughly enjoying herself. At last, however, she grew tired and decided that she had danced enough and that she would go to sleep. But, to her great surprise, she found that she could not stop dancing. When she went to lie down beside the Red Calf, her legs would not let her. They went on capering and prancing and, of course, carrying her with them. Round and round the field she went, leaping and waltzing and stepping on tip-toe.

"Dear me!" she murmured at intervals with a ladylike accent. " How very peculiar!" But she couldn't stop.

In the morning she was still dancing and the Red Calf had to take its breakfast of dandelions all by itself because the Red Cow could not remain still enough to eat.

All through the day she danced, up and down the meadow and round and round the meadow, with the Red Calf mooing piteously behind her. When the second night came, and she was still at it and still could not stop, she grew very worried. And at the end of a week of dancing she was nearly distracted.

" I must go and see the King about it," she decided, shaking her head.

So she kissed her Red Calf and told it to be good. Then she turned and danced out of the meadow and went to tell the King.

She danced all the way, snatching little sprays of green food from the hedges as she went, and every eye that saw her stared with astonishment. But none of them were more astonished than the Red Cow herself.

At last she came to the Palace where the King lived. She pulled the bell-rope with her mouth, and when the gate opened she danced through it and up the broad garden path till she came to the flight of steps that led to the King's throne.

Upon this the King was sitting, busily making a new

set of Laws. His Secretary was writing them down in a little red note-book, one after another, as the King thought of them. There were Courtiers and Ladies-in-Waiting everywhere, all very gorgeously dressed and all talking at once.

"How many have I made to-day?" asked the King, turning to the Secretary. The Secretary counted the Laws he had written down in the red note-book.

"Seventy-two, your Majesty," he said, bowing low and taking care not to trip over his quill pen, which was a very large one.

"H'm. Not bad for an hour's work." said the King, looking very pleased with himself. "That's enough for to-day." He stood up and arranged his ermine cloak very tastefully.

"Order my coach. I must go to the Barber's," he said magnificently.

It was then that he noticed the Red Cow approaching. He sat down again and took up his sceptre.

"What have we here, ho?" he demanded, as the Red Cow danced to the foot of the steps.

"A Cow, your Majesty!" she answered simply.

"I can see *that*," said the King. "I still have my eyesight. But what do you want? Be quick, because I have an appointment with the Barber at ten. He won't wait for me longer than that and I *must* have my hair cut. And for goodness' sake stop jigging and jagging about like that!" he added irritably. "It makes me quite giddy."

"Quite giddy!" echoed all the Courtiers, staring.

"That's just my trouble, your Majesty. I *can't* stop!" said the Red Cow piteously.

"Can't stop? Nonsense!" said the King furiously. "Stop at *once*! I, the King, command you!"

"Stop at once! The King commands you!" cried all the Courtiers.

The Red Cow made a great effort. She tried so hard to stop dancing that every muscle and every rib stood out like mountain ranges all over her. But it was no good. She just went on dancing at the foot of the King's steps.

"I *have* tried, your Majesty. And I can't. I've been dancing now for seven days running. And I've had no sleep. And very little to eat. A white-thorn spray or two—that's all. So I've come to ask your advice."

"H'm—very curious," said the King, pushing the crown on one side and scratching his head.

"Very curious," said the Courtiers, scratching their heads, too.

"What does it feel like?" asked the King.

"Funny," said the Red Cow. "And yet," she paused, as if choosing her words, "it's rather a pleasant

"What have we here, ho?"

feeling, too. As if laughter were running up and down inside me."

" *Extraordinary*," said the King, and he put his chin on his hand and stared at the Red Cow, pondering on what was the best thing to do.

Suddenly he sprang to his feet and said :

" Good gracious!"

" What is it?" cried all the Courtiers.

" Why, don't you see?" said the King, getting very excited and dropping his sceptre. " What an idiot I was not to have noticed it before. And what idiots *you* were!" he turned furiously upon the Courtiers. " Don't you see that there's a fallen star caught on her horn?"

" So there is!" cried the Courtiers, as they all suddenly noticed the star for the first time. And as they looked it seemed to them that the star grew brighter.

" That's what's wrong!" said the King. " Now, you Courtiers had better pull it off so that this—er—lady can stop dancing and have some breakfast. It's the star, madam, that is making you dance," he said to the Red Cow. " Now, come along, you!"

And he motioned to the Chief Courtier, who presented himself smartly before the Red Cow and began to tug at the star. It would not come off. The Chief Courtier was joined by one after another of the other Courtiers, until at last there was a long chain of them, each holding the man in front of him by the waist, and

84

a tug-of-war began between the Courtiers and the star.

"Mind my head!" entreated the Red Cow.

"Pull harder!" roared the King.

They pulled harder. They pulled until their faces were red as raspberries. They pulled till they could pull no longer and all fell back, one on top of the other. The star did not move. It remained firmly fixed to the horn.

"Tch, tch, tch!" said the King. "Secretary, look in the Encyclopædia and see what it says about cows with stars on their horns."

The Secretary knelt down and began to crawl under the throne. Presently he emerged, carrying a large green book which was always kept there in case the King wanted to know anything.

He turned the pages.

"There's nothing at all, your Majesty, except the story of the Cow Who Jumped Over the Moon, and you know all about that."

The King rubbed his chin, because that helped him to think.

He sighed irritably and looked at the Red Cow.

"All I can say," he said, "is that *you'd* better try that too."

"Try what?" said the Red Cow.

" Jumping over the moon. It might have an effect. Worth trying, anyway."

" Me?" said the Red Cow, with an outraged stare.

" Yes, you—who else?" said the King impatiently. He was anxious to get to the Barber's.

" Sire," said the Red Cow, " I beg you to remember that I am a decent respectable animal and have been taught from my infancy that jumping was no occupation for a lady."

The King stood up and shook his sceptre at her.

" Madam," he said, " you came here for my advice and I have given it to you. Do you want to go on dancing for ever? Do you want to go hungry for ever? Do you want to go sleepless for ever?"

The Red Cow thought of the lush sweet taste of dandelions. She thought of meadow grass and how soft it was to lie on. She thought of her weary capering legs and how nice it would be to rest them. And she said to herself: " Perhaps, just for once, it wouldn't matter and nobody—except the King—need know."

" How high do you suppose it is?" she said aloud as she danced.

The King looked up at the Moon.

" At least a mile, I should think," said he.

The Red Cow nodded. She thought so, too. For a moment she considered, and then she made up her mind.

"I never thought that I should come to this, your Majesty. Jumping—and over the moon at that. But —I'll try it," she said and curtseyed gracefully to the throne.

"Good," said the King pleasantly, realising that he would be in time for the Barber, after all. "Follow me!"

He led the way into the garden, and the Red Cow and the Courtiers followed him.

"Now," said the King, when he reached the open lawn, "when I blow the whistle—jump!"

He took a large golden whistle from his waistcoat pocket and blew into it lightly to make sure there was no dust in it.

The Red Cow danced at attention.

"Now—one!" said the King.

"Two!"

"Three!"

Then he blew the whistle.

The Red Cow, drawing in her breath, gave one huge tremendous jump and the earth fell away beneath her. She could see the figures of the King and the Courtiers growing smaller and smaller until they disappeared below. She herself shot upwards through the sky, with the stars spinning around her like great golden plates, and presently, in blinding light, she felt the cold rays of the moon upon her. She shut her eyes as she went over it, and as the dazzling gleam passed behind her and she bent her head towards the earth again, she felt the star slip down her horn. With a great rush it fell off and went rolling down the sky. And it seemed to her that as it disappeared into the darkness great chords of music came from it and echoed through the air.

In another minute the Red Cow had landed on the earth again. To her great surprise she found that she was not in the King's garden but in her own dandelion field.

And she had stopped dancing! Her feet were as steady as though they were made of stone and she walked as sedately as any other respectable cow. Quietly and serenely she moved across the field, beheading her golden soldiers as she went to greet the Red Calf.

"I'm so glad you're back!" said the Red Calf. " I've been *so* lonely."

The Red Cow kissed it and fell to munching the meadow. It was her first good meal for a week. And by the time her hunger was satisfied she had eaten up several regiments. After that she felt better. She soon began to live her life just exactly as she had lived it before.

At first she enjoyed her quiet regular habits very

much, and was glad to be able to eat her breakfast without dancing and to lie down in the grass and sleep at night instead of curtseying to the moon until the morning.

But after a little she began to feel uncomfortable and dissatisfied. Her dandelion field and her Red Calf were all very well, but she wanted something else and she couldn't think what it was. At last she realised that she was missing her star. She had grown so used to dancing and to the happy feeling the star had given her that she wanted to do a Sailor's Hornpipe and to have the star on her horn again.

She fretted, she lost her appetite, her temper was atrocious. And she frequently burst into tears for no reason at all. Eventually, she went to my Mother and told her the whole story and asked her advice.

" Good gracious, my dear!" my Mother said to her. " You don't suppose that only one star ever fell out of the sky! Billions fall every night, I'm told. But they fall in different places, of course. You can't expect two stars to drop in the same field in one lifetime."

" Then, you think—if I moved about a bit——?" the Red Cow began, a happy, eager look coming into her eyes.

" If it were me," said my Mother, " I'd go and look for one."

"I will," said the Red Cow joyously. "I will indeed."

Mary Poppins paused.

"And that, I suppose, is why she was walking down Cherry Tree Lane," Jane prompted gently.

"Yes," whispered Michael, "she was looking for her star."

Mary Poppins sat up with a little start. The intent look had gone from her eyes and the stillness from her body.

"Come down from that window at once, sir!" she said crossly. "I am going to turn on the lights." And she hurried across the landing to the electric light switch.

"Michael!" said Jane in a careful whisper. "Just have one look and see if the cow's still there."

Hurriedly Michael peered out through the gathering dusk.

"Quickly!" said Jane. "Mary Poppins will be back in one minute. Can you see her?"

"No-o-o," said Michael, staring out. "Not a sign of her. She's gone."

"I do hope she finds it!" said Jane, thinking of the

Red Cow roaming through the world looking for a star to stick on her horn.

"So do I," said Michael as, at the sound of Mary Poppins' returning footsteps, he hurriedly pulled down the blind. . . .

Chapter Six

BAD TUESDAY

It was not very long afterwards that Michael woke up one morning with a curious feeling inside him. He knew, the moment he opened his eyes, that something was wrong but he was not quite sure what it was.

"What is to-day, Mary Poppins?" he enquired, pushing the bedclothes away from him.

"Tuesday," said Mary Poppins. "Go and turn on your bath. Hurry!" she said, as he made no effort to move. He turned over and pulled the bedclothes up over his head and the curious feeling increased.

"What did I say?" said Mary Poppins in that cold, clear voice that was always a Warning.

Michael knew now what was happening to him. He knew he was going to be naughty.

"I won't," he said slowly, his voice muffled by the blanket.

Mary Poppins twitched the clothes from his hand and looked down upon him.

"I WON'T."

He waited, wondering what she would do and was surprised when, without a word, she went into the bathroom and turned on the tap herself. He took his towel and went slowly in as she came out. And for the first time in his life Michael entirely bathed himself. He knew by this that he was in disgrace, and he purposely neglected to wash behind his ears.

"Shall I let out the water?" he enquired in the rudest voice he had.

There was no reply.

"Pooh, I don't care!" said Michael, and the hot heavy weight that was within him swelled and grew larger. "I *don't* care!"

He dressed himself then, putting on his best clothes, that he knew were only for Sunday. And after that he went downstairs, kicking the banisters with his feet—a thing he knew he should not do as it waked up everybody else in the house. On the stairs he met Ellen, the housemaid, and as he passed her he knocked the hot-water jug out of her hand.

"Well, you *are* a clumsy," said Ellen, as she bent down to mop up the water. "That was for your father's shaving."

"I meant to," said Michael calmly.

Ellen's red face went quite white with surprise.

"*Meant* to? You *meant*—well, then, you're a very bad heathen boy, and I'll tell your Ma, so I will——"

"Do," said Michael, and he went on down the stairs.

Well, that was the beginning of it. Throughout the

rest of the day nothing went right with him. The hot, heavy feeling inside him made him do the most awful things, and as soon as he'd done them he felt extraordinarily pleased and glad and thought out some more at once.

In the kitchen Mrs. Brill, the cook, was making scones.

"No, Master Michael," she said, "you *can't* scrape out the basin. It's not empty yet."

And at that he let out his foot and kicked Mrs. Brill very hard on the shin, so that she dropped the rolling-pin and screamed aloud.

"You kicked Mrs. Brill? Kind Mrs. Brill? I'm ashamed of you," said his Mother a few minutes later when Mrs. Brill had told her the whole story. "You must beg her pardon at once. Say you're sorry, Michael!"

"But I'm not sorry. I'm glad. Her legs are too fat," he said, and before they could catch him he ran away up the area steps and into the garden. There he purposely bumped into Robertson Ay, who was sound asleep on top of the best rock plants, and Robertson Ay was very angry.

"I'll tell your Pa!" he said threateningly.

"And I'll tell him you haven't cleaned the shoes this morning," said Michael, and was a little astonished at himself. It was his habit and Jane's always to protect Robertson Ay, because they loved him and didn't want to lose him.

But he was not astonished for long, for he had begun to wonder what he could do next. And it was no time before he thought of something.

Through the bars of the fence he could see Miss Lark's Andrew daintily sniffing at the Next Door lawn and choosing for himself the best blades of grass. He called softly to Andrew and gave him a biscuit out of his own pocket, and while Andrew was munching it he tied Andrew's tail to the fence with a piece of string. Then he ran away with Miss Lark's angry, outraged voice screaming in his ears, and his body almost bursting with the exciting weight of that heavy thing inside him.

The door of his Father's study stood open—for Ellen had just been dusting the books. So Michael did a forbidden thing. He went in, sat down at his Father's desk, and with his Father's pen began to scribble on the blotter. Suddenly his elbow, knocking against the inkpot, upset it, and the chair and the desk and the quill pen and his own best clothes were covered with great spreading stains of blue ink. It looked dreadful, and fear of what would happen to him stirred within Michael. But, in spite of that, he didn't care—he didn't feel the least bit sorry.

"That child must be ill," said Mrs. Banks, when she was told by Ellen—who suddenly returned and discovered him—of the latest adventure. "Michael, you shall have some syrup of figs."

"I'm not ill. I'm weller than you," said Michael rudely.

" Then you're simply naughty," said his Mother.
" And you shall be punished."

And, sure enough, five minutes later, Michael found
himself standing in his stained clothes in a corner of the
nursery, facing the wall.

Jane tried to speak to him when Mary Poppins was
not looking, but he would not answer, and put out his
tongue at her. When John and Barbara crawled along
the floor and each took hold of one of his shoes and
gurgled, he just pushed them roughly away. And all
the time he was enjoying his badness, hugging it to him
as though it were a friend, and not caring a bit.

" I *hate* being good," he said aloud to himself, as he
trailed after Mary Poppins and Jane and the perambulator on the afternoon walk to the Park.

" Don't dawdle," said Mary Poppins, looking back
at him.

But he went on dawdling and dragging the sides of
his shoes along the pavement in order to scratch the
leather.

Suddenly Mary Poppins turned and faced him, one
hand on the handle of the perambulator.

" You," she began, " got out of bed the wrong side
this morning."

" I didn't," said Michael. " There is no wrong side to my bed."

" Every bed has a right and a wrong side," said Mary Poppins, primly.

" Not mine—it's next the wall."

" That makes no difference. It's still a side," scoffed Mary Poppins.

" Well, is the wrong side the left side or is the wrong side the right side? Because I got out on the right side, so how can it be wrong?"

" Both sides were the wrong side, this morning, Mr. Smarty!"

" But it has only one, and if I got out the right side——" he argued.

" One word more from you——" began Mary Poppins, and she said it in such a peculiarly threatening voice that even Michael felt a little nervous. " One more word and I'll——"

She did not say what she would do, but he quickened his pace.

" Pull yourself together, Michael," said Jane in a whisper.

" You shut up," he said, but so low that Mary Poppins could not hear.

" Now, sir," said Mary Poppins. " Off you go—in front of me, please. I'm not going to have you stravaiging behind any longer. You'll oblige me by going on ahead." She pushed him in front of her. "And," she continued, "there's a shiny thing sparkling on the path just along there. I'll thank you to go and pick it up and bring it to me. Somebody's dropped their tiara, perhaps."

Against his will, but because he didn't dare not to, Michael looked in the direction in which she was pointing. Yes—there *was* something shining on the path. From that distance it looked very interesting, and its sparkling rays of light seemed to beckon him. He walked on, swaggering a little, going as slowly as he dared and pretending that he didn't really want to see what it was.

He reached the spot and, stooping, picked up the shining thing. It was a small round sort of box with a glass top and on the glass an arrow marked. Inside, a round disc that seemed to be covered with letters swung gently as he moved the box.

Jane ran up and looked at it over his shoulder.

"What is it, Michael?" she asked.

"I won't tell you," said Michael, though he didn't know himself.

"Mary Poppins, what is it?" demanded Jane, as the perambulator drew up beside them. Mary Poppins took the little box from Michael's hand.

"It's mine," he said jealously.

"No, mine," said Mary Poppins. "I saw it first."

"But I picked it up." He tried to snatch it from her hand, but she gave him such a look that his hand fell to his side.

She tilted the round thing backwards and forwards, and in the sunlight the disc and its letters went careering madly inside the box.

"What's it for?" asked Jane.

"To go round the world with," said Mary Poppins.

"Pooh!" said Michael. "You go round the world in a ship, or an aeroplane. *I* know that. The box thing wouldn't take you round the world."

"Oh, indeed—wouldn't it?" said Mary Poppins, with a curious I-know-better-than-you expression on her face. "You just watch!"

And holding the compass in her hand she turned towards the entrance of the Park and said the word "North!"

The letters slid round the arrow, dancing giddily. Suddenly the atmosphere seemed to grow bitterly cold, and the wind became so icy that Jane and Michael shut their eyes against it. When they opened them the Park had entirely disappeared—not a tree nor a green-painted seat nor an asphalt footpath was in sight. Instead, they were surrounded by great boulders of blue ice and beneath their feet snow lay thickly frosted upon the ground.

"Oh, oh!" cried Jane, shivering with cold and sur-

The compass

prise, and she rushed to cover the Twins with their perambulator rug. "What *has* happened to us?"

Mary Poppins sniffed. She had no time to reply, however, for at that moment a white furry head peered cautiously round a boulder. Then, a huge Polar Bear leapt out and, standing on his hind legs, proceeded to hug Mary Poppins.

"I was afraid you might be trappers," he said. "Welcome to the North Pole, all of you."

He put out a long pink tongue, rough and warm as a bath towel, and gently licked the children's cheeks.

They trembled. Did Polar Bears eat children, they wondered?

"You're shivering!" the Bear said kindly. "That's because you need something to eat. Make yourselves comfortable on this iceberg." He waved a paw at a block of ice. "Now, what would you like? Cod? Shrimps? Just something to keep the wolf from the door."

"I'm afraid we can't stay," Mary Poppins broke in. "We're on our way round the world."

"Well, do let me get you a little snack. It won't take me a jiffy."

He sprang into the blue-green water and came up with a herring. "I wish you could have stayed for a chat." He tucked the fish into Mary Poppins's hand. "I long for a bit of gossip."

"Another time perhaps," she said. "And thank you for the fish."

"South!" she said to the compass.

It seemed to Jane and Michael then that the world was spinning round them. As they felt the air getting soft and warm, they found themselves in a leafy jungle from which came a noisy sound of squawking.

"Welcome!" shrieked a large Hyacinth Macaw who was perched on a branch with outstretched wings. "You're just the person we need, Mary Poppins. My wife's off gadding, and I'm left to sit on the eggs. Do take a turn, there's a good girl. I need a little rest."

He lifted a spread wing cautiously, disclosing a nest with two white eggs.

"Alas, this is just a passing visit. We're on our way round the world."

"Gracious, what a journey! Well, stay for a little moment so that I can get some sleep. If you can look after all those creatures"—he nodded at the children—"you can keep two small eggs warm. Do, Mary Poppins! And I'll get you some bananas instead of that wriggling fish."

"It was a present," said Mary Poppins.

"Well, well, keep it if you must. But what madness to go gallivanting round the world when you could stay and bring up our nestlings. Why should *we* spend our time sitting when you could do it as well?"

"Better, you mean!" sniffed Mary Poppins.

Then, to Jane and Michael's disappointment — they would dearly have liked some tropical fruit — she shook her head decisively and said, "East!"

Again the world went spinning round them — or were they spinning round the world? And then, whichever it was ceased.

They found themselves in a grassy clearing surrounded by bamboo trees. Green paperlike leaves rustled in the breeze. And above that quiet swishing they could hear a steady rhythmic sound — a snore, or was it a purr?

Glancing round, they beheld a large furry shape — black with blotches of white, or was it white with blotches of black? They could not really be sure.

Jane and Michael gazed at each other. Was it a dream from which they would wake? Or were they seeing, of all things, a Panda! And a Panda in its own home and not behind bars in a zoo.

The dream, if it was a dream, drew a long breath.

"Whoever it is, please go away, I rest in the

afternoon."

The voice was as furry as the rest of him.

"Very well, then, we *will* go away. And then perhaps" — Mary Poppins's voice was at its most priggish — "you'll be sorry you missed us."

The Panda opened one black eye. "Oh, it's you, my dear girl," he said sleepily. "Why not have let me know you were coming? Difficult though it would have been, for *you* I would have stayed awake." The furry shape yawned and stretched itself. "Ah well, I'll have to make a home for you all. There wouldn't be enough room in mine." He nodded at a neat shelter made of leaves and bamboo sticks. "But," he added, eying the herring, "I will not allow that scaly sea-thing under any roof of mine. Fishes are far too fishy for me."

"We shall not be staying," Mary Poppins assured him. "We're taking a little trip round the world and just looked in for a moment."

"What nonsense!" The Panda gave an enormous yawn. Traipsing wildly round the world when you could stay here with me. Never mind, my dear Mary, you always do what you want to do, however absurd and foolish. Pluck a few young bamboo shoots. They'll sustain you till you get home. And you two" — he nodded at Jane and Michael — "tickle me gently behind the ears. That always sends me to sleep."

Eagerly they sat down beside him and stroked the silky fur. Never again—they were sure of it—would they have the chance of stroking a Panda.

The furry shape settled itself, and as they stroked, the snore—or the purr—began its rhythm.

"He's asleep," said Mary Poppins softly. "We mustn't wake him again." She beckoned to the children, and as they came on tiptoe towards her, she gave a flick of her wrist. And the compass, apparently, understood, for the spinning began again.

Hills and lakes, mountains and forests went waltzing round them to unheard music. Then again the world was still, as if it had never moved.

This time they found themselves on a long white shore, with wavelets lapping and curling against it.

And immediately before them was a cloud of whirling, swirling sand from which came a series of grunts. Then slowly the cloud settled, disclosing a large black and grey Dolphin with a young one at her side.

"Is that you, Amelia?" called Mary Poppins.

The Dolphin blew some sand from her nose and gave a start of surprise. "Well, of all people, it's Mary Poppins! You're just in time to share our sand-bath. Nothing like a sand-bath for cleansing the fins and the tail."

"I had a bath this morning, thank you!"

"Well, what about those young ones, dear? Couldn't they do with a bit of scouring?"

"They have no fins and tails," said Mary Poppins, much to the children's disappointment. They would have liked a roll in the sand.

"Well, what on earth or sea are you doing here?" Amelia demanded briskly.

"Oh, just going round the world, you know," Mary Poppins said airily, as though going round the world was a thing you did every day.

"Well, it's a treat for Froggie and me—isn't it, Froggie? Amelia butted him with her nose, and the young Dolphin gave a friendly squeak.

"I call him Froggie because he so often strays away—just like the Frog that would a-wooing go, whether his mother would let him or no. Don't you, Froggie?" Her answer was another squeak.

"Well, now for a meal. What would you like?" Amelia grinned at Jane and Michael, displaying a splendid array of teeth. "There's cockles and mussels alive, alive-O. And the seaweed here is excellent."

"Thank you kindly, I'm sure, Amelia. But we have to be home in half a minute." Mary Poppins

laid a firm hand on the handle of the perambulator.

Amelia was clearly disappointed.

"Whatever kind of visit is that? Hullo and good-
bye in the same breath. Next time you must stay
for tea, and we'll all sit together on a rock and sing
a song to the moon. Eh, Froggie?"

Froggie squeaked.

"That will be lovely," said Mary Poppins, and
Jane and Michael echoed her words. They had
never yet sat on a rock and sung a song to the
moon.

"Well, au revoir, one and all. By the way, Mary,
my dear, were you going to take that herring with
you?"

Amelia greedily eyed the fish, which, fearing
the worst was about to happen, made itself as limp
as it could in Mary Poppins's hand.

"No. I am planning to throw it back to the sea!"
The herring gasped with relief.

"A very proper decision, Mary," Amelia
toothily smiled. "We get so few of them in these
parts, and they make a delicious meal. Why don't
we race for it, Froggie and me? When you say
'Go!', we'll start swimming and see who gets it
first."

Mary Poppins held the fish aloft.

"Ready! Steady! Go!" she cried.

And as if it were bird rather than fish, the herring swooped up and splashed into the sea.

The Dolphins were after it in a second, two dark striving shapes rippling through the water.

Jane and Michael could hardly breathe. Which would win the prize? Or would the prize escape?

"Froggie! Froggie! Froggie!" yelled Michael. If the herring had to be caught and eaten, he wanted Froggie to win.

"F-r-o-g-g-i-e!" The wind and sea both cried the name, but Michael's voice was the stronger.

"What *do* you think you're doing, Michael?" Mary Poppins sounded ferocious.

He glanced at her for a moment and turned again to the sea.

But the sea was not there. Nothing but a neat green lawn; Jane, agog, beside him; the Twins in the perambulator; and Mary Poppins pushing it in the middle of the Park.

"Jumping up and down and shouting! Making a nuisance of yourself. One would think you had done enough for one day. Step along at once, please!"

"Round the world and back in a minute—what a wonderful box!" said Jane.

"It's a *compass*. Not a box. And it's mine," said

Michael. "I found it. Give it to me!"

"*My* compass, thank you," said Mary Poppins, as she slipped it into her pocket.

He looked as if he would like to kill her. But he shrugged his shoulders and stalked off taking no notice of anyone.

The burning weight still hung heavily within him. After the adventure with the compass it seemed to grow worse, and towards the evening he grew naughtier and naughtier. He pinched the Twins when Mary Poppins was not looking, and when they cried he said in a falsely kind voice:

"Why, darlings, what *is* the matter?"

But Mary Poppins was not deceived by it.

"You've got something coming to *you*!" she said significantly. But the burning thing inside him would not let him care. He just shrugged his shoulders and pulled Jane's hair. And after that he went to the supper table and upset his bread-and-milk.

"And that," said Mary Poppins, "is the end. Such deliberate naughtiness I never saw. In all my born days I never did, and that's a fact. Off you go! Straight into bed with you and not another word!"

He had never seen her look so terrible.

But still he didn't care.

He went into the Night-nursery and undressed. No, he didn't care. He was bad, and if they didn't look out he'd be worse. He *didn't* care. He hated everybody. If they weren't careful he would run away and join a circus. There! Off went a button. Good — there would be fewer to do up in the morning. And another! All the better. Nothing in all the world could ever make him feel sorry. He would get into bed without brushing his hair or his teeth — certainly without saying his prayers.

He was just about to get into bed and, indeed, had one foot already in it, when he noticed the compass lying on top of the chest of drawers.

Very slowly he withdrew his foot and tiptoed across the room. He knew now what he would do. He would take the compass and spin it and go round the world. And they'd never find him again. And it would serve them right. Without making a sound he lifted a chair and put it against the chest of drawers. Then he climbed up on it and took the compass in his hand.

He moved it.

"North, South, East, West!" he said very quickly, in case anybody should come in before he got well away.

A noise behind the chair startled him and he turned round guiltily, expecting to see Mary Poppins. But instead, there were four gigantic figures bearing down upon him—the bear with his fangs showing, the Macaw fiercely flapping his wings, the Panda with his fur on end, the Dolphin thrusting out her snout. From all quarters of the room they were rushing upon him, their shadows huge on the ceiling. No longer kind and friendly, they were now full of revenge. Their terrible angry faces loomed nearer. He could feel their hot breath on his face.

"Oh! Oh!" Michael dropped the compass. "Mary Poppins, help me!" he screamed and shut his eyes in terror.

And then something enveloped him. The great creatures and their greater shadows, with a mingled roar or squawk of triumph, flung themselves upon him. What was it that held him, soft and warm, in its smothering embrace? The Polar Bear's fur coat? The Macaw's feathers? The Panda's fur he had stroked so gently? The mother Dolphin's flipper? And what was he—or it might be she—planning to do to him? If only he had been good—if only!

"Mary Poppins!" he wailed, as he felt himself carried through the air and set down in something still softer.

"Oh, *dear* Mary Poppins!"

"All right, all right. I'm not deaf, I'm thankful to say—no need to shout," he heard her saying calmly.

He opened one eye. He could see no sign of the four gigantic figures of the compass. He opened the other eye to make sure. No—not a glint of any of them. He sat up. He looked round the room. There was nothing there.

Then he discovered that the soft thing that was round him was his own blanket, and the soft thing he was lying on was his own bed. And oh, the heavy burning thing that had been inside him all day had melted and disappeared. He felt peaceful and happy, and as if he would like to give everybody he knew a birthday present.

"What—what happened?" he said rather anxiously to Mary Poppins.

"I told you that was my compass, didn't I? Be kind enough not to touch my things, *if* you please," was all she said as she stooped and picked up the compass and put it in her pocket. Then she began to fold the clothes that he had thrown down on the floor.

"Shall I do it?" he said.

"No, thank you."

He watched her go into the next room, and presently she returned and put something warm into his hands. It was a cup of milk.

Michael sipped it, tasting every drop several times with his tongue, making it last as long as possible so that Mary Poppins should stay beside him.

She stood there without saying a word, watching the milk slowly disappear. He could smell her crackling white apron and the faint flavour of toast that always hung about her so deliciously. But try as he would, he could not make the milk last for ever, and presently, with a sigh of regret, he handed her the empty cup and slipped down into the bed. He had never known it be so comfortable, he thought. And he thought, too, how warm he was and how happy he felt and how lucky he was to be alive.

"Isn't it a funny thing, Mary Poppins," he said drowsily. "I've been so very naughty and I feel so very good."

"Humph!" said Mary Poppins as she tucked him in and went away to wash up the supper things. . . .

Chapter Seven

THE BIRD WOMAN

" PERHAPS she won't be there," said Michael.

" Yes, she will," said Jane. " She's always there for ever and ever."

They were walking up Ludgate Hill on the way to pay a visit to Mr. Banks in the City. For he had said that morning to Mrs. Banks:

" My dear, if it doesn't rain I think Jane and Michael might call for me at the Office to-day—that is, if you are agreeable. I have a feeling I should like to be taken to Tea and Shortbread Fingers and it's not often I have a Treat."

And Mrs. Banks had said she would think about it.

But all day long, though Jane and Michael had watched her anxiously, she had not seemed to be thinking about it at all. From the things she said, she was thinking about the Laundry Bill and Michael's new overcoat and where was Aunt Flossie's address, and why did that wretched Mrs. Jackson ask her to tea on the second Thursday of the month when she knew that was the very day Mrs. Banks had to go to the Dentist's?

Suddenly, when they felt quite sure she would never think about Mr. Banks' treat, she said :

" Now, children, don't stand staring at me like that. Get your things on. You are going to the City to have tea with your Father. Had you forgotten?"

As if they could have forgotten! For it was not as though it were only the Tea that mattered. There was also the Bird Woman, and she herself was the best of all Treats.

That is why they were walking up Ludgate Hill and feeling very excited.

Mary Poppins walked between them, wearing her new hat and looking very distinguished. Every now and then she would look into the shop window just to make sure the hat was still there and that the pink roses on it had not turned into common flowers like marigolds.

Every time she stopped to make sure, Jane and Michael would sigh, but they did not dare say anything for fear she would spend even longer looking at herself in the windows, and turning this way and that to see which attitude was the most becoming.

But at last they came to St. Paul's Cathedral, which was built a long time ago by a man with a bird's name. Wren it was, but he was no relation to Jenny. That is why so many birds live near Sir Christopher Wren's Cathedral, which also belongs to St. Paul, and that is why the Bird Woman lives there, too.

"There she is!" cried Michael suddenly, and he danced on his toes with excitement.

"Don't point," said Mary Poppins, giving a last glance at the pink roses in the window of a carpet-shop.

"She's saying it! She's saying it!" cried Jane, holding tight to herself for fear she would break in two with delight.

And she *was* saying it. The Bird Woman was there and she was saying it.

"Feed the Birds, Tuppence a Bag! Feed the Birds, Tuppence a Bag! Feed the Birds, Feed the Birds, Tuppence a Bag, Tuppence a Bag!" Over and over again, the same thing, in a high chanting voice that made the words seem like a song.

And as she said it she held out little bags of bread-crumbs to the passers-by.

All round her flew the birds, circling and leaping and swooping and rising. Mary Poppins always called them "sparrers" because, she said conceitedly, all birds were alike to her. But Jane and Michael knew that they were not sparrows, but doves and pigeons. There were fussy and chatty grey doves like Grand-mothers; and brown, rough-voiced pigeons like Uncles; and greeny, cackling, no-I've-no-money-to-day pigeons like Fathers. And the silly, anxious, soft blue doves were like Mothers. That's what Jane and Michael thought, anyway.

They flew round and round the head of the Bird Woman as the children approached, and then, as though to tease her, they suddenly rushed away through the air and sat on the top of St. Paul's, laughing and turning their heads away and pretending they didn't know her.

It was Michael's turn to buy a bag. Jane had bought one last time. He walked up to the Bird Woman and held out four halfpennies.

"*Feed* the Birds, Tuppence a Bag!" said the Bird Woman, as she put a bag of crumbs into his hand and tucked the money away into the folds of her huge black skirt.

"Why don't you have penny bags?" said Michael. "Then I could buy two."

"Feed the Birds, *Tuppence* a Bag!" said the Bird Woman, and Michael knew it was no good asking her any more questions. He and Jane had often tried, but all she could say, and all she had ever been able to say was, "Feed the Birds, Tuppence a Bag!" Just as a cuckoo can only say "Cuckoo," no matter what questions you ask him.

Jane and Michael and Mary Poppins spread the crumbs in a circle on the ground, and presently, one by one at first, and then in twos and threes, the birds came down from St. Paul's.

"Dainty David," said Mary Poppins with a sniff, as one bird picked up a crumb and dropped it again from its beak.

But the other birds swarmed upon the food, pushing and scrambling and shouting. At last there wasn't a crumb left, for it is not really polite for a pigeon or a dove to leave anything on the plate. When they were quite certain that the meal was finished the birds rose with one grand, fluttering movement and flew round the Bird Woman's head, copying in their own language the words she said. One of them sat on her hat and pretended he was a decoration for the crown. And another of them mistook Mary Poppins' new hat for a rose-garden and pecked off a flower.

"You sparrer!" cried Mary Poppins, and shook her umbrella at him. The pigeon, very offended, flew back to the Bird Woman, and to pay out Mary Poppins, stuck the rose in the ribbon of the Bird Woman's hat.

"You ought to be in a pie—that's where *you* ought to be," said Mary Poppins to him very angrily. Then she called to Jane and Michael.

"Time to go," she said, and flung a parting glance of fury at the pigeon. But he only laughed and flicked his tail and turned his back on her.

"Good-bye," said Michael to the Bird Woman.

"Feed the Birds," she replied, smiling.

"Good-bye," said Jane.

"Tuppence a Bag!" said the Bird Woman and waved her hand.

They left her then, walking one on either side of Mary Poppins.

"What happens when *everybody* goes away—like us?" said Michael to Jane.

He knew quite well what happened, but it was the proper thing to ask Jane because the story was really hers.

So Jane told him and he added the bits she had forgotten.

"At night when everybody goes to bed——" began Jane.

"And the stars come out," added Michael.

"Yes, and even if they don't—all the birds come down from the top of St. Paul's and run very carefully all over the ground just to see there are no crumbs left, and to tidy it up for the morning. And when they have done that——"

"You've forgotten the baths."

"Oh, yes—they bath themselves and comb their wings with their claws. And when they have done that they fly three times round the head of the Bird Woman and then they settle."

"Do they sit on her shoulders?"

"Yes, and on her hat."

"And on her basket with the bags in it?"

"Yes, and some on her knee. Then she smooths

down the head-feathers of each one in turn and tells it
to be a good bird———"

" In the bird language?"

" Yes. And when they are all sleepy and don't want

to stay awake any longer, she spreads out her skirts,
as a mother hen spreads out her wings, and the birds
go creep, creep, creeping underneath. And as soon as

the last one is under she settles down over them, making little brooding, nesting noises and they sleep there till morning."

Michael sighed happily. He loved the story and was never tired of hearing it.

" And it's all quite true, isn't it?" he said, just as he always did.

" No," said Mary Poppins, who always said " No."

" Yes," said Jane, who always knew everything. . . .

Chapter Eight

MRS. CORRY

"Two pounds of sausages—Best Pork," said Mary Poppins. "And at once, please. We're in a hurry."

The Butcher, who wore a large blue-and-white striped apron, was a fat and friendly man. He was also large and red and rather like one of his own sausages. He leant upon his chopping-block and gazed admiringly at Mary Poppins. Then he winked pleasantly at Jane and Michael.

"In a Nurry?" he said to Mary Poppins. "Well, that's a pity. I'd hoped you'd dropped in for a bit of a chat. We Butchers, you know, like a bit of company. And we don't often get the chance of talking to a nice, handsome young lady like you——" He broke off suddenly, for he had caught sight of Mary Poppins' face. The expression on it was awful. And the Butcher found himself wishing there was a trap-door in the floor of his shop that would open and swallow him up.

"Oh, well——" he said, blushing even redder than usual. "If you're in a Nurry, of course. Two pounds, did you say? Best Pork? Right you are!"

And he hurriedly hooked down a long strip of the sausages that were festooned across the shop. He cut off a length—about three-quarters of a yard—wound it into a sort of garland, and wrapped it up first in white and then in brown paper. He pushed the parcel across the chopping-block.

" *AND* the next?" he said hopefully, still blushing.

" There will be *no* next," said Mary Poppins, with a haughty sniff. And she took the sausages and turned the perambulator round very quickly, and wheeled it out of the shop in such a way that the Butcher knew he had mortally offended her. But she glanced at the window as she went so that she could see how her new shoes looked reflected in it. They were bright brown kid with two buttons, very smart.

Jane and Michael trailed after her, wondering when she would have come to the end of her shopping-list but, because of the look on her face, not daring to ask her.

Mary Poppins gazed up and down the street as if deep in thought, and then, suddenly making up her mind, she snapped :

" Fishmonger !" and turned the perambulator in at the shop next to the Butcher's.

" One Dover Sole, pound and a half of Halibut, pint of Prawns and a Lobster," said Mary Poppins, talking so quickly that only somebody used to taking such orders could possibly have understood her.

The Fishmonger, unlike the Butcher, was a long thin man, so thin that he seemed to have no front to him but only two sides. And he looked so sad that you felt he had either just been weeping or was just going to. Jane said that this was due to some secret sorrow that had haunted him since his youth, and Michael thought that the Fishmonger's Mother must have fed him entirely on bread and water when he was a baby, and that he had never forgotten it.

"Anything else?" said the Fishmonger hopelessly, in a voice that suggested he was quite sure there wouldn't be.

"Not to-day," said Mary Poppins.

The Fishmonger shook his head sadly and did not look at all surprised. He had known all along there would be nothing else.

Sniffing gently, he tied up the parcel and dropped it into the perambulator.

"Bad weather," he observed, wiping his eye with his hand. "Don't believe we're going to get any summer at all—not that we ever did, of course. *You* don't look too blooming," he said to Mary Poppins. "But then, nobody does——"

Mary Poppins tossed her head.

"Speak for yourself," she said crossly, and flounced

to the door, pushing the perambulator so fiercely that it bumped into a bag of oysters.

"The idea!" Jane and Michael heard her say as she glanced down at her shoes. Not looking too blooming in her new brown kid shoes with two buttons—the idea! That was what they heard her thinking.

Outside on the pavement she paused, looking at her list and ticking off what she had bought. Michael stood first on one leg and then on the other.

"Mary Poppins, are we *never* going home?" he said crossly.

Mary Poppins turned and regarded him with something like disgust.

"That," she said briefly, "is as it may be." And Michael, watching her fold up her list, wished he had not spoken.

"*You* can go home, if you like," she said haughtily. "*We* are going to buy the gingerbread."

Michael's face fell. If only he had managed to say nothing! He hadn't known that Gingerbread was at the end of the list.

"That's your way," said Mary Poppins shortly, pointing in the direction of Cherry Tree Lane. "If you don't get lost," she added as an afterthought.

"Oh no, Mary Poppins, *please*, no! I didn't mean it, really. I—oh—Mary Poppins, please——" cried Michael.

" Do let him come, Mary Poppins!" said Jane. " I'll push the perambulator if only you'll let him come."

Mary Poppins sniffed. " If it wasn't Friday," she said darkly to Michael, " you'd go home in a twink— in an absolute Twink!"

She moved onwards, pushing John and Barbara. Jane and Michael knew that she had relented, and followed wondering what a Twink was. Suddenly Jane noticed that they were going in the wrong direction.

" But, Mary Poppins, I thought you said gingerbread—this isn't the way to Green, Brown and Johnson's, where we always get it——" she began, and stopped because of Mary Poppins' face.

" Am I doing the shopping or are you?" Mary Poppins enquired.

" You," said Jane, in a very small voice.

" Oh, really? I thought it was the other way round," said Mary Poppins with a scornful laugh.

She gave the perambulator a little twist with her hand and it turned a corner and drew up suddenly. Jane and Michael, stopping abruptly behind it, found themselves outside the most curious shop they had ever seen. It was very small and very dingy. Faded loops of coloured paper hung in the windows, and on the shelves were shabby little boxes of Sherbet, old Liquorice Sticks, and very withered, very hard Apples-on-a-stick. There was a small dark doorway between the windows, and through this Mary Poppins propelled the perambulator while Jane and Michael followed at her heels.

Inside the shop they could dimly see the glass-topped counter that ran round three sides of it. And in a case under the glass were rows and rows of dark, dry gingerbread, each slab so studded with gilt stars that the shop itself seemed to be faintly lit by them. Jane and Michael glanced round to find out what kind of a person was to serve them, and were very surprised when Mary Poppins called out:

"Fannie! Annie! Where are you?" Her voice seemed to echo back to them from each dark wall of the shop.

And as she called, two of the largest people the children had ever seen rose from behind the counter and shook hands with Mary Poppins. The huge women then leant down over the counter and said, "How de do?" in voices as large as themselves, and shook hands with Jane and Michael.

"How do you do, Miss——?" Michael paused, wondering which of the large ladies was which.

"Fannie's my name," said one of them. "My rheumatism is about the same; thank you for asking." She spoke very mournfully, as though she were unused to such a courteous greeting.

" It's a lovely day——" began Jane politely to the other sister, who kept Jane's hand imprisoned for almost a minute in her huge clasp.

" I'm Annie," she informed them miserably. " And handsome is as handsome does."

Jane and Michael thought that both the sisters had a very odd way of expressing themselves, but they had not time to be surprised for long, for Miss Fannie and Miss Annie were reaching out their long arms to the perambulator. Each shook hands solemnly with one of the Twins, who were so astonished that they began to cry.

" Now, now, now, now! What's this, what's this?" A high, thin, crackly little voice came from the back of the shop. At the sound of it the expression on the faces of Miss Fannie and Miss Annie, sad before, became even sadder. They seemed frightened and ill at ease, and somehow Jane and Michael realised that the two huge sisters were wishing that they were much smaller and less conspicuous.

" What's all this I hear?" cried the curious high little voice, coming nearer. And presently, round the corner of the glass case the owner of it appeared. She was as small as her voice and as crackly, and to the children she seemed to be older than anything in the world, with her wispy hair and her stick-like legs and her wizened, wrinkled little face. But in spite of this she ran towards them as lightly and as gaily as though she were still a young girl.

"Now, now, now—well, I do declare! Bless me if it

isn't Mary Poppins, with John and Barbara Banks. What—Jane and Michael, too? Well, isn't this a nice surprise for me? I assure you I haven't been so surprised since Christopher Columbus discovered America —truly I haven't!"

She smiled delightedly as she came to greet them, and her feet made little dancing movements inside the tiny elastic-sided boots. She ran to the perambulator and rocked it gently, crooking her thin, twisted, old fingers at John and Barbara until they stopped crying and began to laugh.

"That's better!" she said, cackling gaily. Then she did a very odd thing. She broke off two of her fingers and gave one each to John and Barbara. And the oddest part of it was that in the space left by the broken-off fingers two new ones grew at once. Jane and Michael clearly saw it happen.

"Only Barley-Sugar—can't possibly hurt 'em," the old lady said to Mary Poppins.

"Anything *you* give them, Mrs. Corry, could only do them good," said Mary Poppins with most surprising courtesy.

"What a pity," Michael couldn't help saying, "they weren't Peppermint Bars."

"Well, they are, sometimes," said Mrs. Corry gleefully, "and very good they taste, too. I often nibble 'em myself, if I can't sleep at night. Splendid for the digestion."

"What will they be next time?" asked Jane, looking at Mrs. Corry's fingers with interest.

"Aha!" said Mrs. Corry. "That's just the question. I never know from day to day what they will be.

I take the chance, my dear, as I heard William the Conqueror say to his Mother when she advised him not to go conquering England."

"You must be *very* old!" said Jane, sighing enviously, and wondering if she would ever be able to remember what Mrs. Corry remembered.

Mrs. Corry flung back her wispy little head and shrieked with laughter.

"Old!" she said. "Why, I'm quite a chicken compared to my Grandmother. Now, there's an old woman *if* you like. Still, I go back a good way. I remember the time when they were making this world, anyway, and I was well out of my teens then. My goodness, that *was* a to-do, I can tell you!"

She broke off suddenly, screwing up her little eyes at the children.

"But, deary me—here am I running on and on and you not being served! I suppose, my dear"—she turned to Mary Poppins, whom she appeared to know very well—"I suppose you've all come for some Gingerbread?"

"That's right, Mrs. Corry," said Mary Poppins politely.

"Good. Have Fannie and Annie given you any?" She looked at Jane and Michael as she said this.

Jane shook her head. Two hushed voices came from behind the counter.

"No, Mother," said Miss Fannie meekly.

"We were just going to, Mother——" began Miss Annie in a frightened whisper.

At that Mrs. Corry drew herself up to her full height and regarded her gigantic daughters furiously. Then she said in a soft, fierce, terrifying voice:

"Just going to? Oh, *indeed*! That is *very* interesting. And who, may I ask, Annie, gave you permission to give away *my* gingerbread——?"

"Nobody, Mother. And I didn't give it away. I only thought——"

"You only thought! That is *very* kind of you. But I will thank you not to think. *I* can do all the thinking that is necessary here!" said Mrs. Corry in her soft, terrible voice. Then she burst into a harsh cackle of laughter.

"Look at her! Just look at her! Cowardy-custard! Cry-baby!" she shrieked, pointing her knotty finger at her daughter.

Jane and Michael turned and saw a large tear coursing down Miss Annie's huge, sad face, but they did not like to say anything, for, in spite of her tininess, Mrs. Corry made them feel rather small and frightened. But as soon as Mrs. Corry looked the other way Jane seized the opportunity to offer Miss Annie her handkerchief. The huge tear completely drenched it, and Miss

Annie, with a grateful look, wrung it out before she returned it to Jane.

"And you, Fannie—did *you* think, too, I wonder?" The high little voice was now directed at the other daughter.

"No, Mother," said Miss Fannie trembling.

"Humph! Just as well for you! Open that case!"

With frightened, fumbling fingers, Miss Fannie opened the glass case.

"Now, my darlings," said Mrs. Corry in quite a different voice. She smiled and beckoned so sweetly to Jane and Michael that they were ashamed of having been frightened of her, and felt that she must be very nice after all. "Won't you come and take your pick, my lambs? It's a special recipe to-day—one I got from Alfred the Great. He was a very good cook, I remember, though he did once burn the cakes. How many?"

Jane and Michael looked at Mary Poppins.

"Four each," she said. "That's twelve. One dozen."

"I'll make it a Baker's Dozen—take thirteen," said Mrs. Corry cheerfully.

So Jane and Michael chose thirteen slabs of ginger-bread, each with its gilt paper star. Their arms were piled up with the delicious dark cakes. Michael could not resist nibbling a corner of one of them.

"Good?" squeaked Mrs. Corry, and when he nodded she picked up her skirts and did a few steps of the Highland Fling for pure pleasure.

"Hooray, hooray, splendid, hooray!" she cried in her shrill little voice. Then she came to a standstill and her face grew serious.

"But remember—I'm not *giving* them away. I must be paid. The price is threepence for each of you."

Mary Poppins opened her purse and took out three threepenny-bits. She gave one each to Jane and Michael.

"Now," said Mrs. Corry. "Stick 'em on my coat! That's where they all go."

They looked closely at her long black coat. And sure enough they found it was studded with threepenny-bits as a Coster's coat is with pearl buttons.

"Come along. Stick 'em on!" repeated Mrs. Corry, rubbing her hands with pleasant expectation. "You'll find they won't drop off."

Mary Poppins stepped forward and pressed her threepenny-bit against the collar of Mrs. Corry's coat.

To the surprise of Jane and Michael, it stuck.

Then they put theirs on—Jane's on the right shoulder and Michael's on the front hem. Theirs stuck, too.

"How very extraordinary," said Jane.

"Not at all, my dear," said Mrs. Corry chuckling. "Or rather, not so extraordinary as other things I could mention." And she winked largely at Mary Poppins.

"I'm afraid we must be off now, Mrs. Corry," said Mary Poppins. "There is Baked Custard for lunch, and I must be home in time to make it. That Mrs. Brill——"

"A poor cook?" enquired Mrs. Corry interrupting.

"Poor!" said Mary Poppins contemptuously. "*That's* not the word."

"Ah!" Mrs. Corry put her finger alongside her nose and looked very wise. Then she said:

"Well, my dear Miss Poppins, it has been a very pleasant visit and I am sure my girls have enjoyed it as much as I have." She nodded in the direction of her two large mournful daughters. "And you'll come again soon, won't you, with Jane and Michael and the Babies? Now, are you sure you can carry the Gingerbread?" she continued, turning to Michael and Jane.

They nodded. Mrs. Corry drew closer to them, with a curious, important, inquisitive look on her face.

"I wonder," she said dreamily, "what you will do with the paper stars?"

"Oh, we'll keep them," said Jane. "We always do."

"Ah—you keep them! And I wonder *where* you

keep them?" Mrs. Corry's eyes were half closed and she looked more inquisitive than ever.

"Well," Jane began. "Mine are all under my handkerchiefs in the top left-hand drawer and——"

"Mine are in a shoe-box on the bottom shelf of the wardrobe," said Michael.

"Top left-hand drawer and shoe-box in the wardrobe," said Mrs. Corry thoughtfully, as though she were committing the words to memory. Then she gave Mary Poppins a long look and nodded her head slightly. Mary Poppins nodded slightly in return. It seemed as if some secret had passed between them.

"Well," said Mrs. Corry brightly, "that is very interesting. You don't know how glad I am to know you keep your stars. I shall remember that. You see, I remember everything—even what Guy Fawkes had for dinner every second Sunday. And now, good-bye. Come again soon. Come again so-o-o-o-n!"

Mrs. Corry's voice seemed to be growing fainter and fading away, and presently, without being quite aware of what had happened, Jane and Michael found themselves on the pavement, walking behind Mary Poppins who was again examining her list.

They turned and looked behind them.

"Why, Jane," said Michael with surprise, "it's not there!"

"So I see," said Jane, staring and staring.

And they were right. The shop was *not* there. It had entirely disappeared.

"How odd!" said Jane.

"Isn't it?" said Michael. "But the Gingerbread is very good."

And they were so busy biting their Gingerbread into different shapes—a man, a flower, a teapot—that they quite forgot how *very* odd it was.

They remembered it again that night, however, when the lights were out and they were both supposed to be sound asleep.

"Jane, Jane!" whispered Michael. "I hear someone tip-toeing on the stairs—listen!"

"Sssh!" hissed Jane from her bed, for she, too, had heard the footsteps.

Presently the door opened with a little click and somebody came into the room. It was Mary Poppins, dressed in hat and coat all ready to go out.

She moved about the room softly with quick secret movements. Jane and Michael watched her through half-closed eyes without stirring.

First she went to the chest-of-drawers, opened a drawer and shut it again after a moment. Then, on tip-toe, she went to the wardrobe, opened it, bent down and put something in or took something out (they couldn't tell which). Snap! The wardrobe door shut quickly and Mary Poppins hurried from the room.

Michael sat up in bed.

"What was she doing?" he said to Jane in a loud whisper.

"I don't know. Perhaps she's forgotten her gloves or her shoes or——" Jane broke off suddenly. "Michael, listen!"

He listened. From down below—in the garden, it seemed—they could hear several voices whispering together, very earnestly and excitedly.

With a quick movement Jane got out of bed and beckoned Michael. They crept on bare feet to the window and looked down.

There, outside in the Lane, stood a tiny form and two gigantic figures.

"Mrs. Corry and Miss Fannie and Miss Annie," said Jane in a whisper.

And so indeed it was. It was a curious group. Mrs. Corry was looking through the bars of the gate of Number Seventeen, Miss Fannie had two long ladders balanced on one huge shoulder, while Miss Annie appeared to be carrying in one hand a large pail of something that looked like glue and in the other an enormous paint-brush.

From where they stood, hidden by the curtain, Jane and Michael could distinctly hear their voices.

"She's late!" Mrs. Corry was saying crossly and anxiously.

"Perhaps," Miss Fannie began timidly, settling the ladders more firmly on her shoulder, "one of the children is ill and she couldn't——"

"Get away in time," said Miss Annie, nervously completing her sister's sentence.

"Silence!" said Mrs. Corry fiercely, and Jane and Michael distinctly heard her whisper something about "great galumphing giraffes," and they knew she was referring to her unfortunate daughters.

"Hist!" said Mrs. Corry suddenly, listening with her head on one side, like a small bird.

There was the sound of the front door being quietly opened and shut again, and the creak of footsteps on the path. Mrs. Corry smiled and waved her hand as Mary Poppins came to meet them, carrying a market basket on her arm, and in the basket was something that seemed to give out a faint, mysterious light.

"Come along, come along, we must hurry! We haven't much time," said Mrs. Corry, taking Mary Poppins by the arm. "Look lively, you two!" And she moved off, followed by Miss Fannie and Miss Annie, who were obviously trying to look as lively as possible but not succeeding very well. They tramped heavily after their Mother and Mary Poppins, bending under their loads.

Jane and Michael saw all four of them go down Cherry Tree Hill, and then they turned a little to the left and went up the hill. When they got to the top of the hill, where there were no houses but only grass and clover, they stopped.

Miss Annie put down her pail of glue, and Miss Fannie swung the ladders from her shoulder and steadied them until both stood in an upright position. Then she held one and Miss Annie the other.

"What on earth are they going to do?" said Michael, gaping. But there was no need for Jane to reply, for he could see for himself what was happening.

As soon as Miss Fannie and Miss Annie had so fixed the ladders that they seemed to be standing with one end on the earth and the other leaning on the sky, Mrs. Corry picked up her skirts and the paint-brush in one hand and the pail of glue in the other. Then she set her foot on the lowest rung of one of the ladders and began to climb it. Mary Poppins, carrying her basket, climbed the other.

Then Jane and Michael saw a most amazing sight. As soon as she arrived at the top of her ladder, Mrs. Corry dipped her brush into the glue and began slapping the sticky substance against the sky. And Mary Poppins, when this had been done, took something

One end on the earth and the other leaning on the sky

shiny from her basket and fixed it to the glue. When she took her hand away they saw that she was sticking the Gingerbread Stars to the sky. As each one was placed in position it began to twinkle furiously, sending out rays of sparkling golden light.

"They're ours!" said Michael breathlessly. "They're our stars. She thought we were asleep and came in and took them!"

But Jane was silent. She was watching Mrs. Corry splashing the glue on the sky and Mary Poppins sticking on the stars and Miss Fannie and Miss Annie moving the ladders to a new position as the spaces in the sky became filled up.

At last it was over. Mary Poppins shook out her basket and showed Mrs. Corry that there was nothing left in it. Then they came down from the ladders and the procession started down the hill again, Miss Fannie shouldering the ladders, Miss Annie jangling her empty glue pail. At the corner they stood talking for a moment; then Mary Poppins shook hands with them all and hurried up the Lane again. Mrs. Corry, dancing lightly in her elastic-sided boots and holding her skirts daintily with her hands, disappeared in the other direction with her huge daughters stumping noisily behind her.

The garden-gate clicked. Footsteps creaked on the path. The front door opened and shut with a soft clanging sound. Presently they heard Mary Poppins come quietly up the stairs, tip-toe past the nursery and go on into the room where she slept with John and Barbara.

As the sound of her footsteps died away, Jane and Michael looked at each other. Then without a word

they went together to the top left-hand drawer and looked.

There was nothing there but a pile of Jane's handkerchiefs.

" I told you so," said Michael.

Next they went to the wardrobe and looked into the shoe-box. It was empty.

" But how? But why?" said Michael, sitting down on the edge of his bed and staring at Jane.

Jane said nothing. She just sat beside him with her arms round her knees and thought and thought and thought. At last she shook back her hair and stretched herself and stood up.

"What *I* want to know," she said, "is this : Are the stars gold paper or is the gold paper stars?"

There was no reply to her question and she did not expect one. She knew that only somebody very much wiser than Michael could give her the right answer. . . .

Chapter Nine

JOHN AND BARBARA'S STORY

JANE and Michael had gone off to a party, wearing their best clothes and looking, as Ellen the housemaid said when she saw them, " just like a shop window."

All the afternoon the house was very quiet and still, as though it were thinking its own thoughts, or dreaming perhaps.

Down in the kitchen Mrs. Brill was reading the paper with her spectacles perched on her nose. Robertson Ay was sitting in the garden busily doing nothing. Mrs. Banks was on the drawing-room sofa with her feet up. And the house stood very quietly around them all, dreaming its own dreams, or thinking perhaps.

Upstairs in the nursery Mary Poppins was airing the clothes by the fire, and the sunlight poured in at the window, flickering on the white walls, dancing over the cots where the babies were lying.

" I say, move over ! You're right in my eyes," said John in a loud voice.

" Sorry !" said the sunlight. " But I can't help it. I've got to get across this room somehow. Orders is

147

orders. I must move from East to West in a day and
my way lies through this Nursery. Sorry! Shut your
eyes and you won't notice me."

The gold shaft of sunlight lengthened across the
room. It was obviously moving as quickly as it could in
order to oblige John.

"How soft, how sweet you are! I love you," said
Barbara, holding out her hands to its shining warmth.

"Good girl," said the sunlight approvingly, and
moved up over her cheeks and into her hair with a
light, caressing movement. "Do you like the feel of
me?" it said, as though it loved being praised.

"Dee-licious!" said Barbara, with a happy sigh.

"Chatter, chatter, chatter! I never heard such a
place for chatter. There's always somebody talking in
this room," said a shrill voice at the window.

John and Barbara looked up.

It was the Starling who lived on the top of the
chimney.

"I like that," said Mary Poppins, turning round quickly. "What about yourself? All day long—yes, and half the night, too, on the roofs and telegraph poles. Roaring and screaming and shouting—you'd talk the leg off a chair, you would. Worse than any sparrer, and that's the truth."

The Starling cocked his head on one side and looked down at her from his perch on the window-frame.

"Well," he said, "I have my business to attend to. Consultations, discussions, arguments, bargaining. And that, of course, necessitates a certain amount of—er—quiet conversation——"

"Quiet!" exclaimed John, laughing heartily.

"And I wasn't talking to you, young man," said the Starling, hopping down on to the window-sill. "And *you* needn't talk—anyway. I heard you for several hours on end last Saturday week. Goodness, I thought you'd never stop—you kept me awake all night."

"That wasn't talking," said John. "I was——" He paused. "I mean, I had a pain."

"Humph!" said the Starling, and hopped on to the railing of Barbara's cot. He sidled along it until he came to the head of the cot. Then he said in a soft, wheedling voice:

"Well, Barbara B., anything for the old fellow to-day, eh?"

Barbara pulled herself into a sitting position by holding on to one of the bars of her cot.

"There's the other half of my arrowroot biscuit," she said, and held it out in her round, fat fist.

The Starling swooped down, plucked it out of her hand and flew back to the window-sill. He began nibbling it greedily.

"Thank you!" said Mary Poppins, meaningly, but the Starling was too busy eating to notice the rebuke.

"I said 'Thank you!'" said Mary Poppins a little louder.

The Starling looked up.

"Eh—what? Oh, get along, girl, get along. I've no time for such frills and furbelows." And he gobbled up the last of his biscuit.

The room was very quiet.

John, drowsing in the sunlight, put the toes of his right foot into his mouth and ran them along the place where his teeth were just beginning to come through.

"Why do you bother to do that?" said Barbara, in her soft, amused voice that seemed always to be full of laughter. "There's nobody to see you."

"I know," said John, playing a tune on his toes. "But I like to keep in practice. It *does* so amuse the Grown-ups. Did you notice that Aunt Flossie nearly went mad with delight when I did it yesterday? 'The Darling, the Clever, the Marvel, the Creature!'—

didn't you hear her saying all that?" And John threw his foot from him and roared with laughter as he thought of Aunt Flossie.

"She liked my trick, too," said Barbara complacently. "I took off both my socks and she said I was so sweet she would like to eat me. Isn't it funny—when *I* say I'd like to eat something I really mean it. Biscuits and Rusks and the knobs of beds and so on. But Grown-ups never mean what they say, it seems to me. She couldn't have *really* wanted to eat me, could she?"

"No. It's only the idiotic way they have of talking," said John. "I don't believe I'll ever understand Grown-ups. They all seem so stupid. And even Jane and Michael are stupid sometimes."

"Um," agreed Barbara, thoughtfully pulling off her socks and putting them on again.

"For instance," John went on, "they don't understand a single thing we say. But, worse than that, they don't understand what *other* things say. Why, only last Monday I heard Jane remark that she wished she knew what language the Wind spoke."

"I know," said Barbara. "It's astonishing. And Michael always insists—haven't you heard him?—that the Starling says ' Wee-Twe—ee—ee!' He seems not to know that the Starling says nothing of the kind, but speaks exactly the same language as we do. Of course, one doesn't expect Mother and Father to know about it

151

—they don't know *anything,* though they *are* such darlings—but you'd think Jane and Michael would——"

"They did once," said Mary Poppins, folding up one of Jane's nightgowns.

"What?" said John and Barbara together in very surprised voices. "Really? You mean they understood the Starling and the Wind and——"

"And what the trees say and the language of the sunlight and the stars—of course they did! *Once,*" said Mary Poppins.

"But—how is it that they've forgotten it all?" said John, wrinkling up his forehead and trying to understand.

"Aha!" said the Starling knowingly, looking up from the remains of his biscuit. "Wouldn't you like to know?"

"Because they've grown older," explained Mary Poppins. "Barbara, put on your socks at once, please."

"That's a silly reason," said John, looking sternly at her.

"It's the true one, then," Mary Poppins said, tying Barbara's socks firmly round her ankles.

"Well, it's Jane and Michael who are silly," John continued. "I know *I* shan't forget when *I* get older."

"Nor I," said Barbara, contentedly sucking her finger.

"Yes, you will," said Mary Poppins firmly.

The Twins sat up and looked at her.

"Huh!" said the Starling contemptuously. "Look at 'em! They think they're the World's Wonders. Little miracles—I *don't* think! Of course you'll forget —same as Jane and Michael."

"We *won't*," said the Twins, looking at the Starling as if they would like to murder him.

The Starling jeered.

"I say you will," he insisted. "It isn't your fault, of course," he added more kindly. "You'll forget because you just can't help it. There never was a human being that remembered after the age of one—at the very latest—except, of course, Her." And he jerked his head over his shoulder at Mary Poppins.

"But why can she remember and not us?" said John.

"A-a-a-h! She's different. She's the Great Exception. Can't go by *her*," said the Starling, grinning at them both.

John and Barbara were silent.

The Starling went on explaining.

"She's something special, you see. Not in the matter of looks, of course. One of my own day-old chicks is handsomer than Mary P. ever was——"

"Here, you impertinence!" said Mary Poppins crossly, making a dart at him and flicking her apron

" Huh!" said the Starling. " Look at 'em!"

in his direction. But the Starling leapt aside and flew up to the window-frame, whistling wickedly, well out of reach.

"Thought you had me that time, didn't you?" he jeered and shook his wing-feathers at her.

Mary Poppins snorted.

The sunlight moved on through the room, drawing its long gold shaft after it. Outside a light wind had sprung up and was whispering gently to the cherry trees in the Lane.

"Listen, listen, the wind's talking," said John, tilting his head on one side. "Do you really mean we won't be able to hear *that* when we're older, Mary Poppins?"

"You'll hear all right," said Mary Poppins, "but you won't understand." At that Barbara began to weep gently. There were tears in John's eyes, too. "Well, it can't be helped. It's how things happen," said Mary Poppins sensibly.

"Look at them, just look at them!" jeered the Starling. "Crying fit to kill themselves! Why, a starling in the egg's got more sense. Look at them!"

For John and Barbara were now crying piteously in their cots—long-drawn sobs of deep unhappiness.

Suddenly the door opened and in came Mrs. Banks.

"I thought I heard the babies," she said. Then she ran to the Twins. "What is it, my darlings? Oh, my

Treasures, my Sweets, my Love-birds, what is it? Why are they crying so, Mary Poppins? They've been so quiet all the afternoon—not a sound out of them. What can be the matter?"

"Yes, ma'am. No, ma'am. I expect they're getting their teeth, ma'am," said Mary Poppins, deliberately not looking in the direction of the Starling.

"Oh, of course—that must be it," said Mrs. Banks brightly.

"I don't want teeth if they make me forget all the things I like best," wailed John, tossing about in his cot.

"Neither do I," wept Barbara, burying her face in her pillow.

"My poor ones, my pets—it will be all right when the naughty old teeth come through," said Mrs. Banks soothingly, going from one cot to the other.

"You don't understand!" roared John furiously. "I don't *want* teeth."

"It won't be all right, it will be all *wrong*!" wailed Barbara to her pillow.

"Yes—yes. There—there. Mother knows—Mother understands. It will be all right when the teeth come through," crooned Mrs. Banks tenderly.

A faint noise came from the window. It was the Starling hurriedly swallowing a laugh. Mary Poppins gave him one look. That sobered him, and he continued to regard the scene without the hint of a smile.

Mrs. Banks was patting her children gently, first one and then the other, and murmuring words that were meant to be reassuring. Suddenly John stopped crying. He had very good manners, and he was fond of his Mother and remembered what was due to her. It was not *her* fault, poor woman, that she always said the wrong thing. It was just, he reflected, that she did not understand. So, to show that he forgave her, he turned over on his back, and very dolefully, sniffing back his tears, he picked up his right foot in both hands and ran his toes along his open mouth.

" Clever One, oh, Clever One," said his Mother admiringly. He did it again and she was very pleased.

Then Barbara, not to be outdone in courtesy, came out of her pillow and with her tears still wet on her face, sat up and plucked off both her socks.

" Wonderful Girl," said Mrs. Banks proudly, and kissed her.

" There, you see, Mary Poppins! They're quite good again. I can always comfort them. Quite good, quite good," said Mrs. Banks, as though she were singing a lullaby. "And the teeth will soon be through."

" Yes, ma'am," said Mary Poppins quietly; and smiling to the Twins, Mrs. Banks went out and closed the door.

The moment she had disappeared the Starling burst into a peal of rude laughter.

"Excuse me smiling!" he cried. "But really—I can't help it. What a scene! *What* a scene!"

John took no notice of him. He pushed his face through the bars of his cot and called softly and fiercely to Barbara:

"I *won't* be like the others. I tell you I won't. They," he jerked his head towards the Starling and Mary Poppins, "can say what they like. I'll never forget, *never*!"

Mary Poppins smiled, a secret, I-know-better-than-you sort of smile, all to herself.

"Nor I," answered Barbara. "Ever."

"Bless my tail-feathers—listen to them!" shrieked the Starling, as he put his wings on his hips and roared with mirth. "As if they could help forgetting! Why, in a month or two—three at the *most*—they won't even know what my name is—silly cuckoos! Silly, half-grown, featherless cuckoos! Ha! Ha! Ha!" And with another loud peal of laughter he spread his speckled wings and flew out of the window. . . .

It was not very long afterwards that the teeth, after much trouble, came through as all teeth must, and the Twins had their first birthday.

The day after the birthday party the Starling, who

had been away on holiday at Bournemouth, came back to Number Seventeen, Cherry Tree Lane.

"Hullo, hullo, hullo! Here we are again!" he screamed joyfully, landing with a little wobble upon the window-sill.

"Well, how's the girl?" he enquired cheekily of Mary Poppins, cocking his little head on one side and regarding her with bright, amused, twinkling eyes.

"None the better for *your* asking," said Mary Poppins, tossing her head.

The Starling laughed.

"Same old Mary P.," he said. "No change out of *you*! How are the other ones—the cuckoos?" he asked, and looked across at Barbara's cot.

"Well, Barbarina," he began in his soft, wheedling voice, "anything for the old fellow to-day?"

"Be-lah-belah-belah-belah!" said Barbara, crooning gently as she continued to eat her arrowroot biscuit.

The Starling, with a start of surprise, hopped a little nearer.

"I said," he repeated more distinctly, "is there anything for the old fellow to-day, Barbie dear?"

"Ba-loo—ba-loo—ba-loo!" murmured Barbara, gazing up at the ceiling as she swallowed the last sweet crumb.

The Starling stared at her.

"Ha!" he said suddenly, and turned and looked enquiringly at Mary Poppins. Her quiet glance met his in a long look.

Then with a darting movement the Starling flew over to John's cot and alighted on the rail. John had a large woolly lamb hugged close in his arms.

"What's my name? What's my name? What's my name?" cried the Starling in a shrill anxious voice.

"Er-umph!" said John, opening his mouth and putting the leg of the woolly lamb into it.

With a little shake of the head the Starling turned away.

"So—it's happened," he said quietly to Mary Poppins.

She nodded.

The Starling gazed dejectedly for a moment at the Twins. Then he shrugged his speckled shoulders.

"Oh, well—— I knew it would. Always told 'em so. But they wouldn't believe it." He remained silent for a little while, staring into the cots. Then he shook himself vigorously.

"Well, well. I must be off. Back to my chimney. It will need a spring-cleaning, I'll be bound." He flew on to the window-sill and paused, looking back over his shoulder.

"It'll seem funny without them, though. Always liked talking to them—so I did. I shall miss them."

He brushed his wing quickly across his eyes.

"Crying?" jeered Mary Poppins. The Starling drew himself up.

"Crying? Certainly not. I have—er—a slight cold, caught on my return journey—that's all. Yes, a slight cold. Nothing serious." He darted up to the window-pane, brushed down his breast-feathers with his beak and then, "Cheerio!" he said perkily, and spread his wings and was gone. . . .

Chapter Ten

FULL MOON

ALL day long Mary Poppins had been in a hurry, and when she was in a hurry she was always cross.

Everything Jane did was bad, everything Michael did was worse. She even snapped at the Twins.

Jane and Michael kept out of her way as much as possible, for they knew that there were times when it was better not to be seen or heard by Mary Poppins.

" I wish we were invisible," said Michael, when Mary Poppins had told him that the very sight of him was more than any self-respecting person could be expected to stand.

" We shall be," said Jane, " if we go behind the sofa. We can count the money in our money-boxes, and she may be better after she's had her supper."

So they did that.

" Sixpence and four pennies—that's tenpence, and a halfpenny and a threepenny-bit," said Jane, counting up quickly.

" Four pennies and three farthings and—and that's

all," sighed Michael, putting his money in a little heap.

"That'll do nicely for the poor-box," said Mary Poppins, looking over the arm of the sofa and sniffing.

"Oh no," said Michael reproachfully. "It's for myself. I'm saving."

"Huh—for one of those aeryplanes, I suppose!" said Mary Poppins scornfully.

"No, for an elephant—a private one for myself, like Lizzie at the Zoo. I could take you for rides then," said Michael, half-looking and half-not-looking at her to see how she would take it.

"Humph," said Mary Poppins, "what an idea!" But they could see she was not quite so cross as before.

"I wonder," said Michael thoughtfully, "what happens in the Zoo at night, when everybody's gone home?"

"Care killed a cat," snapped Mary Poppins.

"I wasn't *caring*, I was only wondering," corrected Michael. "Do *you* know?" he enquired of Mary Poppins, who was whisking the crumbs off the table in double-quick time.

"One more question from you—and spit-spot, to bed you go!" she said, and began to tidy the Nursery so busily that she looked more like a whirlwind in a cap and apron than a human being.

" It's no good asking her. She knows everything, but she never tells," said Jane.

" What's the good of knowing if you don't tell anyone?" grumbled Michael, but he said it under his breath so that Mary Poppins couldn't hear. . . .

Jane and Michael could never remember having been put to bed so quickly as they were that night. Mary Poppins blew out the light very early, and went away as hurriedly as though all the winds of the world were blowing behind her.

It seemed to them that they had been there no time, however, when they heard a low voice whispering at the door.

" Hurry, Jane and Michael!" said the voice. " Get some things on and hurry!"

They jumped out of their beds, surprised and startled.

" Come on," said Jane. " Something's happening." And she began to rummage for some clothes in the darkness.

" Hurry!" called the voice again.

" Oh dear, all I can find is my sailor hat and a pair of gloves!" said Michael, running round the room pulling at drawers and feeling along shelves.

"Those'll do. Put them on. It isn't cold. Come on."

Jane herself had only been able to find a little coat of John's, but she squeezed her arms into it and opened the door. There was nobody there, but they seemed to hear something hurrying away down the stairs. Jane and Michael followed. Whatever it was, or whoever it was, kept continually in front of them.

They never saw it, but they had the distinct sensation of being led on and on by something that constantly beckoned them to follow. Presently they were in the Lane, their slippers making a soft hissing noise on the pavement as they scurried along.

"Hurry!" urged the voice again from a near-by corner, but when they turned it they could still see nothing. They began to run, hand in hand, following the voice down streets, through alley-ways, under arches and across Parks until, panting and breathless, they were brought to a standstill beside a large turnstile in a wall.

"Here you are!" said the voice.

"Where?" called Michael to it. But there was no reply. Jane moved towards the turnstile, dragging Michael by the hand.

"Look!" she said. "Don't you see where we are? It's the Zoo!"

A very bright full moon was shining in the sky and by its light Michael examined the iron grating and looked through the bars. Of course! How silly of him not to have known it was the Zoo!

"But how shall we get in?" he said. "We've no money."

"That's all right!" said a deep, gruff voice from within. "Special Visitors allowed in free to-night. Push the wheel, please!"

Jane and Michael pushed and were through the turnstile in a second.

"Here's your ticket," the gruff voice said, and, looking up, they found that it came from a huge Brown Bear who was wearing a coat with brass buttons and a peaked cap on his head. In his paw were two pink tickets which he held out to the children.

"But we usually *give* tickets," said Jane.

"Usual is as usual does. To-night you receive them," said the Bear, smiling.

Michael had been regarding him closely.

"I remember you," he said to the Bear. "I once gave you a tin of golden syrup."

"You did," said the Bear. "And you forgot to take the lid off. Do you know, I was more than ten days working at that lid? Be more careful in the future."

"But why aren't you in your cage? Are you always out at night?" said Michael.

" No—only when the Birthday falls on a Full Moon. But you must excuse me. I must attend to the gate." And the Bear turned away and began to spin the handle of the turnstile again.

Jane and Michael, holding their tickets, walked on into the Zoo grounds. In the light of the full moon every tree and flower and shrub was visible, and they could see the houses and cages quite clearly.

" There seems to be a lot going on," observed Michael.

And, indeed, there was. Animals were running about in all the paths, sometimes accompanied by birds and sometimes alone. Two wolves ran past the children, talking eagerly to a very tall stork who was tip-toeing between them with dainty, delicate movements. Jane and Michael distinctly caught the words " Birthday " and " Full Moon " as they went by.

In the distance three camels were strolling along side by side, and not far away a beaver and an American vulture were deep in conversation. And they all seemed to the children to be discussing the same subject.

" Whose Birthday is it, I wonder?" said Michael, but Jane was moving ahead, gazing at a curious sight.

Just by the Elephant Stand a very large, very fat old gentleman was walking up and down on all fours, and on his back, on two small parallel scats, were eight monkeys going for a ride.

"Why, it's all upside down!" exclaimed Jane.

The old gentleman gave her an angry look as he went past.

"Upside down!" he snorted. "Me! Upside down? Certainly not. Gross insult!" The eight monkeys laughed rudely.

"Oh, please—I didn't mean you—but the whole thing," explained Jane, hurrying after him to apologise. "On ordinary days the animals carry human beings and now there's a human being carrying the animals. That's what I meant."

But the old gentleman, shuffling and panting, insisted that he had been insulted, and hurried away with the monkeys screaming on his back.

Jane saw it was no good following him, so she took Michael's hand and moved onwards. They were startled when a voice, almost at their feet, hailed them.

"Come on, you two! In you come. Let's see *you* dive for a bit of orange-peel you don't want." It was a bitter, angry voice, and looking down they saw that it came from a small black Seal who was leering at them from a moonlit pool of water.

"Come on, now—and see how *you* like it!" he said.

"But—but we can't swim!" said Michael.

"Can't help that!" said the Seal. "You should have thought of that before. Nobody ever bothers to find out whether *I* can swim or not. Eh, what? What's that?"

He spoke the last question to another Seal who had emerged from the water and was whispering in his ear.

"Who?" said the first Seal. "Speak up!"

The second Seal whispered again. Jane caught the words "Special Visitors—Friends of——" and then no more. The first Seal seemed disappointed, but he said politely enough to Jane and Michael:

"Oh, beg pardon. Pleased to meet you. Beg pardon." And he held out his flipper and shook hands limply with them both.

"Look where you're going, can't you?" he shouted, as something bumped into Jane. She turned quickly and gave a little frightened start as she beheld an enormous Lion. The eyes of the Lion brightened as he saw her.

"Oh, I say——" he began. "I didn't know it was you! This place is so crowded to-night and I'm in such a hurry to see the humans fed I'm afraid I didn't look where I was going. Coming along? You oughtn't to miss it, you know——"

"Perhaps," said Jane politely, "you'd show us the way." She was a little uncertain of the Lion, but he seemed kindly enough. "And after all," she thought, "everything is topsy-turvy to-night."

"Dee-lighted!" said the Lion in rather a mincing voice, and he offered her his arm. She took it, but to be on the safe side she kept Michael beside her. He was such a round, fat little boy, and after all, she thought, lions are lions——

"Does my mane look nice?" asked the Lion as they moved off. "I had it curled for the occasion."

Jane looked at it. She could see that it had been carefully oiled and combed into ringlets.

"Very," she said. "But—isn't it rather odd for a lion to care about such things? I thought——"

"What! My dear young lady, the Lion, as you know, is the King of the Beasts. He has to remember his position. And I, personally, am not likely to forget it. I believe a lion should *always* look his best no matter where he is. This way."

And with a graceful wave of his forepaw he pointed towards the Big Cat House and ushered them in at the entrance.

Jane and Michael caught their breaths at the sight that met their eyes. The great hall was thronged with animals. Some were leaning over the long bar that separated them from the cages, some were standing on the seats that rose in tiers opposite. There were panthers and leopards, wolves, tigers and antelopes; monkeys and hedgehogs, wombats, mountain goats and giraffes; and an enormous group composed entirely of kittiwakes and vultures.

" Splendid, isn't it?" said the Lion proudly. " Just like the dear old jungle days. But come along—we must get good places."

And he pushed his way through the crowd crying, " Gangway, gangway!" and dragging Jane and Michael after him. Presently, through a little clearing in the middle of the hall, they were able to get a glimpse of the cages.

" Why," said Michael, opening his mouth very wide, " they're full of human beings!"

And they were.

In one cage two large, middle-aged gentlemen in top-hats and striped trousers were prowling up and down, anxiously gazing through the bars as though they were waiting for something.

Children of all shapes and sizes, from babies in long clothes upwards, were scrambling about in another cage. The animals outside regarded these with great interest and some of them tried to make the babies laugh by thrusting their paws or their tails in through the bars. A giraffe stretched his long neck out over the heads of the other animals and let a little boy in a sailor-suit tickle its nose.

In a third cage three elderly ladies in raincoats and goloshes were imprisoned. One of them was knitting, but the other two were standing near the bars shouting at the animals and poking at them with their umbrellas.

"Nasty brutes. Go away. I want my tea!" screamed one of them.

"Isn't she funny?" said several of the animals, and they laughed loudly at her.

"Jane—look!" said Michael, pointing to the cage at the end of the row. "Isn't that——?"

"Admiral Boom!" said Jane, looking very surprised.

And Admiral Boom it was. He was ramping up and down in his cage, coughing, and blowing his nose, and spluttering with rage.

"Blast my gizzard! All hands to the Pump! Land, ho! Heave away there! Blast my gizzard!" shouted the Admiral. Every time he came near the bars a tiger prodded him gently with a stick and this made Admiral Boom swear dreadfully.

"But how did they all get in there?" Jane asked the Lion.

"Lost," said the Lion. "Or rather, left behind. These are the people who've dawdled and been left inside when the gates were shut. Got to put 'em somewhere, so we keep 'em here. He's dangerous—that one there! Nearly did for his keeper not long ago. Don't go near him!" And he pointed at Admiral Boom.

"Stand back, please, stand back! Don't crush!

Make way, please!" Jane and Michael could hear several voices crying these words loudly.

"Ah—now they're going to be fed!" said the Lion, excitedly pressing forward into the crowd. "Here come the keepers."

Four Brown Bears, each wearing a peaked cap, were

trundling trolleys of food along the little corridor that separated the animals from the cages.

"Stand back, there!" they said, whenever an animal got in the way. Then they opened a small door in each cage and thrust the food through on pronged forks.

Jane and Michael had a good view of what was happening, through a gap between a panther and a dingo. Bottles of milk were being thrown in to the babies, who made soft little grabs with their hands and clutched them greedily. The older children snatched sponge-cakes and dough-nuts from the forks and began to eat ravenously. Plates of thin bread-and-butter and wholemeal scones were provided for the ladies in goloshes, and the gentlemen in top-hats had lamb cutlets and custard in glasses. These, as they received their food, took it away into a corner, spread handkerchiefs over their striped trousers and began to eat.

Presently, as the keepers passed down the line of cages, a great commotion was heard.

"Blast my vitals—call that a meal? A skimpy little round of beef and a couple of cabbages! What—no Yorkshire pudding? Outrageous! Up with the anchor! And where's my port? Port, I say! Heave her over! Below there, where's the Admiral's port?"

"Listen to him! He's turned nasty. I tell you, he's not safe—that one," said the Lion.

Jane and Michael did not need to be told whom he meant. They knew Admiral Boom's language too well.

"Well," said the Lion, as the noise in the hall grew less uproarious. "That appears to be the end. And I'm afraid, if you'll excuse me, I must be getting along. See you later at the Grand Chain, I hope. I'll look out for you." And, leading them to the door, he took his leave of them, sidling away, swinging his curled mane, his golden body dappled with moonlight and shadow.

"Oh, please——" Jane called after him. But he was out of hearing.

"I wanted to ask him if they'd ever get out. The poor humans! Why, it might have been John and Barbara—or any of us." She turned to Michael, but found that he was no longer by her side. He had moved away along one of the paths and, running after him, she found him talking to a Penguin who was standing in the middle of the path with a large copy-book under one wing and an enormous pencil under the other. He was biting the end of it thoughtfully as she approached.

"I can't think," she heard Michael saying, apparently in answer to a question.

The Penguin turned to Jane. "Perhaps *you* can tell me," he said. "Now, what rhymes with Mary? I can't use 'contrary' because that has been done before and one must be original. If you're going to say ' fairy,' don't. I've thought of that already, but as it's not a bit like her, it won't do."

" Hairy," said Michael brightly.

" H'm. Not poetic enough," observed the Penguin.

" What about ' wary '?" said Jane.

" Well——" The Penguin appeared to be considering it. " It's not *very* good, is it?" he said forlornly. " I'm afraid I'll have to give it up. You see, I was trying to write a poem for the Birthday. I thought it would be so nice if I began :

' O Mary, Mary——'

and then I couldn't get any further. It's very annoying. They expect something learned from a penguin, and I don't want to disappoint them. Well, well—you mustn't keep me. I must get on with it." And with that he hurried away, biting his pencil and bending over his copy-book.

" This is all very confusing," said Jane. " Whose birthday is it, I wonder?"

" Now, come along, you two, come along. You want to pay your respects, I suppose, it being the Birthday and all!" said a voice behind them, and turning, they saw the Brown Bear who had given them their tickets at the gate.

"Oh, of course!" said Jane, thinking that was the safest thing to say, but not knowing in the least whom they were to pay their respects to.

The Brown Bear put an arm round each of them and propelled them along the path. They could feel his warm soft fur brushing against their bodies and hear the rumblings his voice made in his stomach as he talked.

"Here we are, *here* we are!" said the Brown Bear, stopping before a small house whose windows were all so brightly lit that if it hadn't been a moonlight night you would have thought the sun was shining. The Bear opened the door and gently pushed the two children through it.

The light dazzled them at first, but their eyes soon became accustomed to it and they saw that they were in the Snake House. All the cages were open and the snakes were out—some curled lazily into great scaly knots, others slipping gently about the floor. And in the middle of the snakes, on a log that had evidently been brought from one of the cages, sat Mary Poppins. Jane and Michael could hardly believe their eyes.

"Coupla birthday guests, ma'am," announced the Brown Bear respectfully. The snakes turned their heads enquiringly towards the children. Mary Poppins did not move. But she spoke.

"And where's your overcoat, may I ask?" she demanded, looking crossly but without surprise at Michael.

"And *your* hat and gloves?" she snapped, turning to Jane.

But before either of them had time to reply there was a stir in the Snake House.

"Hsssst! Hsssst!"

The snakes, with a soft hissing sound, were rising up on end and bowing to something behind Jane and Michael. The Brown Bear took off his peaked cap. And slowly Mary Poppins, too, stood up.

"My dear child. My very dear child!" said a small, delicate, hissing voice. And out from the largest of the cages there came, with slow, soft, winding movements, a Hamadryad. He slid in graceful curves past the bowing snakes and the Brown Bear, towards Mary Poppins. And when he reached her, he raised the front half of his long golden body, and, thrusting upwards his scaly golden hood, daintily kissed her, first on one cheek and then on the other.

"So!" he hissed softly. "This is very pleasant— very pleasant, indeed. It is long since your Birthday fell on a Full Moon, my dear." He turned his head.

"Be seated, friends!" he said, bowing graciously to the other snakes, who, at that word, slid reverently to the floor again, coiled themselves up, and gazed steadily at the Hamadryad and Mary Poppins.

The Hamadryad turned then to Jane and Michael, and with a little shiver they saw that his face was smaller and more wizened than anything they had ever seen. They took a step forward, for his curious deep eyes seemed to draw them towards him. Long and narrow they were, with a dark sleepy look in them, and in the middle of that dark sleepiness a wakeful light like a jewel.

" And who, may I ask, are these?" he said in his soft, terrifying voice, looking at the children enquiringly.

" Miss Jane Banks and Master Michael Banks, at your service," said the Brown Bear gruffly, as though he were half afraid. " *Her* friends."

" Ah, *her* friends. Then they are welcome. My dears, pray be seated."

Jane and Michael, feeling somehow that they were in the presence of a King—as they had not felt when they met the Lion—with difficulty drew their eyes from that compelling gaze and looked round for something to sit on. The Brown Bear provided this by squatting down himself and offering them each a furry knee.

Jane said, in a whisper : " He talks as though he were a great lord."

" He *is*. He's the lord of our world—the wisest and

most terrible of us all," said the Brown Bear softly and reverently.

The Hamadryad smiled, a long, slow, secret smile, and turned to Mary Poppins.

"Cousin," he began, gently hissing.

"Is she *really* his cousin?" whispered Michael.

"First cousin once removed—on the mother's side," returned the Brown Bear, whispering the information behind his paw. "But, listen now. He's going to give the Birthday Present."

"Cousin," repeated the Hamadryad, "it is long since your Birthday fell on the Full Moon and long since we have been able to celebrate the event as we celebrate it to-night. I have, therefore, had time to give the question of your Birthday Present some considera-tion. And I have decided"—he paused, and there was no sound in the Snake House but the sound of many creatures all holding their breath—"that I cannot do better than give you one of my own skins."

"Indeed, cousin, it is too kind of you——" began Mary Poppins, but the Hamadryad held up his hood for silence.

"Not at all. Not at all. You know that I change my skin from time to time and that one more or less means little to me. Am I not——?" he paused and looked round him.

"The Lord of the Jungle," hissed all the snakes in

unison, as though the question and the answer were part of a well-known ceremony.

The Hamadryad nodded. "So," he said, "what seems good to me will seem so to you. It is a small enough gift, dear Mary, but it may serve for a belt or a pair of shoes, even a hat-band—these things always come in useful, you know."

And with that he began to sway gently from side to side, and it seemed to Jane and Michael as they watched that little waves were running up his body from the tail to the head. Suddenly he gave a long, twisting, corkscrew leap and his golden outer skin lay on the floor, and in its place he was wearing a new coat of shining silver.

"Wait!" said the Hamadryad, as Mary Poppins bent to pick up the skin. "I will write a Greeting upon it." And he ran his tail very quickly along his thrown skin, deftly bent the golden sheath into a circle, and diving his head through this as though it were a crown, offered it graciously to Mary Poppins. She took it, bowing.

"I just can't thank you enough——" she began, and paused. She was evidently very pleased, for she kept running the skin backwards and forwards through her fingers and looking at it admiringly.

"Don't try," said the Hamadryad. "Hsst!" he

went on, and spread out his hood as though he were listening with it. "Do I not hear the signal for the Grand Chain?"

Everybody listened. A bell was ringing and a deep gruff voice could be heard coming nearer and nearer, crying out:

"Grand Chain, Grand Chain! Everybody to the centre for the Grand Chain and Finale. Come along, come along. Stand ready for the Grand Chain!"

"I thought so," said the Hamadryad, smiling. "You must be off, my dear. They'll be waiting for you to take your place in the centre. Farewell, till your next Birthday." And he raised himself as he had done before and lightly saluted Mary Poppins on both cheeks.

"Hurry away!" said the Hamadryad. "I will take care of your young friends."

Jane and Michael felt the Brown Bear moving under them as they stood up. Past their feet they could feel all the snakes slipping and writhing as they hurried from the Snake House. Mary Poppins bowed towards the Hamadryad very ceremoniously, and without a backward glance at the children went running towards the huge green square in the centre of the Zoo.

"You may leave us," said the Hamadryad to the Brown Bear who, after bowing humbly, ran off with his cap in his hand to where all the other animals were congregating round Mary Poppins.

"Will you go with me?" said the Hamadryad kindly to Jane and Michael. And without waiting for them to reply he slid between them, and with a movement of his hood directed them to walk one on either side of him.

"It has begun," he said, hissing with pleasure.

And from the loud cries that were now coming from the Green, the children could guess that he meant the Grand Chain. As they drew nearer they could hear the animals singing and shouting, and presently they saw leopards and lions, beavers, camels, bears, cranes, antelopes and many others all forming themselves into a ring round Mary Poppins. Then the animals began to move, wildly crying their Jungle songs, prancing in and out of the ring, and exchanging hand and wing as they went as dancers do in the Grand Chain of the Lancers.

A little piping voice rose high above the rest :

"Oh, Mary, Mary,
She's my Dearie,
She's my Dear-i-o!"

And they saw the Penguin come dancing by, waving his short wings and singing lustily. He caught sight of them, bowed to the Hamadryad, and called out :

"I got it—did you hear me singing it? It's not perfect, of course. 'Dearie' does not rhyme *exactly* with Mary. But it'll do, it'll do!" and he skipped off and offered his wing to a leopard.

Jane and Michael watched the dance, the Hamadryad secret and still between them. As their friend the Lion, dancing past, bent down to take the wing of a Brazilian Pheasant in his paw, Jane shyly tried to put her feelings into words.

"I thought, Sir——" she began and stopped, feeling confused, and not sure whether she ought to say it or not.

"Speak, my child!" said the Hamadryad. "You thought?"

"Well—that lions and birds, and tigers and little animals——"

The Hamadryad helped her. "You thought that they were natural enemies, that the lion could not meet a bird without eating it, nor the tiger the hare—eh?"

Jane blushed and nodded.

"Ah—you may be right. It is probable. But not on the Birthday," said the Hamadryad. "To-night the small are free from the great and the great protect the small. Even I——" he paused and seemed to be thinking deeply, "even *I* can meet a Barnacle Goose without any thought of dinner—on this occasion. And

Forming themselves into a ring round Mary Poppins

after all," he went on, flicking his terrible little forked tongue in and out as he spoke, " it may be that to eat and be eaten are the same thing in the end. My

wisdom tells me that this is probably so. We are all made of the same stuff, remember, we of the Jungle, you of the City. The same substance composes us—

the tree overhead, the stone beneath us, the bird, the beast, the star—we are all one, all moving to the same end. Remember that when you no longer remember me, my child."

"But how can tree be stone? A bird is not me. Jane is not a tiger," said Michael stoutly.

"You think not?" said the Hamadryad's hissing voice. "Look!" and he nodded his head towards the moving mass of creatures before them. Birds and animals were now swaying together, closely encircling Mary Poppins, who was rocking lightly from side to side. Backwards and forwards went the swaying crowd, keeping time together, swinging like the pendulum of a clock. Even the trees were bending and lifting gently, and the moon seemed to be rocking in the sky as a ship rocks on the sea.

"Bird and beast and stone and star—we are all one, all one——" murmured the Hamadryad, softly folding his hood about him as he himself swayed between the children.

"Child and serpent, star and stone—all one."

The hissing voice grew softer. The cries of the swaying animals dwindled and became fainter. Jane and Michael, as they listened, felt themselves gently rocking too, or as if they were being rocked. . . .

Soft, shaded light fell on their faces.

"Asleep and dreaming—both of them," said a whispering voice. Was it the voice of the Hamadryad, or their mother's voice as she tucked them in, on her usual nightly round of the Nursery?

"Good." Was that the Brown Bear gruffly speaking, or Mr. Banks?

Jane and Michael, rocking and swaying, could not tell . . . could not tell. . . .

"I had such a strange dream last night," said Jane, as she sprinkled sugar over her porridge at breakfast. "I dreamed we were at the Zoo and it was Mary Poppins' birthday, and instead of animals in the cages there were human beings, and all the animals were outside——"

"Why, that's *my* dream. *I* dreamed that, too," said Michael, looking very surprised.

"We can't both have dreamed the same thing," said Jane. "Are you sure? Do you remember the Lion who curled his mane and the Seal who wanted us to——"

"Dive for orange-peel?" said Michael. "Of course I do! And the babies inside the cage, and the Penguin who couldn't find a rhyme, and the Hamadryad——"

"Then it couldn't have been a dream at all," said
Jane emphatically. "It must have been *true*. And if
it was——" She looked curiously at Mary Poppins,
who was boiling the milk.

"Mary Poppins," she said, "could Michael and I
have dreamed the same dream?"

"You and your dreams!" said Mary Poppins, sniffing. "Eat your porridge, please, or you will have no
buttered toast."

But Jane would not be put off. She *had* to know.

"Mary Poppins," she said, looking very hard at her,
"were you at the Zoo last night?"

Mary Poppins' eyes popped.

"At the Zoo? In the middle of the night? Me?
A quiet orderly person who knows that early to bed,
early to rise makes a man healthy, wealthy and wise?"

"But *were* you?" Jane persisted.

"I have all I need of Zoos in this nursery, thank
you," said Mary Poppins, uppishly. "Hyenas, ourang-
outangs, all of you. Sit up straight, and no more nonsense."

Jane poured out her milk.

"Then it must have been a dream," she said, "after
all."

But Michael was staring, open-mouthed, at Mary
Poppins, who was now making toast at the fire.

"Jane," he said in a shrill whisper, "Jane, look!"
He pointed, and Jane, too, saw what he was looking at.

Round her waist Mary Poppins was wearing a belt
made of golden scaly snake-skin, and on it was written
in curving, snaky writing:

"A Present From the Zoo."

Chapter Eleven

CHRISTMAS SHOPPING

" I SMELL snow," said Jane, as they got out of the Bus.

" I smell Christmas trees," said Michael.

" I smell fried fish," said Mary Poppins.

And then there was no time to smell anything else, for the Bus had stopped outside the Largest Shop in the World, and they were all going into it to do their Christmas shopping.

" May we look at the windows first?" said Michael, hopping excitedly on one leg.

" I don't mind," said Mary Poppins with surprising mildness. Not that Jane and Michael were *really* very surprised, for they knew that the thing Mary Poppins liked doing best of all was looking in shop windows. They knew, too, that while they saw toys and books and holly-boughs and plum cakes, Mary Poppins saw nothing but herself reflected there.

" Look, aeroplanes!" said Michael, as they stopped before a window in which toy aeroplanes were careering through the air on wires.

"And look there!" said Jane. "Two tiny black babies in one cradle—are they chocolate, do you think, or china?"

"Just look at *you*!" said Mary Poppins to herself, particularly noticing how nice her new gloves with the fur tops looked. They were the first pair she had ever had, and she thought she would never grow tired of looking at them in the shop windows with her hands inside them. And having examined the reflection of the gloves she went carefully over her whole person—coat, hat, scarf and shoes, with herself inside—and she thought that, on the whole, she had never seen anybody looking quite so smart and distinguished.

But the winter afternoons, she knew, were short, and they had to be home by tea-time. So with a sigh she wrenched herself away from her glorious reflection.

"Now we will go in," she said, and annoyed Jane and Michael very much by lingering at the Haber-dashery counter and taking great trouble over the choice of a reel of black cotton.

"The Toy Department," Michael reminded her, "is in *that* direction."

"I know, thank you. Don't point," she said, and paid her bill with aggravating slowness.

But at last they found themselves alongside Father Christmas, who went to the greatest trouble in helping them choose their presents.

"That will do nicely for Daddy," said Michael, selecting a clockwork train with special signals. "I will take care of it for him when he goes to the City."

"I think I will get this for Mother," said Jane, pushing a small doll's perambulator which, she felt sure, her Mother had always wanted. "Perhaps she will lend it to me sometimes."

After that, Michael chose a packet of hairpins for each of the Twins and a Meccano set for his Mother, a mechanical beetle for Robertson Ay, a pair of spectacles for Ellen, whose eyesight was perfectly good, and some bootlaces for Mrs. Brill who always wore slippers.

Jane, after some hesitation, eventually decided that a white dickey would be just the thing for Mr. Banks, and she bought *Robinson Crusoe* for the Twins to read when they grew up.

" Until they are old enough, I can read it myself," she said. " I am sure they will lend it to me."

Mary Poppins then had a great argument with Father Christmas over a cake of soap.

" Why not Lifebuoy?" said Father Christmas, trying to be helpful and looking anxiously at Mary Poppins, for she was being rather snappy.

" I prefer Vinolia," she said haughtily, and she bought a cake of that.

" My goodness," she said, smoothing the fur on her right-hand glove. " I wouldn't half like a cup of tea!"

" Would you quarter like it, though?" asked Michael.

" There is no call for you to be funny," said Mary Poppins, in such a voice that Michael felt that, indeed, there wasn't.

" And it is time to go home."

There! She had said the very words they had been hoping she wouldn't say. That was so like Mary Poppins.

" Just five minutes longer," pleaded Jane.

" Ah do, Mary Poppins! You look so nice in your new gloves," said Michael wilily.

But Mary Poppins, though she appreciated the remark, was not taken in by it.

" No," she said, and closed her mouth with a snap and stalked towards the doorway.

" Oh, dear!" said Michael to himself, as he followed her, staggering under the weight of his parcels. " If only she would say ' Yes ' for once!"

But Mary Poppins hurried on and they had to go with her. Behind them Father Christmas was waving his hand, and the Fairy Queen on the Christmas tree and all the other dolls were smiling sadly and saying, " Take me home, somebody!" and the aeroplanes were all beating their wings and saying in bird-like voices, " Let me fly! Ah, do let me fly!"

Jane and Michael hurried away, closing their ears to those enchanting voices, and feeling that the time in the Toy Department had been unreasonably and cruelly short.

And then, just as they came towards the shop entrance, the adventure happened.

They were just about to spin the glass door and go

out, when they saw coming towards it from the pavement the running, flickering figure of a child.

"Look!" said Jane and Michael both together.

"My gracious, goodness, glory me!" exclaimed Mary Poppins, and stood still.

And well she might, for the child had practically no clothes on, only a light wispy strip of blue stuff that looked as though she had torn it from the sky to wrap round her naked body.

It was evident that she did not know much about spinning doors, for she went round and round inside it, pushing it so that it should spin faster and laughing as it caught her and sent her whirling round and round. Then suddenly, with a quick little movement she freed herself, sprang away from it and landed inside the shop.

She paused on tip-toe, turning her head this way and that, as though she were looking for someone. Then, with a start of pleasure, she caught sight of Jane and Michael and Mary Poppins as they stood, half-hidden behind an enormous fir-tree, and ran towards them joyously.

"Ah, *there* you are! Thank you for waiting. I'm afraid I'm a little late," said the child, stretching out her bright arms to Jane and Michael. "Now," she cocked her head on one side, "aren't you glad to see me? Say yes, say yes!"

"Yes," said Jane smiling, for nobody, she felt, could help being glad to see anyone so bright and happy. "But who are you?" she enquired curiously.

"What is your name?" said Michael, gazing at her.

"Who am I? What is my name? Don't say you don't know me? Oh, surely, surely——" The child seemed very surprised and a little disappointed. She turned suddenly to Mary Poppins and pointed her finger.

"*She* knows me. Don't you? I'm sure you know me!"

There was a curious look on Mary Poppins' face. Jane and Michael could see blue fires in her eyes as though they reflected the blue of the child's dress and her brightness.

"Does it—does it," she whispered, "begin with an M?"

The child hopped on one leg delightedly.

"Of course it does—and you know it. M-A-I-A. I'm Maia." She turned to Jane and Michael.

"*Now* you recognise me, don't you? I'm the second of the Pleiades. Electra—she's the eldest—couldn't come because she's minding Merope. Merope's the baby, and the other five of us come in between—all girls. Our Mother was very disappointed at first not to have a boy, but now she doesn't mind."

The child danced a few steps and burst out again in her excited little voice:

"Oh, Jane! Oh, Michael—I've often watched you from the sky, and now I'm actually talking to you. There is nothing about you I don't know. Michael doesn't like having his hair brushed, and Jane has a thrush's egg in a jam-jar on the mantelpiece. And your Father is going bald on the top. I like him. It was he who first introduced us—don't you remember? He said one evening last summer:

"'Look, there are the Pleiades. Seven stars all together, the smallest in the sky. But there is one of them you can't see.'

"He meant Merope, of course. She's still too young to stay up all night. She's such a baby that she has to go to bed very early. Some of them up there call us the Little Sisters, and sometimes we are called the Seven Doves, but Orion calls us 'You girls' and takes us hunting with him."

"But what are you doing here?" demanded Michael, still very surprised.

Maia laughed. "Ask Mary Poppins. I am sure she knows."

"Tell us, Mary Poppins," said Jane.

"Well," said Mary Poppins snappily, "I suppose you two aren't the only ones in the world that want to go shopping at Christmas——"

"That's it," squealed Maia delightedly. "She's quite right. I've come down to buy toys for them all. We can't get away very often, you know, because we're so busy making and storing up the Spring Rains. That's the special job of the Pleiades. However, we drew lots and I won. Wasn't it lucky?"

She hugged herself happily.

"Now, come on. I can't stay very long. And you must come back and help me choose."

And dancing about them, running now to one and now to another, she shepherded them back to the Toy Department. As they went, the crowds of shoppers stood and stared at them and dropped their parcels with astonishment.

"So cold for her. What can her parents be thinking of!" said the Mothers, with voices that were suddenly soft and gentle.

"I mean to say——!" said the Fathers. "It shouldn't be allowed. Must write to *The Times* about it." And their voices were unnaturally gruff and gritty.

The shop-walkers behaved curiously, too. As the little group passed they bowed to Maia as though she were a Queen.

But none of them—not Jane, nor Michael, nor Mary Poppins, nor Maia—noticed nor heard anything extraordinary. They were too busy with their own extraordinary adventure.

"Here we are!" said Maia, as she pranced into the Toy Department. "Now, what shall we choose?"

An Assistant, with a start, bowed respectfully as soon as he saw her.

"I want something for each of my sisters—six of them. You must help me, please," said Maia, smiling at him.

"Certainly, madam," said the Assistant agreeably.

"First—my eldest sister," said Maia. "She's very domestic. What about that little stove with the silver saucepans? Yes. And that striped broom. We are so troubled with star-dust, and she will love having that to sweep it up with."

The Assistant began wrapping the things in coloured paper.

"Now for Taygete. She likes dancing. Don't you think, Jane, a skipping-rope would be just the thing for her? You'll tie them carefully, won't you?" she said to the Assistant. "I have a long way to go."

She fluttered on among the toys, never standing still for a moment, but walking with a light quicksilver step, as though she were still twinkling in the sky.

Mary Poppins and Jane and Michael could not take their eyes off her as she flickered from one of them to another asking their advice.

"Then there's Alcyone. She's difficult. She's so

quiet and thoughtful and never seems to want anything. A book, do you think, Mary Poppins? What is
this Family—the *Swiss-Robinsons*? I think she would
like that. And if she doesn't, she can look at the pictures. Wrap it up!"

She handed the book to the Assistant.

"I know what Celæno wants," she went on. "A
hoop. She can bowl it across the sky in the day-time
and make a circle of it to spin about her at night. She'll
love that red and blue one." The Assistant bowed
again and began to wrap up the hoop.

"Now there are only the two little ones left.
Michael, what would you advise for Sterope?"

"What about a top?" said Michael, giving the question his earnest consideration.

"A humming-top? *What* a good idea! She will
love to watch it go waltzing and singing down the sky.
And what do you think for Merope, the baby, Jane?"

"John and Barbara," said Jane shyly, "have rubber
ducks!"

Maia gave a delighted squeal and hugged herself.

"Oh, Jane, how wise you are! I should never have
thought of that. A rubber duck for Merope, please—a
blue one with yellow eyes."

The assistant tied up the parcels, while Maia ran
round him, pushing at the paper, giving a tug to the
string to make sure that it was firmly knotted.

"That's right," she said. "You see, I mustn't drop anything."

Michael, who had been staring steadily at her ever since she first appeared, turned and said in a loud whisper to Mary Poppins:

"But she has no purse. Who will pay for the toys?"

"None of your business," snapped Mary Poppins.

"And it's rude to whisper." But she began to fumble busily in her pocket.

"What did you say?" demanded Maia with round, surprised eyes. "Pay? Nobody will pay. There is nothing to pay—is there?"

She turned her shining gaze upon the Assistant.

"Nothing at all, madam," he assured her, as he put the parcels into her arms and bowed again.

"I thought not. You see," she said, turning to Michael, "the whole point of Christmas is that things should be *given* away, isn't it? Besides, what could I pay with? We have no money up there." And she laughed at the mere suggestion of such a thing.

"Now we must go," she went on, taking Michael's arm. "We must all go home. It's very late, and I heard your Mother telling you that you must be home in time for tea. Besides, I must get back, too. Come." And drawing Michael and Jane and Mary Poppins after her, she led the way through the shop and out by the spinning door.

Outside the entrance Jane suddenly said:

"But there's no present for *her*. She's bought something for all the others and nothing for herself. Maia has no Christmas present." And she began to search hurriedly through the parcels she was carrying, to see what she could spare for Maia.

Mary Poppins gave a quick glance into the window beside her. She saw herself shining back at her, very smart, very interesting, her hat on straight, her coat nicely pressed and her new gloves just completing the whole effect.

"You be quiet," she said to Jane in her snappiest voice. At the same time she whipped off her new gloves and thrust one on to each of Maia's hands.

"There!" she said gruffly. "It's cold to-day. You'll be glad of them."

Maia looked at the gloves, hanging very large and almost empty upon her hands. She said nothing, but moving close to Mary Poppins she reached up her spare arm and put it round Mary Poppins' neck and kissed her. A long look passed between them, and they smiled as people smile who understand each other. Maia turned then, and with her hand lightly touched the cheeks of Jane and Michael. And for a moment they all stood in a ring at the windy corner gazing at each other as though they were enchanted.

" 'Ere! Come down! We can't 'ave this kind of thing!"

"I've been so happy," said Maia softly, breaking the silence. "Don't forget me, will you?"

They shook their heads.

"Good-bye," said Maia.

"Good-bye," said the others, though it was the last thing they wanted to say.

Then Maia, standing poised on tip-toe, lifted up her arms and sprang into the air. She began to step, climbing ever higher, as though there were invisible stairs cut into the grey sky. She waved to them as she went, and the three of them waved back.

"What on earth is happening?" somebody said close by.

"But it's not possible!" said another voice.

"Preposterous!" cried a third. For a crowd was gathering to witness the extraordinary sight of Maia returning home.

A Policeman pushed his way through the throng, scattering the people with his truncheon.

"Naow, naow. Wot's all this? A Naccident or wot?"

He looked up, his gaze following that of the rest of the crowd.

"'Ere!" he called angrily, shaking his fist at Maia. "Come down! Wot you doing up there? 'Olding up the traffic and all. Come down! We can't 'ave this kind of thing—not in a public place. 'Tisn't natural!"

Far away they heard Maia laughing and saw something bright dangling from her arm. It was the skipping-rope. After all, the parcel had come undone.

For a moment longer they saw her prancing up the airy stair, and then a bank of cloud hid her from their eyes. They knew she was behind it, though, because of the brightness that shone about its thick dark edge.

"Well, I'm jiggered!" said the Policeman, staring upwards, and scratching his head under its helmet.

"And well you might be!" said Mary Poppins, with such a ferocious snap that anyone else might have thought she was really cross with the Policeman. But Jane and Michael were not taken in by that snap. For they could see in Mary Poppins' eyes something that, if she were anybody else but Mary Poppins, might have been described as tears. . . .

"Could we have imagined it?" said Michael, when they got home and told the story to their Mother.

"Perhaps," said Mrs. Banks. "We imagine strange and lovely things, my darling."

"But what about Mary Poppins' gloves?" said Jane.

"We saw her give them away to Maia. And she's not wearing them now. So it must be true!"

"What, Mary Poppins!" exclaimed Mrs. Banks. "Your best fur-topped gloves! You gave them away!"

Mary Poppins sniffed.

"My gloves are my gloves and I do what I like with them!" she said haughtily.

And she straightened her hat and went down to the kitchen to have her tea. . . .

Chapter Twelve

WEST WIND

It was the first day of Spring.

Jane and Michael knew this at once, because they heard Mr. Banks singing in his bath, and there was only one day in the year when he did that.

They always remembered that particular morning. For one thing, it was the first time they were allowed to come downstairs for breakfast, and for another Mr. Banks lost his black bag. So that the day began with two extraordinary happenings.

"Where is my *BAG*?" shouted Mr. Banks, turning round and round in the hall like a dog chasing its tail.

And everybody else began running round and round too—Ellen and Mrs. Brill and the children. Even Robertson Ay made a special effort and turned round twice. At last Mr. Banks discovered the bag himself in his study, and he rushed into the hall with it, holding it aloft.

"Now," he said, as though he were delivering a sermon, "my bag is always kept in one place. Here.

On the umbrella-stand. Who put it in the study?" he
roared.

"You did, my dear, when you took the Income Tax
papers out of it last night," said Mrs. Banks.

Mr. Banks gave her such a hurt look that she wished
she had been less tactless and had said she had put it
there herself.

"Humph—Urrumph!" he said, blowing his nose
very hard and taking his overcoat from its peg. He
walked with it to the front door.

"Hullo," he said more cheerfully, "the Parrot
Tulips are in bud!" He went into the garden and
sniffed the air. "H'm, wind's in the West, I think."
He looked down towards Admiral Boom's house where
the telescope weathercock swung. "I thought so," he
said. "Westerly weather. Bright and balmy. I won't
take an overcoat."

And with that he picked up his bag and his bowler
hat and hurried away to the City.

"Did you hear what he said?" Michael grabbed
Jane's arm.

She nodded. "The wind's in the West," she said
slowly.

Neither of them said any more, but there was a
thought in each of their minds that they wished was not
there.

They forgot it soon, however, for everything seemed

to be as it always was, and the Spring sunlight lit up
the house so beautifully that nobody remembered it
needed a coat of paint and new wallpapers. On the
contrary, they all found themselves thinking that it
was the best house in Cherry Tree Lane.

But trouble began after luncheon.

Jane had gone down to dig in the garden with
Robertson Ay. She had just sown a row of radish-seed
when she heard a great commotion in the Nursery and
the sound of hurrying footsteps on the stairs. Presently
Michael appeared, very red in the face and panting
loudly.

"Look, Jane, look!" he cried, and held out his
hand. Within it lay Mary Poppins' compass, with the
disc frantically swinging round the arrow as it trembled in Michael's shaking hand.

"The compass?" said Jane, and looked at him
questioningly.

Michael suddenly burst into tears.

"She gave it to me," he wept. "She said I could
have it all for myself now. Oh, oh, there must be something wrong! What is going to happen? She has
never given me anything before."

"Perhaps she was only being nice," said Jane to
soothe him, but in her heart she felt as disturbed as
Michael was. She knew very well that Mary Poppins
never wasted time in being nice.

And yet, strange to say, during that afternoon Mary Poppins never said a cross word. Indeed, she hardly said a word at all. She seemed to be thinking very deeply, and when they asked questions she answered them in a far-away voice. At last Michael could bear it no longer.

"Oh, do be cross, Mary Poppins! Do be cross again! It is not like you. Oh, I feel so anxious." And indeed, his heart felt heavy with the thought that something, he did not quite know what, was about to happen at Number Seventeen, Cherry Tree Lane.

"Trouble trouble and it will trouble you!" retorted Mary Poppins crossly, in her usual voice.

And immediately he felt a little better.

"Perhaps it's only a feeling," he said to Jane. "Perhaps everything is all right and I'm just imagining— don't you think so, Jane?"

"Probably," said Jane slowly. But she was thinking hard and her heart felt tight in her body.

The wind grew wilder towards evening, and blew in little gusts about the house. It went pulling and whistling down the chimneys, slipping in through the cracks under the windows, turning the Nursery carpet up at the corners.

Mary Poppins gave them their supper and cleared away the things, stacking them neatly and method-

ically. Then she tidied up the Nursery and put the
kettle on the hob.

" There!" she said, glancing round the room to see
that everything was all right. She was silent for a
minute. Then she put one hand lightly on Michael's
head and the other on Jane's shoulder.

" Now," she said, " I am just going to take the shoes
down for Robertson Ay to clean. Behave yourselves,
please, till I come back." She went out and shut the
door quietly behind her.

Suddenly, as she went, they both felt they must run
after her, but something seemed to stop them. They
remained quiet, with their elbows on the table waiting
for her to come back. Each was trying to reassure the
other without saying anything.

" How silly we are," said Jane presently. " Everything's all right." But she knew she said it more to
comfort Michael than because she thought it was true.

The Nursery clock ticked loudly from the mantelpiece. The fire flickered and crackled and slowly died
down. They still sat there at the table, waiting.

At last Michael said uneasily: " She's been gone a
very long time, hasn't she?"

The wind whistled and cried about the house as if
in reply. The clock went on ticking its solemn double
note.

Suddenly the silence was broken by the sound of the front door shutting with a loud bang.

" Michael!" said Jane, starting up.

" Jane!" said Michael, with a white, anxious look on his face.

They listened. Then they ran quickly to the window and looked out.

Down below, just outside the front door, stood Mary Poppins, dressed in her coat and hat, with her carpet bag in one hand and her umbrella in the other. The wind was blowing wildly about her, tugging at her skirt, tilting her hat rakishly to one side. But it seemed to Jane and Michael that she did not mind, for she smiled as though she and the wind understood each other.

She paused for a moment on the step and glanced back towards the front door. Then with a quick movement she opened the umbrella, though it was not raining, and thrust it over her head.

The wind, with a wild cry, slipped under the umbrella, pressing it upwards as though trying to force it out of Mary Poppins' hand. But she held on tightly, and that, apparently, was what the wind wanted her to do, for presently it lifted the umbrella higher into the air and Mary Poppins from the ground. It carried her lightly so that her toes just grazed along the garden path. Then it lifted her over the front gate and swept her upwards towards the branches of the cherry trees in the Lane.

" She's going, Jane, she's going !" cried Michael, weeping.

" Quick !" cried Jane. " Let us get the Twins. They must see the last of her." She had no doubt now, nor had Michael, that Mary Poppins had gone for good because the wind had changed.

They each seized a Twin and rushed back to the window.

Mary Poppins was in the upper air now, floating away over the cherry trees and the roofs of the houses, holding tightly to the umbrella with one hand and to the carpet bag with the other.

The Twins began to cry quietly.

With their free hands Jane and Michael opened the window and made one last effort to stay Mary Poppins' flight.

"Mary Poppins!" they cried. "Mary Poppins, come back!"

But she either did not hear or deliberately took no notice. For she went sailing on and on, up into the cloudy, whistling air, till at last she was wafted away over the hill and the children could see nothing but the trees bending and moaning under the wild west wind. . . .

"She did what she said she would, anyway. She stayed till the wind changed," said Jane, sighing and turning sadly from the window. She took John to his cot and put him into it. Michael said nothing, but as he brought Barbara back and tucked her into bed he was sniffing uncomfortably.

"I wonder," said Jane, "if we'll ever see her again?"

Suddenly they heard voices on the stairs.

Floating away over the roofs of the houses

Children, children!" Mrs. Banks was calling as she opened the door. "Children—I am very cross. Mary Poppins has left us——"

"Yes," said Jane and Michael.

"You knew, then?" said Mrs. Banks, rather surprised. "Did she tell you she was going?"

They shook their heads, and Mrs. Banks went on:

"It's outrageous. One minute here and gone the next. Not even an apology. Simply said, 'I'm going!' and off she went. Anything more preposterous, more thoughtless, more discourteous—— What is it, Michael?" She broke off crossly, for Michael had grasped her skirt in his hands and was shaking her. "What *is* it, child?"

"Did she say she'd come back?" he cried, nearly knocking his Mother over. "Tell me—did she?"

"You will *not* behave like a Red Indian, Michael," she said, loosening his hold. "I don't remember *what* she said, except that she was going. But I certainly shan't have her back if she does want to come. Leaving me high and dry with nobody to help me and without a word of notice."

"Oh, Mother!" said Jane reproachfully.

"You are a very cruel woman," said Michael, clenching his fist, as though at any minute he would have to strike her.

"Children! I'm ashamed of you—really I am! To

218

want back anybody who has treated your Mother so badly. I'm utterly shocked."

Jane burst into tears.

"Mary Poppins is the only person I want in the world!" Michael wailed, and flung himself on to the floor.

"Really, children, really! I don't understand you. Do be good, I beg of you. There's nobody to look after you to-night. I have to go out to dinner and it's Ellen's Day Off. I shall have to send Mrs. Brill up." And she kissed them absentmindedly, and went away with an anxious little line on her forehead. ...

"Well, if I ever did! Her going away and leaving you pore dear children in the lurch like that," said Mrs. Brill, a moment later, bustling in and setting to work on them.

"A heart of stone, that's what that girl had *and* no mistake, or my name's not Clara Brill. Always keeping herself to herself, too, and not even a lace handkerchief or a hatpin to remember her by. Get up, will you please, Master Michael!" Mrs. Brill went on, panting heavily.

"How we stood her so long, I *don't* know—with her

airs and graces and all. What a lot of buttons, Miss
Jane! Stand still do now, and let me undress you,
Master Michael. Plain she was, too, nothing much to
look at. Indeed, all things considered, I don't know
that we won't be better off, after all. Now, Miss Jane,
where's your nightgown—why, what's this under your
pillow——?"

Mrs. Brill had drawn out a small nobbly parcel.

"What is it? Give it to me—give it," said Jane,
trembling with excitement, and she took it from Mrs.
Brill's hands very quickly. Michael came and stood
near her and watched her undo the string and tear
away the brown paper. Mrs. Brill, without waiting to
see what emerged from the package, went in to the
Twins.

The last wrapping fell to the floor and the thing that
was in the parcel lay in Jane's hand.

"It's her picture," she said in a whisper, looking
closely at it.

And it was!

Inside a little curly frame was a painting of Mary
Poppins, and underneath it was written, " Mary Poppins by Bert."

"That's the Match Man—he did it," said Michael,
and took it in his hand so that he could have a better
look.

Jane found suddenly that there was a letter attached to the painting. She unfolded it carefully. It ran:

" DEAR JANE,
        Michael had the compass so the picture is for you. Au revoir.

                                        MARY POPPINS "

She read it out loud till she came to the words she couldn't understand.

" Mrs. Brill!" she called. " What does ' au revoir ' mean?"

" Au revore, dearie?" shrieked Mrs. Brill from the next room. " Why, doesn't it mean—let me see, I'm not up in these foreign tongues—doesn't it mean ' God bless you '? No. No, I'm wrong. I think, Miss Jane dear, it means ' To Meet Again '."

Jane and Michael looked at each other. Joy and understanding shone in their eyes. They knew what Mary Poppins meant.

Michael gave a long sigh of relief. " That's all right," he said shakily. " She always does what she says she will." He turned away.

" Michael, are you crying?" Jane asked.

He twisted his head and tried to smile at her.

" No, I am not," he said. " It is only my eyes."

She pushed him gently towards his bed, and as he

got in she slipped the portrait of Mary Poppins into his hand—hurriedly, in case she should regret it.

" You have it for to-night, darling," whispered Jane, and she tucked him in just as Mary Poppins used to do. . . .

MARY POPPINS
COMES BACK

They saw before them their own pictured faces

CONTENTS

To PIP,
this keepsake

Chapter One

THE KITE

IT was one of those mornings when everything looks very neat and bright and shiny, as though the world had been tidied up overnight.

In Cherry Tree Lane the houses blinked as their blinds went up, and the thin shadows of the Cherry Trees fell in dark stripes across the sunlight. But there was no sound anywhere, except for the tingling of the Ice Cream Man's bell as he wheeled his cart up and down.

" STOP ME AND BUY ONE "

said the placard in front of the cart. And presently a Sweep came round the corner of the Lane and held up his black, sweepy hand.

The Ice Cream Man went tingling up to him.

" Penny one," said the Sweep. And he stood leaning on his bundle of brushes as he licked out the Ice Cream with the tip of his tongue. When it was all gone, he gently wrapped the cone in his handkerchief and put it in his pocket.

" Don't you eat cones?" asked the Ice Cream Man, very surprised.

" No. I collect them!" said the Sweep. And he picked up his brushes and went in through Admiral Boom's front gate, because there was no Tradesman's Entrance.

The Ice Cream Man wheeled his cart up the Lane

again and tingled, and the stripes of shadow and sunlight fell on him as he went.

"Never knew it so quiet before!" he murmured,
gazing from right to left, and looking out for customers.

At that very moment, a loud voice sounded from
Number Seventeen. The Ice Cream Man cycled
hurriedly up to the gate, hoping for an order.

"I won't stand it! I simply will not stand any more!"
shouted Mr. Banks, striding angrily from the front door
to the foot of the stairs and back again.

"What is it?" said Mrs. Banks anxiously, hurrying out
of the Dining-room. "And what is that you are kicking
up and down the hall?"

Mr. Banks lunged out with his foot and something
black flew half-way up the stairs.

"My hat!" he said between his teeth. "My Best
Bowler Hat!"

He ran up the stairs and kicked it down again. It
spun for a moment on the tiles and fell at Mrs. Banks'
feet.

"Is there anything wrong with it?" said Mrs. Banks,
nervously. But to herself she wondered whether there
was not something wrong with Mr. Banks.

"Look and see!" he roared at her.

Trembling, Mrs. Banks stooped and picked up the
hat. It was covered with large, shiny, sticky patches,
and she noticed it had a peculiar smell.

She sniffed at the brim.

"It smells like boot-polish," she said.

"It *is* boot-polish," retorted Mr. Banks. "Robertson
Ay has brushed my hat with the boot-brush—in fact,
he has polished it."

Mrs. Banks' mouth fell with horror.

"I don't know what's come over this house!" Mr.

Banks went on. "Nothing ever goes right—hasn't for ages! Shaving-Water too hot, Breakfast Coffee too cold. And now—this!"

He snatched his hat from Mrs. Banks and caught up his bag.

"I am going!" he said. "And I don't know that I shall ever come back. I shall probably take a long sea-voyage."

Then he clapped the hat on his head, banged the front door behind him and went through the gate so quickly that he knocked over the Ice Cream Man, who had been listening to the conversation with interest.

"It's your own fault!" said Mr. Banks crossly. "You'd no right to be there!" And he went striding off towards the City, his polished hat shining like a jewel in the sun.

The Ice Cream Man got up carefully, and, finding there were no bones broken, he sat down on the kerb and made it up to himself by eating a large Ice Cream. . . .

"Oh, dear!" said Mrs. Banks as she heard the gate slam. "It is quite true. Nothing *does* go right nowadays. First one thing and then another. Ever since Mary Poppins left without a Word of Warning everything has gone wrong."

She sat down at the foot of the stairs, and took out her hankerchief and cried into it.

And, as she cried, she thought of all that had happened since that day when Mary Poppins had so suddenly and so strangely disappeared.

"Here one night and gone the next—most upsetting!" said Mrs. Banks, gulping.

Nurse Green had arrived soon after and had left at the end of the week because Michael had spat at her. She was followed by Nurse Brown, who went out for a walk one day and never came back. And it was not until later that they discovered that all the silver spoons had gone with her.

And after Nurse Brown came Miss Quigley, the Governess, who had to be asked to leave because she played scales for three hours every morning before breakfast, and Mr. Banks did not care for music.

"And then," sobbed Mrs. Banks to her handkerchief, "there was Jane's attack of measles, and the bathroom geyser bursting, and the Cherry Trees ruined by frost and . . ."

"If you please, m'm!" Mrs. Banks looked up to find Mrs. Brill, the cook, at her side.

"The kitchen flue's on fire!" said Mrs. Brill gloomily.

"Oh, dear. What next?" cried Mrs. Banks. "You must tell Robertson Ay to put it out. Where is he?"

"Asleep, m'am, in the broom cupboard. And when that boy's asleep, nothing'll wake him—not if it's an Earthquake or a regiment of Tom-toms!" said Mrs. Brill, as she followed Mrs. Banks down the kitchen stairs.

Between them they managed to put out the fire, but that was not the end of Mrs. Banks' troubles.

She had no sooner finished Luncheon than a crash, followed by a loud thud, was heard from upstairs.

"What is it now?" Mrs. Banks rushed out to see what had happened.

"Oh, my leg, my leg!" cried Ellen, the housemaid.

She sat on the stairs, surrounded by a ring of broken china, groaning loudly.

"What is the matter with it?" said Mrs. Banks sharply.

"Broken!" said Ellen dismally, leaning against the banisters.

"Nonsense, Ellen! You've sprained your ankle, that's all!"

But Ellen only groaned again.

"My leg is broken! What shall I do?" she wailed, over and over again.

At that moment the shrill cries of the Twins sounded from the Nursery. They were fighting for the possession of a blue celluloid Duck. Their screams rose thinly above the voices of Jane and Michael, who were painting pictures on the wall and arguing as to whether a green horse should have a purple or a red tail. And through this uproar there sounded, like the steady beat of a drum, the groans of Ellen, the housemaid. "My leg is broken! What shall I do?"

"This," said Mrs. Banks, rushing upstairs, "is the Last Straw!"

She helped Ellen to bed, and put a cold water bandage round her ankle. Then she went up to the Nursery.

Jane and Michael rushed at her.

"It should have a red tail, shouldn't it?" demanded Michael.

"Oh, Mother, don't let him be so stupid! No horse has a red tail, has it?"

"Well, what horse has a purple tail? Tell me that!" he screamed.

"*My* Duck!" shrieked John, snatching the Duck from Barbara.

"Mine, mine, mine!" cried Barbara, snatching it back again.

"Children! Children!" Mrs. Banks was wringing her hands in despair. "Be quiet or I shall Go Mad!"

There was silence for a moment as they stared at her with interest. Would she really, they wondered? And what would she be like, if she did?

"Now," said Mrs. Banks, "I will *not* have this behaviour. Poor Ellen has hurt her ankle, so there is nobody to look after you. You must all go into the Park and play there till Tea-time. Jane and Michael, you must look after the little ones. John, let Barbara have the Duck now and you can have it when you go to bed. Michael, you may take your new Kite. Now, get your hats, all of you!"

"But I want to finish my horse——" began Michael crossly.

"Why must we go to the Park?" complained Jane. "There's nothing to do there!"

"Because," said Mrs. Banks, "I *must* have peace. And if you will go quietly and be good children there will be Coconut Cakes for tea."

And before they had time to break out again, she had put on their hats and was hurrying them down the stairs.

"Look both ways!" she called as they went through the gate, Jane pushing the Twins in the perambulator and Michael carrying his Kite.

They looked to the right. There was nothing coming.

They looked to the left. There was nobody there but the Ice Cream Man, who was jingling his bell at the end of the Lane.

Jane hurried across. Michael trailed after her.

"I hate this life!" he said miserably to his Kite. "Everything always goes wrong always."

Jane pushed the perambulator as far as the Lake.

"Now," she said, "give me the Duck!"

The Twins shrieked and clutched it at either end. Jane uncurled their fingers.

"Look!" she said, throwing the Duck into the Lake. "Look, darlings, it's going to India!"

The Duck drifted off across the water. The Twins stared at it and sobbed.

Jane ran round the Lake and caught it and sent it off again.

"Now," she said brightly, "it's off to Southampton!"
The Twins did not appear to be amused.

"Now to New York!" They wept harder than ever.

Jane flung out her hands. "Michael, what *are* we to do with them? If we give the Duck to them they'll fight over it, and if we don't they'll go on crying."

"I'll fly the Kite for them," said Michael. "Look, children, look!"

He held up the beautiful green-and-yellow Kite and began to unwind the string. The Twins eyed it tearfully and without interest. He lifted the Kite above his head and ran a little way. It flapped along the air for a moment and then collapsed hollowly on the grass.

"Try again!" said Jane encouragingly.

"You hold it up while I run," said Michael.

This time the Kite rose a little higher. But, as it floated, its long, tasselled tail caught in the branches of a Lime Tree and the Kite dangled limply among the leaves.

The Twins howled lustily.

"Oh, dear!" said Jane. "Nothing goes right nowadays."

"Hullo, hullo, hullo! What's all this?" said a voice behind them.

They turned and saw the Park Keeper, looking very smart in his uniform and peaked cap. He was prodding up stray pieces of paper with the sharp end of his walking-stick.

Jane pointed to the Lime Tree. The Keeper looked up. His face became very stern.

"Now, now, you're breaking the rules! We don't allow Litter here, you know—not on the ground nor in the trees neither. This won't do at all!"

"It isn't Litter. It's a Kite," said Michael.

A mild, soft, foolish look came over the Keeper's face. He went up to the Lime Tree.

"A Kite? So it is. And I haven't flown a Kite since I was a boy!" He sprang up into the tree and came down holding the Kite tenderly under his arm.

"Now," he said excitedly, "we'll wind her up and give her a run and away she'll go!" He put out his hand for the winding-stick.

Michael clutched it firmly.

"Thank you, but I want to fly it myself."

"Well, but you'll let me help, won't you?" said the Keeper humbly. "Seeing as I got it down and I haven't flown a Kite since I was a boy."

"All right," said Michael, for he didn't want to seem unkind.

"Oh, thank you, thank you!" cried the Keeper gratefully. "Now, I take the Kite and walk ten paces down the green. And when I say 'Go!' you run! See?"

The Keeper walked away, counting his steps out loud.

"Eight, nine, ten."

He turned and raised the Kite above his head.

"Go!"

Michael began to run.

There was a tug at the string as the winding-stick turned in his hand.

"She's afloat!" cried the Keeper.

Michael looked back. The Kite was sailing through the air, plunging steadily upwards. Higher and higher it dived, a tiny wisp of green-and-yellow bounding away into the blue. The Keeper's eyes were popping.

"I never saw such a kite. Not even when I was a boy," he murmured, staring upwards.

A light cloud came up over the sun and puffed across the sky.

"It's coming towards the Kite," said Jane in an excited whisper.

Up and up went the tossing tail, darting through the air until it seemed but a faint, dark speck on the sky. The cloud moved slowly towards it. Nearer, nearer . . .

"Gone!" said Michael, as the speck disappeared behind the thin grey screen.

Jane gave a little sigh. The Twins sat quietly in the perambulator. A curious stillness was upon them all. The taut string running up from Michael's hand seemed to link them all to the cloud, and the earth to the sky. They waited, holding their breaths, for the Kite to appear again.

Suddenly Jane could bear it no longer.

"Michael," she cried. "Pull it in! Pull it in!"

Michael turned the stick and gave a long, strong pull. The string remained taut and steady. He pulled again, puffing and panting.

"I can't," he said. "It won't come."

"I'll help!" said Jane. "Now—pull!"

But, hard as they tugged, the string would not give, and the Kite remained hidden behind the cloud.

"Let me!" said the Keeper importantly. "When I was a boy we did it this way."

And he put his hand on the string, just above Jane's, and gave it a short, sharp jerk. It seemed to give a little.

"Now—all together—pull!"

The Keeper tossed off his hat, and, planting their feet firmly on the grass, Jane and Michael pulled with all their might.

"It's coming!" panted Michael.

Suddenly the string slackened, and a small whirling

242

shape shot through the grey cloud and came floating down.

"Wind her up!" the Keeper spluttered, glancing at Michael.

But the string was already winding round the stick of its own accord.

Down, down came the Kite, turning over and over in the air, wildly dancing at the end of the jerking string.

Jane gave a little gasp.

"Something's happened," she cried. "That's not our Kite! It's quite a different one!"

They stared.

It was quite true. The Kite was no longer green - and - yellow. It had turned colour and was now navy - blue. Down it came, tossing and bounding.

Suddenly Michael gave a shout.

"Jane! Jane! It isn't a Kite at all. It looks like —oh, it looks like——"

"Wind, Michael, wind quickly!" gasped Jane. "I can hardly wait!"

For now, above the tallest trees, the shape at the end of the string was clearly visible. There was no sign of the green-and-yellow Kite, but in its place danced a figure that seemed at once strange and familiar, a figure wearing a blue coat with silver buttons and a straw hat trimmed with daisies. Tucked under its arm was an Umbrella with a parrot's head for a handle, a brown Carpet-bag dangled from one hand, while the other held firmly to the end of the shortening string.

"Ah!" Jane gave a shout of triumph. "It *is* her!"

"I knew it!" cried Michael, his hands trembling on the winding-stick.

"Lumme!" said the Park Keeper, gaping and blinking. "Lumme!"

On sailed the curious figure, its feet neatly clearing the tops of the trees. They could see the face now, and the well-known features—coal-black hair, bright blue eyes, and nose turned upwards like the nose of a Dutch doll.

As the last length of string wound itself round the stick, the figure drifted down between the Lime Trees and alighted primly upon the grass.

In a flash Michael dropped the stick. Away he bounded, with Jane at his heels.

"Mary Poppins, Mary Poppins!" they cried, and flung themselves upon her.

Behind them the Twins were crowing like cocks in the morning, and the Park Keeper was opening and shutting his mouth as though he would like to say something but could not find the words.

"At last! At last! At last!" shouted Michael wildly, clutching at her arm, her bag, her umbrella—anything,

*On sailed the curious figure, its feet neatly clearing the
tops of the trees*

so long as he might touch her and feel that she was really true.

" We knew you'd come back! We found the letter that said *au revoir*!" cried Jane, flinging her arms round the waist of the blue overcoat.

A satisfied smile flickered for a moment over Mary Poppins' face—up from the mouth, over the turned-up nose, into the blue eyes. But it died away swiftly.

" I'll thank you to remember," she remarked, disengaging herself from their hands, " that this is a Public Park and not a Bear Garden. Such goings on! I might as well be at the Zoo. And where, may I ask, are your gloves?"

They fell back, fumbling in their pockets.

" Humph! Put them on, please!"

Trembling with excitement and delight, Jane and Michael stuffed their hands into their gloves and put on their hats.

Mary Poppins moved towards the perambulator. The Twins cooed happily as she strapped them in more securely and straightened the rug. Then she glanced round.

" Who put that Duck in the pond?" she demanded, in that stern, haughty voice they knew so well.

" I did," said Jane. " For the Twins. He was going to New York."

" Well, take him out, then!" said Mary Poppins. " He is not going to New York—wherever that is—but Home to Tea."

And, slinging her Carpet-bag over the handle of the perambulator, she began to push the Twins towards the gate.

The Park Keeper, suddenly finding his voice, blocked her way.

" See here !" he said, staring. " I shall have to report this. It's against the Regulations. Coming down out of the sky like that. And where from, I'd like to know, where from?"

He broke off, for Mary Poppins was eyeing him up and down in a way that made him feel he would rather be somewhere else.

" If I was a Park Keeper," she remarked, primly, " I should put on my cap and button my coat. Excuse me !"

And, haughtily waving him aside, she pushed past with the perambulator.

Blushing, the Keeper bent to pick up his hat. When he looked up again, Mary Poppins and the children had disappeared through the gate of Number Seventeen Cherry Tree Lane.

He stared at the path. Then he stared up at the sky and down at the path again.

He took off his hat, scratched his head, and put it on again.

" I never saw such a thing !" he said shakily. " Not even when I was a boy."

And he went away muttering and looking very upset. . . .

" Why, it's Mary Poppins !" said Mrs. Banks, as they came into the hall. " Where did *you* come from? Out of the blue?"

" Yes," began Michael joyfully, " she came down on the end——"

He stopped short, for Mary Poppins had fixed him with one of her terrible looks.

"I found them in the Park, ma'am," she said, turning to Mrs. Banks, "so I brought them home!"

"Have you come to stay, then?"

"For the present, ma'am."

"But, Mary Poppins, last time you were here you left without a Word of Warning. How do I know you won't do it again?"

"You don't, ma'am," replied Mary Poppins, calmly.

Mrs. Banks looked rather taken aback.

"But—but will you, do you think?" she asked uncertainly.

"I couldn't say, ma'am, I'm sure."

"Oh!" said Mrs. Banks, because, at the moment, she couldn't think of anything else.

And before she had recovered from her surprise, Mary Poppins had taken her Carpet-bag and was hurrying the children upstairs.

Mrs. Banks, gazing after them, heard the Nursery door shut quietly. Then, with a sigh of relief, she ran to the telephone.

"Mary Poppins has come back!" she said happily, into the receiver.

"Has she, indeed?" said Mr. Banks at the other end. "Then perhaps I will, too."

And he rang off.

Upstairs Mary Poppins was taking off her overcoat. She hung it on a hook behind the Night-Nursery door. Then she removed her hat and placed it neatly on one of the bed-posts.

Jane and Michael watched the familiar movements.

Everything about her was just as it had always been. They could hardly believe she had ever been away.

Mary Poppins bent down and opened the Carpet-bag.

It was quite empty except for a large Thermometer.

"What's that for?" asked Jane curiously.

"You!" said Mary Poppins.

"But I'm not ill!" Jane protested. "It's two months since I had measles."

"Open!" said Mary Poppins, in a voice that made Jane shut her eyes very quickly and open her mouth. The Thermometer slipped in.

"I want to know how you've been behaving since I went away!" remarked Mary Poppins sternly.

Then she took out the Thermometer and held it up to the light.

"Careless, Thoughtless and Untidy," she read out.

Jane stared.

"I'm not surprised!" said Mary Poppins, and thrust the Thermometer into Michael's mouth. He kept his lips tightly pressed upon it until she plucked it out and read:

"A very Noisy, Mischievous, Troublesome little Boy."

"I'm not," he said angrily.

For answer she thrust the Thermometer under his nose and he spelt out the large red letters.

"A-V-E-R-Y-N-O-I-S . . ."

"You see?" said Mary Poppins, looking at him triumphantly. She opened John's mouth and popped in the Thermometer.

"Peevish and Excitable." That was John's temperature.

And, when Barbara's was taken, Mary Poppins read out the two words, "Thoroughly Spoilt."

"Humph!" she snorted. "It's about time I came back!"

Then she popped it quickly in her own mouth, left it there for a moment, and took it out.

"A very Excellent and Worthy Person, Thoroughly Reliable in every Particular."

A pleased and conceited smile lit up her face as she read her temperature aloud.

"I thought so," she said, priggishly. "Now—Tea and Bed!"

It seemed to them no more than a minute before they had drunk their milk and eaten their Coconut Cakes and were in and out of the bath. As usual, everything that Mary Poppins did had the speed of electricity. Hooks and eyes rushed apart, buttons darted eagerly out of their holes, sponge and soap ran up and down like lightning, and towels dried with one rub.

Mary Poppins walked along the row of beds tucking them all in. Her starched white apron crackled, and she smelt deliciously of newly-made toast.

When she came to Michael's bed, she bent down and rummaged under it for a minute. Then she carefully drew out her camp-bedstead with her possessions laid upon it in neat piles. The cake of Sunlight soap, the toothbrush, the packet of hairpins, the bottle of scent, the small folding arm-chair and the box of throat lozenges. Also the seven flannel nightgowns, the four cotton ones, the boots, the dominoes, the two bathing-caps and the postcard album.

Jane and Michael sat up and stared.

"Where did they come from?" demanded Michael. "I've been under my bed simply hundreds of times and I know they weren't there before."

Mary Poppins did not reply. She had begun to undress.

Jane and Michael exchanged glances. They knew it was no good asking, because Mary Poppins never explained anything.

She slipped off her starched white collar and fumbled at the clip of a chain round her neck.

"What's inside that?" inquired Michael, gazing at a small gold locket that hung on the end of the chain.

"A portrait."

"Whose?"

"You'll know when the time comes—not before!" she snapped.

"When will the time come?"

"When I go!"

They stared at her with startled eyes.

"But, Mary Poppins," cried Jane, "you won't ever leave us again, will you? Oh, say you won't!"

Mary Poppins glared at her.

"A nice life I'd have," she remarked, "if I spent all my days with *you*!"

"But you will stay?" persisted Jane eagerly.

Mary Poppins tossed the locket up and down on her palm.

"I'll stay till the chain breaks!" she said briefly.

And, popping a cotton nightgown over her head, she began to undress beneath it.

"That's all right," Michael whispered across to Jane. "I noticed the chain and it's a very strong one."

He nodded to her reassuringly. They curled up in their beds and lay watching Mary Poppins as she moved mysteriously beneath the tent of her nightgown. And they thought of her first arrival at Cherry Tree Lane and all the strange and astonishing things that had happened afterwards; of how she had flown away on her umbrella when the wind changed; of the long, weary days without her and of her marvellous descent from the sky this afternoon.

Suddenly Michael remembered something.

"My Kite!" he said, sitting up in bed. "I forgot all about it! Where's my Kite?"

Mary Poppins' head came up through the neck of her nightgown.

"Kite?" she said crossly. "Which Kite? What Kite?"

"My green-and-yellow Kite with the tassels. The one you came down on, at the end of the string."

Mary Poppins stared at him. He could not tell if she was more astonished than angry, but she looked as if she was both.

And her voice when she spoke was worse than her look.

"Did I understand you to say that "—she repeated the words slowly, between her teeth—"that I came down from somewhere on the end of a string?"

"But you did!" faltered Michael. "To-day. Out of a cloud. We saw you!"

"On the end of a string. Like a Monkey or a Spinning-Top? Me, Michael Banks?"

Mary Poppins, in her fury, seemed to have grown to twice her usual size. She hovered over him in her nightgown, huge and angry, waiting for him to reply.

He clutched the bed-clothes for support.

"Don't say any more, Michael!" Jane whispered warningly across from her bed. But he had gone too far now to stop.

"Then—where's my Kite—" he said recklessly. "If you didn't come down—er, in the way I said—where's my Kite? It's not on the end of the string."

"O-ho? And *I* am, I suppose?" she inquired with a scoffing laugh.

He saw then that it was no good going on. He could not explain. He would have to give it up.

"N—no," he said, in a thin voice. "No, Mary Poppins."

She turned and snapped out the electric light.

"Your manners," she remarked tartly, "have not improved since I went away! On the end of a string, indeed! I have never been so insulted in my life. Never!"

And with a furious sweep of her arm, she turned down her bed and flounced into it, pulling the blankets right over her head.

Michael lay very quiet, still holding his bed-clothes tightly.

"She did, though, didn't she? We saw her," he whispered presently to Jane.

But Jane did not answer. Instead, she pointed towards the Night-Nursery door.

Michael lifted his head cautiously.

Behind the door, on a hook, hung Mary Poppins' overcoat, its silver buttons gleaming in the glow of the night-light. And, dangling from the pocket, were a row of paper tassels, the tassels of a green-and-yellow Kite.

They gazed at it for a long time.

Then they nodded across to each other. They knew there was nothing to be said, for there were things about Mary Poppins they would never understand. But—she was back again. That was all that mattered.

The even sound of her breathing came floating across from the camp-bed. They felt peaceful and happy and complete.

" I don't mind, Jane, if it has a purple tail," hissed Michael presently.

" No, Michael!" said Jane. " I really think a red would be better."

After that there was no sound in the Nursery but the sound of five people breathing very quietly. . . .

" *P-p! P-p!*" went Mr. Banks' pipe.

" *Click-click!*" went Mrs. Banks' knitting-needles.

Mr. Banks put his feet up on the study mantelpiece and snored a little.

After a while, Mrs. Banks spoke.

" Do you still think of taking a long sea-voyage?" she asked.

" Er—I don't think so. I am rather a bad sailor. And my hat's all right now. I had the whole of it polished by the Shoe-Black at the corner and it looks as good as new. Even better. Besides, now that Mary Poppins is back, my Shaving-Water will be just the right temperature."

Mrs. Banks smiled to herself and went on knitting.

She felt very glad that Mr. Banks was such a bad sailor and that Mary Poppins had come back. . . .

Down in the Kitchen, Mrs. Brill was putting a fresh bandage round Ellen's ankle.

" I never thought much of her when she was here," said Mrs. Brill. " But I must say that this has been a different house since this afternoon. As quiet as a Sunday and as neat as Ninepence. I'm not sorry she's back."

"Neither am I, indeed!" said Ellen thankfully.

"And neither am I!" thought Robertson Ay, listening to the conversation through the wall of the broom cupboard. "Now I shall have a little peace!"

He settled himself comfortably on the upturned coalscuttle and fell asleep again with his head against a broom.

But what Mary Poppins thought about it nobody ever knew, for she kept her thoughts to herself and never told anyone anything. . . .

Chapter Two

MISS ANDREW'S LARK

I<small>T</small> was Saturday afternoon.

In the hall of Number Seventeen Cherry Tree Lane, Mr. Banks was busy tapping the barometer and telling Mrs. Banks what the weather was going to do.

"Moderate South wind; average temperature: local thunder; sea slight," he said. "Further outlook unsettled. Hullo—what's that?"

He broke off as a bumping, jumping, thumping noise sounded overhead.

Round the bend in the staircase Michael appeared, looking very bad-tempered and sulky as he bumped heavily down. Behind him, with a Twin on each arm, came Mary Poppins, pushing her knee into his back and sending him with a sharp thud from one stair to the next. Jane followed, carrying the hats.

"Well begun is half done. Down you go, please!" Mary Poppins was saying tartly.

Mr. Banks turned from the barometer and looked up as they appeared.

"Well, what's the matter with you?" he demanded.

"I don't *want* to go for a walk! I want to play with my new engine!" said Michael, gulping as Mary Poppins' knee jerked him one stair lower.

"Nonsense, darling!" said Mrs. Banks. "Of course you do. Walking makes such long, strong legs."

"But I like short legs best," grumbled Michael, stumbling heavily down another stair.

" When *I* was a little boy," said Mr. Banks, " I loved going for walks. I used to walk with my Governess down to the second lamp-post and back every day. And I *never* grumbled."

Michael stood still on his stair and looked doubtfully at Mr. Banks.

" Were you *ever* a little boy?" he said, very surprised.

Mr. Banks seemed quite hurt.

" Of course I was. A sweet little boy with long yellow curls and a lace collar and velvet breeches and button-up boots."

" I can hardly believe it," said Michael, hurrying down the stairs of his own accord and staring up at Mr. Banks.

" What was the name of your Governess?" asked Jane, running downstairs after Michael. " And was she nice?"

" She was called Miss Andrew, and she was a Holy Terror!"

" Hush!" said Mrs. Banks, reproachfully.

" I mean——" Mr. Banks corrected himself, " she was —er—very strict. And always right. And she loved putting everybody else in the wrong and making them feel like a worm. That's what Miss Andrew was like!"

Mr. Banks mopped his brow at the mere memory of his Governess.

Ting! Ting! Ting!

The front door bell pealed and echoed through the house.

Mr. Banks went to the door and opened it. On the step, looking very important, stood the Telegraph Boy.

" Urgent Telegram. Name of Banks. Any answer?" He handed over an orange-coloured envelope.

" If it's good news I'll give you sixpence," said Mr.

Banks as he tore the Telegram open and read the message. His face grew pale.

"No answer!" he said shortly.

"And no sixpence?"

"Certainly not!" said Mr. Banks bitterly. The Telegraph Boy gave him a reproachful look and went sorrowfully away.

"Oh, what is it?" asked Mrs. Banks. "Is somebody ill?"

"Worse than that!" said Mr. Banks miserably.

"Have we lost all our money?" By this time Mrs. Banks, too, was pale and very anxious.

"Worse still! Didn't the barometer say thunder? And further outlook unsettled? Listen!"

He smoothed out the telegram and read aloud:

Coming to stay with you for a month. Arriving this afternoon three o'clock. Please light fire in bedroom.

EUPHEMIA ANDREW

"Andrew? Why, that's the same name as your Governess!" said Jane.

"It *is* my Governess!" said Mr. Banks, striding up and down and running his hands nervously through what was left of his hair. "Her other name is Euphemia. And she's coming to-day at three!"

He groaned loudly.

"But I don't call that bad news," said Mrs. Banks, feeling very relieved. "It will mean getting the spare room ready, of course, but I don't mind. I shall like having the dear old soul——"

"Dear old soul!" roared Mr. Banks. "You don't know what you're talking about. Dear old—my Jump-

258

ing Godfathers, wait till you see her, that's all. Just wait till you see her!"

He seized his hat and waterproof.

"But, my dear!" cried Mrs. Banks. "You must be here to meet her. It looks so rude. Where are you going?"

"Anywhere. Everywhere. Tell her I'm dead!" he replied bitterly. And he hurried away from the house looking very nervous and depressed.

"My goodness, Michael, what *can* she be like?" said Jane.

"Curiosity killed the Cat," said Mary Poppins. "Put your hats on, please!"

She settled the Twins into the perambulator and pushed it down the garden path. Jane and Michael followed her out into the Lane.

"Where are we going to-day, Mary Poppins?"

"Across the Park and along the Thirty-Nine bus route, up the High Street, and over the Bridge and home through the Railway Arch!" she snapped.

"If we do that, we'll be walking all night," whispered Michael, dropping behind with Jane. "And we'll miss Miss Andrew."

"She's going to stay for a month," Jane reminded him.

"But I want to see her arrive," he complained, dragging his feet and shuffling along the pavement.

"Step along, please," said Mary Poppins, briskly. "I might as well be taking a stroll with a couple of snails as you two!"

But when they caught up with her she kept them waiting for quite five minutes outside a fried-fish shop while she looked at herself in the window.

She was wearing her new white blouse with the pink

spots, and her face, as she beheld herself reflected back from the piles of fried whiting, had a pleased and satisfied air. She pushed back her coat a little so that more of the blouse was visible and she thought that, on the whole, she had never seen Mary Poppins look nicer. Even the fried fish, with their fried tails curled into their mouths, seemed to gaze at her with round, admiring eyes.

Mary Poppins gave a little conceited nod to her reflection and hurried on. They had passed the High Street now and were crossing the Bridge. Soon they came to the Railway Arch, and Jane and Michael sprang eagerly ahead of the perambulator and ran all the way until they turned the corner of Cherry Tree Lane.

"There's a cab!" cried Michael excitedly. "That must be Miss Andrew's."

They stood still at the corner waiting for Mary Poppins and watching for Miss Andrew.

A Taxi-cab, moving slowly down the Lane, drew up at the gate of Number Seventeen. It groaned and rattled as the engine stopped. And this was not surprising, for from wheel to roof it was heavily weighted with luggage. You could hardly see the cab itself for the trunks on the roof and the trunks at the back and the trunks on either side.

Suit-cases and hampers could be seen half-in and half-out of the windows. Hat-boxes were strapped to the steps, and two large Gladstone bags appeared to be sitting in the Driver's seat.

Presently the Driver himself emerged from under them. He climbed out carefully, as though he were descending a steep mountain, and opened the door.

A boot-box came bounding out, followed by a large brown-paper parcel, and after these came an umbrella and a walking-stick tied together with string. Last of all, a small weighing-machine clattered down from the rack, knocking the Taxi-man over.

" Be careful!" a huge, trumpeting voice shouted from inside the Taxi. " This is valuable luggage!"

" And I'm a valuable driver!" retorted the Taxi-man, picking himself up and rubbing his ankle. " You seem to 'ave forgotten that, 'aven't you?"

" Make way, please, make way! I'm coming out!" called the huge voice again.

And at that moment there appeared on the step of the cab the largest foot the children had ever seen. It was followed by the rest of Miss Andrew.

A large coat with a fur collar was wrapped about her, a man's felt hat was perched on her head, and from the hat floated a long grey veil. With one hand she held up the folds of her skirt and from the other swung a circular object covered with a checked cloth.

The children crept cautiously along by the fence, gazing with interest at the huge figure, with its beaked nose, grim mouth, and small eyes that peered angrily from behind glasses. They were almost deafened by her voice as she argued with the Taxi-man.

"Four and threepence!" she was saying. "Preposterous! I could go half-way round the world for that amount. I shan't pay it. And I shall report you to the Police."

The Taxi-man shrugged his shoulders. "That's the fare," he said calmly. "If you can read, you can read it on the meter. You can't go driving in a Taxi for love, you know, not with this luggage."

Miss Andrew snorted and, diving her hand into her large pocket, took out a very small purse. She handed over a coin. The Taxi-man looked at it and turned it over and over in his hand, as if he thought it a curiosity. Then he laughed rudely.

"This for the Driver?" he remarked, sarcastically.

"Certainly not. It's your fare. I don't approve of tips," said Miss Andrew.

"You wouldn't!" said the Taxi-man, staring at her. And to himself he remarked: "Enough luggage to fill 'arf the Park, and she doesn't approve of tips—the 'Arpy!"

But Miss Andrew did not hear him. The children had arrived at the gate and she turned to greet them, her feet ringing on the pavement and her veil flowing out behind her.

"Well?" she said gruffly, smiling a thin smile. "I don't suppose you know who *I* am?"

"Oh, yes we do!" said Michael. He spoke in his friendliest voice, for he was very glad to meet Miss Andrew. "You're the Holy Terror!"

A dark, purple flush rose up from Miss Andrew's neck and flooded her face.

"You are a very rude, impertinent boy. I shall report you to your Father!"

Michael looked surprised. "I didn't mean to be rude," he began. "It was Daddy who said——"

"Tut! Silence! Don't dare to argue with me!" said Miss Andrew. She turned to Jane.

263

"And you're Jane, I suppose? H'm. I never cared for the name."

"How do you do?" said Jane, politely, but secretly thinking she did not care much for the name Euphemia.

"That dress is much too short!" trumpeted Miss Andrew. "And you ought to be wearing stockings. Little girls in my day never had bare legs. I shall speak to your Mother."

"I don't like stockings," said Jane. "I only wear them in the Winter."

"Don't be impudent. Children should be seen and not heard!" said Miss Andrew.

She leant over the perambulator, and with her huge hand pinched the Twins' cheeks in greeting.

John and Barbara began to cry.

"Tut! What manners!" exclaimed Miss Andrew. "Brimstone and Treacle—that's what they need!" she went on, turning to Mary Poppins. "No, well-brought-up child cries like that. Brimstone and Treacle. And plenty of it. Don't forget."

"Thank you, ma'am," said Mary Poppins, with icy politeness, "but I bring the children up in my own way and take advice from nobody."

Miss Andrew stared. She looked as if she could not believe her ears.

Mary Poppins stared back, calm and unafraid.

"Young woman," said Miss Andrew, drawing herself up, "you forget yourself. How dare you answer me like that! I shall take steps to have you removed from this establishment! Mark my words!"

She flung open the gate and strode up the path, furiously swinging the circular object under the checked cloth, and saying "Tut-tut!" over and over again.

Mrs. Banks came running out to meet her.

"Welcome, Miss Andrew, welcome!" she said politely. "How kind of you to pay us a visit. Such an unexpected pleasure. I hope you had a good journey?"

"Most unpleasant. I never enjoy travelling," said Miss Andrew. She glanced with an angry, peering eye round the garden.

"Disgracefully untidy!" she remarked disgustedly. "Take my advice and dig up those things"—she pointed to the sunflowers—"and plant evergreens. Much less trouble. Saves time *and* money. And looks neater. Better still, no garden at all. Just a plain, cement courtyard."

"But," protested Mrs. Banks gently, "I like flowers best!"

"Ridiculous! Stuff and nonsense! You are a silly woman. And your children are very rude—especially the boy."

"Oh, Michael, I *am* surprised! Were you rude to Miss Andrew? You must apologise at once." Mrs. Banks was getting very nervous and flustered.

"No, Mother, I wasn't. I only——" He began to explain, but Miss Andrew's loud voice interrupted.

"He was most insulting," she insisted. "He must go to a boarding-school at once. And the girl must have a Governess. I shall choose one myself. And as for the young person you have looking after them——" she nodded in the direction of Mary Poppins, "you must dismiss her this instant. She is impertinent, incapable, and totally unreliable."

Mrs. Banks was plainly horrified.

"Oh, surely you are mistaken, Miss Andrew! We think she is such a Treasure."

265

"You know nothing about it. I am *never* mistaken. Dismiss her!"

Miss Andrew swept on up the path.

Mrs. Banks hurried behind her, looking very worried and upset.

"I—er—hope we shall be able to make you comfortable, Miss Andrew," she said, politely. But she was beginning to feel rather doubtful.

"H'm. It's not much of a house," replied Miss Andrew. "And it's in a shocking condition—peeling everywhere, and most dilapidated. You must send for a carpenter. And when were these steps white-washed? They're very dirty."

Mrs. Banks bit her lip. Miss Andrew was turning her lovely, comfortable house into something mean and shabby, and it made her feel very unhappy.

"I'll have them done to-morrow," she said meekly.

"Why not to-day?" demanded Miss Andrew. "No time like the present. And why paint your door white? Dark brown—that's the proper colour for a door. Cheaper, and doesn't show the dirt. Just look at those spots!"

And putting down the circular object, she began to point out the marks on the front door.

"There! There! There! Everywhere! Most disreputable!"

"I'll see to it immediately," said Mrs. Banks faintly. "Won't you come upstairs now to your room?"

Miss Andrew stamped into the hall after her.

"I hope there is a fire in it."

"Oh, yes. A good one. This way, Miss Andrew. Robertson Ay will bring up your luggage."

"Well, tell him to be careful. The trunks are full of medicine bottles. I have to take care of my health!"

Miss Andrew moved towards the stairs. She glanced round the hall.

"This wall needs re-papering. I shall speak to George about it. And why, I should like to know, wasn't he here to meet me? Very rude of him. His manners, I see, have not improved!"

The voice grew a little fainter as Miss Andrew followed Mrs. Banks upstairs. Far away the children could hear their Mother's gentle voice, meekly agreeing to do whatever Miss Andrew wished.

Michael turned to Jane.

"Who is George?" he asked.

"Daddy."

"But his name is Mr. Banks."

"Yes, but his other name is George."

Michael sighed.

"A month is an awfully long time, Jane, isn't it?"

"Yes—four weeks and a bit," said Jane, feeling that a month with Miss Andrew would seem more like a year.

Michael edged closer to her.

"I say——" he began in an anxious whisper, "she can't really make them send Mary Poppins away, can she?"

"No, I don't think so. But she's very odd. I don't wonder Daddy went out."

"Odd!"

The word sounded behind them like an explosion.

They turned. Mary Poppins was gazing after Miss Andrew with a look that could have killed her.

"Odd!" she repeated, with a long-drawn sniff. "*That's* not the word for her. Humph! I don't know how to bring up children, don't I? I'm impertinent, incapable, and totally unreliable, am I? We'll see about that!"

Jane and Michael were used to threats from Mary Poppins, but to-day there was a note in her voice they had never heard before. They stared at her in silence, wondering what was going to happen.

A tiny sound, partly a sigh and partly a whistle, fell on the air.

"What was that?" said Jane quickly.

The sound came again, a little louder this time. Mary Poppins cocked her head and listened.

Again a faint chirping seemed to come from the doorstep.

"Ah!" cried Mary Poppins, triumphantly. "I might have known it!"

And with a sudden movement, she sprang at the circular object Miss Andrew had left behind and tweaked off the cover.

Beneath it was a brass bird-cage, very neat and shiny. And sitting at one end of the perch, huddled between his wings, was a small, light-brown bird. He blinked a little as the afternoon light streamed down upon his head. Then he gazed solemnly about him with a round, dark eye. His glance fell upon Mary Poppins, and, with a start of recognition, he opened his beak and gave a sad, throaty, little cheep. Jane and Michael had never heard such a miserable sound.

"Did she, indeed? *Tch, tch, tch!* You don't say!" said Mary Poppins, nodding her head sympathetically.

"*Chirp-irrup!*" said the bird, shrugging its wings dejectedly.

"What? Two years? In that cage? Shame on her!" said Mary Poppins to the bird, her face flushing with anger.

The children stared. The bird was speaking in no language they knew, and yet here was Mary Poppins carrying on an intelligent conversation with him as though she understood.

"What is it saying——" Michael began.

"*Sh!*" said Jane, pinching his arm to make him keep quiet.

They stared at the bird in silence. Presently he hopped a little way along the perch towards Mary Poppins and sang a note or two in a low, questioning voice.

Mary Poppins nodded. "Yes—of course I know that field. Was that where she caught you?"

The bird nodded. Then he sang a quick, trilling phrase that sounded like a question.

Mary Poppins thought for a moment. "Well," she said, "it's not very far. You could do it in about an hour. Flying South from here."

The bird seemed pleased. He danced a little on his perch and flapped his wings excitedly. Then his song broke out again, a stream of round, clear notes, as he looked imploringly at Mary Poppins.

She turned her head and glanced cautiously up the stairs.

"*Will* I? What do *you* think? Didn't you hear her call me a Young Person? Me!" She sniffed disgustedly.

The bird's shoulders shook as though he were laughing.

Mary Poppins bent down.

"What are you going to do, Mary Poppins?" cried Michael, unable to contain himself any longer. "What kind of a bird is that?"

"A Lark," said Mary Poppins, briefly, turning the handle of the little door. "You're seeing a Lark in a cage for the first time—and the last!"

And as she said that, the door of the cage swung open. The Lark, flapping his wings, swooped out with a shrill cry and alighted on Mary Poppins' shoulder.

"Humph!" she said, turning her head. "That's an improvement, I should think?"

"*Chirr-up!*" agreed the Lark, nodding.

"Well, you'd better be off," Mary Poppins warned him. "She'll be back in a minute."

At that the Lark burst into a stream of running notes, flicking his wings at her and bowing his head again and again.

"There, there!" said Mary Poppins, gruffly. "Don't thank me. I was glad to do it. I couldn't see a Lark in a cage! Besides, you heard what she called me!"

The Lark tossed back his head and fluttered his wings. He seemed to be laughing heartily. Then he cocked his head to one side and listened.

"Oh, I quite forgot!" came a loud voice from upstairs. "I left Caruso outside. On those dirty steps. I must go and get him."

Miss Andrew's heavy-footed tread sounded on the stairs.

"What?" she called back in reply to some question of Mrs. Banks. "Oh, he's my Lark, my Lark, Caruso! I call him that because he used to be such a beautiful singer. What? No, he doesn't sing at all now, not since I trapped him in a field and put him in a cage. I can't think why."

The voice was coming nearer, growing louder as it approached.

"Certainly not!" it called back to Mrs. Banks. "I will fetch him myself. I wouldn't trust one of those impudent children with him. Your banisters want polishing. They should be done at once."

Tramp-tramp. Tramp-tramp. Miss Andrew's steps sounded through the hall.

"Here she comes!" hissed Mary Poppins. "Be off with you." She gave her shoulder a little shake.

"Quickly!" cried Michael, anxiously.

"Oh, hurry!" said Jane.

With a quick movement the Lark bent his head and pulled out one of his wing feathers with his beak.

"*Chirr-chirr-chirr-irrup!*" he sang, and stuck the feather into the ribbon of Mary Poppins' hat. Then he spread his wings and swept into the air.

At the same moment Miss Andrew appeared in the doorway.

"What?" she shouted, when she saw Jane and Michael and the Twins. "Not gone up to bed yet? This will never do. All well-brought-up children"—she looked balefully at Mary Poppins—"should be in bed by five o'clock. I shall certainly speak to your Father."

She glanced round.

"Now, let me see. Where did I leave my——" She broke off suddenly. The uncovered cage, with its open door, stood at her feet. She stared down at it as though she were unable to believe her eyes.

"Why? When? Where? What? Who?" she spluttered. Then she found her full voice.

"Who took off that cover?" she thundered. The children trembled at the sound.

"Who opened that cage?"

There was no reply.

"*Where is my Lark?*"

Still there was silence as Miss Andrew stared from one child to another. At last her gaze fell accusingly upon Mary Poppins.

"You did it!" she cried, pointing her large finger. "I can tell by the look on your face! How dare you! I shall see that you leave this house to-night—bag and baggage! You impudent, impertinent, worthless——"

Chirp-irrup!

From the air came a little trill of laughter. Miss Andrew looked up. The Lark was lightly balancing on his wings just above the sunflowers.

"Ah, Caruso—there you are!" cried Miss Andrew. "Now come along! Don't keep me waiting. Come back to your nice, clean cage, Caruso, and let me shut the door!"

But the Lark just hung in the air and went into peals of laughter, flinging back his head and clapping his wings against his side.

Miss Andrew bent and picked up the cage and held it above her head.

"Caruso—what did I say? Come back at once!" she commanded, swinging the cage towards him. But he swooped past it and brushed against Mary Poppins' hat.

"*Chirp-irrup!*" he said, as he sped by.

"All right!" said Mary Poppins, nodding in reply.

"Caruso, did you hear me?" cried Miss Andrew. But now there was a hint of dismay in her loud voice. She put down the cage and tried to catch the Lark with her hands. But he dodged and flickered past her, and, with a lift of his wings, dived higher into the air.

A babble of notes streamed down to Mary Poppins.

"Ready!" she called back.

And then a strange thing happened.

Mary Poppins fixed her eyes upon Miss Andrew; and Miss Andrew, suddenly spell-bound by that strange dark gaze, began to tremble on her feet. She gave a little gasp, staggered uncertainly forward and, with a thundering rush, she dashed towards the cage. Then—was it that Miss Andrew grew smaller or the cage larger? Jane and Michael could not be sure. All they knew for certain was that the cage door shut to with a little click and closed upon Miss Andrew.

"Oh! Oh! Oh!" she cried, as the Lark swooped down and seized the cage by the handle.

"What am I doing? Where am I going?" Miss Andrew shouted as the cage swept into the air.

"I have no room to move! I can hardly breathe!" she cried.

"Neither could he!" said Mary Poppins quietly.

Miss Andrew rattled at the bars of the cage.

"Open the door! Let me out, I say! Let me out!"

"Humph! Not likely," said Mary Poppins in a low, scoffing voice.

On and on went the Lark, climbing higher and higher and singing as he went. And the heavy cage, with Miss Andrew inside it, lurched after him, swaying dangerously as it swung from his claw.

Above the clear song of the Lark they heard Miss Andrew hammering at the bars and crying:

"I who was Well-Brought-Up. I who was Always Right. I who was Never Mistaken. That I should come to this!"

Mary Poppins gave a curious, quiet little laugh.

The Lark looked very small now, but still he circled upwards, singing loudly and triumphantly. And still Miss Andrew and her cage circled heavily after him, rocking from side to side, like a ship in a storm.

"Let me out, I say! Let me out!" Her voice came screaming down.

Suddenly the Lark changed his direction. His song ceased for a moment as he darted sideways. Then it began again, wild and clear, as, shaking the ring of the cage from his foot, he flew towards the South.

"He's off!" said Mary Poppins.

"Where?" cried Jane and Michael.

"Home—to his meadows!" she replied, gazing upwards.

"But he's dropped the cage!" said Michael, staring.

And well he might stare, for the cage was now hurtling downwards, lurching and tumbling, end over end. They could clearly see Miss Andrew, now standing on her head and now on her feet as the cage turned through the air. Down, down, it came, heavy as a stone, and landed with a plop on the top step.

With a fierce movement, Miss Andrew tore open the door. And it seemed to Jane and Michael as she came out that she was as large as ever and even more frightening.

"Let me out, I say! Let me out!"

For a moment she stood there, panting, unable to speak, her face purpler than before.

"How dare you!" she said in a throaty whisper, pointing a trembling finger at Mary Poppins. And Jane and Michael saw that her eyes were no longer angry and scornful, but full of terror.

"You—you——" stammered Miss Andrew huskily, "you cruel, disrespectful, unkind, wicked, wilful girl—how could you, how could you?"

Mary Poppins fixed her with a look. From half-closed eyes, she gazed revengefully at Miss Andrew for a long moment.

"You said I didn't know how to bring up children," she said, speaking slowly and distinctly.

Miss Andrew shrank back, trembling with fear.

"I—I apologise," she said, gulping.

"That I was imprudent, incapable, and totally unreliable," said Mary Poppins.

"It was a mistake. I—I'm sorry," Miss Andrew stammered.

"That I was a Young Person!" continued Mary Poppins, remorselessly.

"I take it back," panted Miss Andrew. "All of it. Only let me go. I ask nothing more." She clasped her hands and gazed at Mary Poppins, imploringly.

"I can't stay here," she whispered. "No! no! Not here! Let me go!"

Mary Poppins gazed at her, long and thoughtfully. Then, with a little outward movement of her hand— "Go!" she said.

Miss Andrew gave a gasp of relief. "Oh, thank you! Thank you!" Still keeping her eyes fixed on Mary Poppins, she staggered backwards down the steps. Then she turned and went stumbling unevenly down the garden path.

The Taxi-man, who all this time had been unloading the luggage, was starting up his engine and preparing to depart.

Miss Andrew held up a trembling hand.

"Wait!" she cried brokenly. "Wait for me. You shall have a Ten-shilling note for yourself if you will drive me away at once."

The man stared at her.

"I mean it!" she said urgently. "See," she fumbled feverishly in her pocket, "here it is. Take it—and drive on!"

Miss Andrew tottered into the cab and collapsed upon the seat.

The Taxi-man, still gaping, closed the door upon her. Then he began hurriedly re-loading the luggage. Robertson Ay had fallen asleep across a pile of trunks, but the Taxi-man did not stop to wake him. He swept him off on to the path and finished the work himself.

"Looks as though the 'ole girl 'as 'ad a shock! I never saw anybody take on so. Never!" he murmured to himself as he drove off.

But what kind of a shock it was the Taxi-man did not know and, if he lived to be a hundred, could not possibly guess. . . .

"Where is Miss Andrew?" said Mrs. Banks, hurrying to the front door in search of the visitor.

"Gone!" said Michael.

"What do you mean—gone?" Mrs. Banks looked very surprised.

" She didn't seem to want to stay," said Jane.

Mrs. Banks frowned.

"What does this mean, Mary Poppins?" she demanded.

" I couldn't say, m'm, I'm sure," said Mary Poppins calmly, as though the matter did not interest her. She glanced down at her new blouse and smoothed out a crease.

Mrs. Banks looked from one to the other and shook her head.

"How very extraordinary! I can't understand it."

Just then the garden gate opened and shut with a quiet little click. Mr. Banks came tip-toeing up the path. He hesitated and waited nervously on one foot as they all turned towards him.

" Well? Has she come?" he said anxiously, in a loud whisper.

" She has come and gone," said Mrs. Banks.

Mr. Banks stared.

"Gone? Do you mean—really gone? Miss Andrew?"

Mrs. Banks nodded.

"Oh, joy, joy!" cried Mr. Banks. And seizing the skirts of his waterproof in both hands, he proceeded to dance the Highland Fling in the middle of the path. He stopped suddenly.

"But how? When? Why?" he asked.

"Just now—in a taxi. Because the children were rude to her, I suppose. She complained to me about them. I simply can't think of any other reason. Can you, Mary Poppins?"

" No, m'm, I can't," said Mary Poppins, brushing a speck of dust off her blouse with great care.

Mr. Banks turned to Jane and Michael with a sorrowful look on his face.

"You were rude to Miss Andrew? My Governess? That dear old soul? I'm ashamed of you both—thoroughly ashamed." He spoke sternly, but there was a laughing twinkle in his eyes.

"I'm a most unfortunate man," he went on, putting his hands into his pockets. "Here am I slaving day-in and day-out to bring you up properly, and how do you repay me? By being rude to Miss Andrew! It's shameful. It's outrageous! I don't know that I shall ever be able to forgive you. But "—he continued, taking two sixpences out of his pocket and solemnly offering one to each of them—" I shall do my best to forget!"

He turned away smiling.

"Hullo!" he remarked, stumbling against the birdcage. "Where did this come from? Whose is it?"

Jane and Michael and Mary Poppins were silent.

"Well, never mind," said Mr. Banks. "It's mine now. I shall keep it in the garden and train my sweet peas over it."

And he went off, carrying the bird-cage and whistling very happily. . . .

"Well," said Mary Poppins, sternly, as she followed them into the Nursery, "this is nice goings on, I must say. You behaving so rudely to your Father's guest."

"But we weren't rude!" Michael protested. "I only said she was a Holy Terror and he called her that himself."

"Sending her away like that when she'd only just come—don't you call that rude?" demanded Mary Poppins.

"But we didn't," said Jane. "It was you——"

" *I* was rude to your Father's guest?" Mary Poppins, with her hands on her hips, eyed Jane furiously. "Do you dare to stand there and tell me that?"

"No, no! You weren't rude, but——"

"I should think not, indeed!" retorted Mary Poppins, taking off her hat and unfolding her apron. "*I* was properly brought up!" she added sniffing, as she began to undress the Twins.

Michael sighed. He knew it was no use arguing with Mary Poppins.

He glanced at Jane. She was turning her sixpence over and over in her hand.

"Michael!" she said. "I've been thinking."

"What?"

"Daddy gave us these because he thought *we* sent Miss Andrew away."

"I know."

"And we didn't. It was Mary Poppins!"

Michael shuffled his feet.

"Then you think——" he began uneasily, hoping she didn't mean what he thought she meant.

"Yes, I do," said Jane, nodding.

"But—but I wanted to spend mine."

"So do I. But it wouldn't be fair. They're hers, really."

Michael thought about it for a long time. Then he sighed.

"All right," he said regretfully, and took his sixpence out of his pocket.

They went together to Mary Poppins.

Jane held out the coins.

"Here you are!" she said breathlessly, "we think you should have them."

Mary Poppins took the sixpences and turned them

over and over on her palm—heads first and then tails. Then her eye caught theirs and it seemed to them that her look plunged right down inside them and *saw* what they were thinking. For a long time she stood there, staring down into their thoughts.

"Humph!" she said at last, slipping the sixpences into her apron pocket. "Take care of the pennies and the pounds will take care of themselves."

"I expect you'll find them very useful," said Michael, gazing sadly at the pocket.

"I expect I shall," she retorted tartly, as she went to turn on the bath. . . .

Chapter Three

BAD WEDNESDAY

TICK-TACK! Tick-tock!

The pendulum of the Nursery clock swung backwards and forwards like an old lady nodding her head.

Tick-tack! Tick-tock!

Then the clock stopped ticking and began to whir and growl, quietly at first, and then more loudly, as though it were in pain. And as it whirred it shook so violently that the whole mantelpiece trembled. The empty Marmalade Jar hopped and shook and shivered; John's hair-brush, left there over-night, danced on its bristles; the Royal Doulton Bowl that Mrs. Banks' Great-Aunt Caroline had given her as a Christening Present slipped sideways, so that the three little boys who were playing horses inside it stood on their painted heads.

And after all that, just when it seemed as if the clock must burst, it began to strike.

One! Two! Three! Four! Five! Six! Seven!

On the last stroke Jane woke up.

The sun was streaming in through a gap in the curtains and falling in gold stripes upon her quilt. Jane sat up and looked round the Nursery. No sound came from Michael's bed. The Twins in their cots were sucking their thumbs and breathing deeply.

"I'm the only one awake," she said, feeling very pleased. "I can lie here all by myself and think and think and think."

And she drew her knees up to her chin and curled

282

into the bed as though she were settling down into a nest.

"Now I am a bird!" she said to herself. "I have just laid seven lovely white eggs, and I am sitting with my wings over them, brooding. *Cluck-cluck! Cluck-cluck!*"

She made a small, broody noise in her throat.

"And after a long time, say half an hour, there will

be a little cheep, and a little tap and the shells will crack. Then, out will pop seven little chicks, three yellow, two brown, and two——"

"Time to get up!"

Mary Poppins, appearing suddenly from nowhere, tweaked the bedclothes from Jane's shoulders.

"Oh, no, *no*!" grumbled Jane, pulling them up again.

She felt very cross with Mary Poppins for rushing in and spoiling everything.

"I don't want to get up!" she said, turning her face into the pillow.

"Oh, indeed?" Mary Poppins said calmly, as though the remark had no interest for her. She pulled the bed-clothes right off the bed and Jane found herself standing on the floor.

"Oh, dear," she grumbled, "why do I always have to get up first?"

"You're the eldest—that's why!" Mary Poppins pushed her towards the bathroom.

"But I don't *want* to be the eldest. Why can't Michael be the eldest sometimes?"

"Because you were born first—see?"

"Well, I didn't ask to be. I'm tired of being born first. I wanted to think."

"You can think when you're brushing your teeth."

"Not the same thoughts."

"Well, nobody wants to think the same thoughts all the time."

"I do."

Mary Poppins gave her a quick, black look.

"That's enough, thank you!" And, from the tone of her voice, Jane knew she meant what she said.

Mary Poppins hurried away to wake Michael.

Jane put down her toothbrush and sat on the edge of the bath.

"It's not fair," she grumbled, kicking the linoleum with her toes. "Making me do all the horrid things just because I'm the eldest! I won't brush my teeth!"

Immediately she felt surprised at herself. She was usually quite glad to be older than Michael and the Twins. It made her feel rather superior and much more important. But to-day—what was the matter with to-day that she felt so cross and peevish?

"If Michael had been born first I'd have had time to hatch out my eggs!" she grumbled to herself, feeling that the day had begun badly.

Unfortunately, instead of getting better, it grew worse.

At breakfast, Mary Poppins discovered there was only enough Puffed Rice for three.

"Well, Jane must have Porridge," she said, setting out the plates and sniffing angrily, for she did not like making Porridge; there were always too many lumps in it.

"But why?" complained Jane. "I want Puffed Rice."

Mary Poppins darted a fierce look at her.

"Because you're the eldest!"

There it was again. That hateful word. She kicked the leg of her chair under the table, hoping she was scratching off the varnish, and ate her Porridge as slowly as she dared. She turned it round and round in her mouth, swallowing as little as possible. It would serve everybody right if she starved to death. Then they'd be sorry!

"What is to-day?" inquired Michael cheerfully, scraping up the last of his Puffed Rice.

"Wednesday," said Mary Poppins. "Leave the pattern on the plate, please!"

"Then it's to-day we're going to tea with Miss Lark!"

"*If* you're good," said Mary Poppins darkly, as though she did not believe such a thing was possible.

But Michael was in a cheerful mood, and took no notice.

"Wednesday!" he shouted, banging his spoon on the table. "That's the day Jane was born. Wednesday's

Child is full of Woe. That's why she has to have Porridge instead of Rice!" he said, naughtily.

Jane frowned and kicked at him under the table. But
he swung his legs aside and laughed.

"Monday's Child is Fair of Face, Tuesday's Child is
Full of Grace!" he chanted. "That's true, too. The
Twins are full of grace, and they were born on a Tues-
day. And I'm Monday—Fair of Face."

Jane laughed scornfully.

"I am," he insisted. "I heard Mrs. Brill say so. She
told Ellen I was as handsome as Half-a-crown."

"Well, that's not very handsome," said Jane. "Besides, your nose turns up."

Michael looked at her reproachfully. And again Jane
felt surprised at herself. At any other time she would
have agreed with him, for she thought Michael a very
good-looking little boy. But now she said cruelly:

"Yes, and your toes turn in. Bandy-legs! Bandy-
legs!"

Michael rushed at her.

"That will be enough from you!" said Mary Poppins,
looking angrily at Jane. "And if anybody in this house
is a beauty, it's——" She paused, and glanced with a
satisfied smile at her own reflection in the mirror.

"Who?" demanded Michael and Jane together.

"Nobody of the name of Banks!" retorted Mary
Poppins. "So there!"

Michael looked across at Jane as he always did when
Mary Poppins made one of her curious remarks. But,
though she felt his look, she pretended not to notice.
She turned away and took her paint-box from the toy-
cupboard.

"Won't you play trains?" asked Michael, trying to
be friendly.

" No, I won't. I want to be by myself."

" Well, darlings, and how are you all this morning?"

Mrs. Banks came running into the room and kissed them hurriedly. She was always so busy that she never had time to walk.

" Michael," she said, " you must have some new slippers—your toes are coming out at the top. Mary Poppins, John's curls will *have* to come off, I'm afraid. Barbara, my pet, don't suck your thumb! Jane, run downstairs and ask Mrs. Brill not to ice the Plum Cake, I want a plain one."

There they were again, Jane said to herself, breaking into her day! As soon as she began to do anything they made her stop and do something else.

" Oh, Mother, must I? Why can't Michael?"

Mrs. Banks looked surprised.

" But I thought you liked helping! And Michael always forgets the message. Besides, you're the eldest. Run along!"

She went downstairs as slowly as she could. She hoped she would be so late with the message that Mrs. Brill would have already iced the cake.

And all the time she felt astonished at the way she was behaving. It was as if there was another person inside her—somebody with a very bad temper and an ugly face—who was making her feel cross.

She gave the message to Mrs. Brill, and was disappointed to find that she was in plenty of time.

" Well, that'll save a penn'orth of trouble, anyway," Mrs. Brill remarked.

" And, Dearie," she went on, " you might just slip out into the garden and tell that Robertson he hasn't done the knives. My legs are bad, and they're my only pair."

" I can't. I'm busy."

It was Mrs. Brill's turn to look surprised.

"Ah, be a kind girl, then—it's all I can do to stand, let alone walk!"

Jane sighed. Why couldn't they leave her alone? She kicked the kitchen door shut and dawdled out into the garden.

Robertson Ay was asleep on the path with his head on the watering-can. His lank hair rose and fell as he snored. It was Robertson Ay's special gift that he could sleep anywhere, and at any time. In fact, he preferred sleeping to waking. And usually, whenever they could, Jane and Michael prevented him from being found out. But to-day it was different. The bad-tempered person inside her didn't care a bit what happened to Robertson Ay.

"I hate everybody!" she said, and rapped sharply on the watering-can.

Robertson Ay sat up with a start.

"Help! Murder! Fire!" he cried, waving his arms wildly.

Then he rubbed his eyes and saw Jane.

"Oh, it's only you!" he said, in a disappointed voice, as though he had hoped for something more exciting.

"You're to go and do the knives, at once," she ordered.

Robertson Ay got slowly to his feet and shook himself.

"Ah," he said, sadly, "it's always something. If it's not one thing, it's another. I ought to be resting. I never get a moment's peace."

"Yes, you do!" said Jane, cruelly. "You get nothing but peace. You're always asleep."

A hurt, reproachful look came over Robertson Ay's face and at any other time it would have made her feel ashamed. But to-day she wasn't a bit sorry.

" Saying such things!" said Robertson Ay sadly. " And you the eldest and all. I wouldn't have thought it—not if I'd done nothing but think for the rest of my life."

And he gave her a sorrowful glance and shuffled slowly away to the kitchen.

She wondered if he would ever forgive her. And, as if in reply, the sulky creature inside her said, " I don't care if he doesn't!"

She tossed her head and went slowly back to the Nursery, dragging her sticky hands along the fresh, clean, white wall because she had always been told not to.

Mary Poppins was flicking her feather-duster round the furniture.

" Off to a funeral?" she inquired, as Jane appeared.

Jane looked sulky and did not answer.

" I know somebody who's looking for Trouble. And he that seeks shall find!"

" I don't care!"

" Don't Care was made care! Don't Care was hung!" jeered Mary Poppins, putting the duster away.

" And now "—she looked warningly at Jane—" I am going to have my dinner. You are to look after the little ones, and if I hear One Word——" She did not finish the sentence, but she gave a long, threatening sniff as she went out of the room.

John and Barbara ran to Jane and caught her hands. But she uncurled their fingers and crossly pushed them away.

" I wish I were an only child!" she said, bitterly.

" Why don't you run away?" suggested Michael. " Somebody might adopt you."

Jane looked up, startled and surprised.

" But you'd miss me!"

"No, I wouldn't," he said stoutly. "Not if you're always going to be cross. Besides, then I could have your paint-box."

"No, you couldn't," she said jealously. "I'd take it with me."

And just to show him that the paint-box was hers and not his, she got out the brushes and the painting book and spread them on the floor.

"Paint the clock," said Michael, helpfully.

"No."

"Well, the Royal Doulton Bowl."

Jane glanced up.

The three little boys were racing over the field inside the green rim of the bowl. At any other time she would have liked to paint them, but to-day she was not going to be pleasant or obliging.

"I won't. I will paint what *I* want."

And she began to make a picture of herself, quite alone, brooding over her eggs.

Michael and John and Barbara sat on the floor, watching.

Jane was so interested in her eggs that she almost forgot her bad temper.

Michael leaned forward. "Why not put in a hen—just there!"

He pointed to a spare white patch, brushing against John with his arm. Over went John, falling sideways and upsetting the cup with his foot. The coloured water splashed out and flooded the picture.

With a cry, Jane sprang to her feet.

"Oh, I can't bear it. You great Clumsy! You've spoilt everything!"

And, rushing at Michael, she punched him so violently that he too, toppled over and crashed down on top of John. A squeal of pain and terror broke from the Twins, and above their cries rose Michael's voice wailing, "My head is broken! What shall I do? My head is broken!" over and over again.

"I don't care! I don't care!" shouted Jane. "You wouldn't leave me alone and you've spoilt my picture. I hate you, I hate you, I hate——"

The door burst open.

Mary Poppins surveyed the scene with furious eyes.

"What did I say to you?" she inquired of Jane in a voice so quiet that it was terrible. "That if I heard One Word—and now look what I find! A nice party *you'll* have at Miss Lark's, I *don't* think. Not one step will you go out of this room this afternoon, or I'm a Chinaman."

"I don't *want* to go. I'd rather stay here." Jane put her hands behind her back and sauntered away. She did not feel a bit sorry.

"Very good."

Mary Poppins' voice was gentle, but there was something very frightening in it.

Jane watched her dressing the others for the party. And, when they were ready, Mary Poppins took her best hat out of a brown-paper bag and set it on her head at a very smart angle. She clipped her gold locket round her neck, and over it she wound the red-and-white checked scarf Mrs. Banks had given her. At one end was stitched a white label marked with a large *M.P.*, and Mary Poppins smiled at her reflection in the mirror as she tucked the label out of sight.

Then she took her parrot-handled umbrella from the cupboard, popped it under her arm, and hurried the little ones down the stairs.

"Now you'll have time to think!" she remarked tartly, and, with a loud sniff, shut the door behind her.

For a long time Jane sat staring in front of her. She tried to think about her seven eggs. But somehow they didn't interest her any more.

What were they doing now, at Miss Lark's, she wondered? Playing with Miss Lark's dogs, perhaps, and listening to Miss Lark telling them that Andrew had a wonderful pedigree, but that Willoughby was half an Airedale and half a Retriever, and the worst half of both. And presently they would all, even the dogs, have Chocolate Biscuits and Walnut Cake for tea.

"Oh, dear!"

The thought of all she was missing stirred angrily inside Jane, and when she remembered it was all her own fault she felt crosser than ever.

Tick-tack! Tick-tock! said the clock loudly.

"Oh, be quiet!" cried Jane furiously, and picking up her paint-box, she hurled it across the room.

It crashed against the glass face of the clock and, glancing off, clattered down upon the Royal Doulton Bowl.

Crrrrrrrack! The Bowl toppled sideways against the clock.

Oh! Oh! What had she done?

Jane shut her eyes, not daring to look and see.

" I say—that hurt!"

A clear, reproachful voice sounded in the room.

" Jane!" said the voice. " That was my knee!"

She turned her head quickly. There was nobody in the room.

She ran to the door and opened it. Still nobody!

Then somebody laughed.

" Here, Silly!" said the voice again. " Up here!"

She looked up at the mantelpiece. Beside the clock lay the Royal Doulton Bowl with a large crack running right across it and, to her surprise, Jane saw that one of the painted boys had dropped the reins and was bending down, holding his knee with both hands. The other two had turned and were looking at him sympathetically.

" But——" began Jane, half to herself and half to the unknown voice, " I don't understand." The boy in the Bowl lifted his head and smiled at her.

" Don't you? No, I suppose you don't. I've noticed that you and Michael often don't understand the simplest things—do they?"

He turned, laughing, to his brothers.

" No," said one of them, " not even how to keep the Twins quiet!"

" Nor the proper way to draw birds' eggs—she's made them all wriggly," said the other.

" How do you know about the Twins—and the eggs?" said Jane, flushing.

" Gracious!" said the first boy. " You don't think we could have watched you all this time without knowing everything that happens in this room! We can't see into the Night Nursery, of course, or the Bathroom. What coloured tiles has it?"

"Pink," said Jane.

"Ours has blue-and-white. Would you like to see it?"

Jane hesitated. She hardly knew what to reply, she was so astonished.

"Do come! William and Everard will be *your* horses, if you like, and I'll carry the whip and run alongside. I'm Valentine, in case you don't know. We're Triplets. And, of course, there's Christina."

"Where's Christina?" Jane searched the Bowl. But she saw only the green meadow and a little wood of alders, and Valentine, William, and Everard standing together.

"Come and see!" said Valentine persuasively, holding out his hand. "Why should the others have all the fun? You come with us—into the Bowl!"

That decided her. She would show Michael that he and the Twins were not the only ones who could go to a party. She would make them jealous and sorry for treating her so badly.

"All right," she said, putting out her hand, "I'll come!"

Valentine's hand closed round her wrist and pulled her towards the Bowl. And, suddenly, she was no longer in the cool Day Nursery, but out in a wide, sunlit meadow, and instead of the ragged nursery carpet, a springing turf of grass and daisies was spread beneath her feet.

"Hooray!" cried Valentine, William and Everard, dancing round her. She noticed that Valentine was limping.

"Oh," said Jane, "I forgot! Your knee!"

He smiled at her. "Never mind. It was the crack that did it. I know you didn't mean to hurt me!"

Jane took out her handkerchief and bound it round his knee.

"That's better!" he said politely, and put the reins into her hand.

William and Everard, tossing their heads and snorting, flew off across the meadow with Jane jingling the reins behind them.

Beside her, one foot heavy and one foot light, because of his knee, ran Valentine.

And, as he ran, he sang:

> "My love, thou art a nosegay sweet,
>   My sweetest flower I prove thee;
> And pleased I pin thee to my breast,
>   And dearly I do love thee!"

William and Everard's voices came in with the chorus:

> "And deeeee—arly I do lo-o-ve thee!"

Jane thought it was rather an old-fashioned song, but then, everything about the Triplets was old-fashioned—their long hair, their strange clothes, and their polite way of speaking.

"It *is* odd!" she thought to herself, but she also thought that this was better than being at Miss Lark's, and that Michael would envy her when she told him all about it.

On ran the horses, tugging Jane after them, drawing her away from the Nursery.

Presently she pulled up, panting, and looked back over the tracks they had made in the grass. Behind her, at the other side of the meadow, she could see the outer rim of the Bowl. It seemed small and very far away. And something inside her warned her that it was time to turn back.

" I must go now," she said, dropping the jingling reins.

" Oh, no, no!" cried the Triplets, closing round her.

And now something in their voices made her feel uneasy.

" They'll miss me at home. I'm afraid I must go," she said quickly.

" It's quite early!" protested Valentine. " They'll still be at Miss Lark's. Come on. I'll show you my paint-box."

Jane was tempted.

" Has it got Chinese White?" she inquired, for Chinese White was just what her own paint-box lacked.

" Yes, in a silver tube. Come!"

Against her will Jane allowed him to draw her on-wards. She thought she would just have one look at the paint-box and then hurry back. She would not even ask to be allowed to use it.

" But where is your house? It isn't in the Bowl!"

" Of course it is! But you can't see it because it's behind the wood. Come on!"

They were drawing her now under dark alder boughs. The dead leaves crackled under their feet and every now and then a pigeon swooped from branch to branch with a loud clapping of wings. William showed Jane a robin's nest in a pile of twigs, and Everard broke off a spray of leaves and twined it round her head. But, in spite of their friendliness, Jane was shy and nervous and felt very glad when they reached the end of the wood.

" Here it is!" said Valentine, waving his hand.

And she saw rising before her a huge stone house covered with ivy. It was older than any house she had ever seen and it seemed to lean towards her threateningly. On either side of the steps a stone lion crouched, as if waiting the moment to spring.

Jane shivered as the shadow of the house fell upon her.

"I can't stay long," she said, uneasily. "It's getting late."

"Just five minutes!" pleaded Valentine, drawing her into the hall.

Their feet rang hollowly on the stone floor. There was no sign of any human being. Except for herself and the Triplets, the house seemed deserted. A cold wind swept whistling along the corridor.

"Christina! Christina!" called Valentine, pulling Jane up the stairs. "Here she is!"

His cry went echoing round the house and every wall seemed to call back frighteningly, *"Here she is!"*

There was a sound of running feet and a door burst open. A little girl, slightly taller than the Triplets and dressed in an old-fashioned, flowery dress, rushed out and flung herself upon Jane.

"At last, at last!" she cried triumphantly. "The boys have been watching you for ages! But they couldn't catch you before—you were always so happy!"

"Catch me?" said Jane. "I don't understand."

She was beginning to be frightened and to wish she had never come with Valentine into the Bowl.

"Great-Grandfather will explain," said Christina, laughing curiously. She drew Jane across the landing and through the door.

"Heh! Heh! Heh! What's this?" demanded a thin, cracked voice.

Jane stared and drew back against Christina. For at the far end of the room, on a seat by the fire, sat a figure that filled her with terror. The firelight flickered over a very old man, so old that he looked more like a shadow than a human being. From his thin mouth a thin grey beard straggled and, though he wore a smoking-cap, Jane could see that he was as bald as an egg. He was dressed in a long, old-fashioned dressing-gown of faded silk, and a pair of embroidered slippers hung on his thin feet.

" So!" said the shadowy figure, taking a long curved pipe from his mouth. " Jane has arrived at last."

He rose and came towards her smiling frighteningly, his eyes burning in their sockets with a bright steely fire.

" She came through the alder wood with the boys, Great-Grandfather," said Christina.

" Ah? How did they catch her?"

" She was cross at being the eldest. So she threw her paint-box at the Bowl and cracked Val's knee."

" So!" the horrible old voice whistled. " It was temper, was it? Well, well——" He laughed thinly. " Now you'll be the youngest, my dear! My youngest Great-Granddaughter. But I shan't allow any tempers here! Heh! Heh! Heh! Oh, dear, no. Well, come along and sit by the fire. Will you take Tea or Cherry-Wine?"

" No, no!" Jane burst out. " I'm afraid there's been a mistake. I must go home now. I live at Number Seventeen Cherry Tree Lane."

" Used to, you mean," corrected Val triumphantly. " You live here now."

" But you don't understand!" Jane said desperately. " I don't want to live here. I want to go home."

" Nonsense!" croaked the Great-Grandfather. " Num-

The firelight flickered over a very old man

ber Seventeen is a horrible place, mean and stuffy and modern. Besides, you're not happy there. Heh! Heh! Heh! I know what it's like being the eldest—all the work and none of the fun. Heh! Heh! But here "—he waved his pipe—" here you'll be the Spoilt One, the Darling, the Treasure, and never go back any more!"

" Never! " echoed William and Everard, dancing round her.

" Oh, I must. I will! " Jane cried, the tears springing to her eyes.

The Great-Grandfather smiled his horrible, toothless smile.

" Do you think we will let you go? " he inquired. " You cracked our Bowl. You must take the consequences. Besides, you owe us something. You hurt Valentine's knee."

" I will make up to him. I will give him my paint-box."

" He has one."

" My hoop."

" He has out-grown hoops."

" Well——" faltered Jane. " I will marry him when I grow up."

The Great-Grandfather cackled with laughter.

Jane turned imploringly to Valentine. He shook his head.

" I'm afraid it's too late for that," he said sadly. " I grew up long ago."

" Then why, then what—oh, I don't understand. Where am I?" cried Jane, gazing about her in terror.

" Far from home, my child, far from home," croaked the Great-Grandfather. " You are back in the Past— back where Christina and the boys were young sixty years ago!"

Through her tears Jane saw his old eyes burning fiercely.

"Then—how can I get home?" she whispered.

"You cannot. You will stay here. There is no other place for you. You are back in the Past, remember! The Twins and Michael, even your Father and Mother, are not yet born; Number Seventeen is not even built. You cannot go home!"

"No, no!" cried Jane. "It's not true! It can't be." Her heart was thumping inside her. Never to see Michael again, nor the Twins, nor her Father and Mother and Mary Poppins!

And suddenly she began to shout, lifting her voice so that it echoed wildly through the stone corridors.

"Mary Poppins! I'm sorry I was cross! Oh, Mary Poppins, help me, help me!"

"Quick! Hold her close! Surround her!"

She heard the Great-Grandfather's sharp command. She felt the four children pressing close about her.

She shut her eyes tight. "Mary Poppins!" she cried again, "Mary Poppins!"

A hand caught hers and pulled her away from the circling arms of Christina, Valentine, William and Everard.

"Heh! Heh! Heh!"

The Great-Grandfather's cackling laugh echoed through the room. The grasp on her hand tightened and she felt herself being drawn away. She dared not look for fear of those frightening eyes, but she pulled fiercely against the tugging hand.

"Heh! Heh! Heh!"

The laugh sounded again and the hand drew her on, down stone stairs and echoing corridors.

She had no hope now. Behind her the voices of

Christina and the Triplets faded away. No help would come from them.

She stumbled desperately after the flying footsteps and felt, though her eyes were closed, dark shadows above her head and damp earth under her foot.

What was happening to her? Where, oh, where was she going? If only she hadn't been so cross—if only!

The strong hand pulled her onwards and presently she felt the warmth of sunlight on her cheeks and sharp grass scratched her legs as she was dragged along. Then, suddenly, a pair of arms, like bands of iron, closed about her, lifted her up and swung her through the air.

"Oh, help, help!" she cried, frantically twisting and turning against those arms. She would not give in without a struggle, she would kick and kick and kick and . . .

"I'll thank you to remember," said a familiar voice in her ear, "that this is my best skirt and it has to last me the Summer!"

Jane opened her eyes. A pair of fierce blue eyes looked steadily into hers.

The arms that folded her so closely were Mary Poppins' arms and the legs she was kicking so furiously were the legs of Mary Poppins.

"Oh!" she faltered. "It was *you*! I thought you hadn't heard me, Mary Poppins! I thought I should be kept there for ever. I thought——"

"Some people," remarked Mary Poppins, putting her gently down, "think a great deal too much. Of that I'm sure. Wipe your face, please!"

She thrust her blue handkerchief into Jane's hand and began to get the Nursery ready for the evening.

Jane watched her, drying her tear-stained face on the large blue handkerchief. She glanced round the well-known room. There were the ragged carpet and the toy-cupboard and Mary Poppins' arm-chair. At the sight of them she felt safe and warm and comforted. She listened to the familiar sounds as Mary Poppins went about her work, and her terror died away. A tide of happiness swept over her.

"It couldn't have been I who was cross," she said to herself. "It *must* have been somebody else."

And she sat there wondering who the Somebody was. . . .

"But it can't *really* have happened!" scoffed Michael

a little later when he heard of Jane's adventure. "You're much too big for the Bowl."

She thought for a moment. Somehow, as she told the story, it did seem rather impossible.

"I suppose it can't," she admitted. "But it seemed quite real at the time."

"I expect you just thought it. You're always thinking things." He felt rather superior because *he* never thought at all.

"You two and your thoughts!" said Mary Poppins crossly, pushing them aside as she dumped the Twins into their cots.

"And now," she snapped, when John and Barbara were safely tucked in, "perhaps I shall have a moment to myself."

She took the pins out of her hat and thrust it back into its brown-paper bag. She unclipped the locket and put it carefully away in a drawer. Then she slipped off her coat, shook it out, and hung it on the peg behind the door.

"Why, where's your new scarf?" said Jane. "Have you lost it?"

"She couldn't have!" said Michael. "She had it on when she came home. I saw it."

Mary Poppins turned on them.

"Be good enough to mind your own affairs," she said snappily, "and let me mind mine!"

"I only wanted to help——" Jane began.

"I can help myself, thank you!" said Mary Poppins, sniffing.

Jane turned to exchange looks with Michael. But this time it was he who took no notice. He was staring at the mantelpiece as if he could not believe his eyes.

"What is it, Michael?"

"You didn't just think it, after all!" he whispered, pointing.

Jane looked up at the mantelpiece. There lay the Royal Doulton Bowl with the crack running right across it. There were the meadow grasses and the wood of

alders. And there were the three little boys playing horses, two in front and one running behind with the whip.

But—around the leg of the driver was knotted a small, white handkerchief and, sprawling across the grass, as though someone had dropped it as they ran, was a red-and-white checked scarf. At one end of it was stitched a large white label bearing the initials: *M.P.*

" So that's where she lost it!" said Michael, nodding his head wisely. " Shall we tell her we've found it?"

Jane glanced round. Mary Poppins was buttoning on her apron and looking as if the whole world had insulted her.

" Better not," she said, softly. " I expect she knows."

For a moment Jane stood there, gazing at the cracked Bowl, the knotted handkerchief and the scarf.

Then with a wild rush she ran across the room and flung herself upon the starched white figure.

" Oh," she cried. " Oh, Mary Poppins! I'll never be naughty again!"

A faint, disbelieving smile twinkled at the corners of Mary Poppins' mouth as she smoothed out the creases from her apron.

" Humph!" was all she said.

Chapter Four

TOPSY TURVY

"KEEP close to me, please!" said Mary Poppins, stepping out of the Bus and putting up her umbrella, for it was raining heavily.

Jane and Michael scrambled out after her.

"If I keep close to you the drips from your umbrella run down my neck," complained Michael.

"Don't blame me, then, if you get lost and have to ask a Policeman!" snapped Mary Poppins, as she neatly avoided a puddle.

She paused outside the Chemist's shop at the corner so that she could see herself reflected in the three gigantic bottles in the window. She could see a Green Mary Poppins, a Blue Mary Poppins and a Red Mary Poppins all at once. And each one of them was carrying a brand-new leather hand-bag with brass knobs on it.

Mary Poppins looked at herself in the three bottles and smiled a pleased and satisfied smile. She spent some minutes changing the hand-bag from her right hand to her left, trying it in every possible position to see how it looked best. Then she decided that, after all, it was most effective when tucked under her arm. So she left it there.

Jane and Michael stood beside her, not daring to say anything but glancing across at each other and sighing inside themselves. And from two points of her parrot-handled umbrella the rain trickled uncomfortably down the backs of their necks.

"Now then—don't keep me waiting!" said Mary
Poppins crossly, turning away from the Green, Blue and
Red reflections of herself. Jane and Michael exchanged
glances. Jane signalled to Michael to keep quiet. She
shook her head and made a face at him. But he burst
out:

"We weren't. It was you keeping us waiting!——"

"Silence!"

Michael did not dare to say any more. He and Jane

308

trudged along, one on either side of Mary Poppins. The rain poured down, dancing from the top of the umbrella on to their hats. Under her arm Jane carried the Royal Doulton Bowl wrapped carefully in two pieces of paper. They were taking it to Mary Poppins' cousin, Mr. Turvy, whose business, she told Mrs. Banks, was mending things.

"Well," Mrs. Banks had said, rather doubtfully, "I hope he will do it satisfactorily, for until it *is* mended I shall not be able to look my Great-Aunt Caroline in the face."

Great-Aunt Caroline had given Mrs. Banks the bowl when Mrs. Banks was only three, and it was well known that if it were broken Great-Aunt Caroline would make one of her famous scenes.

"Members of *my* family, ma'am," Mary Poppins had retorted with a sniff, "*always* give satisfaction."

And she had looked so fierce that Mrs. Banks felt quite uncomfortable and had to sit down and ring for a cup of tea.

Swish!

There was Jane, right in the middle of a puddle.

"Look where you're going, please!" snapped Mary Poppins, shaking her umbrella and tossing the drips over Jane and Michael. "This rain is enough to break your heart."

"If it did, could Mr. Turvy mend it?" inquired Michael. He was interested to know if Mr. Turvy could mend all broken things or only certain kinds.

"One more word," said Mary Poppins, "and Back Home you go!"

"I only asked," said Michael sulkily.

"Then don't!"

Mary Poppins, with an angry sniff, turned the corner

smartly and, opening an old iron gate, knocked at the door of a small tumble-down building.

" Tap-tap-tappity-tap!" The sound of the knocker echoed hollowly through the house.

" Oh, dear," Jane whispered to Michael, " how awful if he's out!"

But at that moment heavy footsteps were heard tramping towards them, and with a loud rattle the door opened.

A round, red-faced woman, looking more like two apples placed one on top of the other than a human being, stood in the doorway. Her straight hair was scraped into a knob at the top of her head, and her thin mouth had a cross and peevish expression.

" Well!" she said, staring. " It's you or I'm a Dutch-man!"

She did not seem particularly pleased to see Mary Poppins. Nor did Mary Poppins seem particularly pleased to see her.

" Is Mr. Turvy in?" she inquired, without taking any notice of the round woman's remark.

" Well," said the round woman in an unfriendly voice, " I wouldn't be certain. He may be or he may not. It's all a matter of how you happen to look at it."

Mary Poppins stepped through the door and peered about her.

" That's his hat, isn't it?" she demanded, pointing to an old felt hat that hung on a peg in the hall.

" Well, it is, of course—in a manner of speaking." The round woman admitted the fact unwillingly.

" Then he's in," said Mary Poppins. " No member of *my* family ever goes out without a hat. They're much too respectable."

" Well, all I can tell you is what he said to me this

310

morning," said the round woman. "'Miss Tartlet,' he said, 'I may be in this afternoon and I may not. It is quite impossible to tell.' That's what he said. But you'd better go up and see for yourself. I'm not a Mountaineer."

The round woman glanced down at her round body and shook her head. Jane and Michael could easily understand that a person of her size and shape would not want to climb up Mr. Turvy's narrow, rickety stairs very often.

Mary Poppins sniffed.

"Follow me, please!" She snapped the words at Jane and Michael, and they ran after her up the creaking stairs.

Miss Tartlet stood in the hall watching them with a superior smile on her face.

At the top landing Mary Poppins knocked on the door with the head of the umbrella. There was no reply. She knocked again—louder this time. Still there was no answer.

"Cousin Arthur!" she called through the key-hole. "Cousin Arthur, are you in?"

"No, I'm out!" came a far-away voice from within.

"How can he be out? I can hear him!" whispered Michael to Jane.

"Cousin Arthur!" Mary Poppins rattled the door-handle. "I know you're in."

"No, no, I'm not!" came the far-away voice. "I'm out, I tell you. It's the Second Monday!"

"Oh, dear—I'd forgotten!" said Mary Poppins, and with an angry movement she turned the handle and flung open the door.

At first, all that Jane and Michael could see was a large room that appeared to be quite empty except for

311

a carpenter's bench at one end. Piled upon this was a curious collection of articles—china dogs with no noses, wooden horses that had lost their tails, chipped plates, broken dolls, knives without handles, stools with only two legs—everything in the world, it seemed, that could possibly want mending.

Round the walls of the room were shelves reaching from floor to ceiling and these, too, were crowded with cracked china, broken glass and shattered toys.

But there was no sign anywhere of a human being.

"Oh," said Jane in a disappointed voice. "He *is* out, after all!"

But Mary Poppins had darted across the room to the window.

"Come in at once, Arthur! Out in the rain like that, and you with your Bronchitis the winter before last!"

And, to their amazement, Jane and Michael saw her grasp a long leg that hung across the window-sill and pull in from the outer air a tall, thin, sad-looking man with a long, drooping moustache.

"You ought to be ashamed of yourself," said Mary Poppins crossly, keeping a firm hold of Mr. Turvy with one hand while she shut the window with the other. "We've brought you some important work to do and here you are behaving like this!"

"Well, I can't help it," said Mr. Turvy apologetically, mopping his sad eyes with a large handkerchief. "I told you it was the Second Monday."

"What does that mean?" asked Michael, staring at Mr. Turvy with interest.

"Ah," said Mr. Turvy, turning to him and shaking him limply by the hand. "It's kind of you to inquire, very kind. I do appreciate it, really." He paused to wipe his eyes again. "You see," he went on, "it's this way. On the Second Monday of the month everything goes wrong with me."

"What kind of things?" asked Jane, feeling very sorry for Mr. Turvy, but also very curious.

"Well, take to-day!" said Mr. Turvy. "This happens to be the Second Monday of the month. And because I want to be in—having so much work to do—I'm automatically out. And if I wanted to be out, sure enough, I'd be in."

"I see," said Jane, though she really found it very difficult to understand. "So that's why——?"

"Yes." Mr. Turvey nodded. "I heard you coming up the stairs and I did so long to be in. So, of course, as soon as that happened—there I was—out! And I'd be out still if Mary Poppins weren't holding on to me." He sighed heavily.

"Of course, it's not like this all the time. Only between the hours of three and six—but even then it can be very awkward."

"I'm sure it can," said Jane sympathetically.

"And it's not as if it was only In and Out——" Mr. Turvy went on miserably. "It's other things, too. If I try to go upstairs, I find myself running down. I have only to turn to the right and I find myself going to the left. And I never set off for the West without immediately finding myself in the East."

Mr. Turvy blew his nose.

"And worst of all," he continued, his eyes filling again with tears, "my whole nature alters. To look at me now, you'd hardly believe I was really a happy and satisfied sort of person—would you?"

And, indeed, Mr. Turvy looked so melancholy and

distressed that it seemed quite impossible he could ever have been cheerful and contented.

"But, why? Why?" demanded Michael, staring up at him.

Mr. Turvy shook his head sadly.

"Ah!" he said solemnly. "I should have been a Girl."

Jane and Michael stared at him and then at each other. What *could* he mean?

"You see," Mr. Turvy explained, "my mother wanted a girl, and it turned out, when I arrived, that I was a boy. So I went wrong right from the beginning —from the day I was born, you might say. And that was the Second Monday of the month."

Mr. Turvy began to weep again, sobbing gently into his handkerchief.

Jane patted his hand kindly.

He seemed pleased, though he did not smile.

"And, of course," he went on, "it's very bad for my work. Look up there!"

He pointed to one of the larger shelves, on which were standing a row of hearts in different colours and sizes, each one cracked or chipped or entirely broken.

"Now, those," said Mr. Turvy, "are wanted in a great hurry. You don't know how cross people get if I don't send their hearts back quickly. They make more fuss about them than anything else. And I simply daren't touch them till after six o'clock. They'd be ruined—like those things!"

He nodded to another shelf. Jane and Michael looked and saw that it was piled high with things that had been wrongly mended. A china Shepherdess had been separated from her china Shepherd and her arms were glued about the neck of a brass Lion; a Toy Sailor, whom somebody had wrenched from his boat, was firmly stuck to a Willow-pattern plate; and in the boat, with his trunk curled round the mast and fixed there with sticking-plaster, was a grey-flannel Elephant. Broken saucers were riveted together the wrong way of the pattern, and the leg of a wooden Horse was firmly attached to a silver Christening Mug.

"You see?" said Mr. Turvy hopelessly, with a wave of his hand.

Jane and Michael nodded. They felt very, very sorry for Mr. Turvy.

"Well, never mind that now," Mary Poppins broke in impatiently. "What *is* important is this Bowl. We've brought it to be mended."

She took the Bowl from Jane and, still holding Mr. Turvy with one hand, she untied the string with the other.

"H'm!" said Mr. Turvy. "Royal Doulton. A bad crack. Looks as though somebody had thrown something at it."

Jane felt herself blushing as he said that.

"Still," he went on, "if it were any other day, I could mend it. But to-day——" he hesitated.

"Nonsense, it's quite simple. You've only to put a rivet here—and here—and here!"

Mary Poppins pointed to the crack, and, as she did so, she dropped Mr. Turvy's hand.

Immediately, he went spinning through the air, turning over and over like a Catherine wheel.

"Oh!" cried Mr. Turvy. "Why did you let go? Poor me, I'm off again!"

"Quick—shut the door!" cried Mary Poppins. And Jane and Michael rushed across the room and closed the door just before Mr. Turvy reached it. He banged against it and bounced away again, turning gracefully, with a very sad look on his face, through the air.

Suddenly he stopped, but in a very curious position.

Instead of being right-side-up he was up-side-down and standing on his head.

"D e a r, dear!" said Mr. Turvy, giving a fierce kick with his feet. "Dear, dear!"

But his feet would not go d o w n to the f l o o r. They remained waving gently in the air.

"Well," Mr. Turvy remarked in his melancholy voice, "I suppose I should be glad it's no worse. This is certainly better—though not *much* better—than hanging outside in the rain with nothing to sit on and no overcoat. You see," he looked at Jane and Michael, "I want so much to be right-side-up and so—just my luck! —I'm upside-down. Well, well, never mind. I ought to be used to it by now. I've had forty-five years of it. Give me the Bowl."

Michael ran and took the Bowl from Mary Poppins and put it on the floor by Mr. Turvy's head. And, as he did so, he felt a curious thing happening to him. The floor seemed to be pushing his feet away from it and tilting them into the air.

"Oh!" he cried. "I feel so funny. Something most extraordinary is happening to me!"

For by now, he, too, was turning Catherine wheels through the air, and flying up and down the room, until he landed head-first on the floor beside Mr. Turvy.

"Strike me pink!" said Mr. Turvy in a surprised voice, looking at Michael out of the corner of his eye. "I never knew it was catching. You, too? Well, of all the—Hi, Hi, I say! Steady there! You'll knock the goods off the shelves, if you're not careful, and I shall be charged for breakages. What *are* you doing?"

He was now addressing Jane, whose feet had suddenly swept off the carpet and were turning above her head in the giddiest manner. Over and over she went—first her head and then her feet in the air—until at last she came down on the other side of Mr. Turvy and found herself standing on her head.

"You know," said Mr. Turvy, staring at her solemnly, "this is very odd. I never knew it happen to anyone else before. Upon my word, I never did. I do hope you don't mind."

Jane laughed, turning her head towards him and waving her legs in the air.

"Not a bit, thank you. I've always wanted to stand on my head and I've never been able to do it before. It's very comfortable."

"H'm," said Mr. Turvy dolefully. "I'm glad somebody likes it. I can't say *I* feel like that."

317

"I do," said Michael. "I wish I could stay like this all my life. Everything looks so nice and different."

And, indeed, everything *was* different. From their strange position on the floor, Jane and Michael could see that the articles on the carpenter's bench were all upside down—china dogs, broken dolls, wooden stools —all standing on their heads.

"Look!" whispered Jane to Michael. He turned his head as much as he could. And there, creeping out of a hole in the wainscoting, came a small mouse. It skipped, head over heels, into the middle of the room, and, turning upside down, balanced daintily on its nose in front of them.

They watched it for a moment, very surprised. Then Michael suddenly said:

"Jane, look out of the window!"

She turned her head carefully, for it was rather difficult, and saw to her astonishment that everything outside the room, as well as everything in it, was different. Out in the street the houses were standing on their heads, their chimneys on the pavement and their door-steps in the air, and out of the door-steps came little curls of smoke. In the distance a church had turned turtle and was balancing rather top-heavily on the point of its steeple. And the rain, which had always seemed to them to come down from the sky, was pouring up from the earth in a steady, soaking shower.

"Oh," said Jane, "how beautifully strange it all is! It's like being in another world. I'm so glad we came to-day."

"Well," said Mr. Turvy, mournfully, "you're very kind, I must say. You do know how to make allowances. Now, what about this Bowl?"

He stretched out his hand to take it, but at that

318

moment the Bowl gave a little skip and turned upside down. And it did it so quickly and so funnily that Jane and Michael could not help laughing.

"This," said Mr. Turvy miserably, "is no laughing matter for me, I assure you. I shall have to put the rivets in wrong way up—and if they show, they show. I can't help it."

And, taking his tools out of his pocket, he mended the Bowl, weeping quietly as he worked.

"Humph!" said Mary Poppins, stooping to pick it up. "Well, that's done. And now we'll be going."

At that Mr. Turvy began to sob pitifully.

"That's right, leave me!" he said bitterly. "Don't stay and help me keep my mind off my misery. Don't hold out a friendly hand. I'm not worth it. I'd hoped you might all favour me by accepting some refreshment. There's a Plum Cake in a tin on the top shelf. But, there —I'd no right to expect it. You've your own lives to live and I shouldn't ask you to stay and brighten mine. This isn't my lucky day——"

He fumbled for his pocket-handkerchief.

"Well——" began Mary Poppins, pausing in the middle of buttoning her gloves.

"Oh, do stay, Mary Poppins, do!" cried Jane and Michael together, dancing eagerly on their heads.

"You could reach the cake if you stood on a chair!" said Jane, helpfully.

Mr. Turvy laughed for the first time. It was rather a melancholy sound, but still, it *was* a laugh.

"*She'll* need no chair!" he said, gloomily chuckling in his throat. "She'll get what she wants and in the way she wants it—*she* will."

And at that moment, before the children's astonished eyes, Mary Poppins did a curious thing. She raised herself stiffly on her toes and balanced there for a moment. Then, very slowly, and in a most dignified manner, she turned seven Catherine wheels through the air. Over and over, her skirts clinging neatly about her ankles, her hat set tidily on her head, she wheeled up to the top shelf, took the cake, and wheeled down again, landing neatly on her head in front of Mr. Turvy and the children.

"Hooray! Hooray! Hooray!" shouted Michael, delightedly. But from the floor Mary Poppins gave him such a look that he rather wished he had remained silent.

"Thank you, Mary," said Mr. Turvy sadly, not seeming at all surprised.

"There!" snapped Mary Poppins. "That's the last thing I do for you to-day."

She put the cake-tin down in front of Mr. Turvy.

Immediately, with a little wobbly roll, it turned upside down. And each time Mr. Turvy turned it right side up, it turned over again.

"Ah," he said despairingly, "I might have known it. Nothing is right to-day—not even the cake-tin. We shall have to cut it open from the bottom. I'll just ask——"

And he stumbled on his head to the door and shouted through the crack between it and the floor.

"Miss Tartlet! Miss Tartlet! I'm so sorry to trouble you, but could you—would you—do you mind bringing a tin-opener?"

Far away downstairs Miss Tartlet's voice could be heard, grimly protesting.

"Tush!" said a loud croaky voice inside the room. "Tush and nonsense! Don't bother the woman! Let Polly do it! Pretty Polly! Clever Polly!"

Landing neatly on her head in front of Mr. Turvy and the children

Turning their heads, Jane and Michael were surprised to see that the voice came from Mary Poppins' parrot-headed umbrella which was at that moment Catherine-wheeling towards the cake. It landed head downwards on the tin and in two seconds had cut a large hole in it with its beak.

"There!" squawked the parrot-head conceitedly, "Polly did it! Handsome Polly!" And a happy self-satisfied smile spread over its beak as it settled head-downwards on the floor beside Mary Poppins.

"Well, that's very kind, *very* kind!" said Mr. Turvy in his gloomy voice, as the dark crust of the cake became visible.

He took a knife out of his pocket and cut a slice. He started violently, and peered at the cake more closely. Then he looked reproachfully at Mary Poppins.

"This is your doing, Mary! Don't deny it. That cake, when the tin was last open, was a Plum Cake, and now——"

"Sponge is much more digestible," said Mary Poppins, primly. "Eat slowly, please. You're not Starving Savages!" she snapped, passing a small slice each to Jane and Michael.

"That's all very well," grumbled Mr. Turvy bitterly eating his slice in two bites. "But I do like a plum o two, I must admit. Ah, well, this is not my lucky day! He broke off as somebody rapped loudly on the door.

"Come in!" called Mr. Turvy.

Miss Tartlet, looking, if anything, rounder than eve and panting from her climb up the stairs, burst in the room.

"The tin-opener, Mr. Turvy——" she began grim Then she paused and stared.

"My!" she said, opening her mouth very wide ;

322

letting the tin-opener slip from her hand. "Of all the sights I ever did see, this is the one I wouldn't have expected!"

She took a step forward, gazing at the four pairs of waving feet with an expression of deep disgust.

"Upside down—the lot of you—like flies on a ceiling! And you supposed to be respectable human creatures. This is no place for a lady of *my* standing. I shall leave the house this instant, Mr. Turvy. Please note that!"

She flounced angrily towards the door.

But even as she went her great billowing skirts blew against her round legs and lifted her from the floor.

A look of agonised astonishment spread over her face. She flung out her hands wildly.

"Mr. Turvy! Mr. Turvy, Sir! Catch me! Hold me down! Help! Help!" cried Miss Tartlet, as she, too, began a sweeping Catherine wheel.

"Oh, oh, the world's turning turtle! What shall I do? Help! Help!" she shrieked, as she went over again.

But as she turned a curious change came over her. Her round face lost its peevish expression and began to shine with smiles. And Jane and Michael, with a start of surprise, saw her straight hair crinkle into a mass of little curls as she whirled and twirled through the room. When she spoke again her gruff voice was as sweet as honeysuckle.

"What can be happening to me?" cried Miss Tartlet's new voice. "I feel like a ball! A bouncing ball! Or perhaps a balloon! Or a cherry tart!" She broke into a peal of happy laughter.

"Dear me, how cheerful I am!" she trilled, turning and circling through the air. "I never enjoyed my life before, but now I feel I shall never stop. It's the loveliest sensation. I shall write home to my Sister about it, to

323

my Cousins and Uncles and Aunts. I shall tell them that the only proper way to live is upside down, upside down, upside down——"

And, chanting happily, Miss Tartlet went whirling round and round. Jane and Michael watched her with delight and Mr. Turvy watched her with surprise, for he had never known Miss Tartlet to be anything but peevish and unfriendly.

"Very odd! Very odd!" said Mr. Turvy to himself, shaking his head as he stood on it.

Another knock sounded at the door.

"Anyone here name of Turvy?" inquired a voice, and the Post Man appeared in the doorway holding a letter. He stood staring at the sight that met his eyes.

"Holy smoke!" he remarked, pushing his cap to the back of his head. "I must-a come to the wrong place. I'm looking for a decent, quiet gentleman called Turvy. I've got a letter for him. Besides, I promised my wife I'd be home early and I've broken my word, and I thought——"

"Ha!" said Mr. Turvy from the floor. "A broken promise is one of the things I can't mend. Not in my line. Sorry!"

The Post Man stared down at him.

"Am I dreaming or am I not?" he muttered. "It seems to me I've got into a whirling, twirling, skirling company of lunatics!"

"Give me the letter, dear Post Man! Mr. Turvy, you see, is engaged! Give the letter to Topsy Tartlet and turn upside down with me."

Miss Tartlet, wheeling towards the Post Man, took his hand in hers. And as she touched him his feet slithered off the floor into the air. Then away they went, hand

in hand, and over and over, like a pair of bouncing footballs.

"How lovely it is!" cried Miss Tartlet, happily. "Oh, Post Man dear, we're seeing life for the first time. And such a pleasant view of it! Over we go! Isn't it wonderful?"

"Yes!" shouted Jane and Michael, as they joined the wheeling dance of the Post Man and Miss Tartlet.

Presently Mr. Turvy, too, joined in, awkwardly turning and tossing through the air. Mary Poppins and her umbrella followed, going over and over evenly and neatly and with the utmost dignity. There they all were, spinning and wheeling, with the world going up and down outside, and the happy cries of Miss Tartlet echoing through the room.

" The whole of the Town
Is Upside Down!"

she sang, bouncing and bounding.

And up on the shelves the cracked and broken hearts twirled and spun like tops, the Shepherdess and her Lion waltzed gracefully together, the grey-flannel Elephant stood on his trunk in the boat and kicked his feet in the air, and the Toy Sailor danced a hornpipe, not on his feet but his head, which bobbed about the Willow-pattern plate very gracefully.

"How happy I am!" cried Jane, as she careered across the room.

"How happy *I* am!" cried Michael, turning somersaults in the air.

Mr. Turvy mopped his eyes with his handkerchief as he bounced off the window-pane.

Mary Poppins and her umbrella said nothing, but just sailed calmly round, head downwards.

"How happy we *all* are!" cried Miss Tartlet.

But the Post Man had now found his tongue and he did not agree with her.

"'Ere!" he shouted, turning again. "'Elp! 'Elp! Where am I? Who am I? What am I? I don't know at all. I'm lost! Oh, 'elp!"

But nobody helped him and, firmly held in Miss Tartlet's grasp, he was whirled on.

"Always lived a quiet life—I have!" he moaned. "Behaved like a decent citizen, too. Oh, what'll my wife say! And 'ow shall I get 'ome? 'Elp! Fire! Thieves!"

And, making a great effort, he wrenched his hand violently from Miss Tartlet's. He dropped the letter into the cake-tin and went wheeling out of the door and down the stairs, head over heels, crying loudly:

" I'll have the law on them! I'll call the Police! I'll speak to the Post Master General!"

His voice died away as he went bounding farther down the stairs.

Ping, ping, ping, ping, ping, ping!

The clock outside in the Square sounded six.

And at the same moment Jane's and Michael's feet came down to the floor with a thud, and they stood up, feeling rather giddy.

Mary Poppins gracefully turned right side up, looking as smart and tidy as a figure in a shop-window.

The Umbrella wheeled over and stood on its point.

Mr. Turvy, with a great tossing of legs, scrambled to his feet.

The hearts on the shelf stood still and steady, and no movement came from the Shepherdess or the Lion, or the grey-flannel Elephant or the Toy Sailor. To look at them you would never have guessed that a moment before they had all been dancing on their heads.

Only Miss Tartlet went whirling on, round and round the room, feet over head, laughing happily and singing her song.

> " The whole of the Town
> Is Upside Down,
> Upside Down,
> Upside Down!"

she chanted joyfully.

" Miss Tartlet! Miss Tartlet!" cried Mr. Turvy, running towards her, a strange light in his eyes. He took her arm as she wheeled past and held it tightly until she stood upon her feet beside him.

"*What* did you say your name was?" said Mr. Turvy, panting with excitement.

Miss Tartlet actually blushed. She looked at him shyly.

"Why, Tartlet, sir. Topsy Tartlet!"

Mr. Turvy took her hand.

"Then will you marry me, Miss Tartlet, and be Topsy Turvy? It would make up to me for so much. And you seem to have become so happy that perhaps you will be kind enough to overlook my Second Mondays."

"Overlook them, Mr. Turvy? Why, they will be my Greatest Treats," said Miss Tartlet. "I have seen the world upside down to-day and I have got a New Point of View. I assure you I shall look forward to the Second Mondays all the month!"

She laughed shyly, and gave Mr. Turvy her other hand. And Mr. Turvy, Jane and Michael were glad to see, laughed too.

"It's after six o'clock, so I suppose he can be himself again," whispered Michael to Jane.

Jane did not answer. She was watching the mouse. It was no longer standing on its nose but hurrying away to its hole with a large crumb of cake in its mouth.

Mary Poppins picked up the Royal Doulton Bowl and proceeded to wrap it up.

"Pick up your handkerchiefs, please—and straighten your hats," she snapped.

"And now——" She took her umbrella and tucked her new bag under her arm.

"Oh, we're not going yet, are we, Mary Poppins?" said Michael.

"If *you* are in the habit of staying out all night, I am not," she remarked, pushing him towards the door.

"Must you go, really?" said Mr. Turvy. But he seemed to be saying it out of mere politeness. He had eyes only for Miss Tartlet.

But Miss Tartlet herself came up to them, smiling radiantly and tossing her curls.

"Come again," she said, giving a hand to each of them. "Now do. Mr. Turvy and I"—she looked down shyly and blushed—"will be in to tea every Second Monday—won't we, Arthur?"

"Well," said Mr. Turvy, "we'll be in if we're not out—I'm sure of that!"

He and Miss Tartlet stood at the top of the stairs waving good-bye to Mary Poppins and the children— Miss Tartlet blushing happily, and Mr. Turvy holding Miss Tartlet's hand and looking very proud and pompous. . . .

"I didn't know it was as easy as that," said Michael to Jane, as they splashed through the rain under Mary Poppins' umbrella.

"What was?" said Jane.

"Standing on my head. I shall practise it when I get home."

"I wish *we* could have Second Mondays," said Jane dreamily.

"Get in, please!" said Mary Poppins, shutting her umbrella and pushing the children up the winding stairs of the bus.

They sat together in the seat behind hers, talking quietly about all that had happened that afternoon.

Mary Poppins turned and glared at them.

"It is rude to whisper," she said fiercely. "And sit up straight. You're not flour-bags!"

They were quiet for a few minutes. Mary Poppins, half-turning in her seat, watched them with angry eyes.

"What a funny family you've got," Michael remarked to her, trying to make conversation.

Her head went up with a jerk.

"Funny? What do you mean, pray—funny?"

"Well—odd. Mr. Turvy turning Catherine wheels and standing on his head——"

Mary Poppins stared at him as though she could not believe her ears.

"Did I understand you to say," she began, speaking her words as though she were biting them, "that my cousin turned a Catherine wheel? And stood on——"

"But he did," protested Michael nervously. "We saw him."

"On his head? A relation of mine on his head? And turning about like a firework display?" Mary Poppins seemed hardly able to repeat the dreadful statement. She glared at Michael.

"Now this," she began, and he shrank back in terror from her wild darting eyes, "this is the Last Straw. First you are impudent to me and then you insult my relations. It would take very little more—Very Little More—to make me give notice. So—I warn you!"

And with that she bounced round on her seat and sat with her back to them. And even from the back she looked angrier than they had ever seen her.

Michael leaned forward.

"I—I apologise," he said.

There was no answer from the seat in front.

"I'm sorry, Mary Poppins!"

" Humph ! "

" *Very* sorry ! "

" And well you might be ! " she retorted, staring straight ahead of her.

Michael leant towards Jane.

" But it was true—what I said. Wasn't it ? " he whispered.

Jane shook her head and put her finger to her lip. She was staring at Mary Poppins' hat. And presently, when she was sure that Mary Poppins was not looking, she pointed to the brim.

There, gleaming on the black shiny straw, was a scattering crumbs, yellow crumbs from a sponge cake, the kind of thing you would expect to find on the hat of a person who had stood on their head to have Tea.

Michael gazed at the crumbs for a moment. Then he turned and nodded understandingly to Jane.

They sat there, jogging up and down as the bus rumbled homewards. Mary Poppins' back, erect and angry, was like a silent warning. They dared not speak to her. But every time the bus turned a corner they saw the crumbs turning Catherine wheels on the shining brim of her hat. . . .

Chapter Five

THE NEW ONE

"BUT *why* must we go for a walk with Ellen?" grumbled Michael, slamming the gate. "I don't like her. Her nose is too red."

"Sh!" said Jane. "She'll hear you."

Ellen, who was wheeling the perambulator, turned round.

"You're a cruel, unkind boy, Master Michael! I'm only doing my duty, I'm sure. It's no pleasure to me to be going for a walk in this heat—so there!"

She blew her red nose on a green handkerchief.

"Then why do you go?" Michael demanded.

"Because Mary Poppins is busy. So come along, there's a good boy, and I'll buy you a penn'orth of peppermints."

"I don't want peppermints," muttered Michael. "I want Mary Poppins."

Plop-plop! Plop-plop! Ellen's feet marched slowly and heavily along the Lane.

"I can see a rainbow through every chink of my hat," said Jane.

"I can't," said Michael crossly. "I can only see my silk lining."

Ellen stopped at the corner, looking anxiously for traffic.

"Want any help?" inquired the Policeman, sauntering up to her.

"Well," said Ellen, blushing, "if you could take us

across the road, I'd be obliged. What with a bad cold, and four children to look after, I don't know if I'm on my head or my feet." She blew her nose again.

"But you *must* know! You've only got to look!" said Michael, thinking how Perfectly Awful Ellen was.

But the Policeman, apparently, thought differently, for he took tight hold of Ellen's arm with one hand, and the handle of the perambulator with the other, and led her across the street as tenderly as though she were a bride.

"Ever get a Day Off?" he inquired, looking interestedly into Ellen's red face.

"Well," said Ellen. "Half-days, so to speak. Every second Saturday." She blew her nose nervously.

"Funny," said the Policeman. "Those are *my* days, too. And I'm usually just around here at two o'clock in the afternoon."

"Oh!" said Ellen, opening her mouth very wide indeed.

"So!" said the Policeman, nodding at her politely.

"Well, I'll see," said Ellen. "Good-bye."

And she went trudging on, looking back occasionally to see if the Policeman was still looking.

And he always was.

"Mary Poppins never needs a policeman," complained Michael. "What *can* she be busy about?"

"Something important is happening at home," said Jane. "I'm sure of it."

"How do you know?"

"I've got an empty, waiting sort of feeling inside."

"Pooh!" said Michael. "I expect you're hungry! Can't we go faster, Ellen, and get it over?"

"That boy," said Ellen to the Park railing, "has a heart of stone. No, we can't, Master Michael, because of my feet."

"What's the matter with them?"

"They will only go so fast and no faster."

"Oh, *dear* Mary Poppins!" said Michael bitterly.

He went sighing after the perambulator. Jane walked beside him counting rainbows through her hat.

Ellen's slow feet tramped steadily onward. One-two. One-two. *Plop-plop! Plop-plop!*

And away behind them in Cherry Tree Lane the important thing was happening.

From the outside, Number Seventeen looked as peaceful and sleepy as all the other houses. But behind the drawn blinds there was such a stir and bustle that, if it hadn't been Summer-time, a passer-by might have thought the people in the house were Spring-cleaning or getting ready for Christmas.

But the House itself stood blinking in the sunshine, taking no notice. After all, it thought to itself, I have seen such bustlings often before and shall probably see them many times again, so why should *I* bother about it?

And just then, the front door was flung open by Mrs. Brill, and Doctor Simpson hurried out. Mrs. Brill stood dancing on her toes as she watched him go down the garden path, swinging his little brown bag. Then she hurried to the Pantry and called excitedly:

" Where are you, Robertson? Come along, if you're coming!"

She scuttled up the stairs two at a time with Robertson Ay, yawning and stretching, behind her.

" Sh!" hissed Mrs. Brill. " Sh!"

She put her finger to her lips and tip-toed to Mrs. Banks' door.

" *Tch, tch!* You can't see nothing but the wardrobe," she complained, as she bent to look through the key-hole. " The wardrobe and a bit of the winder."

But the next moment she started violently.

" My Glory-goodness!" she shrieked, as the door burst open suddenly, and she fell back against Robertson Ay.

For there, framed against the light, stood Mary Poppins, looking very stern and suspicious. In her arms she carried, with great care, something that looked like a bundle of blankets.

" Well!" said Mrs. Brill, breathlessly. " If it isn't you! I was just polishing the door-knob, putting a shine on it, so to say, as you came out."

Mary Poppins looked at the door-knob. It was very dirty.

" Polishing the key-hole is what *I* should have said!" she remarked tartly.

But Mrs. Brill took no notice. She was gazing tenderly at the bundle. With her large red hand she drew aside a fold of one of the blankets, and a satisfied smile spread over her face.

"Ah!" she cooed. "Ah, the Lamb! Ah, the Duck!

Ah, the Trinket! And as good as a week of Sundays, I'll be bound!"

Robertson Ay yawned again and stared at the bundle with his mouth slightly open.

"Another pair of shoes to clean!" he said mournfully, leaning against the banisters for support.

"Mind you don't drop it, now!" said Mrs. Brill anxiously, as Mary Poppins brushed past her.

Mary Poppins glanced at them both contemptuously.

337

"If I were *some* people," she remarked acidly, "I'd mind my own business!"

And she folded the blanket over the bundle again and went upstairs to the Nursery. . . .

"Excuse me, please! Excuse me!" Mr. Banks came rushing up the stairs, nearly knocking Mrs. Brill over as he hurried into Mrs. Banks' bedroom.

"Well!" he said, sitting down at the foot of the bed. "This is all Very Awkward. Very Awkward indeed. I don't know that I can afford it. I hadn't bargained for five."

"I'm so sorry!" said Mrs. Banks, smiling at him happily.

"You're not sorry, not a bit. In fact, you're very pleased and conceited about it. And there's no reason to be. It's a very small one."

"I like them that way," said Mrs. Banks. "Besides, it will grow."

"Yes, unfortunately!" he replied bitterly. "And I shall have to buy it shoes and clothes and a tricycle. Yes, and send it to school and give it a Good Start in Life. A very expensive proceeding. And then, after all that, when I'm an old man sitting by the fire, it will go away and leave me. You hadn't thought of that, I suppose?"

"No," said Mrs. Banks, trying to look sorry, but not succeeding. "I hadn't."

"I thought not. Well, there it is. But, I warn you! I shall not be able to afford to have the bathroom retiled."

"Don't worry about that," said Mrs. Banks comfortingly. "I really like the old tiles best."

"Then you're a very stupid woman. That's all I have to say."

And Mr. Banks went away, muttering and blustering through the house. But when he got outside the front door, he flung back his shoulders, and pushed out his chest, and put a large cigar into his mouth. And, soon after that, he was heard telling Admiral Boom the news in a voice that was very loud and conceited and boastful. . . .

Mary Poppins stooped over the new cradle between John's and Barbara's cots and laid the bundle of blankets carefully in it.

"Here you are at last! Bless my Beak and Tail-feathers—I thought you were never coming! Which is it?" cried a croaking voice from the window.

Mary Poppins looked up.

The Starling who lived on the top of the Chimney was hopping excitedly on the window-sill.

"A girl. Annabel," said Mary Poppins shortly. "And I'll thank you to be a little quieter. Squawking and croaking there like a packet of magpies!"

But the Starling was not listening. He was turning somersaults on the window-sill, clapping his wings wildly together each time his head came up.

"What a treat!" he panted, when at last he stood up straight. "What a *Treat*! Oh, I could sing!"

"You couldn't. Not if you tried till Doomsday!" scoffed Mary Poppins.

But the Starling was too happy to care.

"A girl!" he shrieked, dancing on his toes. "I've had three broods this season and—would you believe it?—every one of them boys. But Annabel will make up to me for that!"

He hopped a little along the sill. "Annabel!" he burst out again. "That's a nice name! I had an Aunt called Annabel. Used to live in Admiral Boom's chimney, and died, poor thing, of eating green apples and grapes. I warned her! I warned her! But she wouldn't believe me! So, of course——"

"Will you be quiet!" demanded Mary Poppins, making a dive at him with her apron.

"I will not!" he shouted, dodging neatly. "This is no time for silence. I'm going to spread the news."

He swooped out of the window.

"Back in five minutes!" he screamed at her over his shoulder, as he darted away.

Mary Poppins moved quietly about the Nursery, putting Annabel's new clothes in a neat pile.

The Sunlight, slipping in at the window, crept across the room and up to the cradle.

"Open your eyes," it said softly, "and I'll put a shine on them!"

The coverlet of the cradle trembled. Annabel opened her eyes.

"Good girl!" said the Sunlight. "They're blue, I see. My favourite colour! There! You won't find a brighter pair of eyes anywhere!" It slipped lightly out of Annabel's eyes and down the side of the cradle.

"Thank you very much!" said Annabel politely.

A warm Breeze stirred the muslin flounces at her head.

"Curls or straight?" it whispered, dropping into the cradle beside her.

"Oh, curls, please!" said Annabel softly.

"It does save trouble, doesn't it?" agreed the Breeze. And it moved over her head, carefully turning up the feathery edges of her hair, before it fluttered off across the room.

" Here we are! Here we are!"

A harsh voice shrilled from the window. The Starling had returned to the sill. And behind him, wobbling uncertainly as he alighted, came a very young bird.

Mary Poppins moved towards them threateningly.

" Now you be off!" she said angrily. " I'll have no sparrers littering up this Nursery——"

But the Starling, with the young one at his side, brushed haughtily past her.

" Kindly remember, Mary Poppins," he said icily, " that *all* my families are properly brought up. Littering, indeed!"

He alighted neatly on the edge of the cradle and steadied the Fledgling beside him.

The young bird stared about him with round, inquisitive eyes. The Starling hopped along to the pillow.

" Annabel, dear," he began, in a husky, wheedling voice, " I'm very partial to a nice, crisp, crunchy piece of Arrowroot Biscuit." His eyes twinkled greedily. " You haven't one about you, I suppose?"

The curled head stirred on the pillow.

" No? Well, you're young yet for biscuits, perhaps. Your sister Barbara—nice girl, she was, very generous and pleasant—always remembered me. So if, in the future, *you* could spare the old fellow a crumb or two——"

" Of course I will," said Annabel, from the folds of the blanket.

" That's the girl!" croaked the Starling, approvingly. He cocked his head on one side and gazed at her with his round, bright eye. " I hope," he remarked politely, " you are not too tired after your journey."

Annabel shook her head.

341

" Where has she come from—out of an egg?" cheeped the Fledgling suddenly.

" Huh-huh!" scoffed Mary Poppins. " Do you think she's a sparrer?"

The Starling gave her a pained and haughty look.

" Well, what is she, then? And where did she come

from?" cried the Fledgling shrilly, flapping his short wings and staring down at the cradle.

" *You* tell him, Annabel!" the Starling croaked.

Annabel moved her hands inside the blanket.

" I am earth and air and fire and water," she said softly. " I come from the Dark where all things have their beginning."

" Ah, such dark!" said the Starling softly, bending his head to his breast.

" It was dark in the egg, too!" the Fledgling cheeped.

" I come from the sea and its tides," Annabel went on. " I come from the sky and its stars; I come from the sun and its brightness——"

" Ah, so bright!" said the Starling, nodding.

" And I come from the forests of earth."

As if in a dream, Mary Poppins rocked the cradle—
to-and-fro, to-and-fro with a steady swinging movement.

" Yes?" whispered the Fledgling.

" Slowly I moved at first," said Annabel, " always
sleeping and dreaming. I remembered all I had been,
and I thought of all I shall be. And when I had dreamed
my dream, I awoke and came swiftly."

She paused for a moment, her blue eyes full of
memories.

" And then?" prompted the Fledgling.

" I heard the stars singing as I came and I felt warm
wings about me. I passed the beasts of the jungle and
came through the dark, deep waters. It was a long
journey."

Annabel was silent.

The Fledgling stared at her with his bright inquisitive
eyes.

Mary Poppins' hand lay quietly on the side of the
cradle. She had stopped rocking.

" A long journey, indeed!" said the Starling softly,
lifting his head from his breast. " And, ah, so soon
forgotten!"

Annabel stirred under the quilt.

" No!" she said, confidently. " I'll never forget."

" Stuff and Nonsense! Beaks and Claws! Of course
you will. By the time the week's out you won't remember a word of it—what you are or where you came
from!"

Inside her flannel petticoat Annabel was kicking
furiously.

" I will! I will! How could I forget?"

" Because they all do!" jeered the Starling harshly.
" Every silly human, except "—he nodded his head at
Mary Poppins—" her! She's different, she's the Oddity,
she's the Misfit——"

" You Sparrer!" cried Mary Poppins, making a dart
at him.

But with a rude laugh he swept his Fledgling off the
edge of the cradle and flew with him to the window-sill.

" Tipped you last!" he said cheekily, as he brushed
past Mary Poppins. " Hullo, what's that?"

There was a chorus of voices outside on the landing
and a clatter of feet on the stairs.

" I don't believe you! I won't believe you!" cried
Annabel wildly.

And at that moment Jane and Michael and the Twins
burst into the room.

" Mrs. Brill says you've got something to show us!"
said Jane, flinging off her hat.

" What is it?" demanded Michael, gazing round the
room.

" Show me! Me, too!" shrieked the Twins.

Mary Poppins glared at them. " Is this a decent Nursery or the Zoological Gardens?" she inquired angrily.
" Answer me that!"

" The Zoo—er—I mean——" Michael broke off
hurriedly, for he had caught Mary Poppins' eye. " I
mean a Nursery," he said lamely.

" Oh, look, Michael, look!" Jane cried excitedly.
" I told you something important was happening! It's
a New Baby! Oh, Mary Poppins, can I have it to
keep?"

Mary Poppins, with a furious glance at them all,
stooped and lifted Annabel out of the cradle and sat
down with her in the arm-chair.

She sat down in the old arm-chair

"Gently, please, gently!" she warned, as they crowded about her. "This is a baby, not a battleship!"

"A boy-baby?" asked Michael.

"No, a girl—Annabel."

Michael and Annabel stared at each other. He put his finger into her hand and she clutched it tightly.

"My doll!" said John, pushing up against Mary Poppins' knee.

"My rabbit!" said Barbara, tugging at Annabel's shawl.

"Oh!" breathed Jane, touching the hair that the wind had curled. "How very small and sweet! Like a star. Where *did* you come from, Annabel?"

Very pleased to be asked, Annabel began her story again.

"I came from the Dark——" she recited softly.

Jane laughed. "Such funny little sounds!" she cried. "I wish she could talk and tell us."

Annabel stared.

"But I *am* telling you!" she protested, kicking.

"Ha-ha!" shrieked the Starling rudely from the window. "What did I say? Excuse me laughing!"

The Fledgling giggled behind his wing.

"Perhaps she came from a Toy Shop," said Michael.

Annabel, with a furious movement, flung his finger from her.

"Don't be silly!" said Jane. "Doctor Simpson must have brought her in his little brown bag!"

"Was I right, or was I wrong?" The Starling's old dark eyes gleamed tauntingly at Annabel.

"Tell me that!" he jeered, flapping his wings in triumph.

But for answer Annabel turned her face against Mary

Poppins' apron and wept. Her first cries, thin and lonely, rang piercingly through the house.

"There! There!" said the Starling gruffly. "Don't take on! It can't be helped. You're only a human child after all. But next time, perhaps, you'll believe your Betters! Elders and Betters! Elders and Betters!" he screamed, prancing conceitedly up and down.

"Michael, take my feather duster, please, and sweep those birds off the sill!" said Mary Poppins ominously.

A squawk of amusement came from the Starling.

"We can sweep ourselves off, Mary Poppins, thank you! We were just going, anyway! Come along, Boy!"

And with a loud, clucking chuckle, he flicked the Fledgling over the sill and swooped with him through the window. . . .

In a very short time, Annabel settled down comfortably to life in Cherry Tree Lane. She enjoyed being the centre of attraction, and was always pleased when somebody leant over her cradle and said how pretty she was, or how good or sweet-tempered.

"Do go on admiring me!" she would say, smiling. "I like it so much!"

And then they would hasten to tell her how curly her hair was and how blue her eyes, and Annabel would smile in such a satisfied way that they would cry, "How intelligent she is! You would almost think she understood!"

But *that* always annoyed her, and she would turn away in disgust at their foolishness. Which was silly, because when she was disgusted she looked so charming that they became more foolish than ever.

She was a week old before the Starling returned. Mary Poppins, in the dim light of the night-light, was gently rocking the cradle when he appeared.

" Back again?" snapped Mary Poppins, watching him prance in. " You're as bad as a bad penny!" She gave a long disgusted sniff.

" I've been busy!" said the Starling. " Have to keep my affairs in order. And this isn't the *only* Nursery I have to look after, you know!" His beady, black eyes twinkled wickedly.

" Humph!" she said shortly. " I'm sorry for the others!"

He chuckled, and shook his head.

" Nobody like her!" he remarked chirpily to the blind-tassel. " Nobody like her! She's got an answer for everything!" He cocked his head towards the cradle. " Well, how are things? Annabel asleep?"

" No thanks to you, if she is!" said Mary Poppins.

The Starling ignored the remark. He hopped to the end of the sill.

" I'll keep watch," he said, in a whisper. " You go down and get a cup of tea."

Mary Poppins stood up.

" Mind and don't wake her, then!"

The Starling laughed pityingly.

" My dear girl, I have in my time brought up at least twenty broods of fledglings. I don't need to be told how to look after a mere baby."

" Humph!" Mary Poppins walked to the cupboard and very pointedly put the biscuit-tin under her arm before she went out and shut the door.

The Starling marched up and down the window-sill, backwards and forwards, with his wing-tips under his tail-feathers.

There was a small stir in the cradle. Annabel opened her eyes.

"Hullo!" she said. "I was wanting to see you."

"Ha!" said the Starling, swooping across to her.

"There's something I wanted to remember," said Annabel, frowning, "And I thought you might remind me."

He started. His dark eye glittered.

"How does it go?" he said softly. "Like this?"

And he began in a husky whisper: "I am earth and air and fire and water——"

"No, no!" said Annabel impatiently. "Of course it doesn't."

"Well," said the Starling anxiously, "was it about your journey? You came from the sea and its tides, you came from the sky and——"

"Oh, don't be so *silly*!" cried Annabel. "The only journey I ever took was to the Park and back again this morning. No, no—it was something *important*. Something beginning with B."

She crowed suddenly.

"I've got it!" she cried. "It's Biscuit. Half an Arrowroot Biscuit on the mantelpiece. Michael left it there after tea!"

"Is that all?" said the Starling sadly.

"Yes, of course," Annabel said fretfully. "Isn't it enough? I thought you'd be glad of a nice piece of biscuit!"

"So I am, so I am!" said the Starling hastily. "But——"

She turned her head on the pillow and closed her eyes.

"Don't talk any more now, please!" she said. "I want to go to sleep."

The Starling glanced across at the mantelpiece, and down again at Annabel.

"Biscuits!" he said, shaking his head. "Alas, Annabel, alas!"

Mary Poppins came in quietly and closed the door.

"Did she wake?" she said, in a whisper.

The Starling nodded.

"Only for a minute," he said sadly. "But it was long enough."

Mary Poppins' eyes questioned him.

"She's forgotten," he said, with a catch in his croak. "She's forgotten it all. I knew she would. But, ah, my dear, what a pity!"

"Humph!"

Mary Poppins moved quietly about the Nursery, putting the toys away. She glanced at the Starling. He was standing on the window-sill with his back to her, and his speckled shoulders were heaving.

"Caught another cold?" she remarked sarcastically.

He wheeled round.

"Certainly not! It's—ahem—the night air. Rather chilly, you know. Makes the eyes water. Well—I must be off!"

He waddled unsteadily to the edge of the sill. "I'm getting old," he croaked sadly. "That's what it is. Not so young as we were. Eh, Mary Poppins?"

"I don't know about *you*"—Mary Poppins drew herself up haughtily—"but I'm *quite* as young as I was, thank you!"

"Ah," said the Starling, shaking his head, "you're a

Wonder. An Absolute, Marvellous, Wonderful Wonder!" His round eye twinkled wickedly.

"I don't think!" he called back rudely, as he dived out of the window.

"Impudent Sparrer!" she shouted after him, and shut the window with a bang. . . .

Chapter Six

ROBERTSON AY'S STORY

"Step along, please!" said Mary Poppins, pushing the perambulator, with the Twins at one end of it and Annabel at the other, towards her favourite seat in the Park.

It was a green one, quite near the Lake, and she chose it because she could bend sideways, every now and again, and see her own reflection in the water. The sight of her face, gleaming between two water-lilies always gave her a pleasant feeling of satisfaction and contentment.

Michael trudged behind.

"We're always stepping along," he grumbled to Jane in a whisper, taking care that Mary Poppins did not hear him, "but we never seem to get anywhere."

Mary Poppins turned round and glared at him.

"Put your hat on straight!"

Michael tilted his hat over his eyes. It had *H.M.S. Trumpeter* printed on the band, and he thought it suited him very well.

But Mary Poppins was looking with contempt at them both.

"Humph!" she said. "You two look a picture, I must say! Stravaiging along like a couple of tortoises and no polish on your shoes."

"Well, it's Robertson Ay's Half-day," said Jane. "I suppose he didn't have time to do them before he went out."

"*Tch, tch!* Lazy, idle, Good-for-Nothing—that's what he is. Always was and always will be!" Mary Poppins said savagely, pushing the perambulator up against her own green seat.

She lifted out the Twins, and tucked the shawl tightly around Annabel. She glanced at her sunlit reflection in the Lake and smiled in a superior way, straightening the new bow of ribbon at her neck. Then she took her bag of knitting from the perambulator.

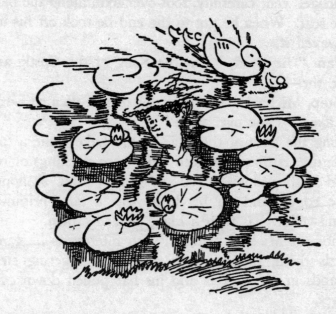

"How do you know he's always been idle?" asked Jane. "Did you know Robertson Ay before you came here?"

"Ask no questions and you'll be told no lies!" said Mary Poppins priggishly, as she began to cast on stitches for a woollen vest for John.

"She never tells us *anything*!" Michael grumbled.

"I know!" sighed Jane.

But very soon they forgot about Robertson Ay and began to play Mr.-and-Mrs.-Banks-and-Their-Two-Children. Then they became Red Indians with John and Barbara for squaws. And after that they changed into Tight-Rope-Walkers with the back of the green seat for a rope.

" Mind my hat—*if* you please!" said Mary Poppins. It was a brown one with a pigeon's feather stuck into the ribbon.

Michael went carefully, foot over foot, along the back of the seat. When he got to the end he took off his hat and waved it.

" Jane," he cried, " I'm the King of the Castle and you're the——"

" Stop, Michael!" she interrupted, and pointed across the Lake. " Look over there!"

Along the path at the edge of the Lake came a tall, slim figure, curiously dressed. He wore stockings of red striped with yellow, a red-and-yellow tunic scalloped at the edges, and on his head was a large-brimmed red-and-yellow hat with a high, peaked crown.

Jane and Michael watched with interest as he came towards them, moving with a lazy, swaggering step, his hands in his pockets and his hat pulled down over his eyes.

He was whistling loudly, and as he drew nearer they saw that the peaks of his tunic and the brim of his hat were edged with little bells that jingled musically as he moved. He was the strangest person they had ever seen, and yet—there was something about him that seemed familiar.

" I think I've seen him before," said Jane, frowning and trying to remember.

"So have I. But I can't think where." Michael balanced on the back of the seat and stared.

Whistling and jingling, the curious figure slouched up to Mary Poppins and leaned against the perambulator.

"'Day, Mary!" he said, putting a finger lazily to the brim of his hat. "And how are you keeping?"

Mary Poppins looked up from her knitting.

"None the better for your asking," she said, with a loud sniff.

Jane and Michael could not see the man's face for the brim of his hat was well pulled down, but from the way the bells jingled they knew he was laughing.

"Busy as usual, I see!" he remarked, glancing at the knitting. "But then, you always were, even at Court. If you weren't dusting the Throne you'd be making the King's bed, and if you weren't doing that you were polishing the Crown Jewels. I never knew such a one for work!"

"Well, it's more than anyone could say for you!" said Mary Poppins crossly.

"Ah," laughed the Stranger, "that's just where you're wrong! I'm always busy. Doing nothing takes a great deal of time! All the time, in fact!"

Mary Poppins pursed up her lips and made no reply.

The Stranger gave an amused chuckle. "Well, I must be getting along," he said. "See you again some day!"

He brushed a finger along the bells of his hat and sauntered lazily away, whistling as he went.

Jane and Michael watched until he was out of sight.

"The Dirty Rascal!"

Mary Poppins' voice rapped out behind them, and they turned to find that she, too, was staring after the Stranger.

" Who was that man, Mary Poppins?" asked Michael, bouncing excitedly up and down on the seat.

" I've just told you," she snapped. " You said you were the King of the Castle—and you're not, not by any means! But that's the Dirty Rascal."

" You mean the one in the Nursery Rhyme?" demanded Jane breathlessly.

" But Nursery Rhymes aren't true, are they?" protested Michael. " And if they are, who *is* the King of the Castle?"

" Hush!" said Jane, laying her hand on his arm.

Mary Poppins had put down her knitting and was gazing out across the Lake with a far-away look in her eyes.

Jane and Michael sat very still, hoping, if they made no sound, she would tell them the whole story. The Twins huddled together at one end of the perambulator, solemnly staring at Mary Poppins. Annabel, at the other end, was sound asleep.

The King of the Castle (began Mary Poppins, folding her hands over her ball of wool and gazing right through the children as though they were not there), the King of the Castle lived in a country so far away that most people have never heard of it. Think as far as you can, and it's even further than that; think as high as you can, and it's higher than that; think as deep as you can, and it's even deeper.

And, she went on, if I were to tell you how rich he was, we'd be sitting here till next year and still be only half-way through the list of his treasures. He was enormously, preposterously, extravagantly rich. In fact, there was only one thing in the whole world that he did not possess.

And that thing was wisdom.

His land was full of gold mines; his people were polite and prosperous and generally splenderiferous. He had a good wife and four fat children—or perhaps it was five. He never could remember the exact number because his memory was so bad.

His Castle was made of silver and granite, and his coffers were full of gold, and the diamonds in his crown were as big as duck's eggs.

He had many marvellous cities, and sailing-ships at sea. And for his right-hand man he had a Lord High Chancellor who knew exactly What was What and What was Not and advised the King accordingly.

But the King himself had no wisdom. He was utterly and absolutely foolish and, what was more, he knew it! Indeed, he could hardly help knowing it for everybody, from the Queen and the Lord High Chancellor downwards, was constantly reminding him of the fact. Even bus-conductors and engine-drivers and the people who served in shops could hardly refrain from letting the King know *they* knew he had no wisdom. They didn't dislike him, they merely felt a contempt for him.

It was not the King's fault that he was so stupid. He had tried and tried to learn wisdom ever since he was a boy. But, in the middle of his lessons, even when he was grown up, he would suddenly burst into tears and, wiping his eyes on his ermine train, would cry:

" I know I shall never be any good at it—never! So why nag at me?"

But still his teachers continued to make the effort. Professors came from all over the world to try to teach the King of the Castle something—even if it was only

Twice-Times-Two or C-A-T cat. But none of them had the slightest effect on him.

Then the Queen had an idea.

"Let us," she said to the Lord High Chancellor, "offer a reward to the Professor who can teach the King a little wisdom! And if, at the end of a month, he has not succeeded, his head shall be cut off and spiked on the Castle gates as a warning to other Professors of what will happen if they fail."

And, as most of them were rather poor and the reward was a large money-prize, the Professors kept on coming, and failing, and losing hope, and also their heads. And the spikes of the Castle gates became rather crowded.

Things went from bad to worse. And at last the Queen said to the King:

"E t h e l b e r t !" (t h a t w a s t h e King's p r i v a t e name), "I really think you had bet- ter l e a v e the government of the Kingdom to me and the Lord High Chancellor, as we both know a good deal about every- thing!"

"But that wouldn't be fair!" said the King, protesting. "After all, it's my Kingdom!"

However, he gave in at last, because he knew she was cleverer than he. But he so much resented being ordered about in his own Castle, and having to use the bent sceptre because he always chewed the knob of the best one, that he went on receiving the Professors and trying to learn wisdom and weeping when he found he couldn't. He wept for their sakes as well as his own, for it made him unhappy to see their heads on the gate.

Each new Professor arrived full of hope and assurance and began with some question that the last had not asked.

"What are six and seven, Your Majesty?" inquired a young and handsome Professor who had come from a great distance.

And the King, trying his hardest, thought for a moment. Then he leant forward eagerly and answered—

"Why, twelve, of course!"

"*Tch, tch, tch!*" said the Lord High Chancellor, standing behind the King's Chair.

The Professor groaned.

"Six and seven are *thirteen,* Your Majesty!"

"Oh, I'm *so* sorry! Try another question, please, Professor! I am sure I shall get the next one right."

"Well, then, what are five and eight?"

"Um—er—let me see! Don't tell me, it's just at the tip of my tongue. Yes! Five and eight are eleven!"

"*Tch, tch, tch!*" said the Lord High Chancellor.

"*THIRTEEN!*" cried the young Professor hopelessly.

"But, my dear fellow, you just said that six and seven were thirteen, so how can five and eight be? There aren't two thirteens, surely?" asked the King.

But the young Professor only shook his head and loosened his collar and went dejectedly away with the Executioner.

"*Is* there more than one thirteen, then?" asked the King nervously.

The Lord High Chancellor turned away in disgust.

"I'm sorry," said the King to himself. "I liked his face so much. It's a pity it has to go on the gate."

And after that he worked very hard at his Arithmetic, hoping that when the next Professor came, he would be able to give the right answers.

He would sit at the top of the Castle steps, just by the drawbridge, with a book of Multiplication Tables on his knees, saying them over to himself. And while he was looking at the book everything went well, but when he shut his eyes and tried to remember them everything went wrong.

"Seven ones are seven, seven twos are thirty-three, seven threes are forty-five——" he began one day. And when he found he was wrong he threw the book away in disgust and buried his head in his cloak.

"It's no good, it's no good! I shall never be wise!" he cried in despair.

Then, because he could not go on weeping for ever, he wiped his eyes and leant back in his golden chair. And as he did that, he gave a little start of surprise. For a stranger had pushed past the sentry at the gate and was walking up the path that led to the Castle.

"Hullo," said the King, "who are you?" For he had no memory for faces.

"Well, if it comes to that," replied the Stranger, "who are *you*?"

"I'm the King of the Castle," said the King, picking up the bent sceptre and trying to look important.

" And I'm the Dirty Rascal," was the reply.

The King opened his eyes wide with astonishment.

" Are you really, though? That's interesting! I'm very pleased to meet you. Do you know Seven times Seven?"

" No. Why should I?"

At that the King gave a great cry of delight and, running down the steps, embraced the Stranger.

" At last, at last!" cried the King, " I have found a friend! You shall live with me! What is mine shall be yours! We shall spend our lives together!"

" But, Ethelbert," protested the Queen, " this is only a Common Person. You cannot have him here."

" Your Majesty," said the Lord High Chancellor sternly, " *it would not do.*"

But for once the King defied him.

" It will do very nicely!" he said royally. " Who is King here—you or I?"

" Well, of course, in a manner of speaking, *you* are, as it were, Your Majesty, but——"

" Very well. Put this man in cap and bells and he can be my Fool!"

" Fool!" cried the Queen, wringing her hands. " Do we need any more of these?"

But the King did not answer. He flung his arm round the Stranger's neck and the two went dancing to the Castle door.

" You first!" said the King politely.

" No, you!" said the Stranger.

" Both together, then!" said the King generously, and they went in side by side.

And from that day the King made no attempt to learn his lessons. He made a pile of all his books and

burnt them in the courtyard while he and his new friend
danced round it singing:

> " I'm the King of the Castle,
> And you're the Dirty Rascal!"

" Is that the only song you can sing?" asked the Fool
one day.

" Yes, I'm afraid it is!" said the King, rather sadly.
" Do you know any others?"

" Oh, dear, yes!" said the Fool. And he sang sweetly:

> " Bright, bright
> Bee, in your flight
> Drop down some Honey
> For Supper to-night!"

and

> " Sweet and low, over the Snow,
> The lolloping, scalloping Lobsters go—
> Did you know?"

and

> " Boys and Girls, come out to play
> Over the Hills and Far Away,
> The Sheep's in the Meadow, the Cow's in the Stall,
> And down will come Baby, Cradle and All!"

" Lovely!" cried the King, clapping his hands. " Now
listen! I've just thought of one myself! It goes like this:

> " All Dogs—Tiddle-de-um!
> Hate Frogs—Tiddle-di-do!"

" H'm!" said the Fool. " Not bad!"

" Wait a minute!" said the King. " I've thought of

another! And I think it's a better one. Listen, carefully!"

And he sang:

> " Pluck me a Flower,
>   And catch me a Star,
>   And braize them in Butter
>   And Treacle and Tar.
>   Tra-la!
>   How delicious they are!"

" Bravo!" cried the Fool. " Let's sing it together!"

And he and the King went dancing through the Castle, chanting the King's two songs, one after the other, to a very special tune.

And when they were tired of singing they fell together in a heap in the main corridor, and there went to sleep.

" He gets worse and worse!" said the Queen to the Lord High Chancellor. " What *are* we to do?"

" I have just heard," replied the Lord High Chancellor, " that the wisest man in the kingdom, the Chief of all the Professors, is coming to-morrow. Perhaps he will help us!"

And the next day the Chief Professor arrived, walking smartly up the path to the Castle, carrying a little black bag. It was raining slightly but the whole Court had gathered at the top of the steps to welcome him.

" Has he got his wisdom in that little bag, do you think?" whispered the King. But the Fool, who was playing knuckle-bones beside the throne, only smiled, and went on tossing.

" Now, if Your Majesty pleases," said the Chief Professor, in a business-like voice, " let us take Arithmetic first. Can Your Majesty answer this? If two Men and a Boy were wheeling a Barrow over a Clover-field, in the middle of February, how many Legs would they have between them?"

The King gazed at him for a moment, rubbing his sceptre against his cheek.

The Fool tossed a knuckle-bone and caught it neatly on the back of his wrist.

"Does it matter?" said the King, smiling pleasantly.

The Chief Professor started violently and looked at the King in astonishment.

"As a matter of fact," he said quietly, "it doesn't. But I will ask Your Majesty another question. How deep is the Sea?"

"Deep enough to sail a ship on."

Again the Chief Professor stared, and his long beard quivered. He was smiling.

"What is the difference, Majesty, between a Star and a Stone, a Bird and a Man?"

"No difference at all, Professor. A Stone is a Star that shines not. A man is a Bird without wings."

The Chief Professor drew nearer, and gazed wonderingly at the King.

"What is the best thing in the world?" he asked quietly.

"Doing Nothing," answered the King, waving his bent sceptre.

"Oh, dear, oh, dear!" wailed the Queen. *"This is dreadful!"*

"Tch! Tch! Tch!" said the Lord High Chancellor.

But the Chief Professor ran up the steps and stood by the King's throne.

"Who taught you these things, Majesty?" he demanded.

The King pointed with his sceptre to the Fool, who was throwing up his knuckle-bones.

" How deep is the Sea?"

"Him," said the King, ungrammatically.

The Chief Professor raised his bushy eyebrows. The Fool looked up at him and smiled. He tossed a knuckle-bone, and the Professor, bending forward, caught it on the back of his hand.

"Ha!" he cried. "I know you! Even in that cap and bells, I know the Dirty Rascal!"

"Ha, ha!" laughed the Fool.

"What else did he teach you, Majesty?" The Chief Professor turned again to the King.

"To sing," answered the King.

And he stood up and sang:

> "A black and white Cow
> Sat up in a Tree
> And if I were she
> Then I shouldn't be me!"

"Very true," said the Chief Professor. "What else?" The King sang again, in a pleasant, quavering voice:

> "The Earth spins round
> Without a tilt
> So that the Sea
> Shall not be spilt."

"So it does," remarked the Chief Professor. "Any more?"

"Oh, Gracious, yes!" said the King delighted at his success. "There's this one:

> "Oh, I could learn
> Until I'm pink,
> But then I'd have
> No time to think.

"Or perhaps, Professor, you'd prefer:

"We won't go round
The World, for then
We'd only come
Back Home again!"

The Chief Professor clapped his hands.

"There's one more," said the King, "if you'd care to hear it."

"Please sing it, Sire!"

And the King cocked his head at the Fool and smiled wickedly and sang:

"Chief Professors
All should be
Drowned in early
Infancee!"

At the end of the song the Chief Professor gave a loud laugh and fell at the King's feet.

"Oh, King," he said, "live for ever! You have no need for me!"

And without another word he ran down the steps and took off his overcoat, coat, and waistcoat. Then he flung himself down upon the grass and called for a plate of Strawberries-and-Cream, and a large glass of Beer.

"*Tch! Tch! Tch!*" said the horrified Lord High Chancellor. For now all the Courtiers were rushing down the steps and taking off their coats and rolling in the rainy grass.

"Strawberries and Beer! Strawberries and Beer!" they shouted thirstily.

"Give *him* the prize!" said the Chief Professor, sucking his Beer through a straw, and nodding in the direction of the Fool.

"Pooh!" said the Fool. "I don't want it. What would I do with it?"

And he scrambled to his feet, put his knuckle-bones in his pocket, and strolled off down the path.

"Hi, where are you going?" cried the King anxiously.

"Oh, anywhere, everywhere!" said the Fool airily, sauntering on down the path.

"Wait for me, wait for me!" called the King, stumbling over his train as he hurried down the steps.

"Ethelbert! What *are* you doing? You forget yourself!" cried the Queen angrily.

"I do not, my dear!" the King called back. "On the contrary, I am remembering myself for the first time!"

He hurried down the path, caught up with the Fool, and embraced him.

"Ethelbert!" called the Queen again.

The King took no notice.

The rain had ceased but there was still a watery brightness in the air. And presently a rainbow streamed out of the sun and curved in a great arc down to the Castle Path.

"I thought we might take this road," said the Fool, pointing.

"What? The rainbow? Is it solid enough? Will it hold us?"

"Try!"

The King looked at the rainbow and its shimmering stripes of violet, blue and green and yellow and orange and red. Then he looked at the Fool.

"All right, I'm willing!" he said. "Come on!" He stepped up to the coloured path.

"It holds!" cried the King, delightedly. And he ran swiftly up the Rainbow, his train gathered in his hand.

"I'm the King of the Castle!" he sang triumphantly.

"And I'm the Dirty Rascal!" called the Fool, running after him.

"But—it's impossible!" said the Lord High Chancellor, gasping.

The Chief Professor laughed and swallowed another strawberry.

"How can anything that truly happens be impossible?" he inquired.

"But it is! It must be! It's against all the Laws!" The face of the Lord High Chancellor was purple with anger.

A cry burst from the Queen.

"Oh, Ethelbert, come back!" she implored. "I don't mind how foolish you are if you'll only come back!"

The King glanced down over his shoulder and shook his head. The Fool laughed loudly. Up and up they went together, steadily climbing the rainbow.

Something curved and shining fell at the Queen's

feet. It was the bent sceptre. A moment later it was followed by the King's crown.

She stretched out her arms imploringly.

But the King's only answer was a song, sung in his high, quavering voice:

> "Say good-bye, Love,
> Never cry, Love,
> You are wise,
> And so am I, Love!"

The Fool, with a contemptuous flick of his hand, tossed her down a knuckle-bone. Then he gave the King a little push, and urged him onwards.

The King picked up his train and ran, and the Fool pounded at his heels. On and on they went up the bright, coloured path, until a cloud passed between them and the earth, and the watching Queen saw them no longer.

> "You are wise,
> And so am I, Love!"

The echo of the King's song came floating back. She

heard the last thin thread of it after the King himself had disappeared.

"*Tch! Tch! Tch!*" said the Lord High Chancellor. "Such things are simply *not done*!"

But the Queen sat down upon the empty throne and wept.

"Aie!" she cried softly, behind the screen of her hands. "My King is gone and I am very desolate, and nothing will ever be the same again."

Meanwhile, the King and the Fool had reached the top of the rainbow.

"What a climb!" panted the King, sitting down and wrapping his cloak about him. "I think I shall sit here for a bit—perhaps for a long time. You go on!"

"You won't be lonely?" the Fool inquired.

"Oh, dear, no! Why should I be? It is very quiet and pleasant up here. And I can always think—or, better still, go to sleep." And as he said that, he stretched himself out upon the rainbow with his cloak under his head.

The Fool bent down and kissed him.

"Good-bye, then, King!" he said softly. "For you no longer have any need of me."

He left the King quietly sleeping, and went whistling down the other side of the rainbow.

And from there he went wandering the world again, as he had done in the days before he met the King, singing and whistling, and taking no thought for anything but the immediate moment.

Sometimes he took service with other Kings and high people, and sometimes he went among ordinary men living in small streets or lanes. Sometimes he would be wearing gorgeous livery and sometimes clothes as poor as anyone ever stood up in. But no matter where he went he brought good fortune and great luck to the house that roofed him. . . .

Mary Poppins ceased speaking. For a moment her hands lay still in her lap and her eyes gazed out unseeingly across the Lake.

Then she sighed and gave her shoulders a little shake and stood up.

" Now then," she said briskly. " Best Feet Forward! And off home!"

She turned to find Jane's eyes fixed steadily upon her.

" You'll know me next time, I hope!" she remarked tartly. " And you, Michael, get down off that seat at once! Do you want to break your neck and give me the trouble of calling a Policeman?"

She strapped the Twins into the perambulator and pushed it in front of her with a quick, impatient movement.

Jane and Michael fell into step behind.

" I wonder where the King of the Castle went when the rainbow disappeared?" said Michael thoughtfully.

" He went with it, I suppose, wherever it goes," said Jane. " But what *I* wonder is—what happened to the Rascal?"

Mary Poppins had wheeled the perambulator into the Elm Walk. And, as the children turned the corner, Michael caught Jane's hand.

" There he is!" he cried excitedly, pointing down the Elm Walk to the Park Gates.

A tall, slim figure, curiously dressed in red and yellow,

was swaggering towards the entrance. He stood for a moment, looking up and down Cherry Tree Lane, and whistling. Then he slouched across to the opposite pavement and swung himself lazily over one of the garden fences.

"It's ours!" said Jane, recognising it by the brick that had always been missing. "He's gone into our garden. Run, Michael! Let's catch up with him!"

They ran at a gallop after Mary Poppins and the perambulator.

"Now then, now then! No horse-play, please!" said Mary Poppins, grabbing Michael's arm firmly as he rushed by.

"But we want——" he began, squirming.

"*What did I say?*" she demanded, glaring at him so fiercely that he dared not disobey. "Walk beside me, please, like a Christian. And Jane, you can help me push the pram!"

Unwillingly Jane fell into step beside her.

As a rule, Mary Poppins allowed nobody to push the perambulator except herself. But to-day it seemed to Jane that she was purposely preventing them from running ahead. For here was Mary Poppins, who usually walked so quickly that it was difficult to keep up with her, going at a snail's pace down the Elm Walk, pausing every few minutes to gaze about her, and standing for at least a minute in front of a basket of litter.

At last, after what seemed to them like hours, they came to the Park Gates. She kept them beside her until they reached the gate of Number Seventeen. Then they broke from her and went flying through the garden.

They darted behind the lilac tree. Not there!

They searched among the rhododendrons and looked

in the glass-house, the tool-shed, and the water-butt. They even peered into a circle of hose-piping. The Dirty Rascal was nowhere to be seen!

There was only one other person in the garden, and that was Robertson Ay. He was sound asleep in the middle of the lawn, with his cheek against the knives of the lawn-mower.

" We've missed him!" said Michael. " He must have taken a short cut and gone out by the back way. Now we'll never see him again."

He turned back to the lawn-mower.

Jane, standing beside it, looked down affectionately at Robertson Ay. His old felt hat was pulled over his face, its crown crushed and dented into a curving peak.

" I wonder if he had a good Half-day!" said Michael, whispering so as not to disturb him.

But, small as the whisper was, Robertson Ay must have heard it. For he suddenly stirred in his sleep and settled himself more comfortably against the lawn-mower. And as he moved there was a faint, jingling sound as though, near at hand, small bells were softly ringing.

With a start Jane lifted her head and glanced at Michael.

" Did you hear?" she whispered.

He nodded, staring.

Robertson Ay moved again and muttered in his sleep. They bent to listen.

" Black-and-white Cow," he murmured indistinctly. " Sat up in a Tree . . . mumble, mumble, mumble . . . it couldn't be me! Hum . . .!"

Across his sleeping body Jane and Michael gazed at each other with wondering eyes.

" Humph! Well to be him, I must say!"

Mary Poppins had come up behind them, and she, too, was staring down at Robertson Ay.

" The lazy, idle, Good-for-Nothing!" she said crossly.

But she couldn't really have been as cross as she sounded, for she took her handkerchief out of her pocket and slipped it between Robertson Ay's cheek and the lawn-mower.

" He'll have a clean face, anyway, when he wakes up. *That'll* surprise him!" she said tartly.

But Jane and Michael noticed how careful she had been not to waken Robertson Ay, and how soft her eyes were when she turned away.

They tip-toed after her, nodding wisely to one another. Each knew that the other understood.

Mary Poppins trundled the perambulator up the steps and into the hall. The front door shut with a quiet little click.

Outside in the garden Robertson Ay slept on. . . .

That night when Jane and Michael went to say Good Night to him, Mr. Banks was in a towering rage. He was dressing to go out to dinner and he couldn't find his best stud.

"Well, by All that's Lively, here it is!" he cried suddenly. "In a tin of stove-blacking—of all things, on my dressing-table! That Robertson Ay's doing. I'll sack that fellow one of these days. He's nothing but a dirty rascal!"

And he could not understand why Jane and Michael, when he said that, burst into such joyous peals of laughter. . .

Chapter Seven

THE EVENING OUT

" WHAT, no pudding?" said Michael, as Mary Poppins, her arms full of plates, mugs, and knives, began to lay the table for Nursery Tea.

She turned and looked at him fiercely.

" This," she snapped, " is my Evening Out. So you will eat bread and butter and strawberry jam and be thankful. There's many a little boy would be glad to have it."

" *I'm* not," grumbled Michael. " I want rice-pudding with honey in it."

" You want! You want! You're always wanting. If it's not this it's that, and if it's not that it's the other. You'll ask for the Moon next."

Michael put his hands in his pockets and moved sulkily away to the window-seat. Jane was kneeling there, staring out at the bright, frosty sky. He climbed up beside her, still looking very cross.

" All right, then! I *do* ask for the Moon. So there!" He flung the words back at Mary Poppins. " But I know I shan't get it. Nobody ever gives me anything."

He turned hurriedly away from her angry glare.

" Jane," he said, " there's no pudding."

" Don't interrupt me, I'm counting!" said Jane, pressing her nose against the window-pane so that it was quite blunt and squashed at the tip.

" Counting what?" he asked, not very interested. His mind was full of rice-pudding and honey.

377

" Shooting stars. Look, there goes another! That's seven. And another! Eight. And one over the Park— that's nine! "

" O-o-h! And there's one going down Admiral Boom's chimney! " said Michael, sitting up suddenly, and forgetting all about the pudding.

" And a little one—see!—streaking right across the Lane. Such frosty lights! " cried Jane. " Oh, *how* I wish we were out there! What makes the stars shoot, Mary Poppins? "

" Do they come out of a gun? " inquired Michael.

Mary Poppins sniffed contemptuously.

" What do you think I am? An Encyclopædia? Everything from A to Z? " she demanded crossly. " Come and eat your teas, please! " She pushed them towards their chairs and pulled down the blind. " And No Nonsense. I'm in a hurry! "

And she made them eat so quickly that they were both afraid they would choke.

" Mayn't I have just *one* more piece? " asked Michael, stretching out his hand to the plate of bread and butter.

" You may not. You have already eaten more than is good for you. Take a Ginger Biscuit and go to bed. "

" But—— "

" But me no buts or you'll be sorry! " she flung at him sternly.

" I shall have indigestion, I know I shall! " he said to Jane, but only in a whisper, for when Mary Poppins looked like that it was wiser not to make any remark at all. Jane took no notice. She was slowly eating her Ginger Biscuit and peering cautiously out at the frosty sky through a chink in the blind.

" Thirteen, Fourteen, Fifteen, Sixteen—— "

"Did I or did I not say *bed*?" inquired the familiar voice behind them.

"All right! I'm just going, Mary Poppins!"

And they ran squealing to the Night Nursery, with Mary Poppins hurrying after them and looking Simply Awful.

Less than half an hour later she was tucking each one in tightly, pushing the sheets and blankets under the mattress with sharp, furious little stabs.

"There!" she said, snapping the words between her lips. "That's all for to-night. And if I hear One Word ——" She did not finish the sentence but her look said all that was necessary.

"There'll be Trouble!" said Michael, finishing it for her. But he whispered it under his breath to his blanket, for he knew what would happen if he said it aloud. She whisked out of the room, her starched apron rustling and crackling, and shut the door with an angry click. They heard her light feet hurrying away down the stairs —*Tap-tap, Tap-tap*—from landing to landing.

"She's forgotten to light the night-light," said Michael, peering round the corner of his pillow. "She *must* be in a hurry. I wonder where she's going?"

"And she's left the blind up!" said Jane, sitting up in bed. "Hooray, now we can watch the shooting stars!"

The pointed roofs of Cherry Tree Lane were shiny with frost, and the moonlight slid down the gleaming slopes and fell soundlessly into the dark gulfs between the houses. Everything glimmered and shone. The earth was as bright as the sky.

"Seventeen-Eighteen-Nineteen-Twenty——" said Jane, steadily counting as the stars shot down. As fast as one disappeared another came to take its place, until it seemed that the whole sky was alive and dancing with the dazzle of shooting stars.

" It is like fireworks," said Michael. " Oh, look at that one! Or the Circus. Do you think they have circuses in Heaven, Jane?"

" I'm not sure!" said Jane doubtfully. " There's the Great Bear and the Little Bear, of course, and Taurus-the-Bull and Leo-the-Lion. But I don't know about a Circus."

" Mary Poppins would know," said Michael nodding wisely.

" Yes, but she wouldn't tell," said Jane, turning again to the window. " Where was I? Was it Twenty-One? Oh, Michael, *such* a beauty—do you see?" She bounced excitedly up and down in her bed, pointing to the window.

A very bright star, larger than any they had yet seen, was shooting through the sky towards Number Seventeen Cherry Tree Lane. It was different from the others for, instead of leaping straight across the dark, it was turning over and over, curving through the air very curiously.

" Duck your head, Michael!" shouted Jane suddenly. " It's coming in here!" They dived down into the blankets and burrowed their heads under the pillows.

" Do you think it's gone now?" came Michael's muffled voice presently. " I'm nearly smothercated."

" Of course I haven't gone!" A small, clear voice answered him. " What do you take me for?"

Very surprised, Jane and Michael threw off the bed-clothes and sat up. There, at the end of the window-sill, perched on its shiny tail and gleaming brightly at them, was the shooting star.

" Come on, you two! Be quick!" it said, shining frostily across the room.

Michael stared at it.

"You mean—we're to come with you?" said Jane.

"Of course. And mind you wrap up. It's chilly!"

They sprang out of their beds and ran for overcoats.

"Got any money?" the star asked sharply.

"There's twopence in my coat pocket," said Jane doubtfully.

"Coppers? They'll be no good! Here, catch!" And with a little sizzling sound, as though a firework squib was going off, the star sent out a shower of sparks. Two of them shot right across the room and landed, one in Jane's hand and one in Michael's.

"Hurry, or we'll be late!"

The star streaked across the room, through the closed door and down the stairs, with Jane and Michael, tightly clasping their starry money, after it.

"Can I be dreaming, I wonder?" said Jane to herself, as she hurried through the garden.

"Follow!" cried the star as, at the end of the Lane, where the frosty sky seemed to come down to meet the pavement, it leapt into the air and disappeared.

"Follow! Follow!" came the voice. "Just as you are, step on a star!"

Jane seized Michael's hand and raised her foot uncertainly from the pavement. To her surprise she found that the lowest star in the sky was easily within her reach. She stepped up, balancing carefully. The star seemed quite steady and solid.

"Come on, Michael!"

They hurried up the frosty sky, leaping over the gulfs between the stars.

"Follow!" cried the voice, far ahead of them. Jane paused, and glancing down, caught her breath to see how high they were. Cherry Tree Lane—indeed, the whole world—was as small and sparkling as a toy on a Christmas Tree.

"Are you giddy, Michael?" she said, springing on to a large, flat star.

"N-o-o. Not if you hold my hand."

They paused. Behind them the great stairway of stars led down to earth, but before them there were no more to be seen, nothing but a thick blue patch of naked sky.

Michael's hand trembled in Jane's.

"W-w-what shall we do now?" he said, in a voice that tried not to sound frightened.

"Walk up! Walk up! Walk up and see the sights! Pay your money and take your choice! The two-Tailed Dragon or the Horse with Wings! Magical Marvels! Universal Wonders! Walk up! Walk up!"

A loud voice seemed to be shouting these words in their very ears. They stared about them. There was no sign of anybody.

"Step along, everybody! Don't miss the Golden Bull and the Comical Clown! World-Famous Troupe of Performing Constellations! Once seen never forgotten! Push aside the curtain and walk in!"

Again the voice sounded close beside them. Jane put out her hand. To her surprise she found that what seemed a plain and starless patch of sky was really a thick, dark curtain. She pressed against it and felt it yield, then gathered up a fold of it and, pulling Michael after her, pushed the curtain aside.

A bright flare of light dazzled them for a moment.

When they could see again they found themselves standing at the edge of a ring of shining sand. The great blue curtain enfolded the ring on all sides and was drawn up to a point above as though it were a tent.

"Now, then! Do you know you were almost too late? Got your tickets?"

They turned. Beside them, his bright feet gleaming in the sand, stood a strange and gigantic figure. He looked like a hunter, for a starry leopard-skin was slung across his shoulders, and from his belt, decorated with three large stars, hung down a shining sword.

"Tickets, please!" He held out his hand.

"I'm afraid we haven't got any. You see, we didn't know——" began Jane.

"Dear, dear, how careless! Can't let you in without a ticket, you know. But what's that in your hands?"

Jane held out the golden spark.

"Well, if that isn't a ticket, I'd like to know what is!" He pressed the spark between his three large stars. "Another shiner for Orion's belt!" he remarked pleasantly.

"Is that who you are?" said Jane, staring at him.

"Of course—didn't you know? But—excuse me, I must attend to the door. Move along, please!"

The children, feeling rather shy, moved on hand in hand. Tier on tier of seats rose up at one side of them and at the other a golden cord separated them from the ring. And the ring itself was crowded with the strangest collection of animals, all shining bright as gold. A Horse with great gold Wings pranced by on glittering hooves. A golden Fish threshed up the dust of the ring with its fin. Three Little Kids were rushing wildly about on two legs instead of four. And it seemed to Jane and Michael, as they looked closer, that all these animals were made of stars. The wings of the Horse were

of stars, not feathers; the Three Kids had stars on their noses and tails, and the Fish was covered with shining, starry scales.

"Good evening!" it remarked, bowing politely to Jane as it threshed by. "Fine night for the performance!"

But before Jane could reply it had hurried past.

"How very strange!" said she. "I've never seen animals like this before!"

"Why should it be strange?" said a voice behind them.

Two children, both boys a little older than Jane, stood there smiling. They were dressed in shining tunics and their peaked caps had each a star for a pom-pom.

"I beg your pardon," said Jane, politely. "But, you see, we're used to—er—fur and feathers, and these animals seem to be made of stars."

"But, of course they are!" said the first boy, opening

his eyes very wide. "What else could they be made of? They're the Constellations!"

"But even the saw-dust is gold . . ." began Michael.

The second boy laughed. "Star-dust, you mean! Haven't you been to a Circus before?"

"Not this kind."

"All circuses are alike," said the first boy. "Our animals are brighter, that's all."

"But who are you?" demanded Michael.

"The Twins. He's Pollux and I'm Castor. We're always together."

"Like the Siamese Twins?"

"Yes. But more so. The Siamese Twins are only joined in body, but we have a single heart and mind between us. We can think each other's thoughts and dream each other's dreams. But we mustn't stay here talking. We've got to get ready—see you later!" And the Twins ran off and disappeared through a curtained exit.

"Hullo!" said a gloomy voice from inside the ring. "I suppose you don't happen to have a Currant Bun in your pocket?"

A Dragon with two large finny tails lumbered towards them, breathing steam from its nostrils.

"I'm sorry, we haven't," said Jane.

"Not a biscuit or two?" said the Dragon eagerly.

They shook their heads.

"I thought not," he grumbled, dropping a golden tear. "It's always the way on Circus nights. I don't get fed till after the performance. On ordinary occasions I have a beautiful maiden for supper."

Jane drew back quickly, pulling Michael with her.

"Oh, don't be alarmed!" the Dragon went on, reassuringly. "You'd be *much* too small. Besides, you're

human and therefore tasteless. They keep me hungry,"
he explained, "so that I shall do my tricks better. But
after the show . . ." A greedy light came into his eyes
and he shuffled away, lolling out his tongue and saying
"Yum-yum" in a soft, greedy, hissing voice.

"I'm glad we're only human," said Jane, turning to
Michael. "It would be *dreadful* to be eaten by a
Dragon!"

But Michael had hurried on ahead and was talking
eagerly to the Three Little Kids.

"How does it go?" he was asking, as Jane caught up
with him.

And the Eldest Kid, which apparently had offered
to recite, cleared his throat, and began:

> "Horn and toe,
> Toe and horn——"

"Now, Kids!" Orion's voice interrupted loudly.
"You can say your piece when the time comes. Get
ready now, we're going to begin! Follow me, please!"
he said to the children.

They trotted obediently after the gleaming figure,
and as they went the golden animals turned to stare at
them. They heard snatches of whispered conversation
as they passed.

"Who's that?" said a starry Bull, as it stopped pawing
the star-dust to gaze at them. And a Lion turned and
whispered something into the Bull's ear. They caught
the words "Banks" and "Evening Out," but heard no
more than that.

But now every seat on every tier was filled with a
shining, starry figure. Only three empty seats remained,
and to these Orion led the children.

"Here you are! We kept these for you. Just under

the Royal Box. You'll see perfectly. Look! they're just beginning!"

And, turning, Jane and Michael saw that the ring was empty. The animals had hurried out while they had been climbing to their seats. The children unbuttoned their overcoats and leaned forward excitedly.

From somewhere came a fanfare of trumpets. A blast of music echoed through the tent, and above the sound could be heard a high, sweet neighing.

"The comets!" said Orion, sitting down beside Michael.

A wild, nodding head appeared at the entrance, and one by one nine comets galloped into the ring, their manes braided with gold, and silver plumes on their heads.

Suddenly the music rose to a great roar of sound, and with one movement the comets dropped upon their knees and bowed their heads. A warm gust of air came wafting across the ring.

"How hot it's getting!" cried Jane.

"Hush! He's coming!" cried Orion.

"Who?" whispered Michael.

"The Ring-Master!"

Orion nodded to the far entrance. A light shone there, eclipsing the light of the constellations. It grew steadily brighter.

"Here he is!" Orion's voice had a curious softness in it.

And as he spoke there appeared between the curtains a towering, golden figure with flaming curls upon his head and a wide, radiant face. And with him came a great swell of warmth that lapped the ring and spread out in ever-widening circles until it surrounded Jane and Michael and Orion. Half-consciously, made dreamy by that warmth, the children slipped off their overcoats.

Orion sprang to his feet holding his right hand above his head.

" Hail, Sun, hail!" he cried. And, from the stars in the tiered seats, the cry came echoing:

" Hail!"

The Sun glanced round the wide dark-tented ring and, in answer to the greeting, swung his long gold whip three times about his head. As the lash turned in the air there was a quick, sharp crack. At once the comets sprang up and cantered out, their braided tails swinging wildly, their plumed heads high and erect.

" Here we are again, here we are again!" cried a loud, hoarse voice. And bouncing into the ring came a comical figure with silver-painted face, wide red mouth and huge silvery frills about his neck.

" Saturn—the Clown!" whispered Orion behind his hand to the children.

" When is a Door not a Door?" demanded the Clown of the audience, turning over and standing on one hand.

" When it's ajar!" answered Jane and Michael loudly.

A disappointed look came over the Clown's face.

" Oh, you know it!" he said, reproachfully. " That's not fair!"

The Sun cracked his whip.

" All right, all right!" said the Clown. " I've got another. Why does a Hen cross the Road?" he asked, sitting down with a bump on the star-dust.

" To get to the other side!" cried Jane and Michael together.

The swinging whip caught the Clown round the knees.

"O-o-h! Don't do that! You'll hurt poor Joey. Look at them laughing up there! But I'll fix them. Listen!"

He turned a double somersault in the air.

"What kind of jam did the Chicken ask for when it came out of the Egg? Tell me that!"

"Mar—me—lade!" yelled Michael and Jane.

"Be off with you!" cried the Sun, catching his whip about the Clown's shoulders; and the Clown went bounding round the ring, head over heels, crying:

"Poor old Joey! He's failed again! They know all his best jokes, poor old fellow, poor old—oh, beg pardon, Miss, beg pardon."

He broke off, for he had somersaulted against Pegasus, the Winged Horse, as it entered carrying a bright, spangly figure on its back.

"Venus, the Evening Star," explained Orion.

Breathlessly, Jane and Michael watched the starry figure ride lightly through the ring. Round and round she went, bowing to the Sun as she passed, and presently the Sun, standing in her path, held up a great hoop covered with thin, gold paper.

She balanced on her toes for a moment. "Hup!" said the Sun. And Venus, with the utmost grace, jumped through the hoop and landed again on the back of Pegasus.

"Hurrah!" cried Jane and Michael; and the audience of stars echoed back "Hurrah!"

"Let me try! Let poor Joey have a go, just a little one to make a cat laugh!" cried the Clown. But Venus only tossed her head and laughed and rode out of the ring.

She had hardly disappeared before the Three Kids came prancing in, looking rather shy and bowing awkwardly to the Sun. Then they stood on their hind legs

389

in a row before him, and, in high, thin voices, recited
the following song:

> "Horn and hoof,
> Hoof and horn,
> Every night
> Three Kids are born,
> Each with a Twinkly Nose,
> Each with a Twinkly Tail.
>
> Blue and black,
> Black and blue
> Is the evening sky
> As the Kids come through,
> Each with a Twinkly Nose,
> Each with a Twinkly Tail.
>
> Gay and bright
> And white as May
> The Three Kids drink
> At the Milky Way,
> Each with a Twinkly Nose,
> Each with a Twinkly Tail.
>
> All night long
> From Dusk till Dawn
> The Three Kids graze
> On the starry lawn,
> Each with a Twinkly Nose,
> Each with a twink-ker-ly T-a-i-l!"

They drew out the last line with a long baa-ing sound
and danced out.

"What's next?" asked Michael. But there was no
need for Orion to reply, for the Dragon was already in

the ring, his nostrils steaming and his two finny tails tossing up the star-dust.

After him came Castor and Pollux, carrying between them a large, white, shining globe faintly figured with a design of mountains and rivers.

" It looks like the Moon!" said Jane.

" Of course it's the Moon!" said Orion.

The Dragon was now on its hind legs and the Twins

were balancing the Moon on his nose. It bobbed up and down uncertainly for a moment. Then it settled, and the Dragon began to waltz. Round he went, very carefully and steadily, once, twice, three times.

" That will do!" said the Sun, cracking his whip. And the Dragon, with a sigh of relief, shook its head and sent the Moon flying across the ring. It landed, with a bumpy thud, right in Michael's lap.

" Good gracious!" said he, very startled. " What shall I do with this?"

" Whatever you like," said Orion. " I thought you asked for it."

And suddenly Michael remembered his conversation

that evening with Mary Poppins. He had asked for the Moon then and now he had got it. And he didn't know what to do with it. How very awkward!

But he had no time to worry about it, for the Sun was cracking his whip again. Michael settled the Moon on his knee, folded his arms around it and turned back to the ring.

"What are two and three?" the Sun was asking the Dragon.

The two tails lashed five times on the star-dust.

"And six and four?" The Dragon thought for a minute. One, two, three, four, five, six, seven, eight, nine—— The tails stopped.

"Wrong!" said the Sun. "Quite wrong! No supper for you to-night!"

At that the Dragon burst into tears and hurried from the ring sobbing.

> "Alas and alack,
> Boo-hoo, boo-hoo!"

he cried bitterly.

> "I wanted a Maiden
> Served in a stew,
> A succulent, seasoned, tasty Girl
> With a star for her eye
> And a comet for curl,
> And I wouldn't have minded if there'd been two,
> For I'm awfully hungry.
> > Boo-hoo!
> > Boo-hoo!"

"Won't they give him even a small maiden?" said Michael, feeling rather sorry for the Dragon.

"Hush!" said Orion, as a dazzling form sprang into the ring.

When the cloud of star-dust had cleared away, the children drew back, startled. It was the Lion, and he was growling fiercely.

Michael moved a little closer to Jane.

The Lion, crouching, moved forward slowly till he reached the Sun. His long, red tongue went out, lolling dangerously. But the Sun only laughed, and, lifting his foot, he gently kicked the Lion's golden nose. With a roar, as though he had been burnt, the starry beast sprang up.

The Sun's whip cracked fiercely on the air. Slowly, unwillingly, growling in his throat, the Lion rose on his hind legs. The Sun tossed him a skipping-rope and, holding it between his forepaws, the Lion began to sing :

> "I am the Lion, Leo-the-Lion,
> The beautiful, suitable, Dandy Lion.
> Look for me up in the starry sky on
> Clear, cold nights at the foot of Orion,
> Glimmering, glittering, gleaming there,
> The Handsomest Sight in the atmosphere!"

And at the end of the song he swung the rope and skipped round the ring, rolling his eyes and growling horribly.

"Hurry up, Leo, it's our turn!" A rumbling voice sounded from behind the curtains.

"Come on, you big cat!" a shrill voice added.

The Lion dropped his skipping-rope and, with a roar, sprang at the curtain, but the two creatures who entered next stepped carefully aside so that the Lion missed them.

" Great Bear and Little Bear !" said Orion.

Slowly the two Bears lumbered in, holding paws and waltzing to slow music. Round the ring they went, looking very serious and solemn, and at the end of their dance they made a clumsy curtsey to the audience and remarked :

" We're the Gruffly bear and the Squeaky Bear,
    O Constellations, has anyone here
    A Honeycomb-Square that they can spare
    For the Squeaky Bear and the Gruffly Bear
    To add to the store in their dark blue lair
    Or to——
            or to——
                    or to——"

The Great Bear and the Little Bear stammered and stumbled and looked at each other.

" Don't you remember what comes next?" rumbled the Gruffly Bear behind his paw.

" No, I don't!" The Squeaky Bear shook his head and stared anxiously down at the star-dust as though he thought the missing words might be there.

But at that moment the audience saved the situation. A shower of Honeycombs came hurtling down, tumbling about the ears of the two Bears. The Gruffly Bear and the Squeaky Bear, looking very relieved, stooped and picked them up.

" Good!" rumbled the Great Bear, digging his nose into a comb.

" *Ex*-cellent!" squeaked the Little Bear, trying another. Then, with their noses streaming with honey, they bowed solemnly to the Sun and lumbered out.

The Sun waved his hand and the music rang triumphantly through the tent.

" The signal for the Big Parade," said Orion, as Castor and Pollux came dancing in with all the Constellations at their heels.

The Bears came back, waltzing clumsily together; and Leo, the Lion, still growling angrily, came sniffing at their heels. In swept a starry Swan, singing a high, clear chant.

" The Swan Song," said Orion.

And after the Swan came the Golden Fish, leading the Three Kids by a silver string, and the Dragon followed, still sobbing bitterly. A loud and terrible sound almost drowned the music. It was the bellowing of Taurus, the Bull, as he leapt into the ring, trying to toss Saturn the Clown from his back. One after another the creatures came rushing in to take their places. The ring was a swaying golden mass of horns and hooves and manes and tails.

" Is this the end?" Jane whispered.

" Almost," replied Orion. "They're finishing early to-night. She has to be in by half-past ten."

" Who has?" asked both the children together. But Orion did not hear. He was standing up in his seat waving his arm.

" Come along, be quick there, step along!" he called.

And in came Venus riding her Winged Horse, followed by a starry Serpent that, with its tail tucked into its mouth, bowled round the ring like a hoop.

Last of all came the comets, prancing proudly through the curtains, swinging their braided tails. The music was louder now and wilder, and a golden smoke rose up from the star-dust as the constellations, shouting, singing, roaring, growling, formed themselves into a ring. And in the centre, as though they dared not go too near his presence, they left a clear, bare circle for the Sun.

He stood, towering above them all, his whip folded in his arms. He nodded lightly to each animal as it passed him with bent head. And then Jane and Michael saw that bright gaze lift from the ring and wander round the audience of stars until it turned in the direction of the Royal Box. They felt themselves growing warmer as his rays fell upon them and, with a start of surprise, they saw him raise his whip and nod his head towards them.

As the lash swung up, every star and constellation turned in its tracks. Then, with one movement, every one of them bowed.

"Are they—can they be bowing to *us*?" whispered Michael, clutching the Moon more tightly.

A familiar laugh sounded behind them. They turned quickly. There, sitting alone in the Royal Box, was a well-known figure in a straw hat and blue coat with a gold locket round its neck.

"Hail, Mary Poppins, hail!" came the massed voices from the Circus Ring.

Jane and Michael looked at each other. So this was what Mary Poppins did on her Evening Out! They could hardly believe their eyes—and yet, there *was* Mary Poppins, as large as life, and looking very superior.

"Hail!" came the cry again.

Mary Poppins raised her hand in greeting.

Then, stepping primly and importantly, she moved out of the box. She did not seem in the least surprised to see Jane and Michael, but she sniffed as she went past.

"How often," she remarked to them across Orion's head, "have you been told that it is rude to stare?"

She passed on and down to the ring. The Great Bear lifted the golden rope. The Constellations drew apart

" *How often,*" she remarked, " *have you been told
that it is rude to stare?*"

and the Sun moved a pace forward. He spoke, and his voice was warm and full of sweetness.

"Mary Poppins, my dear, you are welcome!"

Mary Poppins dropped to her knees in a deep curtsey.

"The Planets hail you, and the Constellations give you greeting. Rise, my child!"

She stood up, bending her head respectfully before him.

"For you, Mary Poppins," the Sun went on, "the Stars have gathered in the dark blue tent, for you they have been withdrawn to-night from shining on the world. I trust, therefore, that you have enjoyed your Evening Out!"

"I never had a better one. Never!" said Mary Poppins, lifting her head and smiling.

"Dear child!" The Sun bowed. "But now the sands of night are running out and you must be in by half-past ten. So, before you depart, let us all, for old times' sake, dance the Dance of the Wheeling Sky!"

"Down you go!" said Orion to the astonished children, giving them a little push. They stumbled down the stairs and almost fell into the star-dust ring.

"And where, may I ask, are your manners?" hissed the well-known voice in Jane's ear.

"What must I do?" stammered Jane.

Mary Poppins glared at her and made a little movement towards the Sun. And, suddenly, Jane realised. She grabbed Michael's arm, and, kneeling, pulled him down beside her. The warmth from the Sun lapped about them with fiery sweetness.

"Rise, children," he said kindly. "You are very welcome. I know you well—I have looked down upon you many a summer's day!"

Scrambling to her feet, Jane moved towards him, but

398

his whip held her back. "Touch me not, Child of Earth!" he cried warningly, waving her further away. "Life is sweet and no man may come near the Sun—touch me not!"

"But are you truly the Sun!" demanded Michael, staring at him.

The Sun flung out his hand.

"O Stars and Constellations," he said, "tell me this. Who am I? This child would know!"

"Lord of the Stars, O Sun!" answered a thousand starry voices.

"He is King of the South and North," cried Orion, "and Ruler of the East and West. He walks the outer rim of the world and the Poles melt in his glory. He draws up the leaf from the seed and covers the land with sweetness. He is truly the Sun."

The Sun smiled across at Michael.

"Now do you believe?"

Michael nodded.

"Then, strike up! And you, Constellations, choose your Partners!"

The Sun waved his whip. The music began again, very swift and gay and dancey. Michael began to beat time with his feet as he hugged the Moon in his arms. But he squeezed it a little too tightly for, suddenly, there was a loud pop and the Moon began to dwindle.

"Oh! Oh! Look what's happening!" cried Michael, almost weeping.

Down, down, down, shrank the Moon until it was as small as a soap bubble, then it was only a wisp of shining light and then—his hands closed upon empty air.

"It couldn't have been a real Moon, could it?" he demanded.

Jane glanced questioningly at the Sun across the little stretch of star-dust.

He flung back his flaming head and smiled gently at her.

"What is real and what is not? Can you tell me or I you? Perhaps we shall never know more than this—that to think a thing is to make it true. And so, if Michael thought he had the real Moon in his arms—why, then, he had indeed."

"Then," said Jane wonderingly, "is it true that we are here to-night, or do we only think we are?"

The Sun smiled again, a little sadly.

"Child," he said, "seek no further! From the beginning of the world all men have asked that question. And I, who am Lord of the Sky—even I do not know the answer. I am only certain that this is the Evening Out, that the Constellations are shining in your eyes, and it is true if you think it is. . . ."

"Come, dance with us, Jane and Michael!" cried the Twins.

And Jane forgot her question as the four of them swung out into the ring in time with the heavenly tune. But they were hardly half-way round before she stumbled and stood still.

"Look! Look! She is dancing with him!"

Michael followed her gaze and stood still on his short, fat legs, staring.

Mary Poppins and the Sun were dancing together. But not as Jane and he were dancing with the Twins, breast to breast and foot to foot. Mary Poppins and the Sun never once touched, but waltzed with arms outstretched, opposite each other, keeping perfect time together in spite of the space between them.

About them wheeled the dancing Constellations, Venus with her arms round the neck of Pegasus, the Bull and the Lion arm-in-arm, and the Three Kids prancing in a row. Their moving brightness dazzled the children's eyes as they stood in the star-dust gazing.

Then suddenly the dance slackened and the music died away. The Sun and Mary Poppins, together yet apart, stood still. And at the same time every animal paused in the dance and stood patiently in its tracks. The whole ring was silent.

The Sun spoke.

"Now," he said quietly, "the time has come. Back to your places in the sky, my Stars and Constellations. Home and to sleep, my three dear mortal guests. Mary Poppins, good-night! I do not say Good-bye for we shall meet again. But—for a little time—Farewell, Farewell!"

Then, with a large and gracious movement of his head, the Sun leaned across the space that separated him from Mary Poppins and, with great ceremony, carefully, lightly, swiftly, he brushed her cheek with his lips.

"Ah!" cried the Constellations, enviously. "The Kiss! The Kiss!"

But as she received it, Mary Poppins' hand flew to her cheek protectingly, as though the kiss had burnt it.

A look of pain crossed her face for a moment. Then, with a smile, she lifted her head to the Sun.

"Farewell!" she said softly, in a voice Jane and Michael had never heard her use.

"Away!" cried the Sun, stretching out his whip. And obediently the Constellations began to rush from the ring. Castor and Pollux joined arms protectingly about the children, that the Great Bear might not brush them as he lumbered by, nor the Bull's horns graze them, nor the Lion do them harm.

But in Jane's ears and Michael's the sounds of the ring were growing fainter. Their heads fell sideways, dropping heavily upon their shoulders. Other arms came round them and, as if in a dream, they heard the voice of Venus saying—"Give them to me! I am the Homeward Star. I bring the lamb to the fold and the child to its Mother."

They gave themselves up to her rocking arms, swinging lightly with her as a boat swings with the tide.

To and fro, to and fro.

A light flickered across their eyes. Was that the Dragon going brightly by or the Nursery candle held guttering above them?

To and fro, to and fro.

They nestled down into soft, sweet warmth. Was it the lapping heat of the Sun? Or the eiderdown on a Nursery bed?

"I think it is the Sun," thought Jane, dreamily.

"I think it is my eiderdown," thought Michael.

And a far-away voice, like a dream, like a breath, cried faintly, faintly—"It is whatever you think it is. Farewell . . . Farewell. . . ."

Michael woke with a shout. He had suddenly remembered something.

"My overcoat! My overcoat! I left it under the Royal Box!"

He opened his eyes. He saw the painted duck at the end of his bed. He saw the mantelpiece with the Clock and the Royal Doulton Bowl and the Jam-jar full of green leaves. And he saw, hanging on its usual hook, his overcoat with his hat just above it.

"But where are the Stars?" he called, sitting up in bed and staring. "I want the Stars and Constellations!"

"Oh? Indeed?" said Mary Poppins, coming into the room and looking very stiff and starched in her clean apron. "Is that all? I wonder you don't ask for the Moon, too!"

"But I did!" he reminded her reproachfully. "And I got it, too! But I squeezed it too tight and it bust!"

"Burst!"

"Well, burst, then!"

"Stuff!" she said, tossing him his dressing-gown.

"Is it morning already?" said Jane, gazing round the room and feeling very surprised to find herself in her own bed. "But how did we get back? I was dancing with the Twin stars, Castor and Pollux."

"You two and your stars!" said Mary Poppins crossly, pulling back the blankets. "I'll star you. Spit-spot out of bed, please! I'm late already."

"I suppose you danced too long last night," said Michael, bundling unwillingly out on to the floor.

"Danced? Humph, a lot of dancing I get a chance for, looking after the five worst children in the world!"

Mary Poppins sniffed and looked very sorry for herself, as if she hadn't had enough sleep.

"But weren't you dancing—on your Evening Out?" said Jane. For she was remembering how Mary Poppins and the Sun had waltzed together in the centre of the star-dust ring.

Mary Poppins opened her eyes wide. " I hope," she remarked, drawing herself up haughtily, " I have something better to do with my Evening Out than to go round and round like a Careering Whirligig."

" But I saw you!" said Jane. " Up in the sky. You jumped down from the Royal Box and went to dance in the ring."

Holding their breaths, she and Michael gazed at Mary Poppins as her face flushed red with fury.

" You," she said shortly, " have been having a nice sort of a nightmare, I must say. Who ever heard of me, a person in my position, jumping down from——"

" But I had the nightmare, too," interrupted Michael, " and it was lovely. Jane and I *saw* you!"

" What, jumping?"

" Er—yes—and dancing."

" In the sky?" He trembled as she came towards him. Her face was dark and terrible. " One more insult——" she said threateningly, " just *one more* and you'll find yourself dancing in the corner. So I warn you!"

He hurriedly looked the other way, and Mary Poppins, her very apron crackling with anger, flounced across the room to wake up the Twins.

Jane sat on her bed staring at Mary Poppins as she bent over the cots. Michael slowly put on his slippers and sighed. " We *must* have dreamt it after all," he said sadly. " I wish it had been true."

" It *was* true," said Jane, in a cautious whisper, her eyes still fixed on Mary Poppins.

" How do you know? Are you sure?"

" Look!" Mary Poppins' head was bent over Barbara's cot. Jane nodded towards it. "Look at her face!" she whispered in his ear.

Michael regarded Mary Poppins' face steadily. There was the black hair looped behind the ears, there the familiar blue eyes so like a Dutch doll's, and there were the turned-up nose and the red, shiny cheeks.

"I can't see anything——" he began, and broke off suddenly. For now, as Mary Poppins turned her head, he saw what Jane had seen.

Burning bright, in the very centre of her cheek, was a small, fiery mark. And, looking closer, Michael saw that it was curiously shaped. It was round, with curly, flame-shaped edges, and like a very small sun.

"You see?" said Jane softly. "That's where he kissed her." Michael nodded—once, twice, three times.

"Yes," he said, standing very still and staring at Mary Poppins. "I do see. I do. . . ."

Chapter Eight

BALLOONS and BALLOONS

" I WONDER, Mary Poppins," said Mrs. Banks, hurrying into the Nursery one morning, "if you will have time to do some shopping for me?"

And she gave Mary Poppins a sweet, nervous smile, as though she were uncertain what the answer would be.

Mary Poppins turned from the fire where she was airing Annabel's clothes.

" I might," she remarked, not very encouragingly.

" Oh, I see——" said Mrs. Banks, and she looked more nervous than ever.

" Or again—I might not," continued Mary Poppins, busily shaking out a woollen jacket and hanging it over the fire-guard.

" Well—in case you *did* have time, here is the list and here is a Pound Note. And, if there is any change left over, you may spend it!"

Mrs. Banks put the money on the chest of drawers.

Mary Poppins said nothing. She just sniffed.

" Oh!" said Mrs. Banks, suddenly remembering something, " and the Twins must walk to-day, Mary Poppins. Robertson Ay sat down on the perambulator this morning. He mistook it for an arm-chair. So it will have to be mended. Can you manage without it—and carry Annabel?"

Mary Poppins opened her mouth and closed it again with a snap.

"I," she remarked tartly, "can manage anything—and more, if I choose."

"I—I know!" said Mrs. Banks, edging towards the door. "You are a Treasure—a perfect Treasure—an absolutely wonderful and altogether suitable Treas——" Her voice died away as she hurried downstairs.

"And yet—and yet—I sometimes wish she wasn't!" Mrs. Banks remarked to her great-grandmother's portrait as she dusted the Drawing-room. "She makes me feel small and silly, as though I were a little girl again. And I'm not!" Mrs. Banks tossed her head and flicked a speck of dust from the Spotted Cow on the mantelpiece. "I'm a very important person and the Mother of five children. She forgets that!"

And she went on with her work, thinking out all the things she would like to say to Mary Poppins, but knowing all the time that she would never dare.

Mary Poppins put the list and the Pound Note into her bag, and in no time she had pinned on her hat and was hurrying out of the house with Annabel in her arms, and Jane and Michael, each holding the hand of a Twin, following as quickly as they could.

"Best foot forward, please!" she remarked, turning sternly upon them.

They quickened their pace, dragging the poor Twins with a shuffling sound along the pavement. They forgot that John's arms and Barbara's were being pulled very nearly out of their sockets. Their only thought was to keep up with Mary Poppins and see what she did with the change from the Pound Note.

"Two packets of candles, four pounds of rice, three of brown sugar, and six of caster; two tins of tomato-soup, and a hearth-brush; a pair of housemaid's gloves,

lf a stick of sealing-wax, one bag of flour, one fire-
hter, two boxes of matches, two cauliflowers, and a
ndle of rhubarb!"

Mary Poppins, hurrying into the first shop beyond
e Park, read out the list.

The Grocer, who was fat and bald and rather short
breath, took down the order as quickly as he could.

"One bag of housemaid's gloves——" he wrote, ner-
ously licking the wrong end of his blunt little pencil.

"Flour, I said!" Mary Poppins reminded him tartly.

The Grocer blushed as red as a mulberry.

"Oh, I'm sorry. No offence meant, I'm sure. Lovely
ay, isn't it? Yes. My mistake. One bag of house——er
—flour."

He hurriedly scribbled it down and added:

"Two boxes of hearth-brushes——"

"Matches!" snapped Mary Poppins.

The Grocer's hands trembled on his pad.

"Oh, of course. It must be the pencil—it seems to
rite all the wrong things. I must get a new one.
Matches, of course! And then you said——?" He
ooked up nervously and then down again at his little
tub of pencil.

Mary Poppins unfolded the list, read it out again in
n angry, impatient voice.

"Sorry," said the Grocer, as she came to the end,
' but the rhubarb's off. Would damsons do?"

"Certainly not. A packet of Tapioca."

"Oh, no, Mary Poppins—not Tapioca. We had that
ast week," Michael reminded her.

She glanced at him and then at the Grocer, and by
he look in her eye they both knew that there was no
ope. Tapioca it would be. The Grocer, blushing redder
han ever, went to get it.

" There won't be any change left if she goes on like this," said Jane, watching the pile of groceries being heaped up on the counter.

" She might have enough left over for an ounce of Acid-drops—but that's all," Michael said mournfully, as Mary Poppins took the Pound Note out of her bag.

" Thank you," she said, as the Grocer handed her the change.

" Thank *you*!" he remarked politely, leaning his arms on the counter. He smiled at her in a manner that was meant to be pleasant, and continued, " Keeps nice and fine, doesn't it?" He spoke proudly, as though he, him-self, had complete charge of the weather and had made it fine for her on purpose.

" We want rain!" said Mary Poppins, snapping her mouth and her hand-bag at the same time.

" That's right," said the Grocer hurriedly, trying not to offend her. " Rain's always pleasant."

" Never!" retorted Mary Poppins, tossing Annabel into a more comfortable position on her arm.

The Grocer's face fell. *Nothing* he said was right.

" I hope," he remarked, opening the door courteously for Mary Poppins, " that we shall be favoured with your further custom, Madam."

" Good-day!" Mary Poppins swept out.

The Grocer sighed.

" Here," he said, scrabbling hurriedly in a box near the door. " Take these. I meant no harm, truly I didn't. I only wanted to oblige."

Jane and Michael held out their hands. The Grocer slipped three Chocolate-drops into Michael's hand and two in Jane's.

" One for each of you, one for the two little ones,

and one for "—he nodded towards Mary Poppins' retreating figure—" her!"

They thanked the Grocer and hurried after Mary Poppins, munching their Chocolate-drops.

"What's that you're eating?" she demanded, looking
at the dark rim round Michael's mouth.

"Chocolates. The Grocer gave us one each. And one
for you." He held out the last Drop. It was very sticky.

"Like his impudence!" said Mary Poppins, but she
took the Chocolate-drop and ate it in two bites as though
she thoroughly enjoyed it.

"Is there much change left?" inquired Michael
anxiously.

"That's as may be."

She swept into the Chemist's and came out with a
cake of soap, a mustard plaster, and a tube of tooth-
paste.

Jane and Michael, waiting with the Twins at the door,
sighed heavily.

The Pound Note, they knew, was disappearing fast.

"She'll hardly have enough left over for a stamp, and,
even if she has, *that* won't be very interesting," said Jane.

"Now to the Cake shop!" said Mary Poppins, examining her list and darting in at a dark door. Through
the window they could see her pointing to a pile of
Macaroons. The assistant handed her a large bag.

"She's bought a dozen at least," said Jane sadly.
Usually, the sight of anybody buying a Macaroon filled
them with delight, but to-day they wished and wished
that there wasn't a Macaroon in the world.

"*Now* where?" demanded Michael, hopping from
one leg to the other in his anxiety to know if there was
any of the Pound Note left. He felt sure there couldn't
be, and yet—he hoped.

"Home," said Mary Poppins.

Their faces fell. There was no change, after all, not even a penny, or Mary Poppins would surely have spent it. But Mary Poppins, as she dumped the bag of Macaroons upon Annabel's chest and strode ahead, had such a look on her face that they did not dare to make any remark. They only knew that, for once, she had disappointed them and they felt they could not forgive her.

"But—this isn't the way home!" complained Michael, dragging his feet so that his toes scraped along the pavement.

"Isn't the Park on the way home, I'd like to know?" she demanded, turning fiercely upon him.

"Yes—but——"

"There are more ways than one of going through a Park," she remarked, and led them round to a side of it they had never seen before.

The sun shone warmly down. The tall trees bowed over the railings and rustled their leaves. Up in the branches two sparrows were fighting over a piece of straw. A fat squirrel hopped along the stone balustrade and sat up on his hindquarters, asking for nuts.

But to-day these things did not matter. Jane and Michael were not interested. All they could think of was the fact that Mary Poppins had spent the whole Pound Note on unimportant things and had kept nothing over.

Tired and disappointed, they trailed after her towards the Gates.

Over the entrance, a new one they had never seen before, spread a tall stone arch, splendidly carved with a Lion and a Unicorn. And beneath the arch sat an old, old woman, her face as grey as the stone itself, and as withered and wrinkled as a walnut. On her little old knees she held a tray piled up with what looked like small coloured strips of rubber; and above her head, tied firmly to the Park railings, a cluster of bright balloons bobbed and bounced and bounded.

"Balloons! Balloons!" shouted Jane. And, loosening her hand from John's sticky fingers, she ran towards the old woman. Michael bounded after her, leaving Barbara alone and lost in the middle of the pavement.

"Well, my deary-ducks!" said the Balloon Woman, in an old, cracked voice. "Which will you have? Take your choice! And take your time!" She leant forward and shook her tray in front of them.

"We only came to look," Jane explained. "We've got no money."

"*Tch, tch, tch!* What's the good of *looking* at a balloon? You've got to feel a balloon, you've got to hold a balloon, you've got to *know* a balloon. Coming to look! What good will that do you?"

The old woman's voice crackled like a little flame. She rocked herself on her stool.

Jane and Michael stared at her helplessly. They knew she was speaking the truth. But what could they do?

"When I was a girl," the old woman went on, "people really *understood* balloons. They didn't just come and look! They took—yes, they *took*! There wasn't a child that went through these gates without one. They wouldn't have insulted the Balloon Woman in those days by just looking and passing by!"

She bent her head back and gazed up at the bouncing balloons above her.

"Ah, my loves and doves!" she cried. "They don't understand you any more—nobody but the old woman understands. You're old-fashioned now. Nobody wants you!"

"We *do* want one!" said Michael stoutly. "But we haven't any money. *She* spent the whole Pound Note on——"

"And who is 'she'?" inquired a voice close behind him.

He turned, and his face went pink.

"I meant—er—that you—er——" he began nervously.

"Speak politely of your betters!" remarked Mary Poppins, and, stretching her arm over his shoulder, she put half-a-crown on the Balloon Woman's tray.

Michael stared at it, shining there among the limp unblown balloons.

"Then there *was* some change left over!" said Jane, wishing she had not thought so crossly of Mary Poppins.

The Balloon Woman, her old eyes sparkling, picked up the coin and gazed at it for a long moment.

"Shiny, shiny, King-and-Crown!" she cried. "I haven't seen one of these since I was a girl." She cocked her head at Mary Poppins. "Do you want a balloon, my lass?"

"*If* you please!" said Mary Poppins, with haughty politeness.

"How many, my deary-duck, how many?"

"Four!"

Jane and Michael, almost jumping out of their skins, turned and flung their arms round Mary Poppins.

"Oh, Mary Poppins, do you mean it? One each? Really?—really?"

"I hope I always say what I mean," she said primly, looking very conceited.

They sprang towards the tray and began to turn over the coloured balloon-cases.

The Balloon Woman slipped the silver coin into a pocket of her skirt. "There, my shiny!" she said, giving the pocket a loving pat. Then, with excited, trembling hands, she helped the children turn over the cases.

"Go carefully, my deary-ducks!" she warned them. "Remember, there's balloons *and* balloons. Take your choice and take your time. There's many a child got the wrong balloon and his life was never the same after."

"I'll have this one!" said Michael, choosing a yellow one with red markings.

"Well, let me blow it up and you can see if it's the right one," said the Balloon Woman.

She took it from him and with one gigantic puff blew it up. Zip! There it was. You could hardly think such a tiny person could have so much breath in her body. The yellow balloon, neatly marked with red, bobbed at the end of its string.

"But, I say!" said Michael, staring. "It's got my name on it!"

And, sure enough, the red markings on the balloon were letters spelling out the two words—"*Michael Banks.*"

"Aha!" cackled the Balloon Woman. "What did I tell you? You took your time and the choice was right!"

"See if mine is!" said Jane, handing the Balloon Woman a limp blue balloon.

She puffed and blew it up, and there appeared across the fat blue globe the words "*Jane Caroline Banks*" in large white letters.

"Is that your name, my deary-duck?" said the Balloon Woman.

Jane nodded.

The Balloon Woman laughed to herself, a thin, old cackling laugh, as Jane took the balloon from her and bounced it on the air.

"Me! Me!" cried John and Barbara, plunging fat hands among the balloon-cases. John drew out a pink one and, as she blew it up, the Balloon Woman smiled. There, round the balloon, the words could clearly be seen. "*John and Barbara Banks—one between them because they are twins.*"

"But," said Jane, "I don't understand. How did you know? You never saw us before."

"Ah, my deary-duck, didn't I tell you there was balloons *and* balloons and that these were extra-special?"

"But did you put the names on them?" said Michael.

"I?" the old woman chuckled. "Nary I!"

"Then who did?"

"Ask me another, my deary-duck! All I know is that the names *are* there! And there's a balloon for every single person in the world if only they choose properly."

"One for Mary Poppins, too?"

The Balloon Woman cocked her head and looked at Mary Poppins with a curious smile.

"Let her try!" She rocked herself on her little stool. "Take your choice and take your time! Choose and see!"

Mary Poppins sniffed importantly. Her hand hovered for a moment over the empty balloons and then pounced on a red one. She held it out at arm's length and, to their astonishment, the children saw it slowly filling with air of its own accord. Larger and larger it grew till it became the size of Michael's. But still it swelled until it was three times as large as any other balloon. And across it appeared in letters of gold the two words *Mary Poppins.*

The red balloon bounced through the air; the old woman tied a string to it, and, with a little cackling laugh, handed it back to Mary Poppins.

Up into the dancing air danced the four balloons. They tugged at their strings as though they wanted to be free of their moorings. Then the wind caught them and flung them backwards and forwards, to the North, to the South, to the East, to the West.

"Balloons *and* balloons, my deary-ducks! One for everybody if only they knew it!" cried the Balloon Woman happily.

At that moment an elderly gentleman in a top-hat, turning in at the Park Gates, looked across and saw the balloons. The children saw him give a little start. Then he hurried up to the Balloon Woman.

"How much?" he said, jingling his money in his pocket.

"Sevenpence-halfpenny. Take your choice and take your time!"

He took a brown one and the Balloon Woman blew it up. The words *"The Honourable William Wetherill Wilkins"* appeared on it in green letters.

"Good gracious!" said the elderly gentleman. "Good gracious, that's *my* name!"

"You chose well, my deary-duck. Balloons *and* balloons!" said the old woman.

The elderly gentleman stared at his balloon as it tugged at its string.

" Extraordinary!" he said, and blew his nose with a trumpeting sound. "Forty years ago, when I was a boy, I tried to buy a balloon here. But they wouldn't let me. Said they couldn't afford it. Forty years—and it's been waiting for me all this time. Most extraordinary!"

And he hurried away, bumping into the Arch because his eyes were fixed on the balloon. The children saw him giving little excited leaps in the air as he went.

" Look at him!" cried Michael, as the Elderly Gentleman bobbed higher and higher. But at that moment his own balloon began pulling at the string and he felt himself lifted off his feet.

" Hello, hello! How funny! Mine's doing it, too!"

" Balloons *and* balloons, my deary-duck!" said the Balloon Woman, and broke into her cackling laugh as the Twins, both holding their balloon by its single string, bounced off the ground.

" I'm going, I'm going!" shrieked Jane as she, too, was borne upwards.

" Home, please!" said Mary Poppins.

Immediately, the red balloon soared up, dragging Mary Poppins after. Up and down she bounced, with Annabel and the parcels in her arms. Through the Gates and above the path the red balloon bore Mary Poppins, her hat very straight, her hair very tidy, and her feet as trimly walking the air as they usually walked the earth. Jane and Michael and the Twins, tugged jerkily up and down by their balloons, followed her.

" Oh, oh, oh!" cried Jane, as she was whirled past the branch of an elm tree. "What a *delicious* feeling!"

" I feel as if I were made of air!" said Michael, knocking into a Park seat and bouncing off it again. "What a lovely way to go home!"

"O-o-h! E-e-e-h!" squeaked the Twins, tossing and bobbing together.

"Follow me, please, and don't dawdle!" said Mary Poppins, looking fiercely over her shoulder, for all the world as if they were walking sedately on the ground instead of being tugged through the air.

Past the Park Keeper's house they went and down the Lime Walk. The Elderly Gentleman was there, bouncing along ahead of them.

Michael turned for a moment and looked behind him.

"Look, Jane, look! Everybody's got one!"

She turned. In the distance a group of people, all carrying balloons, were being jerked up and down in the air.

"The Ice Cream Man has bought one!" she cried, staring and just missing a statue.

"Yes, and the Sweep! And there—do you see?—is Miss Lark!"

Across the lawn a familiar figure came bouncing, hatted and gloved, and holding a balloon bearing the name "*Lucinda Emily Lark.*" She bobbed across the Elm Walk, looking very pleased and dignified, and disappeared round the edge of a fountain.

By this time the Park was filling with people and every one of them had a balloon with a name on it, and everyone was bouncing in the air.

"Heave ho, there! Room for the Admiral! Where's my port? Heave ho!" shouted a huge, nautical voice, as Admiral and Mrs. Boom went rolling through the air. They held the string of a large white balloon with their name on it in blue letters.

"Masts and mizzens! Cockles and shrimps! Haul away, my hearties!" roared Admiral Boom, carefully avoiding a large oak tree.

The crowd of balloons and people grew thicker. There was hardly a patch of air in the park that was not rainbowy with balloons. Jane and Michael could see Mary Poppins threading her way primly among them and they, too, hurried as fast as they could through the throng, with John and Barbara bobbing at their heels.

"Oh, dear! Oh, dear! My balloon won't bounce me. I must have chosen the wrong one!" said a voice at Jane's elbow.

An old-fashioned lady with a quill in her hat and a feather boa round her neck was standing on the path just below Jane. At her feet lay a purple balloon across which was written in letters of gold, *"The Prime Minister."*

"What shall I do?" she cried. "The old woman at the Gates said 'Take your choice and take your time, my deary-duck!' And I did. But I've got the wrong one. *I'm* not the Prime Minister!"

"Excuse me, but I am!" said a voice at her side, as a tall man, very elegantly dressed and carrying a rolled umbrella, stepped up to her.

The lady turned. "Oh, then this is your balloon! Let me see if you've got mine!"

The Prime Minister, whose balloon was not bouncing him at all, showed it to her. Its name was *"Lady Muriel Brighton-Jones."*

"Yes, you have! We've got mixed!" she cried, and handing the Prime Minister his balloon, she seized her own. Presently they were off the ground, and flying among the trees, talking as they went.

"Are you married?" Jane and Michael heard Lady Muriel ask.

And the Prime Minister answered, "No. I can't find the right sort of middle-aged lady—not too young and not too old and rather jolly, because I'm so serious myself."

"Would I do?" said Lady Muriel Brighton-Jones. "I can enjoy myself quite a lot."

"Yes, I think you'd do very nicely," said the Prime Minister and, hand in hand, they joined the tossing throng.

By this time the Park was really rather crowded. Jane and Michael, bobbing across the lawns after Mary Poppins, constantly bumped into other bouncing figures who had bought balloons from the Balloon Woman. A tall man, wearing a long moustache, a blue suit and a helmet, was being tugged through the air by a balloon marked "*Police Inspector;*" and another, bearing the words "*Lord Mayor,*" dragged along a round, fat person in a three-cornered hat, a red overall, and a large, brass necklace.

"Move on, please! Don't crowd the Park. Observe the Regulations! All Litter to be deposited in the Rubbish Baskets!"

The Park Keeper, roaring and ranting, and holding a small, cherry-coloured balloon marked "*F. Smith,*" threaded his way through the crowd. With a wave of his hand he moved on two dogs—a bull-dog, with the word "*Cu*" written on his balloon, and a fox-terrier whose name appeared to be "*Albertine.*"

"Leave my dogs alone! Or I shall take your number and report you!" cried a lady whose balloon said she was "*The Duchess of Mayfield.*"

But the Park Keeper took no notice and went bobbing by, crying "All Dogs on a Lead! Don't crowd the Park!

By this time the Park was really rather crowded

No Smoking! Observe the Regulations!" till his voice was hoarse.

"Where's Mary Poppins?" said Michael, whisking up to Jane.

"There! Just ahead of us!" she replied and pointed to the prim, tidy figure that bounced at the end of the largest balloon in the Park. They followed it homewards.

"Balloons *and* balloons, m y d e a r y - ducks!" cried a cackling voice behind them.

And turning, they saw the Balloon Woman. Her tray was empty and there was not a balloon anywhere near her, but in spite of that she was flying through the air as though a hundred invisible balloons were drawing her onwards.

"Every one sold!" she screamed as she sped by. "There's a balloon for everyone if only they knew it. They took their choice and they took their time! And I've sold the lot! Balloons *and* balloons."

Her pockets jingled richly as she flew by and, standing still in the air, Jane and Michael watched the small, withered figure shooting past the bobbing balloons, past

the Prime Minister and the Lord Mayor, past Mary
Poppins and Annabel, until the tiny shape grew tinier
still and the Balloon Woman disappeared into the distance.

"Balloons *and* balloons, my deary-ducks!" The
faint echo came drifting back to them.

"Step along, please!" said Mary Poppins. They
flocked round her, all four of them. Annabel, rocked
by the movement of Mary Poppins' balloon, nestled
closer to her and went to sleep.

The gate of Number Seventeen stood open, the front
door was ajar. Mary Poppins, leaping neatly and bouncing primly, passed through and up the stairs. The
children followed, jumping and bobbing. And when
they reached the nursery door, their four pairs of feet

clattered noisily to the ground. Mary Poppins floated down and landed without a sound.

"Oh, what a *lovely* afternoon!" said Jane, rushing to fling her arms round Mary Poppins.

"Well, that's more than *you* are, at this moment. Brush your hair, please. I don't care for scarecrows!" Mary Poppins said tartly.

"I feel like a balloon myself," said Michael joyfully. "All airy-fairy-free!"

"I'd be sorry for the fairy that looked like you!" said Mary Poppins. "Go and wash your hands. You're no better than a sweep!"

When they came back, clean and tidy, the four balloons were resting against the ceiling, their strings firmly moored behind the picture over the mantelpiece.

Michael gazed up at them—his own yellow one, Jane's

blue, the Twins' pink and Mary Poppins' red. They were very still. No breath of wind moved them. Light and bright, steady and still, they leaned against the ceiling.

"I wonder!" said Michael softly, half to himself.

"You wonder what?" said Mary Poppins, sorting out her parcels.

"I wonder if it would all have happened if you hadn't been with us."

Mary Poppins sniffed.

"I shouldn't wonder if you didn't wonder much too much!" she replied.

And with that Michael had to be content. . . .

Chapter Nine

NELLIE-RUBINA

" I DON'T believe it will ever stop—ever!"

Jane put down her copy of *Robinson Crusoe* and gazed gloomily out of the window.

The snow fell steadily, drifting down in large soft flakes, covering the Park and the pavements and the houses in Cherry Tree Lane with its thick, white mantle. It had not stopped snowing for a week and in all that time the children had not once been able to go out.

" I don't mind—not very much," said Michael from the floor, where he was busy arranging the animals of his Noah's Ark. " We can be Esquimos and eat whales."

" Silly—how could we get whales when it's too snowy even to go out and buy cough-drops?"

" They might come here. Whales do, sometimes," he retorted.

" How do you know?"

" Well, I don't *know*, exactly. But they might. Jane, where's the second giraffe? Oh, here he is—under the tiger!"

He put the two giraffes into the Ark together.

> " The Animals went in Two-by-Two,
>   The Elephant and the Kangaroo "

sang Michael. And, because he hadn't got a kangaroo, he sent an antelope in with the elephant, and Mr. and Mrs. Noah behind them to keep order.

"I wonder why they never have any relations!" he remarked, presently.

"*Who* don't?" said Jane crossly, for she didn't want to be disturbed.

"The Noahs. I've never seen them with a daughter or a son or an uncle or an aunt. Why?"

"Because they don't have them," said Jane. "Do be quiet."

"Well, I was only remarking. Can't I remark if I want to?"

He was beginning to feel cross now, and very tired of being cooped up in the Nursery. He scrambled to his feet and swaggered over to Jane.

"I only said——" he began, annoyingly, jogging the hand that held the book.

But, at that, Jane's patience gave way and she hurled *Robinson Crusoe* across the room.

"How dare you disturb me?" she shouted, turning on Michael.

"How dare you not let me make a remark?"

"I didn't!"

"You did!"

And in another moment Jane was shaking Michael furiously by the shoulders, and he had gripped a great handful of her hair.

"*What is all this?*"

Mary Poppins stood in the doorway, glowering down at them.

They fell apart.

"She sh-sh-shook me!" wailed Michael, but he looked guiltily at Mary Poppins.

"He p-p-pulled my hair!" sobbed Jane, hiding her head in her arms, for she dared not face that stern gaze.

Mary Poppins stalked into the room. She had a pile

of coats, caps, and mufflers on her arm; and the Twins, round-eyed and interested, were at her heels.

"I would rather," she remarked with a sniff, "have a family of Cannibals to look after. They'd be more human!"

"But she did sh-sh-shake me——" Michael began again.

"Tell-Tale-Tit, Your Tongue shall be slit!" jeered Mary Poppins. Then, as he seemed to be going to protest, "Don't dare answer back!" she said warningly, and tossed him his overcoat. "Get your things on, please! We're going out!"

"Out?"

They could hardly believe their ears! But at the sound of that word all their crossness melted away. Michael, buttoning up his leggings, felt sorry he had annoyed Jane, and looked across to find her putting on her woollen cap and smiling at him.

"Hooray, hooray, hooray!" they shouted, stamping and clapping their woollen-gloved hands.

"Cannibals!" she said fiercely, and pushed them in front of her down the stairs.

The snow was no longer falling but was piled in heavy drifts all over the garden, and beyond, in the Park, it lay upon everything like a thick white quilt. The naked branches of the Cherry Trees were covered with a glistening rind of snow; and the Park railings, that had once been green and slender, were now white and rather woolly.

Down the garden path Robertson Ay was languidly trailing his shovel, pausing every few inches to take a long rest. He was wearing an old overcoat of Mr. Banks' that was much too big for him. As soon as he had shovelled the snow from one piece of path, the coat, drifting behind him, swept a new drift of snow over the cleared patch.

But the children raced past him and down to the gate, crying and shouting and waving their arms.

Outside in the Lane everybody who lived in it seemed to be taking the air.

"Ahoy there, shipmates!" cried a roaring, soaring voice as Admiral Boom came up and shook them all by the hand. He was wrapped from head to foot in a large Inverness cape and his nose was redder than they had ever seen it.

"Good-day!" said Jane and Michael politely.

"Port and starboard!" cried the Admiral. "I don't call *this* a good day. Hur-rrrrrumph! A hideous, hoary, land-lubbery sort of day, I call it. Why doesn't the Spring come? Tell me that!"

"Now, Andrew! Now, Willoughby! Keep close to Mother!"

Miss Lark, muffled up in a long fur coat and wearing a fur hat like a tea-cosy, was taking a walk with her two dogs.

"Good-morning, everybody!" She greeted them fussily. "*What* weather! *Where* has the sun gone? And *why* doesn't the Spring come?"

"Don't ask me, Ma'am!" shouted Admiral Boom. "No affair of mine. You should go to sea. Always good weather there! Go to sea!"

"Oh, Admiral Boom, I couldn't do that! I haven't the time. I am just off to buy Andrew and Willoughby a fur coat each."

A look of shame and horror passed between the two dogs.

"Fur coats!" roared the Admiral. "Blast my binnacle! Fur coats for a couple of mongrels? Heave her over! Port, I say! Up with the Anchor! Fur coats!"

"Admiral! Admiral!" cried Miss Lark, stopping her ears with her hands. "Such *language*! Please, *please* remember I am not used to it. And my dogs are *not* mongrels. Not at all! One has a long pedigree and the other has at least a Kind Heart. Mongrels, indeed!"

And she hurried away, talking to herself in a high, angry voice, with Andrew and Willoughby sidling behind her, swinging their tails and looking very uncomfortable and ashamed.

The Ice Cream Man trundled past on his cycle, going at a terrific rate and ringing his bell madly.

"DON'T STOP ME OR I SHALL CATCH COLD" said the notice in front of his cart.

"Whenever's that there Spring coming?" shouted the Ice Cream Man to the Sweep who at that moment came trudging round the corner. To keep out the cold he had completely covered himself with brushes so that he looked more like a porcupine than a man.

"Bur-rum, bur-rum, bumble!" came the voice of the Sweep through the brushes.

"What's that?" said the Ice Cream Man.

"Bumble!" the Sweep remarked, disappearing in at Miss Lark's Tradesman's Entrance.

In the gateway to the Park stood the Keeper, waving his arms and stamping his feet and blowing on his hands.

"Need a bit of Spring, don't we?" he said cheerfully to Mary Poppins as she and the children passed through.

"*I'm* quite satisfied!" replied Mary Poppins primly, tossing her head.

"*Self*-satisfied, I'd call it," muttered the Keeper. But as he said it behind his hand, only Jane and Michael heard him.

Michael dawdled behind. He stooped and gathered up a handful of snow and rolled it between his palms.

"Jane, dear!" he called in a wheedling voice. "I've got something for you!"

She turned, and the snowball, whizzing through the air, caught her on the shoulder. With a squeal she began to burrow in the snow and presently there were snowballs flying through the air in every direction. And in and out, among the tossing, glistening balls, walked Mary Poppins, very prim and neat, and thinking to herself how handsome she looked in her woollen gloves and her rabbit-skin coat.

And just as she was thinking that, a large snowball grazed past the brim of her hat and landed right on her nose.

"Oh!" screamed Michael, putting up both hands to his mouth. "I didn't mean to, Mary Poppins! I didn't, really. It was for Jane!"

Mary Poppins turned; and her face, as it appeared through the fringe of broken snowball, was terrible.

"Mary Poppins," he said earnestly. "I'm sorry. It was a Naccident!"

"A Naccident or not," she retorted, "that's the end of *your* snowballing. Naccident, indeed! A *Zulu* would have better manners!"

She plucked the remains of the snowball from her neck and rolled them into a small ball between her woollen palms. Then she flung the ball right across the snowy lawn and went stamping haughtily after it.

"Now you've done it!" whispered Jane.

"I didn't mean to," Michael whispered back.

"I know. But you know what she is!"

Mary Poppins, arriving at the place where the snowball had fallen, picked it up and threw it again, a long, powerful throw.

"Where is she going?" said Michael suddenly. For the snowball was bowling away under the trees and, instead of keeping to the path, Mary Poppins was hurrying after it. Every now and then she dodged a little fall of snow as it tumbled softly from a branch.

"I can hardly keep up!" said Michael, stumbling over his own feet.

Mary Poppins quickened her steps. The children panted behind her. And when at last they caught up with the snowball they found it lying beside the strangest building they had ever seen.

"I don't remember seeing this house before!" exclaimed Jane, her eyes wide with surprise.

"It's more like an Ark than a house," said Michael, staring.

The house stood solidly in the snow, moored by a thick rope to the trunk of a tree. Round it, like a veranda, ran a long narrow deck, and its high-peaked roof was painted bright scarlet. But the most curious thing about it was that though it had several windows there was not a single door.

"Where *are* we?" said Jane, full of curiosity and excitement.

Mary Poppins made no reply. She led the way along the deck and stopped in front of a notice that said:

"KNOCK THREE AND A HALF TIMES"

"What is half a knock?" whispered Michael to Jane.

"Sh!" she said, nodding towards Mary Poppins. And her nod said as clearly as if she had spoken— "We're on the brink of an Adventure. Don't spoil it by asking questions!"

Mary Poppins, seizing the knocker that hung above the notice, swung it upwards and knocked three times against the wall. Then, taking it daintily between the finger and thumb of her woollen glove, she gave the merest, tiniest, smallest, gentlest tap.

Like this:

RAP! RAP! RAP! . . . TAP!

Immediately, as though it had been listening and waiting for that signal, the roof of the building flew back on its hinges.

"Goodness Graciousness!" Michael could not restrain the exclamation, for the wind of the roof, as it swung open, nearly lifted his hat off.

Mary Poppins walked to the end of the narrow deck and began to climb a small, steep ladder. At the top she turned, and looking very solemn and important, beckoned with a woolly finger.

"Step up, please!"

The four children hurried after her.

"Jump!" cried Mary Poppins, leaping down from the top of the ladder into the house. She turned and caught the Twins as they came tumbling over the edge with Jane and Michael after them. And as soon as they were all safely inside, the roof closed over again and shut with a little click.

They gazed round them. Four pairs of eyes popped with surprise.

"*What* a funny room!" exclaimed Jane.

But it was really more than funny. It was extraordinary. The only piece of furniture in it was a large counter that ran along one end of the room. The walls were white-washed and, leaning against them, were piles of wood cut into the shape of trees and branches and all painted green. Small wooden sprays of leaves, newly painted and polished, were scattered about the floor. And several notices hung from the walls, saying

"MIND THE PAINT!"
or
"DON'T TOUCH!"
or
"KEEP OFF THE GRASS!"

But this was not all.

In one corner stood a flock of wooden sheep with the dye still wet on their fleeces. Crowded in another were small, stiff groups of flowers—yellow aconites, green-and-white snowdrops, and bright blue scyllas. All of them looked very shiny and sticky as though they had been newly varnished.

So did all the wooden birds and butterflies that were neatly piled in a third corner. So did the flat, white, wooden clouds that leant tidily against the counter.

But the enormous jar that stood on a shelf at the end of the room was not painted. It was made of green glass and filled the brim with hundreds of small flat shapes of every kind and colour.

"You're quite right, Jane," said Michael, staring. "It *is* a funny room!"

"Funny!" said Mary Poppins, looking as though he had said something insulting.

"Well—peculiar."

"*Peculiar?*"

Michael hesitated. He could not find the right word. "What I meant was——"

"I think it's a lovely room, Mary Poppins——" said Jane, hastily coming to the rescue.

"Yes it is," said Michael, very relieved. "And," he added cleverly, "*I* think you look very nice in that hat."

He watched her carefully. Yes, her face was a little softer—there were even faint beginnings of a conceited smile round her mouth.

"Humph!" she remarked, and turned towards the end of the room.

"Nellie-Rubina!" she called. "Where are you? We've arrived!"

"Coming! Coming!"

The highest, thinnest voice they had ever heard seemed to rise up from beneath the counter. And, presently, from the same direction as the voice, a head, topped with a small, flat hat, popped up. It was followed by a round, rather solid body that held in one hand a pot of red paint, and in the other a plain wooden tulip.

Surely, surely, thought Jane and Michael, this was the strangest person they had ever seen!

From her face and size she seemed to be quite young, but somehow she looked as though she were made, not of flesh, but of wood. Her stiff, shiny black hair seemed to have been carved on her head and then painted. Her eyes were like small black holes drilled in her face, and surely that bright pink patch on her shiny cheek was paint!

"Well, Miss Poppins!" said this curious person, her red lips glistening as she smiled. "This *is* nice of you, I must say!" And, putting down the paint and the tulip, she came round the counter and shook hands with Mary Poppins.

Then it was that the children noticed she had no legs at all! She was quite solid from the waist downwards and moved with a rolling motion by means of a round flat disc where her feet should have been.

"Not at all, Nellie-Rubina," said Mary Poppins, with unusual politeness. "It is a Pleasure and a Treat!"

"We've been expecting you, of course," Nellie-Rubina went on, "because we wanted you to help with the——" She broke off, for not only had Mary Poppins flashed her a warning look, but she had caught sight of the children.

"Oh!" she cried, in her high, friendly voice. "You've brought Jane and Michael! And the Twins, too. What a surprise!" She bowled across and shook hands jerkily with them all.

"Do you know us, then?" said Michael, staring at her amazed.

"Oh, dear me, yes!" she trilled gaily. "I've often heard my Father and Mother speak of you. Pleased to make your acquaintance." She laughed, and insisted on shaking hands all round again.

"I thought, Nellie-Rubina," said Mary Poppins, "that maybe you could spare an ounce of Conversations."

"Most certainly!" said Nellie-Rubina, smiling and rolling towards the counter. "To do anything for *you*, Miss Poppins, is an Honour and a Joy!"

" But can you have conversation by the ounce?" said Jane.

" Yes, indeed. By the pound, too. Or the ton, if you like." Nellie-Rubina broke off. She lifted her arms to the large jar on the shelf. They were just too short to reach it. " *Tch, tch, tch!* Not long enough. I must have a bit added. In the meantime, I'll get my Uncle to lift them down. Uncle Dodger! Uncle Dod-*ger*!"

She screamed the last words through a door behind the counter, and immediately an odd-looking person appeared.

He was as round as Nellie-Rubina, but much older, and with a sadder sort of face. He, too, had a little flat hat on his head, and his coat was tightly buttoned across a chest as woodeny as Nellie-Rubina's. And Jane and Michael could see, as his apron swung aside for a moment, that, like his niece, he was solid from the waist downwards. In his hand he carried a wooden cuckoo half-covered with grey paint and there were splashes of the same paint on his own nose.

" You called, my dear?" he asked, in a mild respectful voice.

Then he saw Mary Poppins.

" Ah, here you are at last, Miss Poppins! Nellie-Rubina *will* be pleased. She's been expecting you to help us with——"

He caught sight of the children and broke off suddenly.

" Oh, I beg your pardon. I didn't know there was Company, my dear! I'll just go and finish this bird——"

" You will not, Uncle Dodger!" said Nellie-Rubina, sharply. " I want the Conversations lifted down. Will you be so good?"

Although she had such a jolly, cheerful face, the children noticed that when she spoke to her Uncle she gave orders rather than asked favours.

Uncle Dodger sprang forward as swiftly as anybody could who had no legs.

"Certainly, my dear, certainly!" He lifted his arms jerkily and set the jar on the counter.

"In front of me, please!" ordered Nellie-Rubina haughtily.

Fussily, Uncle Dodger edged the jar along.

"There you are, my dear, begging your pardon!"

"Are *those* the Conversations?" asked Jane, pointing to the jar. "They look more like sweets."

"So they are, Miss! They're Conversation Sweets,"

said Uncle Dodger, dusting the jars with his apron.

"Does one eat them?" inquired Michael.

Uncle Dodger, glancing cautiously at Nellie - Rubina, leaned across the counter.

"*One* does," he whispered behind his hand. "But *I* don't, being only an Uncle-by - Marriage.

But she——" he nodded respectfully towards his niece, " she's the Eldest Daughter and a Direct Descendant !"

Neither Jane nor Michael knew in the least what he meant, but they nodded politely.

" Now," cried Nellie-Rubina gaily, as she unscrewed the lid of the Jar. " Who'll choose first?"

Jane thrust in her hand and brought out a flat, star-shaped sweet rather like a peppermint.

" There's writing on it!" she exclaimed.

Nellie-Rubina shrieked with laughter. " Of course there is! It's a Conversation! Read it."

" *You're My Fancy,*" read Jane aloud.

" How *very* nice !" tinkled Nellie-Rubina, pushing the jar towards Michael. He drew out a pink sweet shaped like a shell.

" *I Love You. Do You Love Me?*" he spelled out.

" Ha, ha! That's a good one! Yes, I do!" Nellie-Rubina laughed loudly, and gave him a quick kiss that left a sticky patch of paint on his cheek.

John's yellow Conversation read, " *Deedle, deedle, dumpling!*" and on Barbara's was written in large letters, " *Shining-bright and airy.*"

" And so you are!" cried Nellie-Rubina, smiling at her over the counter.

" Now you, Miss Poppins!" And as Nellie-Rubina tipped the jar towards Mary Poppins, Jane and Michael noticed a curious, understanding look pass between them.

Off came the large woollen glove and Mary Poppins, shutting her eyes, put in her hand and scrabbled for a moment among the Conversations. Then her fingers closed on a white one shaped like a half-moon and she held it out in front of her.

" *Ten o'clock To-night,*" said Jane, reading the inscription aloud.

Uncle Dodger rubbed his hands together.

"That's right. That's the time when we——"

"Uncle Dod-*ger*!" cried Nellie-Rubina in a warning voice.

The smile faded away from his face and left it sadder than before.

"Begging your pardon, my dear!" he said humbly. "I'm an old man, I'm afraid, and I sometimes say the wrong things—beg pardon." He looked very ashamed of himself, but Jane and Michael could not see that he had done anything very wrong.

"Well," said Mary Poppins, slipping her Conversation carefully into her hand-bag, "if you'll excuse us, Nellie-Rubina, I think we'd better be going!"

"Oh, must you?" Nellie-Rubina rolled a little on her disc. "It has been such a Satisfaction! Still," she glanced out of a window, "it might snow again and keep you imprisoned here. And you wouldn't like that, would you?" she trilled, turning to the children.

"*I* would," said Michael, stoutly. "I would love it. And then, perhaps, I'd find out what these are for." He pointed to the painted branches, the sheep and birds and flowers.

"Those? Oh, those are just decorations," said Nellie-Rubina, airily dismissing them with a jerky wave of her hand.

"But what do you do with them?"

Uncle Dodger leaned eagerly across the counter.

"Well, you see, we take them out and——"

"Uncle Dod-*ger*!" Nellie-Rubina's eyes were snapping dangerously.

"Oh, dear! There I go again. Always speaking out of my turn. I'm too old, that's what it is!" said Uncle Dodger mournfully.

Nellie-Rubina gave him an angry look. Then she turned, smiling, to the children.

"Good-bye," she said, jerkily shaking hands. "I'll remember our Conversations. You're my Fancy, I love You, Deedle-deedle and Shining-bright!"

"You've forgotten Mary Poppins' Conversation. It's 'Ten o'clock To-night,'" Michael reminded her.

"Ah, but *she* won't!" said Uncle Dodger, smiling happily.

"Uncle Dod-*ger*!"

"Oh, begging your pardon, begging your pardon!"

"Good-bye!" said Mary Poppins. She patted her hand-bag importantly and another strange look passed between her and Nellie-Rubina.

"Good-bye, good-bye!"

When Jane and Michael thought about it afterwards, they could not remember how they had got out of that curious room. One moment they were inside it saying good-bye to Nellie-Rubina, and the next they were out in the snow again, licking their Conversations and hurrying after Mary Poppins.

"Do you know, Michael," said Jane, "I believe that sweet was a message."

"Which one? Mine?"

"No. The one Mary Poppins chose."

"You mean . . .?"

"I think something is going to happen at ten o'clock to-night and I'm going to stay awake and see."

"Then so will I," said Michael.

"Come along, please! Keep up!" said Mary Poppins. "I haven't *all* day to waste. . . ."

Jane was dreaming deeply. And in her dream somebody was calling her name in a small, urgent voice. She sat up with a start to find Michael standing beside her in his pyjamas.

"You said you'd stay awake!" he whispered accusingly.

"What? Where? Why? Oh, it's you, Michael! Well, you said you would, too."

"Listen!" he said.

There was a sound of somebody tip-toeing in the next room.

Jane drew in her breath sharply. "Quick! Get back into bed. Pretend to be asleep. Hurry!"

With a bound Michael was under the blankets. In the darkness he and Jane held their breaths, listening.

From the other Nursery, the door opened stealthily. The thin gap of light widened and grew larger. A head came round the edge and peeped into the room. Then somebody slipped through and silently shut the door behind them.

Mary Poppins, wrapped in her fur coat and holding her shoes in her hands, tip-toed through their room.

They lay still, listening to her steps hurrying down the stairs. Far away the key of the front door scraped in its lock. There was a scurry of steps on the garden path and the front gate clicked.

And at that moment the clock struck ten.

Out of bed they sprang and rushed into the other Nursery, where the windows opened on the Park.

The night was black and splendid, lit with high, swinging stars. But to-night it was not stars they were looking for. If Mary Poppins' Conversation had really been a message, there was something more interesting to be seen.

"Look!" Jane gave a little gulp of excitement, and pointed.

Over in the Park, just by the entrance gate, stood the curious ark-shaped building, loosely moored to a tree-trunk.

"But how did it get *there*?" said Michael, staring. "It was at the other side of the Park this morning."

Jane did not reply. She was too busy watching.

The roof of the Ark was open and on the top of the ladder stood Nellie-Rubina, balancing on her round disc. From inside Uncle Dodger was handing up to her bundle after bundle of painted wooden branches.

"Ready, Miss Poppins?" tinkled Nellie-Rubina, passing an armful down to Mary Poppins, who was standing on the deck waiting to receive them.

The air was so clear and still that Jane and Michael, crouched in the window-seat, could hear every word.

Suddenly there was a loud noise inside the Ark as a wooden shape clattered to the floor.

"Uncle Dod-*ger*! Be careful, please. They're fragile!"

said Nellie-Rubina sternly. And Uncle Dodger, as he lifted out a pile of painted clouds, replied apologetically :

" Begging your pardon, my dear !"

The flock of wooden sheep came next, all very stiff and solid. And last of all, the birds, butterflies and flowers.

" That's the lot !" said Uncle Dodger, heaving himself up through the open roof. Under his arm he carried the wooden cuckoo, now entirely covered with grey paint. And in his hand swung a large, green paint-pot.

" Very well," said Nellie-Rubina. " Now, if you're ready, Miss Poppins, we'll begin."

And then began one of the strangest pieces of work Jane and Michael had ever seen. Never, never, they thought, would they forget it, even if they lived to be ninety.

From the pile of painted wood, Nellie-Rubina and Mary Poppins each took a long spray of leaves and, leaping into the air, attached them swiftly to the naked frosty branches of the trees. The sprays seemed to clip on easily, for it did not take more than a minute to attach them. And as each was slipped into place, Uncle Dodger would spring up and neatly dab a spot of green paint at the point where the spray joined the tree.

" My Goodness *Goodness* !" exclaimed Jane, as Nellie-Rubina sailed lightly up to the top of a tall poplar and fixed a large branch there. But Michael was too astonished to say anything.

All over the Park went the three, jumping up to the tallest branch as if they were on springs. And, in no time, every tree in the Park was decked out with wooden sprays of leaves and neatly finished off with dabs of paint from Uncle Dodger's brush.

Every now and then Jane and Michael heard Nellie-Rubina's shrill voice crying, " Uncle Dod-*ger*! *Be careful!* " and Uncle Dodger's voice begging her pardon.

And now Nellie-Rubina and Mary Poppins took up in their arms the flat, white wooden clouds. With these they soared higher than ever before, shooting right above the trees and pressing the clouds carefully against the sky.

" They're sticking, they're sticking!" cried Michael excitedly, dancing on the window-seat. And, sure enough, against the sparkling, darkling sky the flat, white clouds stuck fast.

" Who-o-o-op!" cried Nellie-Rubina as she swooped down. " Now for the sheep!"

Very carefully, on a snowy strip of lawn, they set up the wooden flock, huddling the larger sheep together with the stiff white lambs among them.

" We're getting on!" Jane and Michael heard Mary Poppins say, as she put the last lamb on its legs.

" I don't know what we'd have done without you, Miss Poppins, indeed I don't!" said Nellie-Rubina, pleasantly. Then, in quite a different voice, " Flowers, please, Uncle Dodger! And look sharp!"

" Here, my dear!" He rolled hurriedly up to her, his apron bulging with snowdrops, scyllas and aconites.

" Oh, look! Look!" Jane cried, hugging herself delightedly. For Nellie-Rubina was sticking the wooden shapes round the edge of an empty flower-bed. Round and round she rolled, planting her wooden border and reaching up her hand again and again for a fresh flower from Uncle Dodger's apron.

" That's neat!" said Mary Poppins admirably, and Jane and Michael were astonished at the pleasant, friendly tone of her voice.

" Yes, isn't it?" trilled Nellie-Rubina, brushing the

447

snow from her hands. "Quite a Sight. What's left, Uncle Dodger?"

"The birds, my dear, and the butterflies!" He held out his apron. Nellie-Rubina and Mary Poppins seized the remaining wooden shapes and ran swiftly about the Park, setting the birds on branches or in nests and tossing the butterflies into the air. And the curious thing was that they *stayed* there, poised above the earth, their bright patches of paint showing clearly in the starlight.

"There! I think that's all!" said Nellie-Rubina, standing still on her disc, with her hands on her hips, as she gazed round at her handiwork.

"One thing more, my dear!" said Uncle Dodger.

And, rather unevenly, as though the evening's work had made him feel old and tired, he bowled towards the ash tree near the Park Gates. He took the cuckoo from under his arm and set it on a branch among the wooden leaves.

"There, my bonny! There, my dove!" he said, nodding his head at the bird.

"Uncle Dod-*ger*! When *will* you learn? It's *not* a dove. It's a cuckoo!"

He bent his head humbly.

"A dove of a cuckoo—that's what I meant. Begging your pardon, my dear!"

"Well, now, Miss Poppins, I'm afraid we must really be going!" said Nellie-Rubina; and, rolling towards Mary Poppins, she took the pink face between her two wooden hands and kissed it.

"See you soon, Tra-la!" she cried airily, bowling along the deck of the Ark and up the little ladder. At the top she turned and waved her hand jerkily to Mary Poppins. Then, with a woodeny clatter, she leapt down and disappeared inside.

*" I don't know what we'd have done
without you, Miss Poppins!"*

"Uncle Dod-*ger*! Come along! Don't keep me waiting!" her thin voice floated back.

"Coming, my dear, coming! Begging your pardon!" Uncle Dodger rolled towards the deck, shaking hands with Mary Poppins on the way. The wooden cuckoo stared out from its leafy branch. He flung it a sad, affectionate glance. Then his flat disc rose in the air and echoed woodenly as he landed inside. The roof flew down and shut with a click.

"Let her go!" came Nellie-Rubina's shrill command from within. Mary Poppins stepped forward and unwound the mooring-rope from the tree. It was immediately drawn in through one of the windows.

"Make way, there, please! Make way!" shouted Nellie-Rubina. Mary Poppins stepped back hurriedly.

Michael clutched at Jane's arm excitedly.

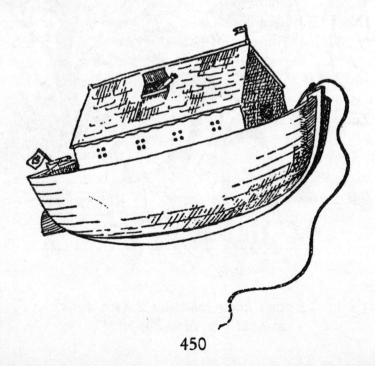

"They're off!" he cried, as the Ark rose from the ground and moved top-heavily above the snow. Up it went, rocking drunkenly between the trees. Then it steadied itself and passed lightly up and over the top-most boughs.

A jerky arm waved downwards from one of the windows, but before Jane and Michael could be certain whether it was Nellie-Rubina's or Uncle Dodger's, the Ark swept into the star-lit air and a corner of the house hid it from view.

Mary Poppins stood for a moment by the Park Gates waving her woollen gloves.

Then she came hurrying across the Lane and up the garden path. The front door key scraped in the lock. A cautious footstep creaked on the stairs.

"Back to bed, quick!" said Jane. "She mustn't find us here!"

Down from the window-seat and through the door they fled and with two quick jumps landed in their beds. They had just time to put the bed-clothes over their heads before Mary Poppins opened the door and quietly tip-toed through.

Zup! That was her coat being hung on its hook. Crackle! That was her hat rustling down into its paper-bag. But they heard no more. For by the time she had undressed and climbed into her camp-bed, Jane and Michael had huggled down under the blankets and were fast asleep. . . .

"Cuckoo! Cuckoo! Cuckoo!"
Across the Lane the soft bird note came floating.

"Jumping Giraffes!" cried Mr. Banks, as he lathered his face. "The Spring is here!"

And he flung down his shaving-brush and rushed out into the garden. He gave one look at it and then, flinging back his head, he made a trumpet with his hands.

"Jane! Michael! John! Barbara!" he called up to the Nursery windows. "Come down! The snow's gone and Spring has come!"

They came tumbling down the stairs and out of the front door to find the whole Lane alive with people.

"Ship ahoy!" roared Admiral Boom, waving his muffler. "Rope and Rigging! Cockles and Shrimps! Here's the Spring!"

"Well," said Miss Lark, hurrying out through her gate. "A fine day at last! I was thinking of getting Andrew and Willoughby two pairs of leather boots each, but now the snow's gone I shan't have to!"

At that Andrew and Willoughby looked very relieved and licked her hand to show they were glad she had not disgraced them.

The Ice Cream Man wheeled slowly up and down, keeping an eye open for customers. And to-day his notice-board read:

"Spring has come,
Rum-ti-tum,
Stop and buy one,
Spring has come!"

And the Sweep, carrying only one brush, walked along the Lane, looking from right to left with a satisfied air, as though he himself had arranged the lovely day.

And in the middle of all the excitement Jane and Michael stood still, staring about them.

Everything shone and glistened in the sunlight. There was not a single flake of snow to be seen.

From every branch of every tree, the tender, pale-green buds were bursting. Round the edge of the flower-beds just inside the Park, fragile green shoots of aconites, snowdrops and scyllas were breaking into a border of yellow, white and blue. Presently the Park Keeper came along and picked a tiny bunch and put them carefully in his button-hole.

From flower to flower brightly-coloured butterflies were darting on downy wings, and in the branches, thrushes and tits and swallows and finches were singing and building nests.

A flock of sheep, with soft young lambs at their heels, went by, baa-ing loudly.

And from the bough of the ash tree by the Park Gates came the clear, double-noted call:

" Cuckoo! Cuckoo!"

Michael turned to Jane. His eyes were shining.

" So that's what they were doing—Nellie-Rubina and Uncle Dodger and Mary Poppins!"

Jane nodded, gazing wonderingly about her.

Among the faint green smoke of buds a grey body rocked backwards and forwards on the ash-bough.

" Cuckoo! Cuckoo!"

" But . . . I thought they were all made of painted wood!" said Michael. " Did they come alive in the night, do you think?"

" Perhaps," said Jane.

" Cuckoo! Cuckoo!"

Jane seized Michael's hand and, as though he guessed the thought in her mind, he ran with her through the garden, across the Lane and into the Park.

"Hi! Where are you going, you two?" called Mr. Banks.

"Ahoy, there, messmates!" roared Admiral Boom.

"You'll get lost!" warned Miss Lark shrilly.

The Ice Cream Man tingled his bell wildly and the Sweep stood staring after them.

But Jane and Michael took no notice. They ran on, right through the Park and under the trees to the place where they had first seen the Ark.

They drew up, panting. It was cold and shadowy here under the dark branches, and the snow had not yet melted. They peered about, seeking, seeking. But there was only a heavy drift of snowflakes spread under the dark green boughs.

"It's really gone, then!" said Michael, gazing round. "Do you think we only imagined it, Jane?" he asked doubtfully.

She bent down suddenly and picked up something from the snow.

"No," she said slowly. "I'm sure we didn't." She held out her hand. In her palm lay a round, pink Conversation Sweet. She read out the words:

" Good-bye till Next Year,
Nellie-Rubina Noah."

Michael drew a deep breath.

" So that's who she was. Uncle Dodger said she was the Eldest Daughter. But I never guessed."

" She brought the Spring!" said Jane dreamily, gazing at the Conversation.

" I'll thank you," said a voice behind them, " to come home at once and eat your breakfast!"

They turned guiltily.

"We were just . . ." Michael began to explain.

"Then don't!" snapped Mary Poppins. She leant over Jane's shoulder and took the Conversation.

"That, I believe, is mine!" she remarked; and, putting it in her apron pocket, she led the way home through the Park.

Michael broke off a spray of green buds as he went. He examined them carefully.

"They seem quite real now," he said.

"Perhaps they always were," said Jane.

And a mocking voice came floating from the ash tree:

"Cuckoo! Cuckoo! Cuckoo!"

Chapter Ten

MERRY-GO-ROUND

IT had been a quiet morning.

More than one person, passing along Cherry Tree Lane, had looked over the fence of Number Seventeen and said, "How very extraordinary! Not a sound!"

Even the House, which usually took no notice of anything, began to feel alarmed.

"Dear me! Dear me!" it said to itself, listening to the silence. "I hope nothing's wrong!"

Downstairs in the Kitchen, Mrs. Brill, with her spectacles on the tip of her nose, was nodding over the newspaper.

On the first-floor landing, Mrs. Banks and Ellen were tidying the linen-cupboard and counting the sheets.

Upstairs in the Nursery Mary Poppins was quietly clearing away the luncheon things.

"I feel very good and sweet to-day," Jane was saying drowsily, as she lay stretched on the floor in a patch of sunlight.

"That must be a change!" remarked Mary Poppins with a sniff.

Michael took the last chocolate out of the box Aunt Flossie had given him last week for his sixth birthday.

Should he offer it to Jane, he wondered? Or to the Twins? Or Mary Poppins?

No. After all, it had been *his* birthday.

"Last, lucky last!" he said quickly and popped it into

456

his own mouth. "And I wish there were more!" he added regretfully, gazing into the empty box.

"All good things come to an end, sometime," said Mary Poppins primly.

He cocked his head on one side and looked up at her.

"*You* don't!" he said daringly. "And you're a good thing."

The beginnings of a satisfied smile glimmered at the corners of her mouth, but it disappeared as quickly as it had come.

"That's as may be!" she retorted. "Nothing lasts for ever."

Jane looked round, startled.

If nothing lasted for ever it meant that Mary Poppins——

"Nothing?" she said uneasily.

"Nothing at all!" snapped Mary Poppins.

And as if she had guessed what was in Jane's mind, she went to the mantelpiece and took down her large Thermometer. Then she pulled her carpet-bag from under the camp-bed and popped the Thermometer into it.

Jane sat up quickly.

"Mary Poppins, why are you doing that?"

Mary Poppins gave her a curious look.

"Because," she said priggishly, "I was always taught to be tidy." And she pushed the carpet-bag under the bed again.

Jane sighed. Her heart felt tight and heavy in her chest.

"I feel rather sad and anxious," she whispered to Michael.

"I expect you had too much Steam Pudding!" he retorted.

"No, it's not that kind of a feeling——" she began, and broke off suddenly for a knock had sounded at the door.

Tap! Tap!

"Come in!" called Mary Poppins.

Robertson Ay stood there yawning.

"Do you know what?" he said sleepily.

"No, what?"

"There's a Merry-go-round in the Park!"

"That's no news to me!" snapped Mary Poppins.

"A Fair?" cried Michael excitedly. "With swinging-boats and a Hoop-la?"

"No," said Roberson Ay, solemnly shaking his head. "A Merry-go-round, all by itself. Came last night. Thought you would like to know."

He shuffled languidly to the door and closed it after him.

Jane sprang up, her anxiety forgotten.

"Oh, Mary Poppins, may we go?"

"Say Yes, Mary Poppins, say Yes!" cried Michael, dancing round her.

She turned, balancing a tray of plates and cups on her arm.

"*I* am going," she remarked, calmly. "Because I have the fare. I don't know about you."

"There's sixpence in my money-box!" said Jane eagerly.

"Oh, Jane, lend me twopence!" pleaded Michael. He had spent all his money the day before on a stick of Liquorice.

They gazed anxiously at Mary Poppins, waiting for her to make up her mind.

"No borrowing or lending in this Nursery, please," she said tartly. "I will pay for one ride each. And one is all you will have."

She swept from the room carrying the tray with its load of cups.

They stared at each other.

"What can be the matter?" said Michael. It was now *his* turn to be anxious. "She's never paid for anything before!"

"Aren't you well, Mary Poppins?" he asked uneasily, as she came hurrying back.

"Never better in my life!" she replied, tossing her head. "And I'll thank you, if you please, not to stand there, peeking and prying at me as if I were a Waxwork! Go and get ready!"

Her look was so stern, and her eyes so fiercely blue and she spoke so like her usual self, that their anxiety vanished away, and they ran, shouting, to get their hats.

Presently the quietness of the house was broken by the noise of slamming doors, screaming voices and stamping feet.

"Dear me! Dear me! What a relief! I was getting quite anxious!" said the House to itself, listening to Jane and Michael and the Twins plunging and tumbling downstairs.

Mary Poppins paused for a moment to glance at her reflection in the hall mirror.

"Oh, do come on, Mary Poppins! You look all right," said Michael impatiently.

She wheeled about. Her expression was angry, outraged and astonished all at once.

All right, indeed! That was hardly the word. All right, in her blue jacket with the silver buttons! All right with her gold locket round her neck! All right with the parrot-headed umbrella under her arm!

Mary Poppins sniffed.

"That will be enough from you—and more!" she said shortly. Though what she meant was that it wasn't nearly sufficient.

But Michael was too excited to care.

"Come on, Jane!" he cried, dancing wildly. "I simply can't wait! Come on!"

They ran on ahead while Mary Poppins strapped the Twins into the perambulator. And presently the garden gate clicked behind them and they were on the way to the Merry-go-round.

Faint sounds of music came floating across from the Park, humming and drumming like a humming-top.

"Good afternoon! And how are *we* to-day?" Miss Lark's high voice greeted them as she hurried down the Lane with her dogs.

But before they had time to reply she went on, "Off to the Merry-go-round, I suppose! Andrew and Willoughby and I have just been. A *very* superior Entertainment. *So* nice and clean. And *such* a polite Attendant!" She fluttered past with the two dogs prancing beside her. "Good-bye! Good-bye!" she called back over her shoulder as she disappeared round the corner.

"All Hands to the Pump! Heave ho, my hearties!"

A well-known voice came roaring from the direction of the Park. And through the gates came Admiral Boom, looking very red in the face and dancing a Sailor's Hornpipe.

"Yo, ho, ho! And a bottle of Rum! The Admiral's been on the Merry-go-round. Bail her out! Cockles and shrimps! It's as good as a long sea voyage!" he roared, as he greeted the children.

"We're going, too!" said Michael excitedly.

"What? *You're* going?" The Admiral seemed quite astonished.

"Yes, of course!" said Jane.

"But—not all the way, surely?" The Admiral looked curiously at Mary Poppins.

"They're having one ride each, Sir!" she explained primly.

"Ah, well! Farewell!" he said in a voice that, for him, was almost gentle.

Then, to the children's astonishment, he drew himself up, put his hand to his forehead, and smartly saluted Mary Poppins.

"*Ur-rrrrrrumph!*" he trumpeted into his handkerchief. "Hoist your sail! And up with your Anchor! And away, Love, away!"

And he waved his hand and went off, rolling from side to side of the pavement and singing :

"Every nice Girl loves a Sailor!"

in a loud, rumbling voice.

"Why did he say Farewell and call you Love?" said Michael, staring after the Admiral as he walked on beside Mary Poppins.

"Because he thinks I'm a Thoroughly Respectable Person!" she snapped. But there was a soft, dreamy look in her eyes.

Again Jane felt the strange sad feeling, and her heart tightened inside her.

"What *can* be going to happen?" she asked herself anxiously. She put her hand on Mary Poppins' hand as it lay on the handle of the perambulator. It felt warm and safe and comforting.

"How silly I am!" she said softly. "There *can't* be anything wrong!"

And she hurried beside the perambulator as it trundled towards the Park.

"Just a moment! Just a moment!" a panting voice sounded behind them.

"Why," said Michael, turning, "it's Miss Tartlet!"

"Indeed, it is not," said Miss Tartlet breathlessly. "It's Mrs. Turvy!"

She turned, blushing to Mr. Turvy. He stood beside her, smiling a little sheepishly.

"Is this one of your Second Mondays?" Jane inquired. He was right-side up, so she did not think it could be.

"Oh, no! Thank goodness, no!" he said hastily. "We—er—were just coming to say—oh, Good Afternoon, Mary!"

"Well, Cousin Arthur?" They all shook hands.

"I wondered if you were going on the Merry-go-round?" he inquired.

"Yes, I am. We all are!"

"All!" Mr. Turvy's eyebrows shot up to the top of his head. He seemed very surprised.

"They're going for one ride each!" said Mary Poppins, nodding at the children. "Sit still, please!" she snapped at the Twins, who had bobbed up excitedly. "You're not Performing Mice!"

"Oh, I see. And then—they're getting off? Well—Good-bye, Mary, and Bon Voyage!" Mr. Turvy raised his hat high above his head, very ceremoniously.

"Good-bye—and thank you for coming!" said Mary Poppins, bowing graciously to Mr. and Mrs. Turvy.

"What does Bon Voyage mean?" said Michael, looking over his shoulder at their retreating figures—Mrs. Turvy very fat and curly, Mr. Turvy very straight and thin.

"Good journey! Which is something *you* won't have unless you walk up!" snapped Mary Poppins. He hurried after her.

The music was louder now, beating and drumming on the air, drawing them all towards it.

Mary Poppins, almost running, turned the perambulator in at the Park Gates. But there a row of pavement pictures caught her eye and she pulled up suddenly.

"What is she stopping for *now*?" said Michael in an angry whisper to Jane. "We'll never get there at this rate!"

The Pavement Artist had just completed a set of fruit in coloured chalks—an Apple, a Pear, a Plum, and a Banana.

Underneath them he was busy chalking the words:

TAKE ONE

"Ahem!" said Mary Poppins, with a lady-like cough.

The Pavement Artist leapt to his feet, and Jane and Michael saw that it was Mary Poppins' great friend, the Match Man.

"Mary! At last! I've been waiting all day!"

The Match Man seized her by both hands and gazed admiringly into her eyes.

Mary Poppins looked very shy and rather pleased.

"Well, Bert, we're off to the Merry-go-round," she said, blushing.

He nodded. "I thought you would be. They going with you?" he added, jerking his thumb at the children.

Mary Poppins shook her head mysteriously.

" Just for a ride," she said quickly.

" Oh——" He pursed up his mouth. " I see."

Michael stared. What else could they do on a Merry-go-round *except* go for a ride, he wondered?

" A nice set of pictures you've got!" Mary Poppins was saying admiringly, as she stood gazing down at the fruit.

" Help yourself!" said the Match Man airily.

And with that Mary Poppins, before their astonished eyes, bent down and picked the painted Plum from the pavement and took a bite out of it.

" Won't you take one?" said the Match Man, turning to Jane.

She stared at him. " But *can* I?" It seemed so impossible.

" Try!"

She bent towards the Apple and it leapt into her hand. She bit into the red side. It tasted very sweet.

" But how do you do it?" said Michael staring.

" I don't," said the Match Man. " It's Her!" He nodded at Mary Poppins as she stood primly beside the perambulator. " It only happens when *she's* around, I assure you!"

Then he bent down and picked the Pear clean out of the pavement and offered it to Michael.

" But what about you?" said Michael, for though he wanted the Pear, he also wanted to be polite.

" That's all right!" said the Match Man. " I can always paint more!" And with that he plucked the Banana, peeled it, and gave half each to the Twins.

A clear, sweet strain of music came floating urgently to their ears.

" Now, Bert, we must really be going!" said Mary

Poppins hurriedly, as she neatly hid her Plum-stone between two Park railings.

"Must you, Mary?" said the Match Man, very sadly. "Well, Good-bye, my Dear. And Good Luck!"

"But you'll see him again, won't you?" said Michael, as he followed Mary Poppins through the Gates.

"Maybe and maybe not!" she said shortly. "And it's no affair of yours!"

Jane turned and looked back. The Match Man was standing by his box of chalks, gazing with all his eyes after Mary Poppins.

"This *is* a curious day!" she said, frowning.

Mary Poppins glared at her.

"What's wrong with it, pray?"

"Well—everyone's saying Good-bye. And looking at you so strangely."

"Speech costs nothing!" snapped Mary Poppins. "And a Cat can look at a King, I suppose?"

Jane was silent. She knew it was no good saying anything to Mary Poppins, because Mary Poppins never explained.

She sighed. And because she was not quite sure why she sighed, she began to run, streaking past Michael and Mary Poppins and the perambulator towards the thundering music.

"Wait for me! Wait for me!" screamed Michael, dashing after her. And behind him came the rumbling trundle of the perambulator as Mary Poppins hurried after them both.

There stood the Merry-go-round on a clear patch of lawn between the Lime Trees. It was a new one, very bright and shiny, with prancing horses going up and down on their brass poles. A striped flag fluttered from the top, and everywhere it was gorgeously decorated with golden scrolls and silver leaves and coloured birds and stars. It was, in fact, everything Miss Lark had said, and more.

The Merry-go-round slowed down and drew to a standstill as they arrived. The Park Keeper ran up officiously and held on to one of the brass poles.

" Come along, come along! Threepence a ride!" he called importantly.

" I know which horse I'll have!" said Michael, dashing up to one painted blue-and-scarlet, with the name " Merry-legs " on its gold collar. He clambered on to its back and seized the pole.

" No Litter Allowed and Observe the By-Laws!" called the Keeper fussily, as Jane sped past him.

" I'll have Twinkle!" she cried, climbing upon the back of a fiery white horse with its name on a red collar.

Then Mary Poppins lifted the Twins from the perambulator and put Barbara in front of Michael, and John behind Jane.

" Penny, Tuppeny, Threepenny, Fourpenny, or Five-penny rides?" said the Merry-go-round Attendant, as he came to collect the money.

" Sixpenny," said Mary Poppins, handing him four sixpenny-bits.

The children stared, amazed. They had never before had a sixpenny ride on a Merry-go-round.

" No Litter Allowed!" called the Keeper, his eye on the tickets in Mary Poppins' hand.

" But aren't you coming?" Michael called down to her.

" Hold tight, please! Hold tight! I'll take the next turn!" she replied, snappily.

There was a hoot from the Merry-go-round's chimney. The music broke out again. And slowly, slowly the horses began to move.

"Hold on, please!" called Mary Poppins sternly.

They held on.

The trees were moving past them. The brass poles slipped up and down through the horses' backs. A dazzle of light fell on them from the rays of the setting sun.

"Sit tight!" came Mary Poppins' voice again.

They sat tight.

Now the trees were moving more swiftly, spinning about them as the Merry-go-round gathered speed. Michael tightened his arm about Barbara's waist. Jane flung back her hand and held John firmly. On they rode, turning ever more quickly, with their hair blowing out behind them, and the wind sharp on their faces. Round and round went Merry-legs and Twinkle, with the children on their backs and the Park tipping and rocking, whirling and wheeling about them.

It seemed as if they would never stop, as if there were no such thing as Time, as if the world was nothing but a circle of light and a group of painted horses.

The sun died in the West and the dusk came fluttering down. But still they rode, faster and faster, till at last they could not distinguish tree from sky. The whole broad earth was spinning now about them with a deep, drumming sound like a humming top.

Never again would Jane and Michael and John and Barbara be so close to the centre of the world as they were on that whirling ride. And, somehow, it seemed as though they knew it.

For—" Never again! Never again!" was the thought in their hearts as the earth whirled about them and they rode through the dropping dusk.

Presently, the trees ceased to be a circular green blur and their trunks again became visible. The sky moved away from the earth, and the Park stopped spinning. Slower and slower went the horses. And at last the Merry-go-round stood still.

" Come along, come along! Threepence a ride!" the Park Keeper was calling in the distance.

Stiff from their long ride, the four children clambered down. But their eyes were shining, and their voices trembled with excitement.

" Oh, lovely, lovely, lovely!" cried Jane, gazing at Mary Poppins with sparkling eyes, as she put John into the perambulator.

" If only we could have gone on for ever!" exclaimed Michael, lifting Barbara in beside him.

Mary Poppins gazed down at them. Her eyes were strangely soft and gentle in the gathering dusk.

"All good things come to an end," she said for the second time that day.

Then she flung up her head and glanced at the Merry-go-round.

"*My* turn!" she cried joyfully, as she stooped and took something from the perambulator.

Then she straightened and stood looking at them for a moment—that strange look that seemed to plunge right down inside them and *see* what they were thinking.

"Michael!" she said, lightly touching his cheek with her hand, "be good!"

He stared up at her uneasily. Why had she done that? What could be the matter?

"Jane! Take care of Michael and the Twins!" said Mary Poppins. And she lifted Jane's hand and put it gently on the handle of the perambulator.

"All aboard! All aboard!" cried the Ticket Collector.

The lights of the Merry-go-round blazed up.

Mary Poppins turned.

"Coming!" she called, waving her parrot-headed umbrella.

She darted across the little gulf of darkness that lay between the children and the Merry-go-round.

"Mary Poppins!" cried Jane, with a tremble in her voice. For suddenly—she did not know why—she felt afraid.

"Mary Poppins!" shouted Michael, catching Jane's fear.

But Mary Poppins took no notice. She leaped gracefully upon the platform, and, climbing upon the back of a dappled horse called Caramel, she sat down neatly and primly.

"Single or Return?" said the Ticket Collector.

For a moment she appeared to consider the question. She glanced across at the children and back at the Collector.

" You never know," she said, thoughtfully. " It might come in useful. I'll take a Return."

The Ticket Collector snapped a hole in a green ticket and handed it to Mary Poppins.

Jane and Michael noticed that she did not pay for it.

Then the music broke out again, softly at first, then loudly, wildly, triumphantly. Slowly the painted horses began to move.

Mary Poppins, looking straight ahead of her, was borne past the children. The parrot's head of her umbrella nestled under her arm. Her neatly-gloved hands were closed on the brass pole. And in front of her, on the horse's neck—

470

"Michael!" cried Jane, clutching his arm. "Do you see? She must have hidden it under the rug! Her Carpet-bag!"

Michael stared.

"Do you think——" he began, in a whisper.

Jane nodded.

"But—she's wearing the locket! The chain hasn't broken! I distinctly saw it!"

Behind them the Twins began to whimper, but Jane and Michael took no notice. They were gazing anxiously at the shining circle of horses.

The Merry-go-round was moving swiftly now, and soon the children could no longer tell which horse was which, nor distinguish Merry-legs from Twinkle.

Everything before them was a blaze of spinning light, except for the dark figure, neat and steady, that ever and again approached them and sped past and disappeared.

Wilder and wilder grew the drumming music. Faster and faster whirled the Merry-go-round. Again the dark shape rode towards them upon the dappled horse. And this time, as she came by, something bright and gleaming broke from her neck and came flying through the air to their feet.

Jane bent and picked it up. It was the gold locket, hanging loosely from its broken golden chain.

"It's true, then, it's true!" came Michael's bursting cry. "Oh, open it, Jane!"

With trembling fingers she pressed the catch and the locket flew open. The flickering light fell across the glass and they saw before them their own pictured faces, clustered about a figure with straight black hair, stern blue eyes, bright pink cheeks, and a nose turning upwards like the nose of a Dutch doll.

> " Jane, Michael, John,
> Barbara, and Annabel Banks
> and
> Mary Poppins "

read Jane from the little scroll beneath the picture.

" So that's what was in it!" said Michael, miserably, as Jane shut the locket and put it in her pocket. He knew there was no hope now. . . .

They turned again to the Merry-go-round, dazzled and giddy in the spinning light, seeing it faintly through a mist of tears. By now the horses were flying more swiftly than ever, and the pealing music was louder than before.

And then a strange thing happened. With a great blast of trumpets, the whole Merry-go-round rose, spinning, from the ground. Round and round, rising ever higher and higher, the coloured horses wheeled and raced with Caramel and Mary Poppins at their head. And the springing circle of light went lifting among the trees, turning the leaves to gold as the light fell upon them.

" She's going!" said Michael.

" Oh, Mary Poppins, Mary Poppins! Come back, come back!" they cried, lifting their arms towards her.

But her face was turned away, she looked out serenely above her horse's head, and gave no sign that she had heard.

" Oh, Mary Poppins! Come back, come back!"

"Mary Poppins!" It was a last despairing cry.

No answer came from the air.

By now the Merry-go-round had cleared the trees and was whirling up towards the stars. Away it went and away, growing smaller and smaller, until the figure of Mary Poppins was but a dark speck in a wheel of light.

On and on, pricking through the sky, went the Merry-go-round, carrying Mary Poppins with it. And at last it was just a tiny, twinkling shape, a little larger but not otherwise different from a star.

Michael sniffed and fumbled in his pocket for his handkerchief.

"I've got a crick in my neck," he said, to explain the sniff. But when Jane was not looking he hurriedly wiped his eyes.

Jane, still watching the bright spinning shape, gave a sigh.

Then she turned away.

"We must go home," she said flatly, remembering that Mary Poppins had told her to take care of Michael and the Twins.

"Come along, come along! Threepence a ride!"

The Park Keeper, who had been putting litter in the baskets, returned to the scene. He glanced at the place where the Merry-go-round had been, and started violently. He looked around him and his mouth fell open. He looked up and his eyes nearly burst out of his head.

"See here!" he shouted. "This won't do. Here one minute and gone the next! It's Against the Regulations! I'll have the Law on you." He shook his fist wildly at the empty air. "I never saw such a thing! Not even when I was a boy. I must make a report! I shall tell the Lord Mayor!"

Silently the children turned away. The Merry-go-round had left no trace in the grass, not a dent in the clover. Except for the Park Keeper, who stood there shouting and waving his arms, the green lawn was quite empty.

"She took a Return," said Michael, walking slowly beside the perambulator. "Do you think that means she'll come back?"

Jane thought for a moment. "Perhaps—if we want her enough, she will," she said slowly.

"Yes, perhaps . . .!" he repeated, sighing a little, and said no more till they were back in the Nursery. . . .

"I say! I say! I say!"

Mr. Banks came running up the path and burst in at the front door.

"Hi! Where's everybody?" he shouted, running up the stairs three at a time.

"Whatever is the matter?" said Mrs. Banks, hurrying out to meet him.

"The most wonderful thing!" he cried, flinging open the Nursery door. "A new star has appeared. I heard about it on the way home. The Largest Ever. I've borrowed Admiral's Boom's telescope to look at it. Come and see!"

He ran to the window and clapped the telescope to his eye.

"Yes! Yes!" he said, hopping excitedly. "There it is! A Wonder! A Beauty! A Marvel! A Gem! See for yourself!"

He handed Mrs. Banks the telescope.

"Children!" he shouted. "Look! There's a new star!"

"I know——" began Michael. "But it's not really a star. It's——"

"You know? And it isn't? What on earth do you mean?"

"Take no notice. He is just being silly!" said Mrs. Banks. "Now, where is this star? Oh, I see! *Very* pretty! Quite the brightest in the sky! I wonder where it came from? Now, children!"

She gave the telescope in turn to Jane and Michael, and as they looked through the glass they could clearly see the circle of painted horses, the brass poles, and the dark blur that ever and again whirled across their sight for a moment and was gone.

They turned to each other and nodded. They knew what the dark blur was—a neat, prim figure in a blue coat with silver buttons, a stiff straw hat on its head, and a parrot-headed umbrella under its arm. Out of the sky she had come, back to the sky she had gone. And Jane and Michael would not explain to anyone, for they knew there were things about Mary Poppins that could never be explained.

A knock sounded at the door.

"Excuse me, Ma'am," said Mrs. Brill, hurrying in, very red in the face. "But I think you ought to know that that there Mary Poppins has gone again!"

"Gone!" said Mrs. Banks unbelievingly.

"Lock, stock, and barrel—gone!" said Mrs. Brill, triumphantly. "Without a word, or By Your Leave. Just like last time. Even her Camp-bed and her Carpet-bag—clean gone! Not even her Postcard-album as a Memento. So there!"

"Dear, dear!" said Mrs. Banks. "How very tiresome! How thoughtless, how—George!" She turned to Mr. Banks. "George, Mary Poppins has gone again!"

"Who? What? Mary Poppins? Well, never mind that! We've got a new star!"

"A new star won't wash and dress the children!" said Mrs. Banks crossly.

"It will look through their window at night!" cried Mr. Banks, happily. "That's better than washing and dressing."

He turned back to the telescope.

"Won't you, my Wonder? My Marvel? My Beauty?" he said, looking up at the star.

Jane and Michael drew close and leaned against him, gazing across the window-sill into the evening air.

And high above them the great shape circled and wheeled through the darkening sky, shining and keeping its secret for ever and ever and ever. . . .

MARY POPPINS IN
CHERRY TREE LANE

To
K.L.T.
and
C.J.T.

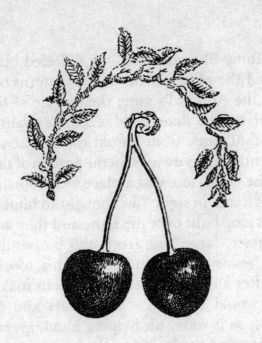

It was Midsummer's Eve. This is the most magical night of the year. Many curious things can happen in it before it gives way to the dawn. But it was not night yet by any means. The sun, still bright, was dawdling to the west, lazily taking his time about it, as though reluctant to leave the world.

He felt that he had done it proud, putting upon it a shine and a polish that would not quickly fade. His own reflection shone back at him from fountains, lakes and window-panes, even from the ripened fruit that hung in the trees of Cherry Tree Lane, a place well known to him.

"Nothing like sunshine," he flattered himself, as he noted the glitter of the ship's lanterns on either side of the Admiral's gate; the sparkle of the brass knocker on the door of Miss Lark's mansion; the gleam that came from an old tin toy, abandoned, apparently, by its owners, in the garden of the smallest house. This, too, was a place well known to him.

"Not a soul in sight," he thought to himself, as he sent his long light over the Lane and then across the open space, large and green and blossoming, that spread beside and beyond it. And this, too, he knew well. After all, he had had a hand in its making. For where would they be – tree, grass and flower – without, as it were, his helping hand, greening the grass, coaxing the leaf from the bare bough, warming the bud into flower?

And here, among lengthening light and shadows, there *was* a soul in sight.

"Who's that, down there in the Park?" he wondered, as a curious figure went back and forth, blowing a whistle and shouting.

Who else could it be but the Park Keeper? It was no wonder, however, that the sun did not recognize him for, in spite of the heavy heat of June, he was wearing a black, felt, sea-faring hat painted with skull-and-crossbones.

"Obey the rules! Remember the bye-laws! All

490

litter to be placed in the baskets!" he bellowed.

But nobody took any notice. People went strolling hand in hand; scattering litter as they went; deliberately sauntering on lawns whose notices said KEEP OFF THE GRASS; failing to observe the rules; forgetting all the bye-laws.

The Policeman was marching to and fro, swinging his baton and looking important, as if he thought he owned the earth and expected the earth to be glad of it.

Children went up and down on the swings, swooping like evening swallows.

And the swallows sang their songs so loudly that nobody heard the Park Keeper's whistle.

Admiral and Mrs Boom, sharing a bag of peanuts between them and dropping the empty shells as they went, were taking the air in the Long Walk.

> "Oh, I'm roaming
> In the gloaming
> With my lassie by my side!"

sang the Admiral, disregarding the signboard's warning NO HAWKERS, NO MUSICIANS.

In the Rose Garden, a tall man, in a cricketing cap a little too small and skimpy for him, was dipping his handkerchief into the fountain and was mopping his sunburnt brow.

Down by the Lake, an elderly gentleman in a hat of folded newpaper stood turning his head this way and that, sniffing the air like a gun dog.

"Coo-ee, Professor!" called Miss Lark, hurrying across the lawns, with her dogs unwillingly dragging behind her, as though they wished they were somewhere else.

For Miss Lark, to celebrate Midsummer's Eve, had tied a ribbon upon each head – pink for Willoughby, blue for Andrew – and they felt ashamed and dejected. What, they wondered, would people think? They might be mistaken for poodles!

"Professor, I've been waiting for you. You must have lost your way."

"Well, that's the way with ways, I suppose. Either you lose them or they lose you. Anyway, you've found me, Miss Sparrow. But alas!" he fanned himself with his hat, "I find the Sahara Desert a little – um – er – hot."

"You are not in the Sahara, Professor. You are in the Park. Don't you remember? I invited you to supper."

"Ah, so you did. To Strawberry Street. I hope it will be cooler there. For you and me and your two – um – poodles."

Andrew and Willoughby hung their.heads. Their

worst fears had been realized.

"No, no. The address is Cherry Tree Lane. And my name is Lucinda Lark. Do try not to be so forgetful. Ah, there you are, dear friends!" she trilled, as she spied the Booms in the distance. "Where are you off to this beautiful evening?"

"Sailing, sailing, over the bounding main," sang the Admiral. "And many a stormy wind shall blow, till Jack comes home again – won't it, Messmate?" he enquired of his wife.

"Yes, dear," murmured Mrs. Boom. "Unless you would like to wait till tomorrow. Binnacle is making Cottage Pie and there will be Apple Tart for dinner."

"Cottage Pie! I can't miss that. Let down the anchor, Midshipman. We'll wait for the morning tide."

"Yes, dear," Mrs Boom agreed. But she knew there would be no morning tide. She also knew that the Admiral, although he was always talking about it, would never go to sea again. It was far too far away from land and it always made him seasick.

"Obey the rules! Observe the bye-laws!" The Park Keeper rushed past, blowing his whistle.

"Ship ahoy there! Heave to, old salt!" The Admiral seized the Park Keeper's sleeve. "That's my hat you're wearing, skipper. I won it in a hand-to-hand fight off the coast of Madagascar. Didn't I, Messmate?" he demanded.

"If you say so, dear," murmured Mrs Boom. It was better, she knew, to agree than to argue. But privately she was aware of the facts – that the hat belonged to Binnacle, a retired pirate who kept the Admiral's ship-shaped house as shipshape as only a pirate could; and, moreover, that neither he nor her husband had ever clapped eyes on Madagascar.

"And I thought I had lost my Skull-and-Crossbones! Where did you find it, you son of a sea-snake?"

"Well, it fell down, sort of, out of the sky." The Park Keeper shuffled uneasily. "And I put it on by mistake, so to say, not meaning any harm, Admiral, sir."

"Nonsense! You're thinking of cannon balls. Pirate hats don't fall from the sky. Hand it over to Mrs Boom. She carries all the heavy things while I spy out the land." The Admiral took out his telescope and fixed it to his eye.

"But what am I going to put on my head?" the Park Keeper demanded.

"Go to sea, my man, and they'll give you a cap. A white thing with H.M.S. Something on it. You can't have my pirate hat, I need it. For away I'm bound to go – oho! – 'cross the wide Missouri."

And the Admiral, singing lustily, dragged his wife and the hat away.

The Park Keeper glanced round anxiously. What if the Lord Mayor came along and found him with his head uncovered? He dared not think of the consequences. If only the long day were over. If only all these crowding people, lolling or strolling hand in hand, would go home to their suppers. Then he could lock the Park Gates and slip away into the dark where his lack of a cap would not be noticed. If only the sun would go down!

But the sun still lingered. No one went home. They merely opened paper bags, took out cakes and sandwiches and threw the bags on to the grass.

"You'd think they thought they owned the Park," said the Park Keeper, who thought he owned it himself.

More people streamed in through the Main Gate, two by two, choosing balloons; or two by two from Mudge's Fairground, buying ice cream from the Ice Cream Man, each one holding the other's hand as the falling sun threw their long shadows before them on the lawns.

And then, through the Lane Gate, came another shadow that preceded through the two pillars a small but formal procession – a perambulator packed with toys and children; at one side a girl who

carried a basket, at the other a boy in a sailor suit with a string bag swinging from his hand.

Basket and bag were both well stocked as though for some lengthy excursion. And, pushing the perambulator, was an upright figure with bright pink cheeks, bright blue eyes and a turned-up nose – a figure that to the Park Keeper was only too familiar.

"Oh, *no*!" he muttered to himself. "Not at this hour, for Heaven's sake! What's she doing setting out when she ought to be going home?"

He crossed the lawn and accosted the group.

"Late, aren't you?" he enquired, trying, as far as he could, to look friendly. If he had been some kind of dog, his tail would have given a modest wag.

"Late for what?" Mary Poppins demanded, looking right through the Park Keeper as though he were a window.

He quailed visibly. "Well, what I meant to say was – you're sort of upside down, so to speak."

The blue eyes grew a shade bluer. He could see he had offended her.

"Are you accusing me," she enquired, "a well-brought-up respectable person, of standing on my head?"

"No, no, of course not. Not on your head. Not like an acrobat. Nothing like that."

The Park Keeper, thoroughly muddled, was now

afraid that he himself was the one that was upside down.

"It's just that it's sort of late in the day, the time when you're usually coming back – tea and bed and that sort of thing. And here you are, sallying forth, as though you were off on a jaunt." He eyed the bulging bag and basket. "With all and sundry, so to speak."

"We are. We're having a supper picnic." Jane pointed to the basket. "There's plenty of everything in here. You never know when a friend will appear – so Mary Poppins says."

"And we're staying up for hours and hours," said Michael, swinging his bag.

"*A supper picnic!*" The Park Keeper winced. He had never heard of such a thing. And was it even permitted, he wondered. His list of bye-laws raced through his head and he promptly gave it tongue.

"Observe the rules!" he warned the group. "All litter to be placed in the proper containers. No eggshells left lying about on the grass."

"Are we cuckoos," demanded Mary Poppins, "to be scattering eggs in every direction?"

"I meant hard-boiled," said the Park Keeper. "There never was a picnic, ever, that didn't have hard-boiled eggs. And where are you going, might I ask?" If the picnic was to be in the Park, he felt he had a right to know.

"We're off to –" Jane began eagerly.

"That will do, Jane," said Mary Poppins. "We will not hob-nob with strangers."

"But I'm no stranger!" The Park Keeper stared. "I'm here every day and Sundays. You know me. I'm the Park Keeper."

"Then why aren't you wearing your hat?" she demanded, giving the perambulator such a forceful push that if the Park Keeper had not jumped backwards, it would have run over his foot.

"Step along, please!" said Mary Poppins. And the little cavalcade stepped along, orderly and purposeful.

The Park Keeper watched till it disappeared, with a swish of Mary Poppins' new sprigged dress, behind the rhododendrons.

"Hob-nob!" he spluttered. "Who does she think she is, I wonder?"

There was no one at hand to answer that question and the Park Keeper dismissed it. Uppity – that's what she was, he thought. And no great bargain to look at either. She could go where she liked for all he cared – the long Walk led to all sorts of places: the Zoo, St Paul's, even the River – it might be any of them. Well, he couldn't patrol the whole of London. His job was to see to the Park. So, ready for any misdemeanour, he cast a vigilant eye about him.

"Hey, you!" he shouted warningly, as the tall man who had washed his face in the fountain bent down to smell a rose – and picked it! "No picking of flowers allowed in the Park. Obey the rules. Remember the bye-laws!"

"I could hardly forget them," the tall man answered. "Considering I was the one who made them."

"Ha, ha! *You* made them! Very funny!" The Park Keeper laughed a mirthless laugh.

"Well, some of them, I admit, are funny. They often make me chuckle. But, have you forgotten, it's Midsummer's Eve? Nobody keeps the bye-laws to-night. And I myself don't *have* to keep them, now or at any time."

"Oh no? And who do you fancy you are then?"

"One doesn't fancy. One just knows. It's the kind of thing one can't forget. I'm the Prime Minister."

The Park Keeper flung back his head and guffawed. "Not in that silly cap, you're not. Prime Ministers wear black shiny hats and white stripes down their trousers."

"Well, I've been having a game of cricket. I know

it's too small. I've grown out of it. But you can't wear a top hat when you're batting – or bowling, for that matter."

"I see. And now you've had your little game, you're off to visit the King, I suppose?" The Park Keeper was sarcastic.

"Well as a matter of fact, I am. An important letter arrived from the Palace as I was leaving home. Now, where did I put the wretched thing? Drat these skimpy flannel pockets! Not in this one, not in that. Can I have lost it? Ah, now I remember!" He wrenched off the offending cap and took from within it an envelope sealed with a large gold crown.

"DEAR PRIME MINISTER," he read out. "IF YOU HAVE NOTHING BETTER TO DO, PLEASE COME OVER TO DINNER. LOBSTER, TRIFLE, SARDINES ON TOAST. I AM THINKING OF MAKING A FEW NEW LAWS AND WOULD BE SO GLAD OF A CHAT."

"There! What did I tell you? And tonight of all nights! One never gets a moment's peace. I don't mind the chat, that's part of my job. But I can't stand lobster. It upsets my digestion. Oh, well, I'll have to go, I suppose. Bye-laws can always be by-passed, but laws have to be kept. And anyway," he said haughtily, folding his arms and looking important, "what has it got to do with you? A perfect stranger accosting me and telling me – *me!* – not to pick the roses! That's the Park Keeper's business."

"I-I *am* the Park Keeper," the Park Keeper said, shuddering from head to foot as he stared at the regal letter. He had made a terrible mistake and he trembled to think where it might lead him.

The Prime Minister lifted his monocle, screwed it firmly into his eye and regarded the figure before him.

"*I am shocked!*" he said, sombrely. "Even stupefied. Almost, I might say, speechless. A public servant in a public place failing to array himself in the uniform provided! I don't know when I have been so displeased. And what, pray, have you done with your hat?"

"I-I dropped it in a litter basket."

"A *litter* basket! A receptacle for orange peel! An employee of the County Council who thinks so little of his hat that he throws it into a – well, really! This kind of thing must not go on. It would bring the country to the verge of ruin. I shall speak to the Lord Mayor."

"Oh, please, your Honour, it just happened. A little slip when my mind was elsewhere. I'll go through the litter tomorrow and find it. Not the Lord Mayor, your Worship, *please*! Think of my

503

poor old mother."

"You should have thought of her yourself. Park Keepers are paid to think. To keep their minds here, not elsewhere. And not to let things just happen. However, as it's Midsummer's Eve – only once a year, after all – I will let the matter pass. On condition – " The Prime Minister glanced at his watch. "Dear me, it's far too late for conditions. You'll just have to solve the problem yourself. I must hurry home and change my trousers."

He bent down to pick up his bat. "You a married man?" he enquired, glancing up at the Park Keeper.

"No, my lord, my Prime – er, no."

"Neither am I. A pity, that. Not from my own point of view, of course. But to think that there's someone dreaming of me – putting a bunch of herbs under her pillow – Lad's Love, Lavender, Creeping Jenny – and then not finding me, poor woman. Alas, alas, what a disappointment! Tonight of all nights – you understand."

And he strode off, swinging his bat and his rose, his white trousers riding up from his ankles as though they had shrunk in the wash.

The Park Keeper did *not* understand. Who would be disappointed, and why? What was so special about tonight – except the fact that everyone seemed to be breaking the bye-laws; using the public park

504

as though it were their own back yard? And who could that be, he asked himself, as a curious figure, walking backwards, feet uncertainly feeling their way, came staggering through the Lane Gate?

It was Ellen from Number Seventeen, Cherry Tree Lane, moving like a sleep-walker, eyes closed, arms outstretched before her, meandering over the newly turfed lawn that he had mown that morning.

The Park Keeper braced himself. He would not stand meekly by while the rules were not only not observed but being illegally flouted. Come what might, this was something he would have to deal with, even without a hat. His eyes fell on a small object lying limply beside the fountain. It was the Prime Minister's cricketing cap, left behind, apparently, when he hurried off to change his trousers. The Park Keeper seized it gratefully. At least, his head would be covered.

"Look where you're going! Be careful, Miss Ellen! Beware of swings and see-saws and such. Steer clear of benches, borders and baskets." He strode towards her shouting his warnings.

Slowly, carefully, sometimes sneezing, Ellen came backing in his direction. Then, just as she was almost upon him, the Policeman, suddenly spying her, neatly inserted himself between them and Ellen landed with a bump against his blue serge jacket.

"Oh!" she cried joyfully, as she turned about and opened her eyes. "I hoped it might be you – and it is! What if I had made a mistake and bumped into the wrong one!"

"What, indeed!" The Policeman beamed. "But you didn't. And I'm the right one, see, and no mistake about it."

"It *is* a mistake to do things like that. You might have knocked someone over or got yourself a broken leg. And then who'd be to blame? Me! No backing allowed in a public park!" the Park Keeper warned her sternly.

"But I have to. It's Midsummer's Eve – atishoo! And if you walk backwards on Midsummer's Eve, after putting a herb or two under your pillow – Marjoram, Sweet Basil, no matter what – you'll back into your own true love as sure as nuts are nuts. Unless it's a gooseberry bush – atishoo! If it is, you have to wait till next year. To try again, I mean."

"Well, I'm no gooseberry bush, am I?" The Policeman took her hand in his. "So you won't have to wait till next year, will you?" He tucked his arm through hers.

"But what if you *never* bump into someone? What if it's *always* a gooseberry bush?" the Park Keeper demanded. It might be an Old Wives' Tale she was telling. But with these, he knew, you had to be careful. Unwise to make a mock of them: they were apt to turn out to be true.

"Oh, it's got to be someone someday – atishoo! There aren't all that many gooseberry bushes. And then there's the cucumber, don't forget!"

"What cucumber?" Was this some further silliness? Were they trying to make a fool of him?

"You don't know *anything*, do you?" said Ellen. "Didn't your grandmother tell you nothing? Mine told it to me and hers told her. And *her* grandmother told it to her, and away and away, right back to Adam."

He had been right, the Park Keeper thought. It *was* an Old Wives' Tale!

"Well, this is what you do," said Ellen. "You rub the juice behind your ears, close your eyes, put out your arms and then start walking backwards. It might be a long time or a short. Atishoo!" She paused to blow her nose. "But at last, if you're lucky, you meet your true love."

She gave the Policeman a blushing glance. "It's witchy," she added, "very witchy. But – you'll see! – it's worth it."

"Nothing like cucumber!" the Policeman grinned. "Luckiest vegetable in the world! Well, you've met yours and I've met mine. So the next thing is to name the day. How about next Thursday?"

He took Ellen firmly by the hand and led her away across the grass, tossing aside, as he did so, a spill of toffee paper.

The Park Keeper sighed as he picked it up and gazed after the lovers.

What was to be his lot, he wondered. The world went strolling past in pairs, two by two, hand in hand. Would such a thing ever happen to him? Had herbs been tucked under someone's pillow in the hope of meeting Frederick Smith, the Park Keeper? Would anyone - Snow White, say, or Cinderella - hide her face in *his* serge jacket?

The sun had now laggardly slipped away, leaving behind the long blue twilight - not day, not night, but something between - the hour that is thronged with fate.

The Prime Minister had disappeared and was even now, very likely, taking his top hat out of its hat box. Everyone else, apparently, was bent on their own affairs, even if those very affairs were ruining the Park. No one, as far as the Park Keeper could see, was looking in his direction.

What if - it was nonsense, of course - but what if he gave the thing a try? It certainly wouldn't do any harm. And it might, oh, it might - ! He crossed his fingers.

Straightening the blue flannel cap, the Park Keeper glanced furtively round, slipped a hand into his pocket and brought out the crumbling remains of his lunch – a scrap of cucumber sandwich. Cautiously, stealthily, he rubbed the scrap behind each ear and felt the juice of the cucumber as it trickled down into his collar. He summoned up his determination and drew a long, deep breath.

"Good luck, Fred!" he said to himself. Then he closed his eyes, stretched out his arms in front of him and began to walk slowly backwards. Easy now! Step by step. He gave himself to the twilight.

He seemed to be in another world. The Park he knew had dissolved itself into the darkness behind his eyes. Voices that had been near and lively grew faint and faded away. Distant music was wafted to him by people singing in chorus – old songs he seemed to have known as a boy, dreamy, gentle as lullabies. And somewhere a hurdy-gurdy was playing. Bert, the Matchman, of course!

Tch, tch! NO MUSICIANS OR HAWKERS ALLOWED IN THE PARK! But now the bye-laws would have to wait. He had something else to do.

From the right – or was it the left of him? – came the sound of splashing water. Oh, why wouldn't people look at the notice? NO SWIMMING PERMITTED IN THE LAKE. But perhaps it was just the fish rising,

which was what they did at this hour of the day. You couldn't really blame them for that. Fish, after all, can't read.

On, on. His feet felt the bending grass beneath them and the spreading roots of trees. The scent of dandelions rose to his nose, something like dandelions brushed his boots. Where was he? In the Wild Garden? He could not tell and dared not look. If he opened his eyes, he might break the spell. On, on. Backward, backward. His destiny was leading him.

And now about him were whispering voices, rustlings and stirrings and stifled laughter.

"Hurry, you boys!" urged a man's deep voice that seemed to come from far above him. "We haven't got much time!"

Good Heavens, thought the Park Keeper. Were people actually up in the trees, breaking the branches as well as the bye-laws? Never mind. He had to go on.

"We're coming!" piping voices answered, from the height of the Park Keeper's shoulder. "It's the others who are lagging behind. Come *on*, Foxy! And you, too, Bear! Why must you always be such a slowcoach?"

Foxes? Bears? The Park Keeper trembled. Could it be that the Keeper of the Zoological Gardens, bewitched by this thing called Midsummer's Eve, had left the cages open? Might he himself, at any moment, be confronted with a jungle beast, a tiger burning bright?

"Oh, help!" he cried, leaping aside, as a furry form brushed his ankle. Not a tiger, he thought, too small and fleecy. A rabbit, it must be, a wild rabbit. No rabbits allowed in the public parks. He would set a trap tomorrow.

There were scurryings now all about him and a sudden swoop and clap of wings as an airy shape flew past.

Something that felt like a cherry-stone rapped on his cap and bounced away. It was as though it had been spat out by someone much taller than himself, imagining him – the Park Keeper! – to be a litter basket. He was humming, this someone, as he strode by, a refrain that sounded familiar. Could it, perhaps, be *Pop Goes the Weasel*? If so, it was out of tune.

The humming died away behind him. All was silent. The world was still, his footsteps the only thing that moved.

The Park Keeper felt lost and lonely. His outstretched arms were beginning to ache. His eyes were weary of seeing nothing.

Even so, back and back he went. All things come to an end, he knew. And he would not fail whoever it was who was dreaming her Midsummer dream.

Blindly stumbling, backwards, backwards. And, after hours, it seemed, and miles – was he even still in the Park? – he heard behind him a distant murmur: nothing festive, no great clamour, merely the friendly, sociable chatter of people at one with each other.

The murmur grew louder as he neared it. Somebody laughed. Voices were raised and then lowered. Conversation went back and forth. How beautiful, the Park Keeper thought, was the sound of human gossip! Whoever these people were, he was sure, the longed-for "she" would be among them. At last, at last, his fate was upon him. The time had come when he, Fred Smith, like everybody else in the world, would go hand in hand, two by two.

Nearer and nearer came the voices. How many more backward steps were needed? Three would do it, the Park Keeper thought. He took them slowly. One. Two. Three.

And, suddenly – bump! There she was! His spine sensed the shape of a curving shoulder, slender and warm, and his heart leapt. All he need do now was turn and face her. He swivelled round upon his heel and a firm hand thrust him sideways.

"I'll thank you not to behave like a carthorse. I am not a lamp-post!" said Mary Poppins.

The voice was only too well known and the Park

Keeper, still with his eyes closed, let out a cry of protest.

"Never no luck for me," he wailed. "I might have known it wouldn't work. Here I come, looking for my true love, and I have to bump into a gooseberry bush!"

A cackle of laughter rent the air. "Some gooseberry bush!" jeered another voice he would rather not have heard.

With a groan, the Park Keeper opened his eyes and, as though unwilling to believe what they told him, hurriedly closed them again.

He was in the Herb Garden, he realized, with its marble seats and its paved path round a square of chamomile lawn. There was nothing new in that, of course. He had planned and planted it himself. But now on the sward he had mown so often, among the remains of a recent picnic – egg-shells, cake, sausage rolls – were Mary Poppins and the Banks children, Mrs Corry and her two daughters, and his own mother sitting on one of the seats, smiling her welcoming smile.

Nothing new in all that either. But had he seen – yes, he had indeed – he could not deny his own eyes – a Bear sitting snugly beside the hedge, licking a trumpet of Honeysuckle; a Fox on its hind legs picking the Foxgloves; and a Hare in the Parsley patch!

And, as if all this were not enough, Jane and Michael, wearing wreaths of green, together with two unknown boys, scantily clad and similarly crowned, were plucking armfuls of herbs; a big man, armed with a club and dressed in strips of leather, a studded belt about his waist and a lion-skin round his shoulders, was decking Mary Poppins' ear with a double stem of cherries; and a large bird, perched on a bough above her – this to him was the last straw! – was being regaled by the Bird Woman with a sprig of flowering Fennel!

"Mother, how *could* you?" the Park Keeper cried. "No picking of herbs allowed in the Park. You know the bye-laws and you break them!"

This was the first time she had failed him and he felt he could never forgive her.

"Well, you got to make allowances, lad. He only comes down once a year."

"I'm not *allowed* allowances, Mum! And birds are coming down all the time. They can't make nests up there in the sky. After all, it stands to reason."

"Nothing stands to reason, Fred – not tonight, it doesn't."

She glanced from the bird to the animals.

"Well, isn't it very reasonable to come and get the things you need? *I* would!" said Michael stoutly.

"But how did they get here to get what they need?

Somebody let them out of the Zoo!" The cages *had* been unlocked! The Park Keeper was sure of it.

"No, no. They came down with Castor and Pollux." Jane waved her hand at the two boys, as she plucked a spray of Solomon's Seal and tucked it into her looped-up skirt.

"Castor and Pollux! Get along! They're characters in a story. Lily-white boys turned into stars. Tamed horses, that's what they did. I read it when I was a boy."

"And we came down with Orion," said the boys, speaking as though with a single voice. "We came to get fresh herbs for our horse, and he to pick cherries in the Lane. He always does on Midsummer's Eve."

"Oh, does he indeed?" The Park Keeper smiled a withering smile. "Just descends, like, out of the sky, to steal what belongs to the County Council! What do you take me for, then – an April Fool in the middle of June? Orion's up there, like he always is." He flung up a pointing finger.

"Where?" demanded the big man. "Show me!"

The Park Keeper craned his head backwards, but all he could see was emptiness, a large, vacant, unanswering sky, blue as the bloom on a plum.

"Well, you'll have to wait. It's not dark enough yet. But he'll be there, don't you worry – up there

519

where he belongs."

Mrs Corry let out a cackle of laughter. "Who's worrying?" she shrieked.

"You're right," said the big man with a sigh, as he sat down on a marble seat and laid his club beside him. "Orion will be where he belongs. He can't do otherwise, poor chap." He took a cherry from the hoard in his hand, ate it and spat out the stone. "But not yet – ah, no, not yet. There's still a little time."

"Well, you'd better get off where *you* belong – a circus tent, I wouldn't wonder, with all that fol de rol fancy dress. *And* you!" the Park Keeper waved at the boys. "Tight-rope walkers or I'm a Dutchman!"

"You're a Dutchman then! We're Gallopers!" The boys burst into a peal of laughter.

"One thing or the other, it makes no difference. Leave the leaves and I'll burn them tomorrow. We don't want no ragamuffins here."

"They're not ragamuffins! Oh, can't you see?" Jane was almost in tears.

"But what will Pegasus do?" cried Michael, angrily stamping his foot. "They wanted a meal of Coltsfoot for him. So I gathered it. I don't *want* it burnt!" He hugged the herb-filling string bag to him, determined to defy the bye-laws.

"Pegasus!" scoffed the Park Keeper. "He's another of them taradiddles. You learn about them

520

when you're at school. *Astronomy for Boys and Girls*. Constellations, comets and such. But whoever saw a horse with wings? He's just a bunch of stars, that's all. And Vulpecula, and Ursa Minor and Lepus – all that lot."

"What important names." The two boys giggled. "We call them Foxy and Bear and Hare."

"Call them anything you like. Just get out of here, the three of you. And take your circus beasts along or I'll go to the Zoo and find the Keeper and have them put behind bars."

"If a gooseberry bush may make a remark –" Mary Poppins broke in. "You did say gooseberry bush, I believe?" she said with icy politeness.

The Park Keeper quailed before her glance.

"It was just a-a kind of manner of speaking. And gooseberry bush is no libel, it's just a sort of – er – spiky shrub. And anyway, put it in a nutshell –" Why shouldn't he speak his mind, he thought. "It isn't as though you're the Queen of Sheba."

The big man sprang from the marble seat.

"Who says she's not?" he demanded sternly, and the lion-skin stiffened on his shoulder, the head showing its fangs.

The Park Keeper hurriedly took a step backwards.

"Well, no one can say she is, can they? What with

521

turned-up nose and turned-out feet and a knob of hair and –"

"What's wrong with them?" The big man glowered, reaching for the club at his side and looming over the Park Keeper, who hurriedly took another step backwards.

Majestically, a pink and white statue, Mary Poppins inserted herself between them. "If you're looking for the Keeper of the Zoological Gardens, he is not in the Zoo. He is in the Lake."

"In the *Lake*?" The Park Keeper stared at her aghast. "D-drownded?" he whispered, pale as a lily. Oh, alas, alas!

"Paddling. With the Lord Mayor and two Aldermen. Fishing for tiddlers to put in a jam jar."

"J-jam-jar? The Lord Mayor? Oh, no! Oh, no! Not tiddlers. It's against the b-bye-laws. Isn't *anyone* observing the rules?" the Park Keeper cried in despair.

The world, as he knew it, had fallen apart. Where now was the lawful authority that he had always served? To whom could he turn for reassurance? The Policeman? No, he was off with Ellen. The Lord Mayor – oh, horrors! – was in the Lake. The Prime Minister was closeted with the King. And he himself, the Park's Park Keeper, important though he undoubtedly was, must carry the burden alone.

"Why should it all depend on me?" He flung his arms wide with the question. "All right, I took off a bit of time, which is owed me, after all. And it wasn't much to ask," he lamented. "Only to find my own true love –"

"Curly Locks, I suppose, or Rapunzel?" Mrs Corry chuckled. "You'll find they're suited, I'm afraid. But I've got a couple of soncy girls – Fannie or Annie, take your pick – and I'll throw in a pound of tea!"

The Park Keeper put the suggestion aside as being beneath his notice.

"To find my true love," he repeated. "And all litter placed in the proper baskets. No stealing of herbs from here, nor cherries from the Lane. No one pretending to be what they're not –" He waved at the intruders. "And everyone keeping the bye-laws."

"If you ask me, that's a lot to ask." The big man looked at him sternly. "True loves don't grow on trees, you know."

"Or gooseberry bushes," Mary Poppins put in.

"And what are cherries for but eating? Herbs, too, if it comes to that." The big man swallowed another cherry, and spat out another stone.

"But you can't just pick them because you want them!" The Park Keeper was scandalized.

"Why else?" enquired the big man, mildly. "If we didn't want them, we wouldn't take them."

"Because you've got to think of others." The Park Keeper, who seldom thought of others himself, was quick to deliver his sermon. "That's why we have the bye-laws, see!"

"Well, we *are* the others, all of us. And so are you, my man."

"Me!" The Park Keeper was indignant. "I'm not somebody else, not me!"

"Of course you are. Everyone's somebody else to someone. And what harm have the wild beasts done? A few green leaves one day in the year! It's true that they're not used to bye-laws. We don't have them up there, thank goodness." The big man nodded at the sky.

"And as for pretending to be what we're not – or what you presume to think we're not – how about yourself? Making all this fuss and pother, meddling in things that don't concern you – isn't it rather presumptuous? You're behaving as though you owned the place. Why not look after your own affairs and leave the Park to the Park Keeper? He seems a sensible sort of chap. I always enjoy looking down at him – mowing the lawns, putting waste paper into containers, faithfully going about his job."

The Park Keeper stared.

"But it's *my* job he's going about . I mean that *I'm* going about it. Don't you see? He's me!"

"Who's you?"

"Him. I mean me. *I'm* the Park Keeper."

"Nonsense! I've seen him often enough. A decent young fellow, neat and natty. Wears a peaked hat with P.K. on it, not a silly little blue flannel top-knot."

The Park Keeper clapped his hand to his head. The Prime Minister's cap! He had quite forgotten. Perhaps he should never have worn it.

"Look here," he said, with the fearful calm of one who is near to his wits' end. "I'm the same man, aren't I, whatever my cap?" Surely it was obvious. Had circus people no brains at all?

"Well, *are* you? Only you can give an answer to that. And it's not an easy question. I wonder –" The big man was suddenly thoughtful. "I wonder, would I be the same person without my belt and lion-skin?"

"*And* your club. *And* your faithful dog-star. Don't forget Sirius, Orion!" The two boys laughed and teased him. "Sirius can't come down with us," they explained to Jane and Michael. "He'd be chasing all the cats in the Lane."

"Yes, yes, the fellow has a point. Even so," the big man went on, "I can't believe the Keeper I know,

526

that watchful, conscientious servant, would go walking backwards through the Park, eyes closed, hands
outstretched, and bits of crust behind his ears. And
on top of that – without a 'By your leave' or 'I beg
your pardon' – go bumping into an elegant lady as
though she were a lamp-post."

The Park Keeper put his hands to his ears. It was
true. They were decked with scraps of sandwich!

"Well," he blustered, "how was I to know she was
there? And it wasn't the bread that was important.
What I wanted was cucumber."

"A proper Park Keeper doesn't go about bumping. And he knows how to get just what he wants. If
cucumber, then why bread? You should be more
precise."

"I know what *I* want," said a voice from the
hedge. "A little of something sweet."

"Have a finger!" Mrs Corry shrieked, as she broke
off one from her left hand and offered it to the Bear.
"Don't worry, it will grow again!"

His small eyes widened with surprise. "Barley
Sugar!" he exclaimed with delight, and stuffed it
into his mouth.

"Nothing for nothing!" said Mrs Corry. "Put a
shine on my coat for luck!"

The Bear put his paw upon her collar. "It'll shine,
when it's time – just wait!" he said.

"What I want is a pair of gloves. I'm going to a party tonight and I like to look well-dressed." The Fox prinked and pranced beside the Foxgloves, as he tried on flower after flower.

"Parsley!" said the Hare from the Parsley patch.

"For his rheumatism," the big man explained. "It's often cold up there and draughty. And Parsley's good for it."

"Coo-roo, coo-roo," the great Bird crooned as he munched his Fennel.

"I do
Like a herb
Or two,
Don't you?"

The Park Keeper's eyes, as large as soup plates, swivelled in all directions.

Had he seen? Had he heard? A finger turned into Barley Sugar? Animals speaking in human voices? No, of course he hadn't! Yes, he had! Was it a dream? Had he gone mad?

"It's the cucumber!" he cried wildly. "I shouldn't have done it. Not behind the ears. She said it would be witchy. And it is! But whether it's worth it, I'm not sure. Maybe I'm not the Park Keeper. Maybe I *am* somebody else. Everything's head over heels tonight. I don't know nothing, not any more."

528

And snatching the cricket cap from his head, he flung himself, sobbing, across the lawn and buried his face in his mother's skirt.

She smoothed his ruffled hair with her hand. "Don't take on so vainly, Fred. It'll come right – you'll see."

The big man regarded him broodingly.

"A sprig of Heartsease or Lemon balm – either of them would be soothing. Probably needs a rest from himself, whoever he is, poor chap! I even get tired of being Orion." He sighed and shook his head.

"*We* don't need a rest from ourselves, do we?" Castor and Pollux exchanged a grin.

"Ah, that's because you've got each other. But it's often lonely, away up there."

"I never get tired of being myself. I like being Michael Banks," said Michael. "And so does Mary Poppins. I mean, she likes being Mary Poppins. Don't you, Mary Poppins?"

"Who else would I want to be, pray?" She gave him one of her haughty looks. The very idea was absurd.

"Ah, well, but you're the Great Exception. We can't all be like you, can we?" Orion gave her a sidelong glance and picked out another pair of cherries. "That's for your other ear, my dear."

"I've no complaints," the Bear bumbled. "I like

530

showing sailors the way home."

"I'm going to be a sailor," said Michael. "Aunt Flossie sent me this suit for my birthday."

"Well, you'll need the star in my tail to guide you. I am always there."

"Not if I have Mary Poppins' compass. I can go right round the world with that. And she can stay here and look after my children."

"Thank you, Michael Banks, I'm sure. If I've nothing better to do than that," she gave a loud, affronted sniff, "I'll be sorry for myself."

"Come to the party, that's something better – me in my beautiful foxgloves and you in your new pink dress." The Fox danced on his hind legs and held up his foxgloved paws. "The handsome Mr Vulpecula, arm in arm with Miss Mary Poppins!"

"Handsome is as handsome does." Mary Poppins, with a toss of her head, tossed aside the invitation.

"There's poison in Foxgloves," said Michael, glibly. "Mary Poppins never let us wear them in case we happen to lick our fingers and then have to go to bed, and be sick."

"Foxes do not lick their paws, nothing so vulgar," said the Fox. "They merely wash them in the evening dew."

"Parsley," said a voice from the Parsley patch, with a coughing, choking sound.

531

Orion sprang from his marble seat.

"Be careful, Lepus, don't eat it! Spit it out, whatever it is! Ah, that's better. There's a good Hare!" He fossicked among the curling fronds and held up a shiny circular object. "A half-crown piece, by all that's lucky! And he nearly swallowed it."

The four children clustered about it, gazing greedily at the coin.

"What will you spend it on?" Jane asked.

"How could I spend it? There's nothing to buy. There are no ice cream carts in the sky, no peppermint horses, no balloons, not even ..." he glanced at Mrs Corry, "not even a gingerbread star."

"Well, what *is* up there? Nothing but nothing?" Michael found that hard to believe.

"Just space." Orion shrugged his shoulders. "Though you can't exactly say space is nothing."

"And there's lots of room," said Castor and Pollux. "Pegasus gallops everywhere and we take it in turns to ride him."

Michael felt a twinge of envy. He wished he could ride a horse through the sky.

"Room? Who wants room?" Orion grumbled. "Down here you have no room at all. Everything's close to something else. Houses leaning against each other. Trees and bushes crowding together. Pennies and half-pennies clinking in pockets. Friends and neighbours always at hand. Someone to talk to, someone to listen. Ah, well," he sighed, "each to his fate."

He tossed the silver coin in the air.

"Tails up, and you two can have it." He nodded at Jane and Michael. "Heads, and I keep it myself."

Down came the coin on his outstretched palm. "Heads it is. Hooray!" he cried. "If I can't spend it, at least I can wear it. I like a bit of bric-a-brac."

He pressed the half-crown against his belt in line with the three studs already there. "How does it look? Too flimsy? Too vulgar?"

"Oh, it's lovely!" all four children exclaimed.

"Neat enough," said Mary Poppins. "You'll need to keep it polished."

"Gingerbreadish, I'd say," giggled Mrs Corry. "A souvenir to remember us by."

"Souvenir!" Orion growled. "As if I needed reminding."

"He's right. He doesn't," said Castor and Pollux. "He pines all the year for Midsummer's Eve – this is our one night of magic – and the Park and the cherries and the music."

"Don't you have music up there?" asked Jane.

"Well," said Orion, "the morning stars sing together, of course. Same old plainsong day in and day out. But none of your cheerful, homely things.

Polly Wolly Doodle, Skip to my Lou, Pop Goes the What-you-call-it - all that stuff. Listen! They're singing down by the Lake. Don't tell me, I'll get it in a minute. Ah, yes - *Green Grow the Rushes-O.*" He hummed a line of the song.

"He can't sing in tune," the two boys whispered. "But he doesn't know it and we don't tell him."

"And then there's the music of the spheres, a sort of steady, droning sound. Rather like that spinning thing I saw you with today."

"My humming top! I'll get it," said Jane.

She ran to the perambulator that was like an over-crowded bird's nest, with John and Barbara and Annabel asleep on each other's shoulders.

Jane thrust in her hand and rummaged among them.

"It's not here. Oh, I've lost my top!"

"No, you haven't," said a gloomy voice, as a thin man and a fat woman came hand in hand into the Garden. "It fell out on to the Long Walk and we found it as we came by."

"It's Mr and Mrs Turvy!" cried Michael, as he dashed away to greet them.

"Well, it may be and it may not. You can't be certain of anything. Not today, you can't. You think you're this and you find you're that. You want to hurry, so you crawl like a snail." The thin man gave a doleful sigh.

"Oh, Cousin Arthur," Mary Poppins protested. "It's not your Second Monday, not one of your upside-down days!"

"I'm afraid it is, Mary, my dear. And tonight of all nights, when I want to go looking for my own true love, just like everyone else."

"But you've already found her, Arthur!" Mrs Turvy reminded him.

"So you say, Topsy. And I'd like to believe it. But nothing's sure on the Second Monday."

"You'll be sure tomorrow. Tomorrow's Tuesday."

"And what if tomorrow never comes? It would be just like it to stay away." Mr Turvy was unconvinced. "Well, here's your top and much good may it do you." He turned aside, wiping an eye, as Jane set the coloured top on the path.

"Not yet, not yet!" Orion cried, suddenly cupping his hand to his ear.

From somewhere among the surrounding trees a bird gave a quick enquiring chirp that was followed by a rush of half-notes, not so much song as a series of kisses.

"A nightingale tuning up. Oh, glory!" Orion's face was alight with joy.

"It belongs to Mr Twigley," said Michael. "It's

the only one in the Park."

"Some people do have all the luck. To own a nightingale! Think of it! Come on, come on, my lovely boy! Spin your old humming top, Jane! He'll out-sing it, be sure."

The four children fell on the shining toy, shouldering each other aside, arguing and complaining.

"I'll start it! No, you won't, it's mine! Me! Me! Me!" they all shouted.

"Is this a Herb Garden or a Bear Pit?" demanded Mary Poppins.

"Certainly not a Bear Pit. Bears are better behaved," said the Bear.

"But, Mary Poppins, it's not fair!" Castor and Pollux protested. "We haven't got a top up there. They might give us a chance."

"Well, we haven't got a flying horse!" Jane and Michael were equally indignant.

Mary Poppins folded her arms and favoured them all with her fierce blue glance.

"Hooligans, the lot of you!" she said. "You haven't got this and you haven't got that. Tops or horses – take what you're given. Nobody has everything."

And in spite, or perhaps because of her fierceness that embraced them all equally, their anger melted away.

Castor and Pollux sat back on their heels. "Not

even you, Mary Poppins?" they teased her. "With your new pink dress and your daisy hat?"

"And your carpet bag! And your parrot umbrella!" Jane and Michael joined in.

She preened a little at the compliment as she gave her characteristic sniff. "That's as may be," she retorted. "And no affair of yours either. I will start the top myself!"

She stooped to seize the handle, and pumped it briskly up and down.

Slowly the top began to turn and as it turned, it hummed – faintly at first but gradually, as it gathered speed, the sound became one long deep note, filling the Herb Garden with its music, a bee-like humming and drumming.

"A ring! Make a ring!" cried Castor and Pollux. "The Grand Chain, everyone!"

And at once they all came into a circle, formally moving round the top as the earth moves round the sun. Right hand to right hand, left hand to left – the Bear with his sugar-stick in his mouth, the Fox dapper in his Foxgloves, the Hare nib-nibbling a sprig of Parsley.

Round and round. Hand to hand. Mary Poppins and the two Banks children, Mrs Corry, her daughters and the Bird Woman, Mr Turvy dragging his feet, Mrs Turvy dancing.

Round and round. Hand to hand. Orion girt with his lion-skin, Pollux with his tunic full of herbs, and Michael's string bag, bursting with Coltsfoot, slung about Castor's neck.

Round and round, each hand taking the hand of each, and the big Bird flying among them. The top spun and the circle spun round it, and the Park round the circle, the earth round the Park and the darkening sky round the earth.

The Nightingale, now the night was come, came to the full of his song. *Jug, jug, jug, tereu!* it went, over and over, from the elder tree, outsinging the hum of the top. The song would never be done, it seemed, and the top would never stop spinning. The circle of humans and constellations would go on turning forever..

But suddenly the bird was silent and the top, with a last musical cry, slowed down and toppled sideways.

Clang! The tin shape crashed upon the flagstones.

And the Park Keeper sat up with a start.

He rubbed his eyes as though waking from sleep. Where was he? What had been happening? He had hidden himself from the fading day and all its unbearable problems. And now the day had disappeared. It had passed through its long blue twilight hour and had almost become the night.

But that was not all. The Herb Garden he knew so well was now another garden. There, in a ring, were people he knew, the familiar solid and substantial shapes of Mary Poppins and her charges, Mrs Corry and her two large daughters, his Mother in her shabby shawl. But who were the others, the bevy of transparent figures, the creatures that seemed to be made of light – insubstantial luminous boys hand in hand with substantial children; a man in a lionskin, bright as the sun, bending towards Mary Poppins; a Bear and a Hare, both shimmering, a big Bird lifting wings of light and a sparkling Fox with flowers on his paws?

And suddenly, like a man who has lost, and regained, his senses, the Park Keeper understood. He had known those figures when he was a boy, and many more besides. And he had forgotten what he had known, denied it, made it a thing of naught, something to be sneered at! He put his hands up to his eyes to hide the springing tears.

Mary Poppins stooped and picked up the top.

"It's time," she said quietly. "The day is gone. You are needed now elsewhere. Castor, put your wreath on straight. And you, Pollux, fasten your collar. Remember who you are!"

"And who *you* are, Mary Poppins!" they teased her. "With your 'Spit spot and away you go!' As if we could ever forget!" They gathered their loads of greenstuff to them.

"Till next year, Jane and Michael," they cried. "We'll be coming to get more Coltsfoot!"

They flung up shining hands as they spoke and then, like the day, they were gone.

"And another pair of gloves!" said the Fox.

"More Barley Sugar!" the Bear bumbled.

"Parsley!" The one word came from the Hare.

And they, too, disappeared.

> *"Coo-roo, coo-roo,*
> *This is for you!"*

The great Bird swooped to Mary Poppins, stuck a wing feather into her hat and then became air and starlight.

Mary Poppins straightened the glowing feather and glanced up at Orion.

"Do not linger!" she warned him.

> *"Linger longer, Lucy,*
> *Linger longer, Lou,*
> *How I long to linger long,*
> *To linger longa you."*

Orion sang tunelessly, and gave her a rueful glance.

"Don't worry, I'll be where I belong, just as that fellow said. "But – to leave all this –" He flung out his arms, as if to embrace the whole width of the Park. "Oh, well – the law's the law! But it's no easy thing to obey it." He gobbled up his remaining cherries, spat out the stones on the chamomile lawn, and took her hand and kissed it.

"Fare thee well, my fairy fay," he said gruffly. And then, like a candle flame blown out, he was there no longer.

"Next year!" cried Jane and Michael shrilly, to the emptiness he had left.

And at that the Park Keeper leapt to his feet.

"No, *now*!" he cried. "They can have them now – all they want, and more."

In a frenzy he dashed from bed to bed, plucking green branches of every kind and tossing them into the air.

"Take them! I'll let the bye-laws be! Rosemary for Remembrance, Mister. All the fodder you need, lads, for the horse! Foxgloves for Foxy! Sweet savours for the beasts and the Bird."

He flung the herbs wildly towards the sky. And to the surprise of Jane and Michael, not a leaf, not a branch, came down – except a small spray of something that Mary Poppins caught in her hand and tucked into her belt.

"Forgive me, friends! I didn't reckernize you!" the Park Keeper called to the nothingness. "And I didn't reckernize meself, neither. I forgot what I knew when I was a boy. It needed the dark to show things plain. But I know who you are now, all of you. And I know who I am, Orion, sir! Cucumber or no cucumber, I'm the Park Keeper with or without my hat!"

And off he darted among the herbs, gathering, bellowing their names, tossing them into the air.

"St John's Wort! Marigold! Coriander! Cornflower! Dandelion! Marjoram! Rue!"

"Really, Smith, you should be more careful! You might have knocked my eye out."

Mr Banks, entering the Herb Garden, removed a sprig of Marjoram from the brim of his bowler hat. "And of course you are the Park Keeper! Whoever said you weren't?"

The Park Keeper took no notice. On he went, madly tossing and yelling. "Good King Henry! Rampion! Sage! Sweet Cicely! Rocket! Basil!"

Up into the air went leaves and flowers and none of them came down.

Mr Banks stared after him.

"What's he doing, throwing herbs around? A Park Keeper breaking the bye-laws! The poor chap must have lost his wits."

"Or found them!" said the Bird Woman softly.

"Aha! So this is where you are!" Mr Banks turned

543

and raised his hat. "I missed you as I came by St Paul's. Your birds were making an awful to-do. Don't they ever stop eating? And no one was there to take my tuppence, so now, of course, they're starving. Well, what are all of you doing here?"

He held out his arms to his children. "A Midsummer picnic, I presume. You might have left me a sausage roll." He picked up a discarded piece of pastry and munched it hungrily.

"Are you looking for your own true love?" Jane asked, hugging his arm.

"Of course not. I know where she is. I'm on my way to her now, as it happens. And how are *you*, Mary Poppins?" he asked, glancing at the upright figure as it rocked the perambulator. "You're looking very sprightly tonight, with a spray of forget-me-not in your belt and your cherry earrings and Sunday-best hat. That feather must have cost a pretty penny!"

"Thank you, I'm sure." She tossed her head, and smiled her self-satisfied smile. Compliments were no more than her due and she always accepted them calmly.

He gave her a thoughtful, puzzled glance. "You never get older, Mary Poppins, do you? What's the secret? Tell me!" he teased her.

"Ah, that's because she's eaten Fern seed!" The

Bird Woman eyed him slyly.

"Fern seed? Nonsense! An Old Wives' Tale. 'Eat Fern seed and you'll live for ever', they told me when I was a boy. And I used to come and look for it, here in this very garden."

"I can't imagine you as a boy." Jane measured her height against his waistcoat button.

"I don't see why not." Mr Banks was hurt. "I was a very charming boy – about as high as you are now – in brown velveteen and a white collar and black stockings and button-up boots. 'Fern seed, fern seed, where are you?' I'd say. But of course I never found it. I'm not even sure that it exists." Mr Banks looked sceptical.

"And, what was worse, I lost something – the first half-crown I ever had. Oh, the dreams I dreamed of that half-crown. I was going to buy the world with it. But it must have dropped out of a hole in my pocket."

"That must be the one Orion found. He took it away with him," said Michael. "Just before you came."

"O'Ryan? A friend of Smith's, I suppose! Those Irish fellows have all the luck. He's probably spent it by now, the wretch! If I had turned up earlier, I'd have made him give it back. I can't afford to lose pennies, let alone half-crowns."

Mary Poppins regarded him sagely. "All that's lost is somewhere," she told him.

Mr Banks stared at her. For a moment he seemed quite mystified and then, of a sudden, his face cleared. He flung back his head and laughed.

"Of course! Why didn't I think of that? It couldn't fall out of the universe, could it? Everything has to be somewhere. Even so," he sighed, "it would have been useful. Well, no good crying over spilt milk. I must get on. I'm late already."

A hen-like screech rent the air. "You always were!" a voice cackled. "Late in the morning. Late at night. You'll be late for your funeral, if you don't look out!"

Mr Banks, startled, peered through the dusk and saw, half-hidden by the elder-tree, a little old woman in a black coat that was covered with – could it be? – threepenny bits! And beside her two large, formless shapes that might, or might not, be younger ladies.

It was true. He had to admit it. He *was* in the habit of not being on time. But how did this old person know it? And what right had she, a complete stranger, to meddle in his affairs?

"Well," he began defensively, "I'm a busy man, I'd have you know. Making money to keep my family; often working late at the office – it's hard to wake up in the morning –"

"Early to bed, early to rise, makes a man healthy and wealthy and wise. I said that to Ethelred the Unready. But, of course, he wouldn't listen."

"*Ethelred the Unready!*" Mr Banks was astonished. "But he was around ten hundred and something!" She's dotty, poor thing, he thought to himself, I must humour her. "And what about Alfred the Great?"he asked. "Was he a friend of yours, too?"

"Ha! He was worse than Ethelred. Promised to watch my cakes, he did. 'No need to move them' I said to him. 'Just keep the fire going – and watch!' And what did he do? Piled up the logs and then forgot. Just sat there, brooding over his kingdom, while my gingerbread stars were cooked to a crisp."

"*Gingerbread stars!*" Whatever next? Really, Mr Banks told himself, Mary Poppins certainly had a gift for making peculiar friends!

"Well, never mind," he said soothingly. "You've still got the real stars, haven't you? They can't get cooked or move from their places."

He ignored her scream of mocking laughter as he glanced up at the sky.

"Ah, there's the first one! Wish on it, children. And another! They're coming thick and fast. Good Lord, they are so bright tonight!" His voice was soft with rapture.

547

"Star light, star bright," he murmured. "It's as though they were having a party up there. Polaris! Sirius! The Heavenly Twins! And where is – ah, yes, there he is! I can always tell him by his belt with its three great stars in a row. Great Heavens!" He gave a start of surprise. "There are *four* in a row, or my eyesight's failing. Jane! Michael! Can you see it? An extra star beside the others?"

Their eyes followed his pointing finger. And, sure enough, faint and small, there was a something – not, perhaps, to be claimed as a star – and yet, and yet, a something!

They blinked at it, half-afraid to believe but, even so, half-believing.

"I *think* I see it," they both whispered. They did not dare to be sure.

Mr Banks threw his hat into the air. He was beside himself with joy.

"A new star! Clap your hands, world! And I, George Banks, of Number Seventeen Cherry Tree Lane, have been the first to spot it. But let me be calm, yes, calm's the word – let me be cool, composed and placid."

But, far from being any of these, he was feverish with excitement. "I must go at once to the Admiral and ask for the use of his telescope. Verify it. Tell the Astronomer Royal. You'll find your way, won't

you, Mary Poppins? This is important, you understand. Goodnight, Mrs Smith!" He bowed to the Bird Woman. "And goodnight to you, Madam – er – hum –"

"Corry," said Mrs Corry, grinning.

Mr Banks, already streaking away, stopped dead in his tracks.

When had he heard that name before? He stared at the oddity before him and turned, for some reason, to Mary Poppins.

The two women were regarding him gravely, silent and motionless as pictured figures in a book, looking out from the page.

Suddenly, Mr Banks was flooded with a sense of being somewhere else. And, also, of being someone else who was, at the same time, himself.

White-collared and velvet-suited, he was standing tip-toe in button-up boots, his nose just reaching a glass-topped counter, over which he was handing to someone he could hardly see, a precious threepenny bit. The place smelt richly of gingerbread; an ancient woman was slyly asking, "What will you do with the gold paper?" and a voice that seemed to be his own was saying, "I keep them under my pillow." "Sensible boy," the old creature croaked, exchanging a nod with someone behind him, someone wearing a straw hat with a flower or two springing from it.

"George, where are you?"

Another and younger voice cried his name. "George! George!"

And the spell was broken.

With a start, Mr Banks returned to the Herb Garden and all familiar things. It had been nothing, he told himself, a moment's madness, a slip of the mind.

"Impossible!" He laughed nervously, as he met Mary Poppins' glance.

"All things are possible," she said, primly.

His eyebrows went up. Was she mocking him?

"Even the impossible?" he asked, mocking her in return.

"Even that," she assured him.

"George!" The calling voice held a note of panic.

"I'm here," he answered. "Safe and sound!" He turned away from the moonstruck moment, the trance, the dream, whatever it was.

"After all," he thought, "it's Midsummer's Eve. One expects to be bewitched."

"Oh, George," cried Mrs Banks, wringing her hands, "the children are off on a supper picnic. And I can't find them. I'm afraid they are lost!"

He strode towards the fluttering shape that was crossing the lawn towards him.

"How could they be lost? They're with Mary Poppins. We can trust her to bring them home. For you're coming with me, my true love. Wonderful news! Guess what it is! I think I've discovered a new star and I want to look at it through a spy-glass. If it's true, I'll be made Star-Gazer-in-Chief and you shall be Queen of the May."

"Don't be silly, George," she giggled. "You and your stars! You're always making fun of me." But she didn't mind him being silly and she liked being called his true love.

"Admiral! Admiral! Wait for us! We want to look through your tel-es-co-pe!"

Mr Banks' voice, a fading echo, came floating back to the Herb Garden. And, at the same moment, the chorus of singers by the Lake came to the end of their song.

> *Two, two are the lily-white boys,*
> *A-clothed all in green-o*
> *One is one and all alone*
> *And ever more shall be so!*"

"Ever more," the Bird Woman murmured, glancing up at the sky. "Well, I must be getting along. I've a dish of Irish stew on the hob and he'll be hungry when he gets home."

She nodded in the direction of the Park Keeper

who was still tossing up twigs and branches and crying their names to the air.

"Good King Henry! Mistletoe! Lovage! All you want, Sir and lads!"

And none of them came down.

"Come, Arthur," said Mrs Turvy. "It's time we were going home."

"If we *have* a home," grumbled Mr Turvy, still very down in the dumps. "What about fires and earthquakes, Topsy? Anything could have happened."

"Nothing has happened to it – you'll see. Come to tea on Thursday, Mary. Things will be better then." Mrs Turvy led her husband away, guiding him through the shadows.

"Wait for me, Mrs Smith, my dear!" Mrs Corry gave her bird-like shriek. The threepenny bits on her coat were a-twinkle and the spot on her collar where the Bear had touched it now shone like a glowing button. "I have to get my beauty sleep or what will Prince Charming say – tee-hee?" She grinned at her two large daughters.

"Stir your stumps, Fannie and Annie," she said. "Come home and stuff some herbs under your pillows – Sowbread and Cuckoo's Meat might do the trick! – and perhaps I'll get you off my hands. Handsome husbands and ten thousand a year. Shake a leg, you galumphing giraffes! Pull up your socks! Skedaddle!"

She made a curtsey to Mary Poppins who received it with a gracious bow. Then away she went, prancing in her elastic boots between her plodding daughters, with the Bird Woman sailing along beside them, like a full-rigged ship, on the grass.

The Herb Garden, so lately full of light and movement, was still now, a pool of darkness.

"Jane, take your top," said Mary Poppins. "It is time we, too, were going home." And the many-coloured tin planet that had hummed and spun so harmoniously was stowed away with the picnic things, silent and motionless, as Jane swung the basket from her hand.

Michael looked round for his string bag and suddenly remembered.

"I've nothing to carry, Mary Poppins," he complained.

"Carry yourself," she told him briskly, as she turned to the perambulator and gave it a vigorous push. "Step along, please, and best foot forward."

"Which is the best foot, Mary Poppins?"

"The one that's in front, of course!"

"But it's sometimes the left and sometimes the right. They can't both be the best," he protested.

"Michael Banks!" She gave him one of her savage

looks. "If you are determined to argle-bargle, you can stay here and do it all by yourself. *We* are going home."

He did, indeed, want to argle-bargle and, if he could, get the better of her. But he knew that she always won in the end. And, anyway, it would be no fun to argue with the empty air since it could not answer back.

He decided he would carry himself. But how did one do that, he wondered. He could do it more easily, he thought, with something in his hand. So he seized on the handle of the perambulator and, to his surprise, became a boy who was carrying himself.

Jane came to the other side so that, with Mary Poppins between, all three were pushing together. They were suddenly glad to feel her nearness in the wide unfamiliar darkness.

For this was no longer their daytime Park, their intimate ordinary playground. They had never before been up so late nor understood that night changes the world and makes the known unknown. The trees that, by daylight, were merely trees – something to shade you from the sun or swing on when the Park Keeper was not looking – were now strange beings with a life of their own, full of secrets never disclosed, holding their breath till you went past.

Camellias, Rhododendrons, Lilacs, that by day were clustering shapes of green, were now nameless creatures full of menace, lying in wait, ready to spring.

The night itself was a whole new country, unmapped and unexplored, where the only thing that could not be doubted was the steady moving shape between them; flesh and bone under its cotton dress, the well-worn handbag and parrot umbrella aswing from the crook of its arm. They felt it rather than saw it, for they dared not lift their eyes. Nor could they be sure, in this crowding darkness, of the brightness they had seen. Or had they really seen it at all? Might they not have dreamed it?

To the right of them a bush moved. It muttered and mumbled to itself. Was it about to pounce?

They huddled closer to the cotton dress.

"It must be somewhere,"the bush was saying. "I had to take it off, I remember, in order to find the letter."

With an effort the children lifted their heads and nervously peered through the dark. They had come, they saw, to the Rose Garden. And the bush, edging forward as if to spring, became, by magic, a man. Ceremoniously clad, in top hat, black jacket and striped trousers, he was crawling about on hands and knees, clearly looking for something.

"I've lost my cricket cap," he told them. "Here, by the fountain or under the roses. I don't suppose any of you have seen it?"

"It's in the Herb Garden," said Mary Poppins.

The Prime Minister sat back on his heels. '*In the Herb Garden!* But that's at the other end of the Park! However could it have got there? Cricket caps can't fly. Or maybe –" He glanced around uneasily. "Maybe they can on a night like this. Strange things happen, you know, on Midsummer's Eve." He scrambled to his feet.

"Well, I've just got time," he looked at his watch, "to fetch it and get to the Palace." He doffed his hat to Mary Poppins, stumbled away into the darkness and bumped into a clump of bushes that was stealthily moving towards him.

"Really!" The Prime Minister uttered the exclamation as he hurriedly jumped aside. "You shouldn't go creeping about like that – as though you were tracking tigers or something. It gave me quite a start."

"Hssssst!" hissed a bush. "Where's the Park Keeper?"

"My dear fellow, how should I know? I don't keep Park Keepers in my pocket. Nothing's in its right place tonight. He could be anywhere. Why do you want him?"

The clump shuffled a little nearer and became the Lord Mayor and two Aldermen. Their robes were looped up round their waists and their bare legs shone whitely in the dark.

"That's just it. I *don't* want him. We need to get safely out of the Park without him getting his eyes on these." The Lord Mayor drew back a fold of his cloak and revealed a large glass jam jar.

"Tiddlers! You'll catch it if he finds you. The Lord Mayor breaking his own bye-laws! Ask that lady over there." The Prime Minister nodded at Mary Poppins. "She told me where to find my cap. And I must be off to get it. Goodnight!"

The Lord Mayor turned. "Why, it's you, Miss Poppins. How fortunate!" He glanced around warily and tip-toed over the grass.

"I wonder," he whispered into her ear, "if by any chance you've come across –"

"The Park Keeper?" Mary Poppins enquired.

"Sh! Not so loud. He might hear you."

"No, he won't." She favoured him with a Sphinx-like look. "He's far away at the end of the Park."

Gooseberry bush or no gooseberry bush, she was not going to disclose the fact that the Park Keeper, if only for tonight, was letting bye-laws be.

"Splendid!" The Lord Mayor beckoned the Alder-

men to him. "We can nip off home along the Lane and help ourselves ..." he winked at them, "to a cherry or two as we go!"

"I think you will find they have all been picked," Mary Poppins informed them.

"What – *all*?" The three were scandalized. "Vandalism! We must speak to the King. What can the world be coming to?" They spoke to each other in outraged whispers as they scurried off with the jam jar.

The perambulator creaked on its way. Tall, ghostly shapes loomed up before it and turned into swings as it came nearer. A thick black shadow went past sneezing and then revealed itself as Ellen who, wrapped in the Policeman's jacket, was being escorted home. Another moved out from among the trees and was seen to be a solid mass comprising Miss Lark and the Professor, with the two dogs huddling against them, as though anxious not to be seen.

"Goodnight, all!" chirruped Miss Lark, as she spied the little group. "And *what* a good night!" She waved at the sky. "Did you ever see such a sparkle, Professor?"

The Professor tilted back his head. "Dear me! Someone seems to be setting off fireworks. Can this be the Fifth of November?"

"Goodnight," called Jane and Michael shrilly, and looked, for the first time, upwards. They had been so intent on the darkness around them and the changes the night had wrought in the earth, that they had forgotten the sky. But the blaze above them, of stars that bent so bright and near – the party evidently in full swing – that, too, was the work of the night. True, the night had created the frightening shapes but then, as though to make amends, had changed them into familiar figures. And what but the night was bringing them, with each turn of the perambulator's wheel, each best foot, – left or right, – thrust forward, to the place from which they had started?

Ahead of them, beyond the line of cherry trees, lights began to appear – not so bright as the ones above but, for all that, bright enough. It seemed as though each house in the Lane, leaning so closely to the next, had lit itself from its neighbour. There were constellations both below and above, the earth and the sky were next door to each other.

"Now, no more day-dreaming, Professor. We want our supper. So do the dogs." Miss Lark seized the arm of her friend, who was raptly gazing into the darkness.

"My dear Miss Wren, I am *not* day-dreaming. I am looking at a fallen star. See! Over there, on that lady's hat." He swept the newspaper from his head and bowed to Mary Poppins.

Miss Lark put on her lorgnette.

"Nonsense, Professor! Falling stars just fizzle out. They never reach the earth. That's just a common pigeon feather – covered with luminous paint, or something. Magicians use things like that for their tricks."

And she whisked him through the Lane Gate.

"Is that you, Professor?" called Mr Banks, racing full tilt along the Lane, with Mrs Banks at his heels.

The Professor looked uncertain. "I suppose it is. People tell me so. I'm never quite sure myself."

"Well, I've glorious news. I've found a new star!"

"You mean the one on that hat? I've seen it."

"No, no! On the Belt, my dear chap. Up till now it has had just three – a trio of shiners in a row. But, tonight, I've distinctly seen a fourth."

"Miss Partridge says it's just luminous paint."

"Paint? Absurd! You can't put paint on the sky, man! It's there, as large as life – and solid. I've verified it. So has Admiral Boom. We've looked at it through his telescope. And who's Miss Partridge, anyway?"

"Lark!" said Miss Lark. "Do remember, Professor!"

"No, no it's not just a lark! He means it. He's seen

562

it through a telescope and telescopes don't lie."

"Of course they don't. They reveal the facts. So, we're off to the Planetarium. The news must be spread abroad."

"But, George, the children!" Mrs Banks broke in.

"Don't worry. They're all right, I tell you. Put on a hat and I'll change my tie." Mr Banks was panting with excitement. "Perhaps they'll call it after me. Imagine it! Fame at last! A heavenly body by the name of Banks!"

And the happy astronomer dashed away, dragging Mrs Banks by the hand, to the door of his own house.

"Why Banks, I wonder? I always thought his name was Cooper. And I could have sworn it was hat, not belt. But my memory is not what it was – if, indeed, it was ever what it was." Vague and perplexed, yet still hopeful, the Professor looked round for his fallen star.

But Miss Lark was having no more nonsense. She took her friend firmly by the arm and hurried him off to supper.

The Professor, however, need not have worried. His memory was what it had been. His fallen star, even now, was making its way towards the Lane Gate. The feather glowed among the daisies and its light was reflected in the pairs of cherries that hung below the hat brim.

Jane and Michael looked up at it and then from the feather to the sky. Half-dazzled by the resplendent light, they searched for, and found, what they sought. Ah, there! They needed no telescope to tell them.

Among the celestial ornaments, Orion's Belt gleamed on its unseen wearer – three large stars in a slanting line, and beside them, small, modest, but bright as a glow-worm, a fourth piece of bric-a-brac!

Neither the feather nor the extra star had been there when they set out. Their adventure had, indeed, been true. At last they could believe it. And, meeting Mary Poppins' eyes, they knew that she knew what they knew. All things, indeed, were possible – sky-light upon an earthy hat-brim, earth-light on a skyey girdle.

They craned their necks as they straggled beside her, and gazed at the conflagration. How was the party going, they wondered. Was someone strutting in his new-found sparkle; another boasting of his elegant mittens; the others displaying their treasure-trove? And was there anyone up there to remind them, with a toss of the head, that handsome was as handsome did? No! There was only one such person and she was walking between them.

Behind them, Mr Twigley's bird burst into song

again. Before them lay the Lane Gate. And as the perambulator creaked towards it they could see a necklace of shining windows beyond the cherry trees. The front door of Number Seventeen, left open by their excited parents, threw a long light down the garden path, as if to welcome them.

"Mary Poppins," said Jane, as they pushed their way on the last lap of the day's excursion. "What will you do with your earrings?"

"Eat them," said Mary Poppins promptly. "Along with a cup of strong tea and a slice of buttered toast." What else were cherries for, after all?

"And what about my string bag?" Michael hugged her sleeve.

"Kindly do not swing on my arm. I am not a garden gate, Michael!"

"But where is it? Tell me!" he demanded. Was Pegasus, even now, he wondered, munching a meal of Coltsfoot?

Her shoulders went up with their characteristic shrug.

"String bags – pooh! – they're two a penny. Lose one and you can get another."

"Ah! But perhaps it's not lost!" He gave her a darting, sidelong glance. "And neither will you be, Mary Poppins, when you skedaddle off."

She drew herself up, insulted.

"I'll thank you, Michael Banks, to mind your manners. I am not in the habit of skedaddling."

"Oh yes you are, Mary Poppins," said Jane. "One day here and the next day gone, without a word of warning."

"But she's not nowhere, even so. And neither is my string bag," said Michael. "But where? Where, Mary Poppins?" Every place, surely, had a name! "How shall we know how to find you?"

They held their breaths, waiting for an answer. She looked at them for a long time and her blue eyes sparkled with it. They could see it dance on to her tongue, all agog to make its disclosure. And then – it danced away. Whatever the secret was, she would keep it.

"Ah!" she said. And smiled.

"Ah! Ah! Ah! Ah!" repeated the Nightingale from its branch.

And above, from every quarter of the sky, there came an echoing "Ah!" The whole world was ringing with the riddle. But nothing, and nobody, answered it.

They might have known! She would not tell them. If she had never explained before, why should she do so now?

Instead, she gave them her haughty glance.

"I know where you two will be in a minute. And

that's into bed, spit spot!"

They laughed. The old phrase made them feel warm and secure. And even if there was no answer, there had been a reply. Earth and sky, like neighbours chatting over a fence, had exchanged the one same word. Nothing was far. All was near. And bed, they now realized, was exactly where they wanted to be, the safest place in the world.

Then Michael made a discovery.

"Well, bed's somewhere!" he exclaimed, surprised at his own cleverness. Plain, ordinary bed was Somewhere. He had never thought of that before! *Everything* had to be somewhere.

"And so will you be, Mary Poppins, with your carpet-bag and parrot umbrella, sniffing and being important!"

He gave her a mischievous, questioning glance, daring her to deny it.

"And well-brought-up and respectable too!" Jane added her teasing to his.

"Impudence!"

She swung her handbag at them, and missed.

For already they were darting away to what was waiting for them.

Wherever she was, she would not be lost. That was answer enough.

"Somewhere! Somewhere! Somewhere!" they cried.

And, leaving the dark Park behind, they ran, laughing, across the Lane, through the gate and up the path and into the lighted house . . .

A. M. G. D.

THE HERBS
IN THE STORY
and their botanical, local and Latin names

SOUTHERNWOOD Old man, Lad's love   *Artemisia abrotanum*

LAVENDER *Lavandula vera*

MONEYWORT Creeping Jenny, Herb twopence
Lysimachia nummularia

SWEET BASIL *Ocimum basilicum*

DANDELION Dens leonis, Swine's snout   *Taraxacum officinale*

CHAMOMILE *Anthemis nobilis*

HONEYSUCKLE Woodbind   *Lonicera caprifolium*

FOXGLOVE Folk's glove, Fairy thimbles   *Digitalis purpurea*

PARSLEY *Petroselinum crispum*

FENNEL *Foeniculum vulgare*

SOLOMON'S SEAL Lady's seals   *Polygonatum multiflorum*

COLTSFOOT Ass's foot, Coughwort   *Tussilago farfara*

GOOSEBERRY Feverberry, Goosegogs   *Ribes grossularia*

RAMPION *Campanula rapunculus*

CUCUMBER Cowcumber   *Cucumis sativus*

HEARTSEASE Love in idleness, Herb constancy   *Viola tricolor*

LEMON BALM Herb livelong   *Melissa officinalis*

ELDER Pipe tree, Black elder   *Sambucus nigra*

ROSEMARY Polar plant, Compass-weed   *Rosmarinus officinalis*

FORGET-ME-NOT *Myosotis symphytifolia*

ST JOHN'S WORT All heal   *Hypericum perforatum*

MARIGOLD   Ruddes, Mary Gowles, Oculis Christi
Calendula officinalis

CORIANDER   *Coriandrum sativum*

CORNFLOWER   Bluebow, Bluebottle, Hurtsickle *Centaurea cyanis*

MARJORAM   Knotted Margery   *Origanum majorana*

RUE   Herb of grace, Herbygrass   *Ruta graveolens*

GOOD KING HENRY   Goosefoot, Fat hen   *Chenopodium Bonus Henricus*

SWEET CICELY   Chervil, Sweet fern   *Myrrhis odorata*

ROCKET   Dame's violet, Vesper flower   *Hesperis matronalis*

BRACKEN   Brake fern, Female fern   *Pteris aquilana*

MISTLETOE   Birdlime mistletoe, Herbe de la Croix   *Viscum album*

LOVAGE   *Levisticum officinale*

CYCLAMEN   Sowbread   *Cyclamen hederaefolium*

SORREL   Cuckoo's meat, Sour suds   *Rumex acetosa*

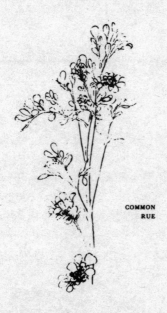

COMMON
RUE

P. L. Travers was born in Queensland, Australia. She was brought up in the deep country, simply, but traditionally. Life was arduous, and there were few luxuries, but it was full of rich impressions, and poetry and myth were very much part of life.

She began her writing career in Australia, publishing many poems, than came to England and wrote for newspapers in Ireland and England. She began Mary Poppins 'out of the blue'. A friend saw the first few chapters and took it to a publisher who at once offered a contract for the whole book.

The first Mary Poppins book was published in 1934 and was an immediate success. It was followed by another five books.